AMERICAN SURRENDER

MICHAEL BRADY

AMERICAN SURRENDER

A NOVEL

DELACORTE PRESS/NEW YORK

Published by
Delacorte Press
1 Dag Hammarskjold Plaza
New York, N.Y. 10017

This work was first published in Great Britain by Michael Joseph Ltd.

Manufactured in the United States of America

First U.S. printing

Designed by Laura Bernay

Library of Congress Cataloging in Publication Data

Brady, Michael.
   American surrender.

   I. Title.
PZ4.B81214Am   [PS3552.R2436]   813'.5'4   79–391
ISBN 0–440–00469–1

Total war between capitalism and communism is inevitable. Naturally we are not yet strong enough to undertake it at the present time. We still have to lull the suspicions of the bourgeoisie and to this end we must organize the most spectacular pacifist movement which has ever existed.

We shall make fabulous propositions and concessions. The decadent and credulous capitalist countries will rush to accept our offers of friendship and will thus contribute to their own destruction. As soon as their vigilance has been allayed and they have lost their protective shield, we shall destroy them with our powerful fist.

DIMITRI MANUILSKY
head of the Comintern in the 1930s

PART
ONE

CHAPTER
ONE

It was hot that summer in crowded Moscow. As often as possible Zimin would escape from his town apartment to seek the shade and quiet of his country dacha at Zhukovka, twenty miles west of the city. There he would swim in the large pool or play tennis with one of the many guards who took such good care of him. Most of all, he liked to walk in the still forests heavy with the smell of pine and, in the evenings, to sit on the high hill and watch the soothing and timeless flow of the Moscow River below.

Chairman Zimin had great need of these retreats, these spells of solitude. His task was not an easy one. As head of the KGB he controlled the largest and most complex intelligence apparatus in the world. He was justly proud of their achievements. With ruthless efficiency they disciplined the Russian people to serve the rulers in the Kremlin. By subversion, sabotage, and terrorism they robbed the capitalist nations of information and territory. Most important of all, they steadily eroded the faith of the capitalist nations in their society and the will of their people to fight for their countries.

But Zimin was not content. They were merely gnawing at the bodies of their enemies. Given time, he knew, they would reach the inner marrow of their bones and destroy them. But gnawing was a slow business. There would not be time! He must find some way to use the power of the KGB to tear out the very heart of their enemies before it was too late.

It was a question he brooded upon. It haunted him like an unsolved mystery—the solution there, somewhere in his mind, but always eluding capture. He had a feeling that when he did find the answer, it would be in the peaceful solitude of his dacha.

Toward the end of that summer, on a sweltering Friday afternoon, he was summoned to the Kremlin to attend a meeting of the Politburo. The Party leader wanted him present while they discussed the implications of the deteriorating situation on the border with China. The problem concerned units of the 300,000 strong Border Guards of the KGB who were called upon to deal with the provocative incursions of Chinese troops into Soviet territory.

It was hot. The air conditioning could not compete with the blazing sun outside. Zimin was bored as he waited for his item to come up for discussion. He listened impatiently to the familiar argument over the allocation of scarce resources between the military and the domestic needs of the people. This time it was copper and nickel; it was always something! Why didn't they shut their stupid mouths, he thought irritably. There was no argument. After the Cuban missile crisis, and their humiliating backdown in the face of American military superiority, the decision had been taken. They would match their enemies' strength, no matter what the cost. The people would have to wait.

Voices rose as tempers became frayed. Zimin cursed inwardly as that old fool Toropov suddenly thumped the table. "And exactly what do we do, comrades," he demanded, "when we are as strong as America? It will be no more than stalemate. Is that what the people have sacrificed for? For so many years! And what if Volodin was right?"

They all knew Toropov, the Party pessimist. He was old. He should have been put out to pasture years ago. Usually they ignored his idiotic outbursts. But with his reference to Volodin an uneasy silence fell on the meeting. All eyes turned to the Party leader at the end of the table.

"Comrade Toropov," he said, "it is hot and you are overexcited. This time I will be lenient. I will forget what you said. But remember, if you have so much sympathy for Volodin perhaps it is time you, too, had a taste of solitude."

The meeting continued but Zimin wasn't listening. Toropov might be an old fool, but his outburst had reminded him once again of the warnings of Party ideologist Volodin. He himself had interrogated Volodin. In branding him as an enemy of the people, he had done no more than his duty. Beyond doubt, his views were treasonable; they called into question the very foundations of Party policy. Now the matter was officially closed. Only the walls of his dacha, where Volodin would remain imprisoned for the rest of his life, could hear his predictions of disaster and his slanderous attacks on Party leaders.

But for Zimin the matter was far from closed. For during the interrogation he had become convinced Volodin was right. If Ivan Andrevich Lensky ever gained control of the Party, once Russia achieved military equality with America war *was* inevitable. A war neither country could win. The only victors would be the Chinese. Unless . . . unless he, Zimin, could find the answer to the question that had plagued him for so long. The KGB must do what military power alone could not do. He felt a sudden urgency to get back to the peace of his dacha. He must think.

From the road the village of Zhukovka was like any other village in Russia—a small collection of log cabins with broken-down outhouses and well-tended vegetable gardens. Only the exceptionally large village store suggested it might be unusual. It was filled with a variety of quality merchandise, much of it imported from Western countries, and never seen even in the largest of Moscow's department stores.

Zhukovka was at the center of one of the most exclusive dacha areas in Russia. The clientele of the store were not the villagers but the occupants of the luxurious summer houses set deep in the forests on either side of the road: the privileged elite of Russia, the New Class, as they were called—high-ranking Party members, senior officers of the military, top scientists, writers, and artists. The dachas, and the right to buy the merchandise in the store at vastly reduced prices, were their reward for unwavering loyalty to the Party.

But it was not the attraction of such luxuries which preoccupied Zimin as his chauffeur-driven Zil limousine sped through the village late that Friday evening, then slowed and turned right down the narrow road leading to his dacha. He was eager to be alone, to think, to brood.

All through Saturday he tramped the quiet forests, stopping for a brief while to eat a light lunch of dry bread and smoked salmon under the branches of a giant fir tree. Toward evening he was drawn to his favorite spot on the hill overlooking the Moscow River. There he sat, motionless, the reflection of the setting sun rippling in the water below. Deep in thought he became aware of the chill breeze which had sprung up like a whisper from nowhere. He rose stiffly to his feet to return home. It was then that the idea slipped into his mind, as unexpectedly and mysteriously as the rising breeze.

All that night he sat in the dark of his study, his mind probing and assessing the imponderables of the future. He had to be sure his idea would work; there were many uncertainties and risks to be weighed in the balance. But then, changing the course of history could never be an easy matter!

Through the autumn he continued to reflect on his plan and to gather information. To be successful, much would depend on the military preparedness and strategic intentions of both his own country and of their enemies in the years ahead. Discreetly, using his contacts in the GRU (the Intelligence Directorate of the Soviet General Staff), he sought out the information he needed. It was not difficult to find. Although ostensibly the GRU was an independent military intelligence agency, they were in fact subservient to, and controlled by, the KGB. However, he proceeded carefully, avoiding the quicker, but more revealing, method of directly questioning the senior members of the GRU and General Staff.

Such secrecy was not only innate to him, it was also politically imperative. Like all men who rise to power in a dictatorship founded on terror, Zimin had many enemies. To reveal a plan of such audacity and then fail in its achievement would be to present his head to them on a plate. Until he was as certain of success as he could be, until he needed the agreement and cooperation of the Politburo for the consummation of his plans, his preparations must be cloaked in darkest secrecy.

But he could not work entirely alone. He needed an utterly professional and competent man to carry out his instructions. A man who would not attract attention by his activities. A man not senior enough to be enmeshed in the political intrigues within the KGB. Above all, a man he could trust. The name of Colonel Aleksandr Sakov came into his mind.

Colonel Sakov arrived at his office in Higher Intelligence School 101 located on the outskirts of Moscow at 7:15 A.M. As he walked to his desk, a slight limp did nothing to detract from the obvious power of his solidly built, muscular frame. A power reflected in the bold cheekbones and firm rugged chin of his handsome Slavic face.

The colonel sat at his desk, unlocked a drawer, and took out a sheaf of typed pages. For a moment he studied the last page with thoughtful, deep-blue eyes, before inserting a blank sheet of paper in the typewriter. He passed the fingers of one hand through short-cropped iron-gray hair, then began to type.

He had nearly two hours to work on the textbook he was writing, *Recruiting and Controlling American Agents in the U.S.A.*, before he was due to give his first lecture.

Sakov had had no official brief to write this book. But he was bored with his duties as an instructor. Also, having recently returned from America, he was dissatisfied with the current textbook in use; it was out of date. Things changed so quickly in America. The telephone rang.

"Colonel Sakov?"

"Yes."

"You will come to my apartment immediately!"

"Who is speaking?" Sakov asked, disguising the unease he felt at the peremptory tone.

"Chairman Zimin."

Sakov stiffened. For a moment his mind was a blank. Then, with relief, he realized the mistake. There was a KGB general also called Sakov. Obviously, the telephone operator had made an error.

"Chairman Zimin," he said deferentially, "this is *Colonel* Sakov. May I suggest it is not me you wish to see." He emphasized his rank to make his meaning clear.

"Comrade *Colonel* Sakov, I have been known to want to see peasants . . . live ones. They have not refused me. Perhaps you will extend the same courtesy to me."

Chairman Zimin was well known for his caustic sense of humor. He was better known for having organized the orderly killing of untold thousands of peasants who chose death rather than enslavement within the USSR.

"Of course, Comrade Chairman, I will come immediately," Sakov replied hurriedly. "Do you require me to bring anything with me?"

There was a silence, then the cutting reply. "Your wits, Colonel, just your wits. You appear to have mislaid them."

Sakov was about to put the telephone down when Zimin spoke again. "You will tell no one you are seeing me. Do you understand . . . *no one*." The line went dead.

Sakov felt bemused . . . apprehensive. He was an atheist but he would have been less surprised if his caller had been God, summoning him to some celestial appointment.

As he drove to Zimin's apartment in Kutuzovsky Prospekt, his apprehension grew. What possible reason could Zimin have for wanting to see him? He was only a colonel. He wondered about his textbook. Certainly the criticism it implied of the existing book could cause him serious trouble. To avoid this he had planned to offer it to a senior officer for publication under his name. Perhaps one of his colleagues had found out about it and informed on him. He dismissed the notion as ridiculous: it was hardly the kind of matter to be dealt with by the chairman himself.

The nearer he drew to Zimin's apartment, the more uneasy he became. He examined his past life for some flaw. An unwise act or association. A careless word to one of his brother officers. Perhaps he had talked with too much admiration of the material achievements of America. With rising suspicion he went over the friends he had made since his return to Moscow.

Nowhere was the smell of suspicion stronger, the antennae more keenly attuned to detect the minutest deviation from Party doctrine—in thought or act—than amongst the officers of the KGB staff. Dog ate dog. For it was the nourishment of such strong meat which ensured only the strong, the ruthless, and the cunning survived to fulfill their role as the "Sword and Shield" of the Party.

But he could think of nothing to account for his summons.

At the door of Zimin's apartment a craggy-featured guard examined his papers. Once inside, the guard pointed to the far end of the long, thickly carpeted corridor. "There," was all he said.

Half a dozen doors led off from each side of the corridor, all closed except for one. As he passed it Sakov caught a glimpse of a large and fully equipped kitchen. It reminded him of his time in America. He had not seen anything like it since he had returned to Russia. Bending over the sink in gray trousers and a white shirt, a tall man with sallow skin was rinsing a plate under the faucet. A blue apron was strung around his waist. Despite his tenseness, Sakov smiled. He would be Zimin's valet and personal bodyguard, a KGB officer ranking major or above.

He reached the end of the corridor, hesitated for a moment, then knocked firmly on the door. A voice from inside instructed him to enter.

Sakov's trained eye took in the room, though his gaze was fixed on the man behind the large ornate desk. The furnishings reflected Zimin's power and position. Antiques mostly, many of them received as gifts from grateful Eastern European Communist governments for "services rendered." In contrast to the magnificent antiques, an array of elaborate electronic equipment occupied the full length of one wall.

Sakov approached the desk. Zimin was small and slightly built, the features of his face thin and delicate, almost ascetic. Without raising his eyes from the file on his desk, he waved a fine-boned hand, indicating that Sakov sit down.

Zimin lifted cold, blue, penetrating eyes and looked at Sakov in silence. When he eventually spoke, there was unmistakable menace in the quiet stillness of his voice.

"I have your personal dossier in front of me, and there are a few questions I would like to ask."

Sakov nodded guardedly.

"You were born in Kiev," Zimin began. "You joined the Young Communist League. The reports made on you by your superiors show you were zealous in your dedication to the Party—*to the point of fanaticism*. Why was this? Did you hope to curry favor by this apparent dedication for your own selfish advancement? To *use* the Party rather than to serve it? Such motives are not uncommon. Examine your conscience carefully. It is still not too late to speak the truth. After all, each one of us has some human weakness."

A chill ran through Sakov. Not because he was unable to answer Zimin with honesty and honor. But because he recognized all too well the opening gambit of a political interrogation. He should: he had used it frequently enough himself!

The technique was as effective as it was simple. A completely praiseworthy act was turned inside out and presented as self-interest—a nebulous form of treason against the Party. Next the trap was baited. Self-interest was a normal human failing. Why not admit it? Forgiveness could well be the reward for an honest admission of guilt. *After all, each one of us has some human weakness.* How often had he used these very words himself.

Usually the bait proved irresistible and the trap would snap shut. For once the first confession was extracted, no matter how trivial the real or invented crime, the victim was lost. He could then be accused of anything. There would be no defense. Who would believe the protestations of a self-confessed traitor against the Party . . . about anything!

Sakov steeled himself for the opening stages of the trial that lay ahead. He was fortunate. Zimin's first move would not be hard to counter.

He said, "Comrade Chairman, I understand very well what

you are suggesting. However, may I be permitted to point out that such zealous support for the Party was not uncommon amongst the young of my day. I, moreover, had a very special reason for my devotion to our cause. My father was killed by the White Russians when they, together with the troops from imperialist countries, tried to crush our glorious Revolution. My mother was carrying me at the time he was killed. Hatred of our enemies came to me with her milk. It is still with me."

"Is it not curious, then," Zimin went on, "that in 1941 when you were serving as a lieutenant on the front at Smolensk, you should have surrendered and been taken prisoner? Am I to believe *surrender* is an act of hatred?"

"I did not surrender," Sakov retorted, trying to suppress his anger. "I was captured while unconscious. A German antitank shell tore my tank apart as if it were a tin can. My crew was killed. I was lucky. And—as you will see from my file—I escaped within three hours, leaving two dead Germans behind as a memento of my brief stay with the German army."

Zimin's features moved, almost imperceptibly. It might have been the faintest flicker of a smile. "Very heroic, very heroic. But then that was no more than the duty of a soldier in the Red Army, was it not?"

"Yes. His duty . . . no more."

"Then you took part in the great counteroffensive, which drove the Germans back from Moscow in early 1942."

"That is correct, Comrade Chairman."

Zimin leaned forward confidingly. "That was a great battle. I was there, in Moscow. Did you know that?"

Sakov nodded. Everyone in the KGB knew Zimin had been a general in the NKVD, the name given to the security forces during the war.

"A great battle," Zimin continued as if he were reminiscing. "All but a few of the commanding generals defending Moscow were officers of the NKVD. We organized the civilian population into people's militia and volunteer divisions. We sent them, badly armed and untrained, to hold the German divisions at bay on the outskirts of the city. They were slaughtered, but they held the city until the Red Army had regrouped and reequipped and was strong enough to counterattack. Those people, Colonel, the ordinary people of Russia, do you think they were brave?" The question sounded casual.

"Yes, they were brave. It is not easy for civilians to die," Sakov answered.

Zimin sat upright abruptly. His tone changed. Now he spoke with ice-cold intensity. "No. *They were not brave.* They died because of us, the NKVD. Our young officers led them from the front and showed them by their example how to fight and die. But for many that was not enough. So we placed our men behind them. Those who retreated were shot. The carrot in front and the stick behind—that is the way to make people rise above themselves. And never forget, the stick is always the stronger. Today we tell the people they work and sacrifice for the benefit of future generations and the glory of communism. But without the stick—fear—they would not do it. We in the KGB are that stick."

Sakov said nothing. He did not know whether he had been merely reprimanded or if he had failed a serious ideological test. Only Zimin knew that, because only Zimin knew the purpose of the questions about his past.

His silence seemed to be the correct response, for Zimin changed the subject. "You were wounded in August 1943 during the great Kharkov tank battle."

"Yes." Sakov remembered in vivid detail the suicidal assault on the entrenched 88-mm guns protecting the flank of the German tank armies. He recalled the searing pain of his burning body as he hurled himself through the hatch of his blazing tank. From that day he had walked with a limp.

"And you met your wife while recovering in hospital?"

"Yes. She was a nurse."

"Her father was a member of Smersh."

"Yes, although I did not know it at the time." He did not think it necessary to explain just how powerful he had later discovered his future father-in-law had been. A senior officer in Smersh, *smert shpionam* ("death to spies"). The elite of the counterintelligence services. Secretive and deadly. His father-in-law had been well trained for his profession. He had been a member of the Cheka, formed in 1917 and responsible for the Red Terror when the Chekists had the authority to execute suspects without trial. To have been a Chekist was still an accolade in the KGB. Zimin had been a Chekist.

"When you left the hospital you transferred to the Political Directorate on the First Ukrainian Front."

Sakov nodded, wondering what further trap Zimin was leading him toward. He did not have to wait long to find out.

"I would not consider that transfer the action of a patriot filled with hatred of his enemies. To become a political spy and propagandist amongst his own soldiers! That was your job as a member of the Political Directorate, was it not? Surely there is a camaraderie amongst true soldiers which makes betrayal of one's brothers repugnant?" The contempt Zimin conveyed was unmistakable. "Why did you not return to the front?"

Sakov tried to suppress his feelings and reply with a calmness he did not feel. Zimin's scathing taunt had hurt him deeply. "I was transferred to the Political Directorate. I did not *choose* it. But as a true patriot I carried out my duties resolutely—no matter how much pain or distaste it caused me. I killed many more Germans through the . . ." He paused, searching for the appropriate words ". . . the enthusiasm and fear I created amongst my men than could any one single tank commander."

Though Sakov had spoken the truth, he searched Zimin's face anxiously for his reaction. Perhaps Zimin's taunt had struck too deep and his resentment had shown—for there *had* been times when he had despised himself for punishing men broken by the cauldron of battle, their courage spent. Maybe it had been a mistake to *admit* his distaste for such work. He did not know.

Zimin said, "It appears you have decided to speak truthfully."

Sakov relaxed. A mistake. Zimin had not finished. "Do you think," he continued, "it is wise to be so truthful?"

"Yes," Sakov replied. There was no other answer. Though he knew such a question could only be a trap.

"Then tell me, Colonel, do you know *why* you were transferred to the Political Directorate?"

Sakov winced. The trap had shut with a vengeance. For he had not told the *whole* truth and there was no way he could prove his reasons had been honorable. For an instant he considered trying to bluff his way out. To deny he knew why he had been transferred. There were no records. It had all been done on the "old boy" net.

Zimin's cold, implacable gaze was on him and he realized there could be no greater danger than to attempt to deceive such a man.

He spoke openly but with reluctance. "Yes, I do know why I was transferred to the Political Directorate. I did not mention it because I did not think it necessary. Nor did I wish to speak of things which might tarnish the memory of my father-in-law. A brave man who died serving his country."

He paused, searching Zimin's face for any sign that he already knew of the events he was about to relate. He found none. "Shortly after I joined the directorate I received a letter from my fiancée. She wrote how pleased she was about my new appointment and how grateful she was to her father for keeping me out of combat—women do not understand how a man feels. I was very angry. I did not know my transfer had been arranged. I . . ."

Sakov wanted to go on to explain how he had immediately written his father-in-law thanking him for his intended kindness, but demanding to be transferred back to his tank unit. His father-in-law sent for him from the front—an indication of just how much influence he had. After a lengthy argument he had been persuaded that his personal feelings were of no importance, that in working for the Political Directorate he was serving his country in the best way possible. And when his father-in-law finally said, a smile creeping over his grim face, "If you prove too troublesome, I shall have you transferred to a safe transport command in Moscow," he knew it would be futile to argue further.

But Zimin was not interested in hearing his explanation. "There is no need to continue. I know all I wish to know." Slowly he closed the file in front of him. "There is no need to continue as I already know a great deal about you . . . much more than there is in this file. You see, I knew your father-in-law very well. We were Chekists together after the Revolution. It was through *me* he arranged your transfer and I knew it was not to your liking."

He continued, "I know every detail of your history in the security services. Your father-in-law spoke of you quite often. He regarded you as a true son and a true Soviet. There are few men whose opinion I valued more highly. It is a great sorrow to me he had to die in the service of his country. I could do no more than avenge his death. The CIA lost two good men." A malevolent smile flickered across his face. "I attended to the arrangements personally. My hope is their widows and children still grieve for them."

This reference to the nature of his father-in-law's death startled Sakov. Till that moment all he had known was contained in the short official note sent to his wife's mother. It had stated that her husband had met with a fatal accident somewhere in the Middle East. That was all. This brief information had been followed by details of her pension entitlement. Nor had he had any inkling of the friendship between his father-in-law and Zimin.

"I have kept you in mind since then, Colonel. In case I needed someone I could trust implicitly—for some special assignment. Now I have such an assignment. But I needed to meet you first, for there are some things a personal file or even a trusted father-in-law cannot tell."

He smiled thinly.

Sakov attempted to smile in return. His throat was dry.

"I know you can lie, for without that ability you would not have been a successful agent. What I needed to discover was whether you knew when to tell the truth. Whether *I* could trust you. I knew you were unaware of my relationship with your father-in-law. That you could not have guessed I had knowledge of the favor he did you in arranging for your safe appointment to the Political Directorate. You *could* have lied about that—there are no records—and it would have put you in a better light."

He paused, eyes fixed on Sakov, and in those eyes Sakov glimpsed an inhuman essence—a being not entirely of this world. And when he said, "The other thing I wanted . . . to see into your very soul," Sakov believed him. Zimin *would* be able to see into souls—even of the dead.

He waited, silent.

"And now, Colonel, I want to ask you a question. Let us imagine there are two powerful animals, exactly matched in their strength. They are together on an island without food. Which one of them will survive?"

"They will fight," Sakov answered, "each trying to kill so as to live off the other's flesh."

"And the probable result?"

"If they are exactly matched in strength, they will both die of their wounds. Neither will survive."

"Precisely. But what if one of the two animals is aware of this?"

"If *only* one is aware of it, then he is the more intelligent. He will use cunning to overcome his adversary."

Zimin smiled appreciatively. "Exactly. And now to your assignment, for which I need your skills and your cunning. Together, Colonel, we are going to capture the United States of America *intact*. We need her flesh!"

CHAPTER
TWO

Madame Leberge removed her pince-nez with an air of finality and slowly looked around at her audience. Her flint-gray eyes took in every detail of the fifty-four young ladies occupying the nine rows of pewlike benches, ranged in front of the high rostrum on which she stood. Madame wore her perfectly tailored dark-gray suit, her flat-heeled, lace-up, black leather shoes, and her gray stockings like a uniform. Indeed, it was Madame's austere appearance, enhanced by the gray hair, tightly scraped around her head into a small bun, which did much to persuade parents to part with a small fortune to send their daughters to one of Switzerland's most exclusive finishing schools. Some hoped their daughters would emerge at the end of a year as poised young women; others, more ambitious, hoped that under the school's strict supervision their daughters would be saved, for at least another year, from the deflowering bed of some rapacious paramour.

Madame's scrutiny of the recent arrivals revealed nothing new to her. There was the usual large Oriental contingent, most of them from India, Burma, and another contingent from Arab countries. Despite the ripeness of their physical maturity, she knew they were still bound by the strictness of their religious and social upbringing. They could be relied upon to be docile and chaste. The Chinese twins, daughters of a wealthy Hong Kong banker, would also, she knew, behave with the admirable decorum innate to their race. Even the Italian and French girls would cause little difficulty, if properly handled; their countries still retained some semblance of parental discipline.

It was the American and English girls she would, as usual, have to watch. Why was it, she wondered, that from the minute these girls arrived in Switzerland, they were determined to make a gift of their virginity to one—any one!—of the all too many predators who swarmed around L'École de Lystre like bees around a pot of honey. Not that they were all virgins by any means, but it was the tradition of the school to assume that all their young ladies were untouched—by male hands at least.

Madame Leberge replaced her pince-nez and continued her introductory address. "And now, ladies, we come to the question of your social life. You must remember that, above all, the reason for your being here is to complete your education. To prepare yourselves to take your proper place in the highest society of your countries. To be a credit to your parents, who have made such sacrifices to send you to L'École de Lystre."

"Shit!" the fair-haired girl sitting next to Cathy Jackson exclaimed, muffling her words with a cupped hand. "Doesn't this little ole lady know ma pappy could buy the who-*ole* little ole L'École with jus one week's losings at Vegas?" She mimicked a southern accent.

"Shush," Cathy hushed her. She wasn't so sure about her own "pappy." He wasn't exactly poor, but looking at the sleekly expensive clothes of the girls around her, she had an idea that an honest senator wouldn't rate too high in the financial stakes at this school.

"But," Madame continued, her eyes flicking for an instant toward the whispering girls, "we do not expect you to work all the time. There will be organized excursions to various places of interest in and around Geneva once a week. Every month there will be a ball, here at the school, to which we will invite suitable . . ." She paused after the word, giving it a wealth of meaning. ". . . young men. However, I would ask you to remember that there is one rule to which we allow no exceptions. Unless you have special permission from your mistress, you must be back to the school no later than ten o'clock in the evening. Any breach of this rule will result in your being confined to the school until I see fit to trust you again."

"Jesus, I'll bet they have more fun in a nunnery," Susan said with dejected exasperation, flicking her long fair hair from her face as she sat on Cathy's bed, looking at the ceiling. The address from Madame over, they had gone to their small but comfortable furnished rooms to unpack. Susan had unpacked in her usual style: just emptied her case onto the floor, then thrown the various items of her expensive wardrobe into whatever looked like a good place. Hell, she could always buy some more.

Cathy was still methodically unpacking. She did everything that way, the way her mother had taught her; the way the houses, the neat treelined streets, and the well-kept gardens were laid out in her hometown. Orderliness and cleanliness might not be *right* next to godliness in Sanville, but they weren't all that far apart either. Cathy's neat features puckered into a frown as she caught sight of a few straggling curls hanging loose from her short, naturally curly, chestnut-brown hair, reflected in the mirror over the basin.

"What's a healthy, normal red-blooded American girl supposed to do in a nunnery like this?" Susan moaned. "Wear her fingers to the bone!"

"Oh, come on, it won't be that bad." Cathy laughed.

"Not that bad!" She looked at Cathy with wide-eyed amazement. "Maybe you don't know just how bad it can get."

She was right; Cathy didn't know. At eighteen, she was still a virgin and she had every intention of remaining that way until the right time. Back in Sanville they still believed there *was* a right time and it wasn't just as soon as you knew what it was for.

"I tell you what, Susan," Cathy said, "as we came through the gates to this den of virtue I saw this guy, a porter or something, I guess, and I swear to you he wasn't a day over sixty. If you play it right, I'll bet we can fix something up."

"Yeah, and I'll bet *you* something," Susan replied wryly. "We'd need splints to do it."

Cathy laughed good-naturedly. She had met Susan on the flight over and, although their backgrounds and temperaments were so different, she was immediately attracted by her uninhibited openness.

During the following months, the two girls became good friends. For Cathy the time flew by. She was fascinated by the new insights the lectures and excursions gave her into art, architecture, music appreciation, political economy, and many other subjects she had never had time to study properly at home. To Susan it was one big frustrating yawn.

They were sitting drinking coffee in one of the many downtown cafés. It was Saturday afternoon. The café was half-full. With a fifty percent foreign population in Geneva, the conversation around them was in half a dozen languages.

Suddenly Susan touched Cathy's arm, her eyes riveted on the door. "Get that!" she said, a reverential awe in her voice.

Cathy followed her gaze. He was standing motionless just inside the door—tall, lithe, and muscular. There was a magnetism about him which no woman could fail to sense. His dark suit was immaculately tailored. As he looked slowly around the café, his light blue eyes had the same contained restlessness as his body. A deep suntan matched the color of his thick wavy hair.

"Santa baby . . . gimme, gimme." Susan's voice had an unmistakably hoarse and urgent sensuality about it.

He walked past them and sat two tables away. A waitress hurried over and took his order while he lit a cigarette. He seemed unaware of the two girls watching his every move as he stirred his coffee. Then, without any indication of his intention, he got up and casually walked over to their table.

"It would give me great pleasure if I could join you, mesdemoiselles." He bowed slightly as he spoke and, without waiting for a reply, sat down.

"You are English?" he asked. His voice was rich, soft, with an accent neither of them could place.

"Hell no," Susan said, regaining her composure. "American."

"Forgive me," he answered, smiling.

"Anything . . . anything at all." Susan's meaning was clear. She knew the name of this game . . . just let it be quick.

"And you are here in Geneva on holiday?" he asked.

"Not exactly. More like serving a prison sentence," Susan replied, wondering how long the preliminaries were going to last.

"A prison sentence?" he raised his eyebrows inquiringly.

"Yeah, a prison sentence. Ever hear of L'École de Lystre?"

He laughed. "Ah, now I understand. Yes, I've heard of it. . . . It has a very good reputation."

"I know," said Susan bitterly, "and that's what's wrong with it."

"I'm sorry. I don't understand." He looked puzzled.

Shit! thought Susan. *Here he is . . . big, beautiful, and more than able and now I've got language problems. What kind of a mating dance do they do around here anyway?* Maybe she should take her pants off and wave them at him or he'd end up thinking something stupid, like she was a nice girl or something. Hell no. He couldn't be that dumb.

"Let's put it this way," she said, leaning toward him, "it has a very good reputation for turning out well-bred young ladies. But it's a bit like a nunnery...."

"Oh yes, now I understand," he answered solemnly. "But you have many, many years for making love and only one year to learn so much about the other beautiful things in life."

"Like what?" Susan asked flatly.

"Oh, many things ... art, for example."

"You're kidding," Susan replied with disgust.

Until then he had addressed all his remarks to Susan, and Cathy was profoundly thankful that he had. She was way out of her depth. She wouldn't even know how to start to talk to him ... about anything. Not that she would have to; it wasn't she who attracted him.

So when he turned to her and asked, "What about you, mademoiselle, do you not like art?" she was embarrassingly conscious of the blush that betrayed her confusion.

"Art!" she exclaimed, sounding as if she hadn't heard the word before. "Oh yes, it's beautiful. . . . Well, some art is," she added hastily, realizing how foolish she sounded.

"Permit me to disagree, mademoiselle. All great art is beautiful. Brueghel and Bosch painted the inhuman side of life with the stark reality of a horrific nightmare, but their artistry is beautiful. Their *art*, if I may express my personal opinion, is far more beautiful than the sentimental romanticism of Rossetti or Millais." He looked at Cathy thoughtfully. "I wonder," he said, "which painters you admire most."

Cathy felt slightly more at ease. At least the conversation had got away from sex. And she really did care about art.

"My favorites . . ." she started, but he held his hand up in an imperious yet polite gesture and interrupted.

"No, let me guess."

He gazed deep into her eyes and she felt the throbbing at the pit of her stomach.

"I know," he said, "the Impressionists—Monet, Renoir, Degas, and the rest of them. You like their superb sense of color, the way they take their raw material, paint, and use it to express their feelings. Right?"

"Yes, yes, you are right," she agreed eagerly. "But how did you know?"

He shrugged. "There are things a man knows about some women ... women who are special."

What on earth is so special about me? Cathy thought. How she would have loved to have asked. But this wasn't the time or the place. And what was more, there never would be. Without Susan, he would never have even noticed she existed. Her brief moment of pleasure would soon be over.

He was looking into her eyes again. "I have a confession to make, mademoiselle. I cheated . . . just a little bit. You see, I am an art dealer. I have a gallery here in Geneva, so perhaps I have a better insight into people's artistic tastes than most."

They were all silent. He seemed thoughtful; Cathy couldn't think what to say; Susan was wondering what the hell had happened to her scene.

At last he said, "Since you are so interested in art, would you like to visit my gallery? Both of you, of course," he added hurriedly. "I cannot offer you the Impressionists but I have some very good originals by modern painters which may interest you." He looked at Cathy expectantly.

Cathy looked at Susan. Susan shrugged. "Sure, why not," she said.

"Next Saturday afternoon," Cathy suggested. Susan nodded.

"Good," he said, and handed Cathy a card from his inside pocket.

Cathy read, "Carl Heindrick, Galerie Siental, fifteen Rue du Lac."

"Oh," Cathy exclaimed as she put the card in her bag, "we haven't introduced ourselves. This is Susan Stafford and I'm Cathy Jackson."

He rose to his feet and bowed to each of them in turn. *"Enchanté, mesdemoiselles, au 'voir* till Saturday."

As he walked away, Susan shook her head slowly from side to side in wonderment. "Art! Would you believe it." She smiled at Cathy. "Come on, sexy," she said, "now you're all fixed up, how about me and those splints for that old porter at the school?"

On the way back in the taxi, Susan wondered how she'd blown it. The more she thought about it, the more she realized she hadn't blown it. It had happened the way Carl Heindrick had wanted it . . . all the way.

Susan had many faults, but jealousy wasn't one of them. You won some, lost some; as long as you tried often enough, you won often enough. Why was it, then, she wondered, as she lay in bed having a last cigarette, that something about the events of the afternoon, something about Mr., Monsieur, Herr, or whatever,

Carl Heindrick, disturbed her. He'd called all the shots; he'd achieved exactly what he wanted with . . . She caught her breath. That was it. *Achieved.* As if he had known what he wanted to do even before he entered the café. *Weird.* . . . It didn't make sense. *Shit!* She killed her cigarette, put out the light, and fell into a restless sleep.

Susan knew a setup when she saw one, but Cathy thought it wonderful the way it all worked out so well when they visited Carl the next Saturday. As Carl finished showing them around his exclusive gallery in the little street leading down to the deep blue waters of Lac Leman, a friend of his arrived, Jean Pierre, an artist. He took an instant tumble for Susan, and the two of them went off together. Then Carl led her up the steep narrow stairs to his apartment above the gallery and showed her his private collection of paintings. They discussed the great painters of the past. He talked of their work and their lives with such enthusiasm, she felt they were more alive and real to him than the modern world he lived in. Caught up in the power of his feelings, she too felt transported into his world. Then, abruptly, he said,

"Forgive me, I must be boring you. What is it you say in America . . . even your best friends won't tell you? And I am sure you are far too polite to tell me when I get tedious."

She started to protest, for the truth was she could have gone on listening to him all evening . . . all her life! But he dismissed her protestations as yet another sign of her politeness.

"Now I will feed your body. I am sure your soul must have indigestion by now. There is a quiet little restaurant by the riverside at Nyon about twenty-five kilometers from here. La Carrosse . . . do you know it?"

She shook her head.

"Good. Then you will enjoy a new experience. The food is superb, especially as the proprietor is a good friend of mine," he laughed. "And his wife, Madame Satre, she does all the cooking herself. Magnificent!"

He drove the Mercedes coupe with the same confident style that marked everything he did. They hardly talked at all as Cathy took in the breathtaking views of the lake between gaps in the pine forest, which covered the mountainside with a mantle of rich greens. She felt so at ease. It seemed the most natural thing in the world that she should be sitting next to this man.

Monsieur Satre greeted them warmly and guided them to a

quiet table by the window, overlooking the lake. He called for Madame and there followed an animated conversation. They spoke in French so rapidly, and accompanied by such extravagant gestures, Cathy was soon lost. When it was over, Madame departed for the kitchen after wishing them *bon appétit*.

While they ate, Carl manipulated the conversation skillfully and Cathy found she was talking about herself. Trivial things, which had marked the progress of her uneventful life, seemed worth talking about and sharing with this man. The evening flew by . . . too fast. Cathy looked at her watch.

"Oh my god!" she said in a panic, "it's already eleven o'clock. I'm supposed to be back at the school by ten. Madame Leberge will probably lock me up for the rest of the year."

To her consternation he laughed. "Don't worry, I have slain bigger dragons than your Madame Leberge. But if you are worried, we will go now."

At the entrance to the school Carl told her to wait. He got out of the car and had a short conversation with the porter. Cathy could see them both quite clearly in the electric light over the entrance gate. She was certain no money was passed. He returned to her and said, "Don't worry. Everything is all right now. I will see you again next Saturday at the gallery. You won't forget."

"I don't get it," Susan said the next evening, as she took up her usual position on Cathy's bed and, as usual, gazed vacantly at the ceiling. "I just don't get it," she repeated, shaking her head. "So he wants me off his back, okay. Not every guy's got what it takes to recognize a good screw when he sees one. . . . Shit, I'm sorry, Cathy, but you know what I mean. Your virginity sticks out like Jean Pierre's prick. But while I'm humping my ass off with lover boy, I'm missing orgasms worrying about what's happening to you. Your Carl is either hung up on virgins, or a rapist, I'm thinking, so what kind of friend does that make me, leaving you alone with him?"

She lowered her gaze from the ceiling and faced Cathy. "Look me straight in the eyes, young lady, and say it again. *You-are-still-a-virgin.*"

"I'm still a virgin," Cathy replied, laughing.

"Yeah, I guess you are," Susan said, fixing her eyes on the ceiling again. "So what does that make him, a faggot?"

Cathy bristled. "Susan, there's a limit to . . ."

"Relax, baby, I know he isn't. That guy can find his way around a woman's body better than his own. I'd swear it."

"Look," Cathy said seriously. "I think he just likes talking to me. It's as simple as that."

Susan wanted to say that with guys it was never as simple as that. Especially it wasn't with smooth operators like Carl Heindrick. She didn't say it. Warning Cathy was one thing; hurting her was another.

"Hey," she said brightly, "you haven't been putting me on . . . I mean, all that bit about your father being a poor, honest senator. You sure he hasn't got the odd few million stashed away somewhere . . . like in a Swiss bank."

"No, Susan, I promise." Cathy laughed and shook her head. She could never be mad with Susan for long.

"Then he's not planning to kidnap you. Pity. *That* I could understand."

"Why don't you give up, Susan? Admit for once you've met a man you don't understand."

"Yeah, why don't I?" said Susan wryly.

As the months went by, Cathy and Susan saw less and less of each other. Susan had plugged into Geneva's artistic set and devoted her free time to familiarizing herself with their beds. Cathy was totally absorbed by her love.

She didn't really understand Carl. All she knew was his mother had been French, his father Austrian. He had grown up in Vienna and studied at the academy in Berlin. But when she tried to press him for more details of his past—she wanted to know so much, to know everything about him—he would just shrug and say, "When I reminisce about my past, Cathy, you will know I'm getting old." And then he would guide the conversation to some other subject.

But she did know she loved him. There was a magnetism about his inner being that both excited and comforted her, a force to which she gladly surrendered. And when they first made love, it seemed natural, inevitable, and completely right.

Carl had suggested they make the long drive to Zurich to see some of the paintings of Cézanne and Manet on view at the Bührle Foundation. To her delight, Madame Leberge willingly gave Cathy permission to be away for the day, saying, "Yes, of course, mademoiselle. We have so few great paintings in Switzerland, you must see what we do have for your education."

The day had been swelteringly hot. On their return to his apartment, she had slumped, exhausted, onto the sofa. "Oh, Carl," she said, "I feel like a soaking wet rag."

He walked into the bedroom and came back with his bathrobe. "Here," he said, "take a shower while I make you something long and cool to drink." She emerged refreshed, his long bathrobe trailing around her ankles. He handed her a tall glass full of ice and pieces of fruit. It tasted delicious.

"What is it?" she asked, holding the ice-cold glass against her forehead. "A Carl Heindrick special," he answered, smiling. "Dry vermouth with a dash of slivovitz and kirsch, stir gently and add pieces of orange and peach *et voilà*! It makes a new person. You agree?" She did.

He watched her silently while she sipped her drink feeling completely relaxed and refreshed. "Stand up, Cathy." His voice was soft but commanding. He stood before her and slowly removed her robe.

"Beautiful! You are a very beautiful woman," he said softly as he gazed at her body with undisguised admiration. Cathy felt no embarrassment. She thrilled to give him so much pleasure. He picked her up in his arms and carried her to the bed. As he caressed her with his strong yet so gentle hands, he whispered, "You do not have to tell me, little one, I know . . . you are still a virgin. I will not hurt you." His sure hands moved down her body and gently stroked the soft flesh between her legs and she felt the wetness flood inside her. Tenderly and lovingly, his fingers opened her and his pulsating organ was penetrating her with a patient massagelike movement, gradually opening her into a state of breathless readiness to receive his full hard maleness. And then he was deep inside her and she gasped, overwhelmed by a joy she had never known before. He moved rhythmically and she responded with a hungry, increasing urgency until she was lost in a frenzy of ecstasy as their bodies were one, abandoned in a world of consuming and insatiable passion. The end came like a shattering explosion as her body vibrated and convulsed with uncontrollable violence, and when she cried out, the sound came from a part of her being she hadn't known existed.

She lay still, unbelieving, clasping his spent body. Slowly she released him and looked up into his eyes. "Oh, Carl, Carl, I love you," she whispered, her voice trembling.

"And I love you, my little Cathy," he said softly. "I will never let you leave me. We will be together always."

"Always," she murmured.

Cathy's year at L'École de Lystre was almost over the day she knocked hesitantly on the door of Susan's room. A voice said to come in. Susan was sitting on her bed in pants and bra, painting her nails. "Susan, please, I must speak to you," she said, her voice unnaturally calm.

"Okay, okay, honey . . . but make it quick," Susan answered without looking up. "I've got a date with a guy who's got the fastest Maserati you did ever see. I have an orgasm every time he takes it around those mountain bends like they weren't there."

"Susan . . . I—I'm pregnant," Cathy blurted.

The brush fell from Susan's hand.

"I'm pregnant," Cathy repeated more calmly.

"Here, sit down." Susan gestured toward the small chair by the window. She got down on her hands and knees, reached under the bed, and produced a half-full bottle of whiskey and a couple of glasses. She poured a large slug into each glass and handed one to Cathy. "Sink it," she said.

"Now, from the beginning. You're pregnant, or you think you're pregnant?"

"I *know* I'm pregnant," Cathy answered.

"And the lucky father?" Susan asked, sipping at her glass.

"Carl. . . . Carl Heindrick."

Susan pulled a face. "Yeah. Who else," she said. "Tell me about it."

And out it all came: how Carl had taken her to a doctor friend of his in town who had examined her and put her on the Pill. How they'd made marvelous love nearly every time they met, and how she loved him and he was the most kind and considerate man in the world.

Susan interrupted. "The pregnant bit," she said flatly. "You were on the Pill. The odds against getting pregnant are higher than I can count."

"That's it," said Cathy. "I never missed and when I told Carl he couldn't believe it either. But I've seen the doctor and it's true."

Susan lit a cigarette and waited in silence.

Cathy blushed. "Carl *wants* to marry me but he can't . . . not yet anyway. He's due to inherit a real fortune under a trust arrangement, but it's on condition he's unmarried at the time. He has to wait another year."

"Great, so that leaves an abortion. Maybe that doctor friend of Carl's can fix it. Come to think of it, maybe he can't. Luck doesn't seem to be his thing. We'll have to find someone else."

"Oh no," Cathy said with horror. "I'd never do that. It's our baby."

Susan reached for the bottle and refilled their glasses.

"And what about your parents when their sweet young daughter comes back all poised, but mostly pregnant. Some education, they'll think. You can get that in your own backyard, without even lying down. Believe me, I know."

She looked at her watch. "There goes my date!"

"I'm sorry, Susan, you don't have to . . ." Cathy said hurriedly.

"Don't give it a thought, baby. He can fuck his Maserati for all I care. I doubt he'd know the difference. But what about your father? Didn't you say he was coming up for reelection shortly? What a ticket. Me and my family—the legit and the illegit side. Shit! No way can you go back to the good old U.S. of A. packaging that bundle of joy."

"I've thought of all that, Susan," Cathy said. "That's why we plan to go to Vienna."

"Oh my god." Susan sighed and drained her glass. "Tell me."

"Well," Cathy started, "Carl has another gallery in Vienna. He suggested I write my family that I'm going to spend a couple of months in Vienna after school finishes, with a girl friend I met here. I'm only just over two months pregnant, and school ends next month so it won't show. Then I'll write to say how much I like Vienna, and how I've got a job to stay on for a while. That way, I'll stall them off until we can get married and go back to the States."

"Uh-huh. And how do you explain to your family how come there were three of you at the wedding? The one they didn't get asked to."

"Oh, that's all right," Cathy said brightly. "Carl says he has all kinds of influence in Vienna and he can fix to have the marriage certificate backdated."

"And the bit about how you've been married for a year without telling your folks?"

"It won't be easy but Carl says we can work something out

when the time comes. And I know my parents. They'll be so pleased to have the baby, and Carl . . . and I know I can trust him to explain things to them somehow."

"Yeah, he's smooth enough. That's what worries me, honey."

"Oh, Susan, you *know* I can trust Carl. Why should he take so much trouble to keep the baby if he didn't love me and want to marry me? If he'd wanted to, he could have persuaded me to have an abortion. *I* know that."

Susan sighed. "What can I say, Cathy. I can't think of a better idea. Only one thing—get it in writing."

Cathy laughed. "Your trouble is you don't trust any man. If only you knew Carl as I do, Susan, you'd understand."

"Okay, baby. So he's the one who's different. I really do believe you. Here." She passed the bottle. "Help yourself."

Susan listened while Cathy talked on about Carl. But Susan kept thinking how it just didn't make sense. Carl Heindrick was mature, sophisticated, and rich. He could have any woman he liked—for the night or for all time. Geneva was full of elegant and experienced women. So what was he doing with a kid like Cathy?

Susan didn't understand Carl Heindrick and it worried her.

It was late when Cathy put the glass down and stood up. "Night, Susan. Thanks for being so patient. One thing though— Carl made me swear not to tell anyone about our plans, but I had to tell you. You won't tell anyone, will you? Promise?"

"I promise," said Susan. And as Cathy went through the door to return to her own room, she felt she wanted to go with her and tuck her into bed.

Cathy didn't want to have any secrets from Carl. It was bad enough she had broken her promise to him. She owned up to telling Susan about the baby and their future plans. It was only for a fleeting second, but for the first time ever she saw real anger on his face. "That was very wrong of you," he said, holding her arms so tightly they hurt. "You must never, never break your promise to me again. Is that understood?"

"Oh, Carl." She was on the verge of tears. "I'm so sorry, but Susan is my friend. She won't tell anyone."

"That was what you promised *me*," he answered curtly.

Cathy felt frightened, lost.

"Please, Carl . . ." She burst into tears.

He released his grip on her. "All right, my little one. No more tears." He dabbed her wet cheeks tenderly. She looked up. He was smiling. It was all she could do not to burst into tears again.

Four days before school ended Carl told Cathy they would have to leave for Vienna a couple of days early. For business reasons. She would have to skip the last two days at the school.

The next day Cathy made her excuses to Madame Leberge, whose only comment was to say she hoped Cathy had profited from her year at L'École de Lystre.

"Oh yes, Madame, I have," she replied truthfully.

Saying good-bye to Susan was not easy. She was very fond of her. She said she would write from Vienna and made her promise once more not to tell *anyone* about Carl or the baby.

"Sure, honey, I promise," Susan said. "And you promise me one thing. Always remember, nobody can really take care of you, except yourself."

CHAPTER
THREE

Six months later Cathy's baby daughter was born in Vienna.

They decided to call her Anette.

Hans, Carl's manservant, turned out to be the perfect nanny. "Madame Cathy," he said, a form of address she found hard to get used to, "I was taken prisoner by the Russians. When I returned home, I found my wife had been killed in the bombing, but my baby was spared. I brought her up by myself."

"Well, now we both have a new baby to look after," Cathy said fondly.

"Yes—for a while," he answered and turned away.

A few days later Carl sent a message to Colonel Sakov at KGB headquarters in Moscow. "All going to plan" was the brief report.

They stayed on in Vienna for three months until Carl's trust settlement was due to be finalized in Geneva. Carl suggested they get married right after the settlement was wrapped up, in Geneva where they had first met. Cathy was delighted. And to add to her excitement they were to fly there in a private plane belonging to a friend of Carl's. Cathy's only regret was that Susan would not be at the wedding. She had written inviting her but the letter had been returned unopened.

On the morning they were to fly to Geneva, Cathy woke up feeling tense with excitement. They were due to take off at noon. Carl left early before breakfast saying he had some last-minute arrangements to make. Hans would look after her and he would meet them at the airport.

A few minutes before the Mercedes limousine was due to arrive to take them to the airport, Cathy was waiting impatiently. Anette gurgled happily, cradled in her arms.

There was a knock on the door and Hans came in carrying a

silver tray with a little box and a glass of water on it. "Excuse me, Madame Cathy," he said as he approached her. "Herr Heindrick left the strictest instructions that I was to make sure you took two tablets immediately before we left for the airport. He said you would be feeling nervous, and they will calm you down."

Cathy looked at the tablets, hesitating. It wasn't that she didn't feel grateful for Carl's thoughtfulness. It was simply that she didn't like taking any sort of tablets.

"Now, Madame Cathy," Hans said, waving a reproving finger at her, "you must do what Herr Heindrick says. He will ask me if you took them. He is always most strict about his instructions."

"All right, Hans, for your sake," she said, smiling. She swallowed the tablets. "Are we ready now, Hans?" she asked.

"Yes, now we are ready, Madame Cathy," he answered, turning quickly and leading the way to the door.

Carl opened the door as the limousine drew up by the plane. "How are you feeling? Did Hans give you the tablets?" he greeted her.

She nodded. "Yes, thank you, Carl," she said.

"Good. Now you will be better."

They had been in the air about one and a half hours when the pains came. Sharp tearing pains in her stomach. She cried out. "Carl, I'm in agony . . . my stomach. Hans, take Anette . . . quick, please." Hans reached across and took the baby from her arms.

"What is it? What kind of pains?" Carl turned around sharply in his seat in the front next to Claude Sites, his friend who was piloting the plane.

"I don't know. . . . I don't know." She gritted her teeth as the pain made her break out in a cold sweat. "I've never felt such pain."

Carl looked at her face closely. "How far have we come?" Cathy heard him ask.

"A little less than halfway," Claude Sites replied.

"Too far. Where is the nearest airport?"

"Munich. We are less than fifty kilometers to the south."

"Land there," Carl directed. "Radio them to have an ambulance standing by. It may be a burst appendix."

The plane banked steeply to the right as Claude contacted Munich airport.

Cathy vomited violently. The pains continued to come in waves of increasing intensity. She doubled over, her eyes screwed tight, aware of nothing except the excruciating pain.

The events that followed were just a blur. The landing, being lifted into the ambulance, the screaming of the siren, the jolting on the stretcher, the voices of the doctor and Carl. And the pain! Then nothing.

For the next days or weeks time did not exist for Cathy. She lay in a twilight world. Vague shapes loomed and disappeared again. Once she thought she recognized Hans, then he, too, vanished.

And that is how it was until the day her mind struggled back to full consciousness and she saw Hans sitting by her bed. Feebly, she stretched her hand toward him. He took hold of it and gently stroked it.

"What happened?" she asked weakly. "What happened?"

"You have been very ill. Your appendix burst. They had to operate." At his words she became aware of the soreness of her stomach.

"Where's Carl?" she asked sleepily.

Hans remained silent. "Carl, where is he?" she repeated.

Hans's voice was tight. "I—I have very bad news, Madame Cathy. They have all been killed . . . Herr Heindrick, little Anette, and Monsieur Sites. They crashed . . . in the mountains near Lucerne. . . . It was instant. There is nothing I can say. . . . My heart cries with you." His eyes filled with tears.

Cathy stared, her mind numb, unable to take in the horror of his words. Then she screamed, "No . . . no . . . no!" A desperate pitiable scream of anguish. Swiftly a waiting nurse moved to her side. She lost consciousness.

Three days later she came out of heavy sedation and Hans explained that Carl had had to keep his appointment in Geneva. Carl had taken Anette but insisted Hans stay on in Munich to look after Cathy. It was on the flight to Geneva that the plane had crashed.

Two more weeks passed before Cathy was strong enough to leave the hospital. She stood alone, in front of the new graves, the tears streaming from her eyes. "Farewell, my loves. Farewell, my life," she murmured. Hans waited for her near the old church. He took her arm and they walked away in silence.

A voice over the loudspeaker announced the departure of TWA flight 643 to Washington. Cathy put her arms around Hans and held him tightly as passengers began to make their way to the departure gate.

"Good-bye, Hans," she said calmly. "And thank you. We shan't meet again. *Tout passe, tout casse, tout lasse.*"

"Yes, everything passes," he answered. "It is the sorrow of life. Now you must make a new life for yourself."

And they parted.

Thirty thousand feet above the Atlantic, most of the passengers were trying to sleep, hoping to beat the jet lag of the long day ahead. Cathy sat perfectly still. After the agony and the despair had come a calmness. Carl had taught her to be a woman physically, but he had always looked after her as if she were a little girl. His death and Anette's had brought full maturity.

Cathy decided she would tell no one of her life with Carl. It was *hers*. A part of her life which, however tragic, she would never regret and would not share. It belonged to the three of them and only them.

As they came in to land at Dulles airport, she braced herself to meet her parents. She knew one thing. She wasn't their little girl anymore; she wasn't anyone's little girl.

The bulk of her baggage arrived by freight a couple of weeks later. The deliverymen carried the cases up to her room. Cathy locked the door, steeling herself for the pain she knew she would have to endure. She opened the nearest case and stood in puzzled surprise. She opened the others with increasing urgency. They were all the same, half-empty, the space filled with crumpled newspapers. She rummaged through each one with mounting dismay; every single thing that would remind her of her past had gone! Carl's presents, little mementos, the dress she was to have been married in, all Anette's little things, every single photograph of Carl and Anette. Everything!

"Oh, Hans, you dear fool," she cried out. And she remembered how Hans had talked in his fatherly way, telling her she must not cling to the past but must look only to the future.

She fell on the bed, sobbing. Gradually, as she began to think more clearly, her resolution returned. Now her secret really was secure, even more her own, even more precious. She must, she *would* make a new life for herself.

Cathy decided to work in her father's office and soon became immersed in the minutiae of politics. She learned what "looking after the folks back home" really meant. She dealt with the complaints and problems, no matter how trivial, which poured in. As often as not she'd stay working late into the evening.

At first it was simply a drug to stop her thinking. In time, however, she began to develop a real interest in the wider aspects of politics. She mentioned it to her father one morning.

He laughed. "Tell you what. Senator Brown is coming over to dinner. He's powerful on the Agriculture and Forestry Committee and I want to sweet-talk him into helping me. Trouble is, he's bringing his wife and daughter . . . always does. Your mother can take care of his wife. You keep the daughter happy and I'll be free to work on the senator. It won't be easy. Your mother says she's the most boring young lady this side of anywhere. Now, that's a *real* political challenge. Keeping people happy who bore the pants off you."

Senator Brown was a quiet-spoken man with a dry sense of humor. Cathy wished she could have listened to him instead of having to talk to his idiot daughter. The girl was "into" everything, from jazz to ecology, but actually knew nothing about anything. The conversation began to die.

Suddenly the girl's face brightened. "Say," she said, "weren't you at that draggy finishing school in Switzerland? Can't remember the name. My mother was thinking of sending *me*. . . . Can you imagine!"

"L'École de Lystre," Cathy prompted.

"Yeah. That's it. Boy, what a blowout. I had a friend there and the way she wrote me, they kept you so locked up you'd think the place was surrounded by rapists."

"Not quite that bad." Cathy brightened up. It was good to talk about the place.

"Well, Susan said—"

Cathy cut her off. "Susan. Susan who?"

"Susan Stafford. Her dad and mine are friends. You knew her, huh?"

"Of course," Cathy said. "How is she?"

"Y'mean you don't know?" The girl looked startled.

"Know what?"

"Hell, she killed herself. The day she was due to leave, would you believe! Threw herself out of a window. How come you didn't know?"

Cathy didn't answer. She was on her way upstairs to her room. She locked the door behind her to shut out . . . she didn't know what. Just to feel safe. Susan. Killed herself! It was impossible. Susan—cheerful, boisterous Susan. Then an ice-cold chill flowed through her, reaching deep into her bones, as she realized she wasn't as shocked by the news as she should have been. Somehow there was an awful inevitability about it. A pattern. Every person who had been close to her in Europe was dead.

In his office at KGB headquarters in Moscow, Colonel Sakov looked at the neat pile of thick files on the desk in front of him. They were all up-to-date. More than fifty of them, each concerning a separate person who, with luck and manipulation, might be in the right place for some future use. They were known as "random shots," in KGB terminology. It was surprising how often they paid off.

Two years had passed since Chairman Zimin had first briefed him on his assignment. Progress was promising. It was slow, but there was no other way.

Sakov reached forward, removed the top file from the pile on his desk, and looked at the title on the front cover: "CASE SII— CATHY JACKSON." He began to browse through the pages, a slightly rueful smile on his face. He had taken a lot of trouble with Cathy Jackson. He hoped his assessment of her would prove right. When Madame Leberge had sent her appraisal of the new intake of students two years ago, Sakov's instinctive assessment of people had told him the American Cathy Jackson was worth special attention. Her background was right; her character was right. He had singled her out for the most careful and painstaking treatment. It had been a good investment to set up L'École de Lystre all those years ago, he thought. Now, with its fine reputation, it attracted girls from influential families all over the globe. Away from home, at a vulnerable age, the girls could be manipulated in many ways. And Madame Leberge did a first-class job. She deserved her rank as major in the KGB.

Sakov reached the last page in the file and read the blue copy of the instructions he had issued on the day Cathy Jackson had returned to her home in America.

FOR IMMEDIATE ACTION—CASE SII

1) AGENT KGB224, ALIAS CARL HEINDRICK. TO BE RESTRICTED TO INTERNAL OPERATIONS ONLY—DURATION, TILL DEATH —ACTION, FIRST CHIEF DIRECTORATE (4TH DEPARTMENT).

2) AGENT KGBL62, ALIAS HANS SCHULTZ. NOW UNRELIABLE, TO BE RECALLED FROM AUSTRIA—SUGGEST TRANSFERRED TO

ADMINISTRATION DIRECTORATE—ACTION, FIRST CHIEF DI-
RECTORATE (4TH DEPARTMENT)/ADMINISTRATION DIREC-
TORATE.

3) AGENT, FOREIGN MI533, ALIAS CLAUDE SITES. RELIABLE
BUT FIRST-PRIORITY SECURITY—IMMEDIATE ELIMINATION
—ACTION, FIRST DIRECTORATE (DEPARTMENT V).

4) AGENT, FOREIGN L312, ALIAS FREDERICK SCHWARTZ. RE-
SPONSIBLE FOR ACQUIRING SUITABLE BODIES AEROPLANE
BURNOUT AND ELIMINATION OF AMERICAN SUSAN STAF-
FORD—RELIABLE BUT FIRST-PRIORITY SECURITY—IMMEDI-
ATE ELIMINATION—ACTION, FIRST CHIEF DIRECTORATE
(DEPARTMENT V).

5) AMERICAN CATHY JACKSON. TO BE KEPT UNDER SURVEIL-
LANCE—ACTION, FIRST CHIEF DIRECTORATE (1ST DEPART-
MENT).

Sakov sat back thoughtfully, the file still open in front of him.
Yes, a great deal of trouble had been taken with Cathy Jackson.
And there were twelve other women among his files. All Americans. All at some time or other having committed acts of indiscre-
tion. Each of them now vulnerable to his manipulation if the need
or opportunity arose.

Sakov's eyes returned to Cathy Jackson's file as a disquieting
thought entered his mind. It was unlikely but what if one of these
women turned out to be vital to the achievement of his assignment? From his long experience he knew women responded to a
particularly subtle form of manipulation. The sort of manipulation only another woman can supply. And he did not have such a
woman in America.

The KGB had always been prejudiced against employing
women as deep-cover agents in foreign countries. They considered women too emotionally unstable; suitable only to be used as
secretaries and filing clerks.

Sakov smiled wryly. They were going to have to change their
attitude. And with the backing of Chairman Zimin he could make
them do it. He had to have the right kind of woman in America.
A Russian woman and a dedicated patriot whom he could rely
upon utterly. A very special woman. Young, beautiful, and with
the patience and nerve to play the long, lonely game of a deep-

cover agent . . . and the ability to act unhesitatingly with ruthless violence should circumstances demand it.

Taking a pad from the tray beside his desk he began to write:

INFORMATION REQUESTED ON EXCEPTIONAL YOUNG PARTY MEMBERS SUITABLE FOR TRAINING AS ILLEGAL AGENTS IN THE UNITED STATES.

He paused, then added the single word: FEMALE.

CHAPTER
FOUR

Anna Zasoravna sat alone in her study. She was working on her latest report, to be sent off that evening. Anna was head of Rostov University's network of secret KGB informers.

There was a knock on the door. This puzzled Anna. Except when she was lecturing or at meetings, she was left well alone by both staff and students. They feared her, with cause. As a fanatical Party member, she remorsely sought out anyone in the university who showed the slightest criticism of the Party—or sympathy for the West.

The head of Administration entered. "Someone to see you," he said.

Anna looked up. She didn't bother to cover her work. Though she was only assistant head of the language department, there was not one person in Rostov University who would have dared challenge her.

"From the authorities," the administrator explained.

Anna put down her pen. "The authorities? Who?"

"He wouldn't say. But he's important."

She raised her brows. "How do you know?"

He shrugged. "It's not a difficult thing to guess."

"Tell him I'll be there in a moment," Anna said.

She locked away her report. Then she tidied herself at the small mirror on the wall. She tucked a stray lock of golden hair back into the severe bun at the nape of her neck, and straightened her blouse. But the drab hairstyle and the soberly dull clothes could not conceal the loveliness of her face and figure.

Anna was totally unaware of her beauty. Remote and detached in her behavior, she had never allowed anyone close enough to make even the slightest personal comment. As a little girl of six,

Anna had been found wandering the streets of Stalingrad in total shock. She had been unable to tell of the horror she had witnessed in the cellar—which had left her an orphan. Anna had grown up in the cold impersonality of a succession of institutions —a true child of the state.

A tall man rose to his feet as she entered, and politely invited her to sit down. His manner was friendly, but he neither introduced himself nor intimated the purpose of his visit. Anna knew better than to ask.

They talked on a variety of subjects. He had a curious way of initiating some topic with enthusiasm, then stopping abruptly and looking at her with an expectant smile. Anna felt compelled to reply quickly, to fill the silence. She realized it was a deliberate and effective technique to make her talk unguardedly.

At the end of the interview he asked, "Would you be prepared to dedicate your life to the work of an illegal agent in America?" His keen eyes searched her face for every nuance of reaction.

Anna was enthralled—that she should take her place at the very forefront of the fight against the capitalists! She answered with a firm voice, "Yes, comrade, that is something to which I could truly dedicate my life."

For three months she heard nothing. Bitterly she began to fear she may have failed to satisfy her deceptively benign inquisitor. But one cold, dark morning, the gray skies above the city heavy with unburdened snow, she was summoned again just as classes were due to begin.

The meeting was brief. "I am pleased to inform you of your selection to work for the intelligence services. Your training will start tomorrow in Moscow. You will prepare yourself to catch the late-afternoon flight." His manner was abrupt. Gone was the warm confiding smile. Major Romanovitch of the KGB was not one to waste time on pleasantries once they had served their purpose.

"It has all been arranged. There is no need to speak to anyone of your departure," he said curtly.

"My colleagues . . . I must say good-bye."

"Comrade," he said, "I have arranged for you to leave without seeing your colleagues. It is a cold world you are entering. It is as well you get used to it quickly."

He opened his briefcase and took out a brown envelope.

"Here, your ticket and papers."

Anna took the envelope, then asked hesitantly, "What shall I do when I get to Moscow?"

"You will be taken care of," he replied dismissingly. "Now go to your room and pack and"—he held out his hand—"good luck, comrade. We shan't meet again."

Anna stood amongst the hurrying crowds of Moscow airport, bemused. It was almost midnight. A giant of a man with the close-set, darting eyes of a rat came lumbering toward her. He was brushing the fresh snow from his thick, shaggy overcoat with obvious distaste, as if the snowflakes were a swarm of irritating ants. He held a photograph in one hand.

"Anna Zasoravna?" He loomed above her, blinking alternately down at her and then at the photograph.

"Yes."

"Come." He picked up her luggage in one arm and turned. Anna followed the massive form as he led her through the milling crowds and official checkpoints. They were not stopped.

Outside, he opened the rear door of a waiting Chaika limousine, threw her baggage on the backseat, beckoned her to get in, then sat himself next to the driver.

It was snowing heavily, the streets almost deserted. They drove in silence broken only by the rasping cough of the driver—a dwarf beside his companion—methodically choking himself on the succession of cigarettes that dangled from his lips.

Off the road and through a high stone archway, the driver stopped the car. The giant rolled effortlessly out, opened the rear door across from Anna, and scooped up her baggage. She followed him up the gray stone steps, worn down by the feet of half a century.

In the dimly lit hallway, the dark-brown walls glistening with condensation, Anna saw the motionless form of the *upravdom* sitting behind his bare wooden desk. The *upravdom* was a man of many parts—a combination of janitor, rent collector, and apartment manager. Above all, he was an informer, reporting regularly to the militia and the KGB on the activities of the occupants. Normally he would have scrutinized the new arrivals with open insolence, but he kept his head lowered as the big man passed, only raising his eyes to steal a glance at Anna.

On the first floor, they stopped in front of the door directly opposite the head of the stairs. Reaching deep into his overcoat pocket with his free hand, Anna saw her KGB guardian—for that was surely who he must be—withdraw a key and delicately insert it into the keyhole. The lock clicked and he shouldered the door open. In the darkness, his hand moved to the light switch with the certainty of familiarity.

Anna stood at the door, overawed. She had never seen such luxury before. The high-ceilinged room was enormous. Heavy velvet drapes were already drawn around the two bay windows to the left. In front of her, a six-foot-high ornate marble fireplace with a wrought-iron electric fire filling the grate. Above it, the inevitable picture of Lenin. The furniture was covered with the unmistakable richness of real leather. In the center of the thick-carpeted floor a low, pink marble table, and standing on it, an exquisitely designed vase filled with an array of brilliant and exotic flowers. A television set stood in one corner.

Only one thing struck an incongruous note: the rows of dark-stained wood bookshelves along one wall, all completely bare.

Anna became aware of the blinking gaze of her companion. He stood silently to one side of the low table, her baggage neatly placed on the floor by his feet.

"Passport," he demanded, holding out his hand. Anna reached into her bag, then hesitated. It was a serious offense to travel anywhere without carrying her internal passport, a thick document containing complete details of ethnic origin (Russian, Ukrainian, Jewish, etc.), social class, marital status, a complete record of employment, the births and deaths of all close relatives and details of every place lived in or visited for more than three days. Anna knew the internal passport was a necessary precaution of the militia and the KGB to protect the people against enemies of the state. But she also knew that, by law, she must register her passport in person with the militia in Moscow.

"The militia . . ." she objected.

He looked at her with puzzlement, then snorted. "The militia!" She handed over her passport.

"You will be ready for your first meeting at eight-thirty tomorrow morning," he said. Then he left, shutting the door quietly behind him.

She sank into a deep chair, exhausted. So much had happened so quickly. From the well-regulated life of a language teacher in a provincial city . . . to Moscow . . . to this! She picked up the bag containing her night things and went into the bedroom. She fell asleep instantly, knowing she would wake with the dawn as she had every day of her life.

But wakefulness came before the full light of dawn. It came with her nightmare. Anna Zasoravna awoke screaming: "Pigs, pigs . . . pigs"—the last cries of her dying mother. She sat bolt upright in bed, drenched in sweat, her whole body shaking with fear and hatred. She fought to free herself of the hideous images which had haunted her dreams since that day when her six-year-old mind had been savaged, leaving an open wound which could only be healed by revenge.

Slowly she gained control of her fear, forcing the terrifying images of the night from her mind. Gradually her trembling body and pounding heart calmed. Throwing off the bedclothes, she leaped up and stumbled across the dark room toward the pale streak of light which chinked between the drapes, and threw them open. The vague hulk of the building opposite was menacing in the early light of the dawn. Everything had been made icily lucent by the thick mantle of freshly fallen snow which lay over the street and rooftops.

As she peered out, her face pressed against the glass, thick snowflakes drifted silently from the darkness toward her, hitting the window with the eerie touch of soft, unseen fingertips. She heard the faint whistle of a train, muted by the heavy stillness of the city and, somewhere high above her, a feeble yellow light appeared at a window of the building across the street.

Anna shivered, though the room was warm enough. She closed the drapes, switched on the bedside light, and looked at her simple metal wristwatch: 6:30 A.M. Her pillow was wet with perspiration. She turned it over, dry side up, and climbed back into bed. With the second match, her still shaking hands managed to light a cigarette. She swept back the thick golden hair which clung to the dampness of her face. She pulled the covers over her and inhaled deeply, savoring the bite of the harsh black tobacco.

The sickening aftermath of the nightmare was still with her. She tried to recall what had triggered it. Since she had channeled her energies and drives into her work as a secret informer for the Party, it had recurred less and less frequently. Then she remembered: the casual words of the KGB interviewer talking about the work of an illegal. She had let them flow over her at the time; the subject was not one her conscious mind was prepared to contemplate.

As a woman illegal, you will be expected to make full use of your main asset—your body. This will be a most important part of your training.

A chilling cold gripped her and she pulled the bedclothes close for comfort. Her nightmare had emerged from her subconscious to remind her. Now there could be no escape. She would have to face the greatest fear of her life: physical contact with a man.

Anna tossed her head back with a gesture of defiance. She would face that challenge when it came. It would be a small price to pay to revenge her mother's brutal rape and death at the hands of the three German soldiers. The horror she had witnessed in the cellar so many years ago must be avenged.

She stubbed out her half-smoked cigarette impatiently, got out of bed, and pulled her nightgown off. A full-length mirror, set in the door of the wardrobe against the wall, caught the reflection of her naked body. She turned to face it.

Anna had never examined her body carefully before. She looked at herself with objective curiosity. Long golden hair framed an oval face with wide-set green eyes. High cheekbones and a full mouth gave her the appearance of sexual assertiveness. Her breasts were full and firm, the nipples prominent. Even in bare feet her legs looked long and elegant, her lithe thighs cupping her pubic hair with perfect symmetry.

Abruptly she turned away and spat. "Men. . . . Pigs."

Colonel Sakov sat hunched in the back of the car. His driver, eyes glued on the road ahead, skillfully negotiated the ice-rutted roads, quietly cursing from time to time as the car skidded and bounced its way forward. After one particularly adroit piece of driving, he swiveled his head quickly for some sign of appreciation from his passenger. Sakov gave a perfunctory nod; he had other things to occupy his mind.

He had appointed himself chief instructor for the new illegal recruit, Anna Zasoravna.

And with good reason. His initiation of the search for a suitable woman to train as an illegal agent had met with great opposition from within the KGB establishment. Only Chairman Zimin's intervention on his behalf had made it possible.

He had meticulously studied more than a hundred dossiers on possible candidates. Finally he had selected Anna Zasoravna. Not only because her obvious qualifications were outstanding—an I.Q. of 156, fluent English, total dedication to the Party, and great physical beauty—but also because of one special and unique attribute: her aversion to men. Sakov knew that the trained experts of the KGB could condition her to overcome her *physical* aversion, but her psychiatrist's report had suggested that the possibility of her ever becoming emotionally attached to a man was remote.

Anna Zasoravna was the perfect candidate. He was going to make certain that her training was the most thorough the KGB could provide. And Colonel Sakov was the ideal man to do this, for he himself had started his long career in the intelligence services as an illegal agent in America, posing as a watch-repairer in New York.

His shop was in a poor neighborhood of the city and his customers developed a special affection for the sturdy yet insignificant "Serge," with his spectacles held together at the bridge by sticking plaster. He was as poor as they, being more interested in his craft than in collecting payment for his work.

What they didn't know was hidden from the world in the room above his dingy premises. The clandestine meetings with agents late at night. The shortwave radio on which he received instructions from KGB headquarters in Moscow. The other electronic and chemical equipment vital for the work of a highly trained illegal agent. For poor, eccentric "Serge" controlled the largest network of Soviet agents operating in the United States.

Sakov was taken aback when Anna opened the door. The young woman who smiled expectantly at him was far more beautiful than her photograph showed. Was she too beautiful to be an illegal, he wondered?

Speaking in English, he came straight to the point: "You are to receive instruction by some of the most experienced members of the security services. Your country is making a costly and time-consuming investment in you. In return you will be expected to work hard. In the cupboard"—he pointed across the room—"is a projector and screening equipment. Throughout your training you will be supplied with American films and television programs. Observe them closely. They will be exactly the same films and television programs the Americans watch. You can learn a great deal from them, particularly their accents and use of colloquial speech. Though your formal English is perfect, you must learn to speak as a native American."

"I catch on fast," Anna replied, repeating an expression she had heard.

"No doubt," Sakov answered with a touch of acidity. "This

afternoon a specialist in dress and cosmetics, Nina Nikolayevna, will visit you. She will teach you to dress and look like an American." He rose. "Study hard. And remember, in the fight against the capitalists, *our agents are perhaps our most vital asset.*"

Later in the day a crate of books was delivered, mostly popular novels. Anna glanced through several. She was revolted. The Americans! They were obsessed with sex and money; they really *were* decadent.

Nina Nikolayenva arrived, a short, plump, dowdily dressed woman. Her manner was brusque and businesslike. After taking Anna's measurements she announced, "Tomorrow I come with a complete wardrobe of American clothes in your size."

"So quickly?" Anna was surprised.

"We have an extensive and up-to-date stock of American clothes, cosmetics, and other material trivia," she told Anna curtly. "I will select what is right for your age in America. Every item has been purchased in New York. And now that I have seen you, I will bring the most suitable cosmetics and teach you how to use them."

Ten minutes after Nina Nikolayevna had left, Anna's instructor in the political philosophy of intelligence arrived, a lean, angular man with a pronounced stoop. He had more of the air of a professor than of an intelligence agent—a deception he had used to good effect in many Western countries.

"You must understand," he began, "that intelligence operations are not a thing apart from the mainstream of history. Still less are they silly games played by irresponsible buffoons, the way they are so often depicted. They are integral to the history of all nations. No doubt it will surprise you to learn that Stalin was informed by our agents of Hitler's impending attack on our country. He chose to ignore this information. Had he not, history would have been different."

Anna's eyes widened. He was right. She was surprised.

"One of the chief advisors to President Nasser was a KGB agent," he continued. "You can imagine the influence this had on events in the Middle East. Without the achievements of our intelligence services, it would have taken us years longer to develop the atomic bomb. There are many more examples of how intelligence operations have determined the course of history. I will tell you about them later. But first I want to explain why the work of our agents is of such importance to our country and to the progress of international communism.

"America is still the greatest power in the world. She has great industrial and military strength. This is no accident. It is the result of an intelligent and industrious people, combined with an abundance of natural resources. It is also the result of her capitalistic system, which has allowed the people to exploit her resources so rapidly. You must remember, *even political aberrations like capitalism have their temporary place in history*. However, as they are not in the true long-term interests of the people, they inevitably decline and perish.

"It is our task to hasten this decline by taking from America's strength and exploiting her weaknesses. Technologically she is more advanced than we, so we use espionage to obtain her knowledge. Her politicians and businessmen are corrupt; we exploit this corruption, not only to obtain information, but to weaken the belief of the American people in their society. In these ways, we fulfill our duty to hasten the day when the world will truly belong to the people."

Anna continued to listen intently. By the end of the session she was elated. He had put her bitter, personal hatred of capitalism into the broad context of history, ennobling it and giving her an even greater sense of purpose.

The next day Nina Nikolayevna duly appeared loaded down with clothes and cosmetics. Anna looked at the delicate, softly clinging underwear. She studied her made-up face in the mirror. So this, she thought, is the way American women treated their men. They turn themselves into dolls to be played with.

Anna devoted herself to perfecting her American image and familiarizing herself with the way Americans behaved and lived. She sat through films and television programs as they were run and rerun time after time. Her instructors explained why various things were happening: why the characters said what they said, what they would be feeling beneath the words they used. She came to realize the purpose of this detailed examination of American behavior, and why it was such an essential part of her training. The American cultural ethos was completely alien from her own.

Separate instructors taught her American history, law, geography, industrial structure, and politics.

At the end of the course she was examined—verbally and in writing. She was not worried about the results. She had become two entirely separate, but completely balanced, people: the one

—herself—a Communist and a Russian; the other, which was to be her armor and her sword, an American in thought, word, and deed.

A week later Colonel Sakov came to see her. "Congratulations, Anna. I am pleased to tell you that the results of your examinations are excellent—so excellent that even the directorate is impressed! In fact, I think they were tempted to check your background to make sure you weren't an American double agent." Sakov's warm smile did not fully express the pleasure he felt at her success. Now he knew he had been right to choose her from among so many possible candidates. And already he was beginning to envisage situations which might develop in America which a woman such as she could exploit toward the achievement of his momentous assignment.

Anna returned his smile politely. "It is all too slow, comrade," she said. "How much more do I have to learn?"

"You must be patient, Anna. You still have a lot to do. Next you must train to be a good American secretary."

Learning to be a secretary wasn't as simple as she'd thought. Shorthand and typing came easily. But when she sat at the desk specially installed in her apartment and her instructor acted the part of an angry boss wanting her to organize flying trips across the world at a minute's notice, or arrange a banquet, including selecting the menu for forty guests, she began to understand just how hazardous the life of a secretary could be.

She learned a great deal about the practicalities of American life which she had not picked up from films, television, or reading. She was not surprised when Colonel Sakov told her later that her instructor had been a highly successful businessman while himself an illegal in America.

Her one relaxation was dancing. "To keep you fit," Colonel Sakov explained. The instructor taught her everything from twist and rock to the very latest modern routines. She found she could extemporize to the music, dancing with a passionate abandon which aroused feelings she had not known existed and did not understand.

After the secretarial training, Colonel Sakov visited her again. "Now, Anna, it is time to learn the basic techniques of espionage. How to decipher messages; how to select and use 'drops,' places where you can hide messages to be picked up by other agents you wish to contact, or to be transmitted by various means to the Center in Moscow. You must become proficient in the art of microphotography—reducing long messages to the size of a period on a letter or postcard—and in the use of invisible writing. You must be able to keep people under surveillance without being detected, as well as being able to evade detection yourself. You will have to master these and many other techniques of communication and surveillance."

Anna worked hard, both at the theory and practice of espionage. She spent days in the streets of Moscow, selecting drops and using them to deposit messages she had enciphered. She received letters and postcards with hidden messages directing her to go to other drops and pick up messages she had to decipher. Photographs of "targets" arrived in the mail, with instructions indicating that they would be at a certain location in Moscow at a specific time. She had to spot them and follow them without being detected, and without them evading her. Other times the roles were reversed and she had to escape from surveillance. Anna decided the greatest asset an agent could have was a pair of comfortable, hard-wearing shoes!

She continued with her reading and Colonel Sakov added *Time, Newsweek, The Washington Post,* and *The New York Times* to her reading list. He went through them with her, pointing out how cleverly they perverted the truth and misrepresented events in their own and in other countries. She continued watching films and television and in her spare time she danced.

It was May and the freezing grip of winter had relaxed its hold on Moscow, giving way to the warm air of spring.

In her apartment Anna watched as Colonel Sakov sat himself in one of the comfortable chairs opposite her. She sensed a certain tenseness in his manner. He remained silent while he lit a cigarette, inhaled deeply, then let the smoke drift out slowly from his mouth and nostrils. At last he spoke, his blue eyes meeting hers. "Now, Anna, we come to a vital part of your training. Your medical reports indicate that you are . . . sexually inexperienced, shall we say."

Anna caught her breath. She braced herself for what was to come.

"In fact," he continued, "it appears you have some kind of aversion to sex. Why this should be, your psychiatrists failed to discover. They suggest it may be a result of having no parents, of being raised in state institutions. However, these are only theories. The fact is, we know, that you are perfectly normal physically. So it is a problem which can be . . . remedied.

"As you are aware from your studies of American culture, apart from money, sex is the main preoccupation of the people. Clearly, if you are to live as an American you must be able to participate in this obsession. Even more important, you must be able to exploit it. The way to an American man's heart is not, as the saying goes, through his stomach, but through his genitals—the American man's Achilles' heel, so to speak. You understand what I'm saying, Anna?" He looked at her steadily.

Anna put on a show of indifference. "I understand. I have no . . . aversion . . . as you call it, to sex." She shrugged. "I have never found it very interesting, that's all. There are so many more important things."

"Not for a female illegal," Sakov replied emphatically. "It will be one of your main weapons."

"Very well," Anna answered calmly, "then I will become expert in the use of this weapon."

"You will indeed, Anna. You are going to a special school where we teach our women to be swallows."

"Swallows?"

"Yes, swallows. That's what we call women who work for us to compromise foreigners. These women are not like you. Their only skill is in the use of their sex. They are, of course, attractive and intelligent, for they have to be able to entice the most reluctant of men."

"From my knowledge of Americans that shouldn't be too difficult," said Anna.

"More difficult than you think, Anna. Foreign governments are familiar with our methods. They warn people coming to our country of the dangers. Swallows have to be more than prostitutes. They must be able to effect an apparently casual meeting with their target—the man they have to trap—then develop what seems like a spontaneous relationship of the heart. To do this they must be able to assess a man very quickly. Identify his needs and his weaknesses—emotional, not sexual, at first. In this way a perfectly natural affair develops so the target suspects nothing. Only then can she complete her work."

"Complete her work?" Anna tried not to sound too apprehensive.

"Yes. They must be photographed together making love. Most of our hotels have special rooms with hidden cameras for this purpose. Or one of our men posing as an irate husband will break in on them and threaten a scandal. Sometimes it is enough for the swallow to take her target along a lonely street. Then suddenly she will scream rape and waiting KGB men appear and threaten to arrest the man unless he "cooperates" with us. The *coup de grâce* is very simple; it is the entrapment that calls for skill and experience."

"It sounds simple enough to me," Anna said with bravado.

"Not always, Anna. And for you it will be more difficult. These entrapments are quick businesses. In America you may have to live with, perhaps marry, a man you despise, all the time pretending you like being with him, even love him. Above all, satisfying his sexual needs, whatever they are. It may not be easy."

"I will do whatever is necessary, comrade. You may depend on it."

"*Whatever* is necessary, Anna," Sakov repeated.

CHAPTER
FIVE

The school for swallows was situated some twenty kilometers outside the city. A complex of modern single-story buildings surrounded by a high wire fence, and standing alone in a bleak landscape. Anna showed her papers and was conducted to her room by a taciturn woman.

She felt confident. She would approach the whole business clinically. She could fight pain, she knew; she would fight her revulsion of men in the same way. At 10:30 P.M. she switched off the bedside lamp. For a while she lay awake, wondering about the next day. Lectures on human biology, perhaps, and tiresome pictures of sexual techniques. Well, she could cope with that. She closed her eyes and was soon asleep.

Breakfast arrived at 8 A.M. It was followed, half an hour later, by the blonde woman who had shown Anna her room when she arrived. "I am Dr. Voronim," she introduced herself. "Come with me. Please." Anna followed her along several corridors and then into a brightly lit room. There were two couches—reminding Anna of those psychiatrists' couches she had read about in American novels—placed a few feet apart and occupying the central space. The only other furniture was a small table with two wooden chairs. Dr. Voronim seated herself on one of the chairs, motioned Anna to sit opposite her, then began methodically to scan the pages of a file.

Late thirties probably, still very attractive, Anna thought, as she examined the intent face of the doctor. She'd be even more attractive when she let her tightly drawn-back hair hang free. Beautiful white skin and good features. Something odd about her eyes, though, something unpleasant. No doubt she was a psychoanalyst and would soon be prying into her past life to find out why she was still a virgin. Well, that was one piece of information which would never find its way into her file. Why didn't they get down to the business of teaching about sex?

The doctor shut the file. "You're twenty-eight, attractive, physically normal, yet you have never had a man," she said flatly. "You have some deep-seated resistance to penetration. To men. You will require special treatment."

Anna said nothing.

"Take your clothes off."

Anna hesitated.

"Take them *off*. Here. Like me." Dr. Voronim started to disrobe. Anna reluctantly obeyed, undressing slowly, until they were both naked.

"Now do as I do," the doctor ordered, lying down on one of the couches, her legs wide apart. Moving woodenly, Anna obeyed the doctor's command. As her head touched the pillow, the door opened and two men came in, both wearing robes. Without speaking they walked to the end of the couches. Anna slammed her legs together and shot upright, her arms clamped around her knees, her eyes shut tight.

"Lie down. Open your legs!" the doctor shouted. But Anna couldn't move, couldn't bring herself to look at the man standing in front of her.

The doctor nodded briefly. "Nikolai."

The man called Nikolai took off his robe, stepped forward, and with one knee on the couch inserted his rigid penis into the doctor's open vulva. Slowly he began to move, backward and forward.

"Anna," the doctor said more gently, "look. Look at *me*."

Anna turned her head and, taking a deep breath, forced herself to open her eyes. She recoiled in horror. It was hideous!

"Now, Anna," the doctor's voice was coaxing, "look at my *face*."

Anna obeyed. The doctor was smiling, totally relaxed.

"Now look at Nikolai's face."

Again Anna obeyed. Nikolai turned to smile at her—a warm, gentle smile from a boyishly handsome face.

"Now. How can it be so terrible?" the doctor said, still smiling.

"I don't know. I don't know," Anna moaned, rocking from side to side, her arms still clasped tightly around her knees.

"Lie back, Anna." The doctor spoke softly but firmly.

Anna lowered herself, her eyes and legs shut, and waited, every fiber in her body tense and quivering. She felt strong female hands placed firmly on her shoulders. Then slowly but inexorably her legs were forced apart. Anna willed herself to stay quite still, to control her horror, to learn what she must. She felt the pressure between her legs and clenched her teeth repeating over and over again to herself, "You must, Anna, you must." The pressure increased, a sharp pain which made her cry out, then the thing was deep inside her, moving up and down. The force of the movements increased, a violent lunge, then the thing was out. For several minutes she lay frozen, motionless.

"That wasn't so bad, was it, Anna?" The doctor spoke from behind her.

Anna sat up and looked around. The men had gone. The doctor was writing in her file. "Get dressed," she said without looking up.

Anna's mind was blank except for one inconsequential thought. She hadn't even seen her "man."

"Go back to your room now." The doctor spoke again. "On the shelves you will find a selection of men's magazines and pornographic books and photographs which are freely available in America. Study them thoroughly. There are many different kinds of sex to learn about. You must become expert in them all."

At first, Anna was appalled by what she read and saw. She studied the faces of the "actors" in the photographs. There was no doubt the men were enjoying themselves. But the women! How could they? Yet some of them obviously were. Perhaps they were *very* good actresses? Or was it because they would be paid a lot of money?

The more she looked at the photographs, the more she became used to the sight of the sexual acts. It was the women who fascinated her. If they could do all those things for money, she decided, then, she, Anna Zasoravna, could certainly learn to do them for her country.

Shortly after 6:30 P.M. there was a knock on her door and the young man Nikolai entered.

"How's your study?" he asked, grinning at the pornography covering her bed.

Anna couldn't help smiling. "Not very good." Then she blushed, recalling the events of the morning. "I have a lot to learn."

"I have come to teach you a little more," he replied, quickly taking off his clothes. "Now you"—he nodded to Anna, who was fully clothed—"in front of me . . . take your clothes off. Slowly."

Anna blushed again, but complied. Nikolai studied each part

of her body as she exposed it. Then he fell on her and took her brutally, like an animal. He lay beside her, panting. "Again," he said. Anna was stunned. She had been raped! She looked at him with bewilderment, then anger.

"No," she said. "*Not* again."

The blow from his hand sent her reeling across the bed. He looked down at her. Gone was his engaging boyish smile: here was the face of a sadist. "Again," he repeated. Anna suppressed her rage and hurt and lay back. "No," he said, "*you* make me." She tried, doing the things she had seen in the photographs, but nothing worked. He got up from the bed, the soft-faced boy again. "You did very well, Anna. For a learner." He left the room, grinning.

The next morning Anna found herself in a theater with a group of women. They all knew one another. She supposed they were a class of swallows. A white-coated woman entered and immediately dimmed the lights. A pornographic film. Anna had an odd sensation she had seen the "actress" before. Then with a shock she realized *the girl in the film was sitting two rows in front of her*. How could she do it? Anna wondered. And how must it feel to be watching yourself . . . with a group of other women? The lights went up. Anna leaned forward to peer curiously at the girl. She showed not the slightest sign of embarrassment.

The woman in the white coat was complimentary about the girl's performance but made a few suggestions as to how she could improve on certain techniques. The girl listened attentively, then the lights dimmed again and another film was shown. And so on. Some performances were much better than others. One unfortunate girl, an attractive redhead, was severely reprimanded and told if she didn't improve she would be dismissed. The girl burst into tears.

Anna found she was soon able to make her own assessments of the performances and was pleased she was beginning to lose some of her inhibitions. Then she saw the unbelievable. Herself! And her clumsy attempts to arouse the young man the previous day. She sat in agony. The lights went up and she forced herself not to run away in shame. The girls were looking at her, some unable to stop themselves from laughing. The instructress spoke. "Our comrade is new," she said. "Do not forget some of you were worse when you first came."

Anna was told to stay behind when the other girls left. "You must not be too upset, comrade," the instructress said. "The girls you watched have almost completed their training. They are very experienced. But you see how much you have to learn?"

Anna nodded, then asked, "The film. Of me. How was it done?"

"There are two-way mirrors in all the bedrooms. Whenever you practice sex you will be filmed, so we can correct and improve your techniques, like this morning. You must also get used to having sex while you know you are being filmed."

Anna resolved that never again would she perform so badly that other women could laugh at her. She was given a succession of partners, some experienced and virile, others far older and requiring great skill to arouse. She learned to cater to perversions, to sadists and masochists. And always to maneuver her partners so the hidden camera had a clear view of their faces. At the end of four weeks she no longer regarded her body as private and personal, but as a weapon to be used like a machine. She still despised men as sexual animals. But she no longer feared them. Their sexual needs made them vulnerable like children.

Anna learned how to fake orgasms. But she never experienced one. She was glad. It meant she was always in control of the situation—never an animal!

On her return to Moscow Colonel Sakov was waiting for her. "You did well, Anna. I have your report here. Congratulations. I know it was not easy for you."

"It was my duty."

"Yes, but not an easy one," Sakov answered, not for the first time impressed by her complete and unquestioning dedication. "However, at least you can be glad the worst of your training is over. The next thing we have to do is build your 'legend,' your fictitious past as an American citizen."

Anna listened, fascinated to learn about her new identity.

"You were born in a small town in Iowa. Tell me what you remember about Iowa from your studies."

She did and he was satisfied.

"Sit where you can see the screen." He slipped a cassette into the projector and dimmed the lights. On the screen she saw the front view of small houses on either side of a street. The picture moved down the street. The image was shaky, like a home movie, and she guessed it had been taken from the back of a slow-moving vehicle. The picture stopped and focused on one house. "That is where you were born and lived until you were eighteen." In the same way she saw the main street, the school she attended, the little river outside town where she used to swim in the hot summers.

"When you get to America, you will go there and familiarize yourself completely with the town," he told her. "Your name was Jane Mantel. When you were eighteen you went to the university and worked your way through, studying French and Russian."

"Russian!" Anna exclaimed. "That could be dangerous."

"Quite the opposite. It may turn out that your knowledge of Russian will be useful to you in America. Who knows? It is also a good precaution. The fact that you speak Russian could come out by accident. These things happen. It would be hard to explain unless you had studied it. Besides," he added, "Jane Mantel *did* study Russian."

"You mean Jane Mantel existed?"

"Of course. Everything about your past life in America *has* to be fact."

"What happened to her?"

Colonel Sakov frowned. "Be patient and you will find out. Shortly before you graduated, your parents were killed in an automobile accident. They drove head-on into a wall in broad daylight."

Anna raised her eyebrows.

"*Fact*," Colonel Sakov said in reply to her unspoken skepticism. "Your father was a liquor salesman. He was also an alcoholic and a violent man. Sometimes he beat up your mother and even you, his daughter. Your mother was one of those women who could take anything except divorce. There are women like that. In time she found refuge from the awfulness of her life in drink and she too became an alcoholic. At the inquiry into the accident, witnesses said they had both been drinking heavily and arguing at an out-of-town club. They were thrown out. Later, other witnesses saw them actually fighting in the car seconds before they hit the wall."

"I guess I had a happy childhood," Anna said wryly. "How do you know so much about 'me'?"

"From your student days. We have agents on many campuses. Disturbed or discontented students make a fruitful hunting ground for recruits to communism. One of our agents, a Professor Wolfe, picked you out, as you were so obviously emotionally disturbed. He took a 'special' interest in you and your work. After your parents were killed and you graduated, it was he who suggested you needed a complete break from your environment if you were to regain your emotional stability. He persuaded you to take a secretarial course in New York . . . so you could go to Europe and work."

"Did she get to Europe?"

"Yes. She spent two weeks in England, then went to East Germany and disappeared. She has not been heard of since."

"What happened?"

"That is all you need to know," Colonel Sakov said tersely. "Except you need never fear she will turn up again in America. Her past is *yours*."

Anna knew him well enough by now not to pursue the matter further. She said, "And what did *I*, the *new*, fictitious Jane Mantel, do?"

"You stayed in London for a year working as a free-lance typist in the daytime and a barmaid in public houses in the evenings. Both can be done without producing a work permit. After London, you spent a further year traveling around France, living cheaply, using the money you had saved from your two jobs. Then you went to Spain and taught French and English at a private school for the children of foreigners living there."

"But a school would keep records of their permanent staff," Anna said questioningly.

Colonel Sakov smiled. "Yes, but fortunately it had to close down for financial reasons. There were only ten staff and most of them have returned to their own countries—including the owner of the school. There is no one left to know where the records are. Most probably they have been destroyed anyway."

"You mean this school really existed?"

"Of course. It closed down six weeks ago. Foreign schools are rarely successful in Spain—bad administration, too few pupils, unqualified staff. Note the last point. Nobody is going to be surprised you were given a teaching post."

Anna couldn't help asking, "How do you know of this school?"

"It is part of our agents' work to send reports to the Center of any event which could be useful for building legends for our illegals. Bankrupt businesses, fires which destroy employee records, the simultaneous death of a husband and wife, apartment blocks which are demolished, and so on."

"Apartment blocks . . ."

"While you were in New York taking your secretarial course, you had to live somewhere. The block you lived in was demolished to make way for an office complex. If your legend were to be checked out, there are no neighbors left to testify whether or not you were actually there."

"Very thorough," Anna commented.

"Merely a basic precaution. I have been trying for some time to complete your legend and the closure of the school in Spain is the perfect solution. You will now have been away from America for four years. Your parents are dead. When they were alive they had no contact with their kin. They were not exactly family people! It will not be surprising that you have no friends in America."

Colonel Sakov sat back. "Yes," he said contentedly, "a most satisfactory legend."

But Anna was far from relaxed. "What about these countries I am supposed to have lived and worked in?" she asked anxiously. "I know nothing about them."

"Do you imagine that is something we will not take care of?" he rebuked her mildly. "When you finish your training you will spend two weeks in London familiarizing yourself with the city and the public houses you worked in. I have an itinerary of the places you visited in France and of the town and its environs where you worked in Spain. You will visit all these places. In Spain our agent will take you to the empty school and give you a rundown on the staff and the school's history. He will also teach you all the Spanish you would be expected to know." Colonel Sakov gathered up his papers. "Yes," he repeated, "a most satisfactory legend.

"However"—he leaned forward and spoke earnestly—"you must remember almost *any* legend can be broken down by an experienced counterintelligence service, once you are under suspicion. The purpose of a legend is to satisfy ordinary Americans of your legitimacy and to avoid attracting the attention of the FBI. Once you are under suspicion you are of no use to us anyway. In fact, you become a threat."

"What would happen then?"

"If we knew you were under suspicion you would be recalled to Moscow immediately. Otherwise the Americans would keep you under surveillance until they had identified any agents working with you."

"And then?"

"They might try to persuade you to become a double agent— as an alternative to sending you to trial on espionage charges. Or they might try to exchange you for one of their own agents whom we are holding." He shrugged. "It would depend on many things." Then a hard glint entered his eyes. "But why this talk of failure?"

"Curiosity, comrade. How else can I know about something I will never experience?"

A smile of appreciation spread slowly across his face.

To complete her training, Anna was sent to the special spy school near Kiev. It consisted of two small "replica" towns completely surrounded by heavily guarded wire fences. One town was typically American; the other British. Anna lived on her own in an apartment in the American town and was given an allowance of dollars. During the day she practiced the mundane things of everyday living in America: shopping in a supermarket; buying clothes in American sizes; sending telegrams; making phone calls; taking buses and cabs; cooking American food; eating in restaurants; attending and giving American-style parties; using a bank account; and so on. She also learned how to drive.

The other occupants of the town were either illegals like herself finishing their training, or permanent instructors who staffed the various facilities they used.

On alternate evenings she crossed into the British town and served in the public house. She learned how to take orders and pour drinks; how to shortchange customers and serve beer from the dispenser so there was too much froth on top, giving a short measure of beer—all the tricks of a good bartender.

The other evenings were filled with instruction on the handling and use of pistols—at static and moving targets. Using lethal gas pistols; using poisons and drugs.

In her apartment on the second evening after her return to Moscow, Anna was restless. The following morning she was due to set out on the long journey to familiarize herself with the legend of her new self to be—Jane Mantel. Anna felt curiously unsettled, as if something were missing. She slumped into a chair and tried to concentrate on the latest edition of *Newsweek* only to find she wasn't taking in anything she was reading.

Eventually she forced herself to admit what it was that was troubling her. Colonel Sakov had not come to say good-bye to her. Not that there was any reason why he should. That morning, she had received her papers and instructions from an officious young officer with the face of a weasel. But she wished Sakov had come, just to wish her luck.

Then she recalled the words of the KGB man who had recruited her at Rostov University. It seemed a lifetime ago, but his words came back to her as if it had been yesterday: "It is a cold world you are entering, comrade. It is as well you get used to it quickly."

"Yes, Anna," she said to herself, almost as if bidding herself farewell, "a cold world. You must learn to make your own good-byes, your own little celebrations." She filled a glass with vodka. "Good-bye, my Russia. . . . Good-bye, Colonel Sakov," she said in a whisper. "Welcome, Jane Mantel." She drained the glass.

Then she was overcome with a strange and exhilarating excitement. Now she was completely and absolutely alone. Untouched and untouchable.

A mile away, in the KGB officers club in Dzerzhinsky Square, Colonel Sakov sat alone at a table, a half-empty bottle of vodka in front of him. With a curt shake of his head he declined the invitation to join a group of brother officers at a nearby table. He raised his glass and stared at it for a few moments. "Good luck, my Anna," he said silently, emptying the glass. Hurriedly he refilled it.

As the plane took off from Moscow for Copenhagen the next morning, Anna knew nothing of the plans for her future—only the thrill of anticipation. She had been warned she would feel nervous when she first arrived in a Western country: the strangeness, the fear of detection. But as she thought of walking the streets of her enemies, living with them openly yet hidden, she felt no fear—only power.

She stayed overnight in Copenhagen, where she tore up and flushed down the toilet the forged British passport she had used to enter the country. The next morning she boarded a flight to London with an American passport under the name of Betty Watson.

The plane circled over Heathrow airport outside London and, looking down on the neat clusters of houses with their little gardens, separated by green fields the size of pocket handkerchiefs, Anna sensed the bourgeois complacency of the British people.

Like all good American tourists, she had bought some inexpensive souvenirs in Copenhagen airport—glassware and a wood-carved replica of Denmark's national symbol, a mermaid sitting on a rock.

"Anything to declare, miss?" the customs officer asked politely. "Nothing expensive," Anna replied. "Just a few souvenirs." "That's all right, miss. I hope you enjoy your stay in England." He marked the bags and waved her through. It had been the same at passport control. A stern-faced official took the forged American passport, opened it at the photograph, gave her a quick glance, then rubber-stamped it and handed it back. It was all so easy.

She took the airport bus into London, then a taxi to a small hotel in Kensington. Once inside the room she fell on the bed laughing, amazed at the feeble controls which allowed her to enter an enemy country so simply.

After familiarizing herself with the pubs and other places on the itinerary drawn up for her, she spent what remained of the two weeks visiting the usual tourist spots—Buckingham Palace, the Tower of London, Hampton Court, and a day trip to the Shakespeare Festival at Stratford-on-Avon.

The day before she was due to leave, she visited the British Museum where Marx had written most of his early works on communism. It was five o'clock when she left and she decided to walk down to Leicester Square to see a new American movie. After walking for about five minutes she had the feeling she was being followed. She didn't know why. Maybe her long training in the streets of Moscow had given her a sixth sense. She stopped to buy an evening newspaper and glanced down the street. It was crowded with people pouring out of offices on their way home. About twenty yards from her, a young man stood preoccupied, looking into a shop window. She walked on and crossed the street; the young man followed. At Leicester Square she went down one of the entrances to the subway and came up out of another. He was still with her.

The pubs were opening. She entered the nearest one, sat on a stool at the bar, and ordered an iced Coke. The young man came in, ordered a Scotch, and sat next to her.

"You're American?" he asked.

She looked him over. Blond wavy hair, good regular features. Too good—slightly feminine. A well-tailored suit. "That's right. How come you know?"

"Your clothes, something about your face. I usually get women right." He offered her a cigarette; she refused; he lit one.

"How long are you here for?"

"A few more days."

"How do you like it?"

"I like your country," she answered. "The people are so friendly."

"How friendly is friendly?" The slight smile made the innuendo obvious.

"Friendly enough," she replied coolly.

"Depends on what you fancy, I suppose." He spoke in the slightly bored tones which come naturally to the English upper class. "There's a few things going on over here you might have missed." He leaned toward her, a sensuous leer on his face, and she caught the cloying smell of his expensive after-shave lotion.

Anna looked at him innocently. "What kind of things?"

"Oh, this and that." He twisted the ring on his finger. "Look here, I'm giving an intimate party tonight. Couple of Jamaican girls, a few chaps from here and there. Come along. Here's my address." He took out a card.

Anna tapped it on the bar counter. "I'll think about it," she said.

"You think about it," he repeated. Anna forced herself not to flinch as he laid his hand lightly on her neck. "It could just turn you on. I've known it to happen to the nicest girls." He left.

Pig! Anna thought and put the card in her bag.

The apartment was in an exclusive area of Hampstead. Loud music flowed out when he opened the door. "You thought about it," he quoted her. "Name's Gerald."

"Betty," she said. "Betty Watson." She walked in. There were half a dozen couples, some in chairs, some on the floor, sharing joints and drinks.

"Wrap yourself around this, Betty, and come over here." He handed her a drink, led her to an empty chair, and pulled her down onto his knee.

One of the girls was doing a slow strip to the beat of the music, her movements suggestive, some obscene. He said, "Your turn next, nice girl," his eyes bright with anticipation.

She got to her feet and slowly poured her drink onto his face. "I don't play with children," she said evenly, and before he could reply she bent down and whispered, "And tell them this, because I'm going to tell them anyway. You're no good. You're clumsy and obvious. You can't even follow someone in the street without being detected. Can't they get more efficient crap than you?" She dropped her glass into his lap.

As she sat in the taxi heading downtown, she felt good. She had known all along it was a setup, a test. The KGB wanted to find out if she was vulnerable to the sexual permissiveness of the West. Whether she could use with discretion the sexual skills they had developed for her.

Well, now they had their answer.

She flew to Paris and spent a week exploring the city and visiting the mandatory "shrines" on every tourist's itinerary.

Hiring a car, she set out on the zigzag course that was part of her legend, ending up at the luxury resort of Biarritz, where she watched the "beautiful people" of Europe enjoying an endless round of pleasure in the hot summer's sun. She crossed the Spanish border at Irún on the edge of the Pyrenees and headed south across the parched landscape of Spain. Through Madrid to Córdoba and down to Málaga on the Costa del Sol. Sixty kilometers along the south coast and she was in Marbella. There she met the KGB agent: a taxi driver. Tall, dark, with black flashing eyes, he frequented the foreign bars where he was known as El Romántico. And where he built his clientele amongst the tourists and resident foreigners.

He took Anna through the still empty school where she had taught. He gave her detailed descriptions of the teachers who had been her colleagues. Speaking English, French, and German, there was little he didn't know about their private lives—especially the women's. In the evenings he drove her to little restaurants in the craggy mountains behind the town, and over simple food taught her "foreigner's" Spanish. A vocabulary of a few hundred words, all verbs present tense only. She soon mastered it.

On the evening before she left, she asked him about himself. "Look at me," he said. "How old am I?"

She studied his face. "About forty, I guess."

He smiled. "Over fifty. Old enough to have fought against Franco and his German and Italian Fascist allies in the civil war in '36. The only friends we had were the Russians and a few Communist volunteers from other countries. It was a bitter war. More than a million Spanish dead. My village was destroyed by Italian bombers. My family wiped out. I remember. I wait. I will have my revenge."

"But here, in a tourist's paradise, what can you do?"

Again the flashing smile of El Romántico. "Many rich foreigners have holiday villas here. The sun seduces them. They drink too much. They commit indiscretions. I make sure our people know of them so they can be used against them when they return to their home countries. There are other things. The British base at Gibraltar is not far. It guards the entrance to the Mediterranean. It looks no more than a bleak rock peninsula jutting out into the sea. But underneath that rock are miles of underground passages and caverns. It is my business to know what goes on in those subterranean shelters. It's not difficult. The British forces stationed there get very bored. You understand?"

Anna nodded.

"There is also the American nuclear submarine base at Rota, near Cádiz. So you see, I'm very busy one way and another. Not like a tourist."

Anna parted from El Romántico feeling proud. It was good to know there were people like him, nationals of their own countries, fighting for the same cause as she.

She took the coast road along the Mediterranean and crossed back into France near Perpignan, continuing on to Marseilles, Nice, and Cannes. Then back to Paris via Lyon and Dijon.

From Paris she flew TWA to New York. It was early afternoon when they approached the city. Looking down at the endless expanse of gigantic concrete buildings, she sensed the power of America. For a second she was awed by the enormity of the task confronting her people—to destroy such power! Then she looked at the soft, overfed faces of her fellow passengers and her confidence was renewed.

She took a cab to a cheap hotel off Broadway. Her first act was to destroy the forged passport in the name of Betty Watson. There was another passport in her luggage, Jane Mantel's, correctly stamped according to her legend. *Anna Zasoravna was now Jane Mantel.*

The next day Jane Mantel rented a car—she wanted to get the feel of America, meet people—and made the long journey to her alleged hometown and university. At the university she had a long session with the KGB agent, Professor Wolfe.

On the way back to New York Jane stopped off at a motel. She washed, put on fresh clothes, and drove downtown. She had set herself one more task to complete.

She selected a bar—not too up-market, not too cheap. Inside, she looked around.

Ed Peterson sat alone at the end of the bar staring vacantly at his seventh shot of bourbon, an unlit cigarette in his mouth. He was thinking.

It was all over between him and Lorna. She'd met a guy who was something in computers and she'd decided she loved him and they were going to get married. Ed hoped she would be happy; he really did. Everybody got married—everybody except Ed Peterson.

He took a long sip of bourbon and wondered about it, not for the first time. During his short life he had respected, cherished, and even on occasion obeyed a number of women, including Lorna. The one thing he could not bring himself to do was marry them. His married friends envied him his freedom. What they were never able to understand was just how incredibly boring it was to always be hunting, finding, courting, then settling with a woman only to end up out in the cold because he wouldn't marry them. One unending merry-go-round to nowhere. Maybe one day he'd find someone who would knock him right off that merry-go-round, head over heels in love . . . whatever that was!

He smelled Jane's perfume as she slid onto the stool beside him and ordered a vodka martini. She'd been watching him. About thirty, she guessed. A sort of boyish openness about his face, with fair hair hanging over his forehead. She imagined women would find him very attractive. But that wasn't what she was interested in. All she cared about was that he was alone and drinking.

He pushed his empty glass toward the bartender and a flame appeared at the end of his unlit cigarette. He twisted around and focused on her. "You watch the late-late shows too?"

Jane smiled. A warm, reassuring smile with just enough behind it to show. "Only if I have to," she said.

"That shouldn't be too often," he observed, thinking what a goddamn shame it was he didn't like his women to be too well packaged.

"How about you?" she asked. "You like to drink alone?"

"There are times," he said meaningfully.

Jane twisted the stem of her glass slowly between her fingers. She was calculating her next move. He wasn't giving a thing, not even a smile. Over his shoulder she saw a group of people coming in: a tall man, heavy shoulders, black hair, the center of attention.

"Who's that?" she asked, playing for time.

He followed her gaze. "The tall one?"

"Yes."

"Senator John Hurst. He's just given a speech down the street to some outfit of his called the American League of Freedom." He shrugged. "Matter of fact, I should have been there."

Jane raised her eyebrows questioningly.

"I'm political correspondent for a newspaper syndicate out here. Only the senator always says the same thing, so I filed six paragraphs on him before I left the office."

"He's that boring?"

He looked at her sharply. "Not to me, he isn't."

"So why weren't you there?"

Ed Peterson grunted briefly, then looked at her as if he wished she'd go away. "Because it hurts too much to see all the empty seats every time he speaks."

Jane shook her head. "I don't understand."

"Nor do most people," he answered. "Let's just say the senator and I have something in common. . . . We're both scared of the Russians."

"Scared. Of the Russians?" Jane's surprise was genuine.

"Yeah. Senator Hurst figures détente is no more than a smoke screen the Russians have thrown up to hide their real intentions, which are distinctly hostile. . . . So do I."

Jane laughed. "You don't really believe all that stuff about the Russians."

"Yes. I do believe all that *stuff*, as you call it"—He bit off his words—"for a lot of reasons, and one of them is I took time out for Vietnam and what I saw scared me to death."

"What . . . ?"

"Communists aren't afraid to die. That's what scared me."

Jane decided to make one more attempt to get through to him. She leaned forward and placed her hand on his arm. "Why so serious? Afraid of me?"

He smiled brilliantly, showing even, white teeth. "Not even a little bit."

Jane braced herself and took the plunge. "Then don't let's waste time. Let's screw."

His smile faded and he looked at her with suspicion. "You a professional lady?"

"No. Just passing through, and bored. Strictly amateur."

"But skilled?"

"Very."

"That's what they all say."

"Try me."

Ed Peterson shrugged and drained his glass. "Why not?" he said as he helped her off the stool. She stood next to him and reaching up, cupped his face in her hands and kissed him very gently. "You know why I'm doing this?" she said.

"You're bored?"

"No. Because there are two things about a man I can never resist. Flattery and enthusiasm."

He smiled broadly and she saw just how attractive he could be. "Okay. You're right," he said. "Let's just say I've had a rough day."

"It could get better."

"Sure it could," he said, gliding her toward the door.

They walked the four blocks to his place. Jane talked nonstop to relieve the tension. She hadn't felt so nervous since that day in the sex school.

He wasn't really listening, but he caught her name and the fact she'd been visiting her old university. He was thinking about Lorna. Mouse-colored hair, skinny, with an overly full mouth and slightly protruding teeth, she wasn't beautiful at all. He glanced at the classic profile of the woman by his side. She'd be better than sinking bourbon; but only just.

"Drink?" he asked as he closed the door of his apartment.

She shook her head and moved toward him. She knelt down in front of him and then he was lying on the bed groaning with pleasure as she played with him. He seized hold of her, tore off her pants and was into her until he came with a violent spasm. Ed Peterson collapsed, spent and eternally grateful.

She waited awhile, then aroused him again, using the techniques she had been so thoroughly trained in. She took him to the edge of his climax, calmed him, then on again, until he cried out, "For chrissake, baby, a man could die this way."

At last she mounted him and, as she looked down into his helpless face, she repeated to herself, "Pigs, pigs, pigs." Suddenly she felt an explosion inside her as she came with him. She lay beside him, content. She *could* do it for real . . . not just in the clinical setting of the training school. *And* her first orgasm. She knew why: the thrill of power. She had milked him as if he were an obedient cow.

He was still sleeping as she hastily dressed and left him without a glance. For Jane Mantel it was the conclusion of an experiment, but for Peterson it was a beginning.

CHAPTER
SIX

Cathy Jackson did not think being twenty-eight years old and unmarried was exactly a crisis situation. Her mother, who took a rather more orderly view of life, did. A woman of twenty-eight *ought* to be married. There was no doubt about it.

"For heaven's sake, Cathy," she'd say. "I know it's none of my business, but you can't go on like this forever. You'll have to get married sometime. Everybody does! What's wrong with Tony Milard, for instance? He'll soon be made partner in one of the best law firms in Washington. He's kind and considerate . . . attractive. . . . There isn't a girl who wouldn't marry him if she got the chance . . . and he wants to marry you!"

"I know, Mother," Cathy would answer, whether it was Tony Milard, Bob Standish, or whoever happened to be pursuing her at the time. "But I don't love him."

Inevitably these conversations would end with her mother in a state of exasperation, exclaiming, "Heaven knows, everyone else seems to find someone they can love. Why can't you?"

Cathy didn't know about everyone else, but she did know about Cathy Jackson. She liked men. She had light affairs with some. But "love and marriage," as the saying goes, was another thing. And she was not going to marry until she found someone she could love the way she had loved Carl.

Sometimes she wondered if Carl hadn't spoiled other men for her. For, as the years had gone by, those two brief, incredibly beautiful years ending in tragedy had become even more private, more personal, more dear to her.

But Cathy was not unhappy. She didn't doubt that sooner or later she would fall in love again and marry.

In the meantime she was content with her life.

Her father, Bill Jackson, seemed to understand. He sensed that the woman who returned from Vienna was a very different person from the young daughter who had gone off to finishing school in Switzerland.

He had an inner calmness which Cathy found soothing. As a senior senator he was under constant pressure, but he never showed signs of strain. Cathy enjoyed working in his office as a research aide, and sometimes at the end of the day they would sit and talk politics.

"I don't know how, Cathy," he would say, "but somehow or other this crazy Constitution of ours works . . . most of the time anyway." Then he would smile and the lines would soften around his alert eyes. "Come on, young lady, your mother likes to see us sometimes, you know."

And that was how it was—until she walked into Senator John Hurst. It was the anniversary of the day she was to have married Carl. Every year since her return she went to the National Gallery and stood gazing at the pastel of Madame Michel-Levy which Carl had said they would see together when they went to the States. It was the one day each year when she allowed herself to feel self-pity. And as she looked, the frame filled with the images of Carl and Anette. She closed her eyes and the tears welled out. Blindly she turned to go before the pain made her sob out loud . . . and she walked into him. He had been standing behind her, looking at the same picture.

"Oh! I'm—I'm sorry," she said, not looking up, embarrassed by the tears streaming down her face.

"My fault, ma'am," he said, and the softness of his voice was like another echo from the past—the same rich timbre as Carl's. "I guess you could use this."

Through a haze of tears she saw the white handkerchief he held toward her, but not his face. "Thank you," she blurted out, and ran down the gallery hiding her face in the handkerchief.

The telephone buzzed in her office the next morning. She picked it up.

"Cathy Jackson?" The voice sounded familiar.

"Yes."

"My name's John Hurst. We met, briefly, at the gallery yesterday. Remember?"

"The man with the handkerchief?"

"That's me."

Cathy felt a mixture of resentment and embarrassment. Resentment because, although he had tried to be helpful, he had trespassed into her private world. And embarrassment because he had seen her lost in grief.

"Glad I was there to help," he continued, the soft tones again reminding her of Carl. "If you don't mind, I'd like to collect my handkerchief from you . . . personally."

"That's not necessary," Cathy answered. "I wouldn't want to put you to that trouble."

"No trouble at all," he persisted. "In fact, I'll be passing your way this evening. We're sort of neighbors in Georgetown. I'll drop by seven o'clock and pick you up. We're going to dinner, so be good and hungry."

"Not so fast—" Cathy began.

"I'll be around anyway," he cut in. "You can always throw my handkerchief from out of your window!" He laughed, a soft, good-natured laugh, then hung up.

Shortly after seven a car drew up and a man got out and shut the door behind him, all in one easy movement. Cathy opened the door. "I'm John Hurst," he said. The name clicked and Cathy recognized him. "*Senator* John Hurst?" She'd seen him a couple of times around Capitol Hill.

"That's right," he said.

His clear blue eyes contrasted vividly with his jet black hair. She supposed his features could be called craggy, good-looking. But not in the way movie stars of that type were; their features always had a soft patina that told of too much easy living. His face had the hardness of a man who wouldn't know how to compromise. He was tall and heavily built, but as he escorted her to the car he moved smoothly and freely.

As he opened the car door she said, "So you're the one who's causing all the stir on the Hill about the Russians."

He smiled. "That's me."

They drove the short distance to Chez Odette on M Street. He didn't speak on the way, but she wasn't embarrassed by the silence, nor did she feel pressured to break it. She saw the hard, taut veins on the back of his strong hands holding the wheel and felt at ease.

She was glad they were dining at Chez Odette. She liked the French cuisine. The gingham curtains and plates hanging on the wall reminded her of the bistros she had been to with Carl.

The waiter escorted them to a corner table and asked what they would like to drink. He looked at her. "Dry sherry," she said. He ordered a Scotch for himself.

"Don't you think you have some explaining to do?" Cathy said.

"Explaining?"

"Yes. Like how you knew my name. How you knew where to telephone me. How you knew my home address. Like what we're doing here now!"

"I made a few inquiries and found out who you are. . . . So here we are!"

"Just like that." Cathy raised her eyebrows.

"Just like that," he repeated. "Does it have to be more complicated?"

"It usually is," Cathy said.

Hurst ignored this. "Any more questions?" he asked with formal politeness.

Cathy held on to the initiative while she still had it. She said, "What were you doing in the National Gallery?"

"Same as you, I imagine. Looking at the paintings."

"You're interested in art?" she asked.

"No. Know nothing about it. But when I get sick of the smell up there on Capitol Hill, I visit the gallery and look at the paintings. I feel a whole lot cleaner and it gives me hope. . . . I guess it's like having a fix."

The waiter arrived to take their order. Cathy selected carefully from the varied menu. Hurst glanced at it and ordered one of the day's specials.

"Well," Cathy said as the waiter withdrew, "you know the saying—if you don't like the heat, get out of the kitchen. If you think politics smells that bad, what are you doing in the Senate?"

"I guess I'm a plumber at heart. If I smell something bad, I have to fix it."

"Oh come on," Cathy said, as the waiter arrived with the food, "it's not that bad."

"The way I see it, it is. If we don't stop fighting each other all the time over who gets the biggest slice of cake in this country, we're going to wake up one day and find the Russians have taken the whole goddamn cake away from us."

"Pessimist," Cathy said.

He laughed. "Okay. But let's concentrate on the important things in life . . . like you. What turns you on, Cathy Jackson?"

"Oh, I don't know," Cathy mused. "Being alive. The blossoms in spring. The brilliant colors in the fall. Sitting and watching tourists from all over the world pass by. The exhibitions and art galleries. Walking around Woodland Plantation and smelling the flowers. Swimming at Patrick Bay. You know . . . all the exciting things in life."

"And art? You were looking at that painting yesterday as if it really meant something to you."

"It does. But that's a part of me I don't talk about . . . even to strangers!"

"And that's Cathy Jackson," he said. "Period."

"That's all you're getting . . . right now," she said.

"I'll settle for that, right now," he answered.

"And what about you?" she asked. "Apart from politics, that is."

"Just an all-American boy, I guess. Disturbed upbringing, like all the best people. Mother died when I was ten. Brought up by a rich father with three interests in life—money, women, and alcohol. You pick the order, he wasn't that bothered! Spent a couple of years bumming around the world, seeing how the other ninety-nine percent live. Came home and started a lumber company. Got interested in local politics, then got myself elected to Congress. On the domestic side, I was married. . . . My wife died of leukemia seven years ago." Cathy detected the fleeting shadow of sadness that passed over his face. "Now I'm living in an old up and down townhouse here in Georgetown. End of story."

Cathy wanted to keep the conversation away from herself. Everything about his manner told her that John Hurst didn't chase after women and take them to dinner just to pass the time or even talk politics. Everything about him was purposeful, deliberate.

She said: "And your plans for the future . . . political, I mean."

"Political? To become President." Then he laughed. "But that might take a little time. Right now I have only one plan in mind. To marry you."

Cathy's mouth was about to close on a piece of pastry. It stayed open.

"I mean exactly what I said. I want to marry you," he repeated.

"Don't be ridiculous!" Cathy said.

"It's not ridiculous. It's the most sensible thing I've said in my life. I knew it the moment I saw you."

"That was just sentimental pity," Cathy answered, "because I was upset."

"People don't all cry the same way. When the barriers are down, you can see what they are really like."

"You don't know a thing about me."

"I don't know how you like your eggs done, or how many children you want, or where you like to vacation, or whether you think Off-Off Broadway is just plain off. Apart from a few other details like that, I know all I need to know."

"It's still ridiculous," Cathy repeated.

He looked at her intently, then very quietly said, "No, it's not, Cathy."

"There's just one little thing," Cathy replied. "Whether I want to marry you."

"You will," he answered.

"You're impossible," Cathy laughed.

It was several months later when she went into her father's office to see if he was through for the day. "Sit down, Cathy," he said. "Drink?"

She was surprised: he rarely drank in the office. "Scotch," she answered, "with a little water . . . and a lot of Scotch."

He poured the drinks and sat in the high-backed chair behind his desk. "This John Hurst—you've been seeing him quite frequently," he began. "But you haven't mentioned him to me."

"I haven't been trying to hide him, Dad. For goodness' sake! I've been so wrapped up in my own thoughts, I haven't got around to it somehow." She didn't add that she had the same sense of her relationship with him being a very personal and private thing as she had about her life with Carl. John Hurst was very different from Carl in so many ways, but they shared something: a calculating purposiveness combined with personal warmth and spontaneity. And Cathy had that same feeling of being completely safe when she was with him.

"I know you haven't been trying to hide him," her father said. "But your not talking about him made me think your interest may be more than a passing fancy. Not that I disapprove. Lord knows, he's an improvement on the young men your mother's thrown at you."

"I know that," Cathy said, sipping her drink. Her father had taken her at her word about the water.

"Just how serious are you about John Hurst?"

"Pretty," Cathy admitted.

"Thinking of marriage?"

She nodded.

He crossed to give her his usual kiss on top of the head but this time he kissed her cheek and then, for a brief moment, held her against him. And Cathy thought how lucky she'd been with the three men in her life!—her father, Carl, and now John.

Cathy Jackson married John Hurst in the spring.

In Moscow, Sakov's eyes stopped halfway down page fifteen of the report specially prepared for him each month. It had been waiting for him when he arrived at his office. Twenty-four pages detailing the most recent activities of more than five hundred illegals, agents, and American citizens whose past and present indiscretions might be useful to him in the furtherance of his assignment.

He had noted the usual sexual adventures of a dozen or so highly placed politicians, members of the military, and industrial bosses of defense plants. Nothing very unusual. He put a tick against a name here and there. He would return to them later.

It was entry number 312 which riveted his attention. Cathy Jackson had married the anti-Soviet John Hurst!

This was what he had been waiting for. The numbers game— the more you tried, the more you scored—was paying off. A pair! The ambitious senator and Cathy Jackson . . .

He sent for the file on Senator Hurst.

The file was thick. The man Hurst was becoming the leader of the anti-Soviet movement in the United States—and gaining increasing support. Sakov whistled soundlessly through his teeth while his mind raced.

He pondered for a long time. He would have to go to America.

Taking a notepad, he wrote the draft of a memorandum for personal discussion with Chairman Zimin. His hand shook very slightly as he wrote, for what Colonel Sakov of the KGB was now proposing was the most audacious coup ever perpetrated by one nation against another.

PART
TWO

CHAPTER
SEVEN

On the flight to New York, Sakov settled down in a window seat. He adjusted the position of his stiff leg to make himself more comfortable. He would sleep as much as possible to reduce the tedium of the long flight and the tiring effects of jet lag.

The plane leveled out at thirty thousand feet. There was nothing to be done until he met Jane Mantel. He closed his eyes and was soon asleep.

Had he known that at that very moment Jane Mantel was engaged on her first active assignment, an assignment which would lead to complications he could never have foreseen, Sakov would not have slept so well. He would not have slept at all.

It had started two days before when Jane was watching the early evening newscast.

For nine months she had worked as a secretary in an insurance company. Living the life of a typical American girl in New York. She had plenty of friends but now that she had got over the thrill of living among her enemies, she was bored. She realized it was essential she be totally assimilated into the American way of life, and it took time. But she was impatient to start.

The telephone rang. The conversation was brief. When she put the receiver down her heart was racing. Grabbing a coat, she ran down the three flights of stairs, too excited to wait for the elevator. Outside she hailed a cab and named a street in Queens. She paid the driver and walked the last four blocks to the house.

It was a safe house. One of the many the KGB used in New York for secret meetings and for other activities of a rather different nature.

She identified herself to the taciturn man who opened the door and followed him upstairs to a comfortably furnished sitting room.

An elegantly dressed man was waiting for her. Jane noticed the graying hair at the sides of the long sardonic face. His name was Valentin Shvets, officially a senior member of the Soviet U.N. delegation. In fact, he was Lieutenant General Shvets, KGB resident for New York in charge of all intelligence operations in the city.

He gestured for her to sit and then started to explain why he had summoned her.

"A Russian writer named Anatole Deniskin has defected," said Shvets. "The CIA have got him."

"Where were we?" Jane asked angrily.

"Asleep. . . . The CIA moved too fast for us. Your job is to get him back. That's what you're here for."

"Just tell me what to do," Jane said eagerly.

Shvets explained. When Jane rose to go he said, "It will be good experience for you."

CIA agent James Hadley was bored. He'd just come back from three years in the Middle East. There'd been some nice action. Won a few, lost a few . . . but never bored. What with the KGB and Mossad—boy, those Israeli security guys sure were one helluva smart bunch. And those Arabs—Jesus, they were on everybody's payroll. They had the answer to unemployment—multi-employment! You couldn't go for a quiet crap but that you'd find everyone had changed sides three times. Yes, sir, it sure made New York a quiet town. And guarding some long-haired Russian screwball writer Deniskin, who wanted to defect to the U.S. "Don't get it wrong, Hadley," they'd said at CIA headquarters out at Langley, "he's the hottest property we've got. . . . That's why we've put an experienced operator like you on him."

So who was going to steal him? The KGB weren't exactly going to come busting in, tommy guns blazing. They were sensitive guys; they cared about their image. And the FBI—shit, man, you could stuff the guy up their assholes, sharp pencil and all, and they still wouldn't be able to find him. As for the guy himself, no way was he going to break out. Barred windows, locked doors, and good old Hadley sitting downstairs with nothing to do except break the arms off the first itinerant Russian writer who tried to walk past him.

The doorbell rang. Hadley groaned. He opened the door on the chain. The night was dark; the girl was beautiful. Tall, stacked, long black hair.

"You want something?" he said lazily.

"Open this goddamn door and let me in."

"You collecting for the Salvation Army?"

"You don't let me in and you'll be collecting a zero salary from Franklin."

"Franklin. Now, why do you have to mention him? He's the dude at Langley who put me on this job. Any friend of his is no friend of mine."

"Stop the wisecracks, Hadley, and let me in. We've got to get the Russian out of here, quick."

"Who said? And how the hell do you know my name?" His brain switched into gear.

"Franklin said and the KGB, both."

Suddenly Hadley was wide awake and in New York and just a little bit worried. "Who the hell are you?" he snapped.

"Let me in, will you, and I'll explain."

"Give me one good reason why I should." He peered at her more closely through the jar and saw the car parked in the road behind her.

"Here, take a look at this."

He took the piece of paper and scanned it. It was a handwritten note from Franklin: Most urgent he follow instructions of bearer, Judy Sinclair, five-six tall, black hair, mole on left cheek. . . . KGB going to bust in. . . . Move Deniskin. Hadley recognized the writing and the signature. He should. Franklin sent a lot of Christmas cards with handwritten personal greetings and the KGB went to a lot of trouble to collect Christmas cards sent by people like him. The note was a perfect forgery.

He let Jane Mantel in and locked the door.

"Mind if I search you?" he said, and without waiting for a reply ran his hands over and under her with the slickness of a conjuror.

"Do that once more, Hadley, and I'll break your neck and leave you here for the KGB to stamp all over." She glared at him.

"And the bag," he demanded.

She opened it.

"Okay. Now tell me about it."

"I told you. The KGB are going to bust in . . . any minute. Got it?"

"How the hell d'you know?"

"If I could answer that, I'd be doing Franklin's job."

"Why did he send you? Can't he use a telephone?"

"You don't have a telephone."

"The hell I don't. I used it fifteen minutes ago."

"It's one way only—out. How long since you took a call? We tried to contact you. Your telephone is dead. The KGB have done some delicate engineering. That's why I'm here."

He looked at her. "Jesus!" was all he could say.

"And what's the betting the telephone is dead both ways by now?"

He rushed and picked the telephone up, then slammed it down.

"I'm getting through?" she asked sarcastically.

"You got. Stay here while I collect the Russian."

He ran up the stairs three at a time. One minute later he was on his way down with the elderly, frightened-looking Russian. Deniskin was protesting loudly but Hadley had a gun on him. "Sorry, pal," he said, "but I don't have time to explain."

They bundled Deniskin into the car. "Christ," said Jane, looking back, "I left the house door open. Shut it, or they'll know we've blown."

As he shut the door, the tires screeched and the car accelerated away. Inside the car, Deniskin looked at Jane Mantel uncomprehendingly. As the needle sank into his arm, his eyes glazed over and he slumped forward. Next to him, Jane withdrew the needle and took her black wig off. She had never felt better in her life.

Sakov's flight touched down at exactly eight-fifteen the next morning.

As an accredited member of the Russian Embassy with diplomatic immunity, he made his way rapidly through to the nearest phone booth. He called the resident at his home and was surprised to learn he had left an hour earlier for his office. He dialed again and got through to the resident's assistant at the U.N.

"Put me on to Comrade Shvets," he said, naming the resident.

"Who is speaking?"

Sakov told him.

The assistant tensed. They had already received instructions from the Center in Moscow. The newly appointed Advisor on American Affairs, Colonel Sakov, was to be given all possible help and his orders to be obeyed without question. But he had not expected to hear from Sakov so soon.

"I'm afraid that will not be possible, Comrade Colonel. He's not available."

"Perhaps *you* can help me?" Sakov wanted to be tactful about the extent of his new authority.

"If I can, comrade."

"I want to meet agent eleven-twenty immediately," Sakov said. The possibility the phone was tapped was remote. But "remote" wasn't enough insurance. He wanted to meet Jane Mantel while he was in New York—before catching the shuttle to Washington.

Under normal circumstances the assistant would have had to refer to the files to link the number with the name. But circumstances were not normal.

"Sorry. That will be difficult. . . . The agent has an assignment."

"In New York?"

"Yes."

"Meet me in front of the Met at Lincoln Center. Be there with a car immediately." Sakov slammed the phone down and hurried to get a cab.

The assistant was waiting when he arrived at the Met. As soon as he learned where Jane was, Sakov instructed the driver to take them there as fast as possible. Then he sat back and listened to the assistant's account of Jane's activities.

She had done well to recover Deniskin from the CIA; it had taken nerve. But Sakov was profoundly thankful that the most dangerous part was safely over. Jane Mantel was too valuable to be put at risk in a direct confrontation with American security services. He would put her under wraps immediately when this was over. As for her part in the rest of the operation, there was little risk involved and it would give him an opportunity to observe her in action.

"How did we know where the CIA were keeping Deniskin?" he asked.

"We were fortunate," the assistant replied. "The CIA took him directly to one of their own safe houses. Our men were able to follow them."

They reached the house in Queens and the assistant led the way to a small room, bare except for a circle of hard-backed chairs facing a wooden panel, about six feet high and three feet wide, set on the wall. Three men were talking.

Sakov was surprised to find the resident himself among them.

After the introductions he drew Shvets to one side, out of earshot of the others. "Why is Deniskin so important?" he asked quietly. "Why are we taking such trouble with a defecting writer?"

"Direct orders from Chairman Zimin," the resident replied. "Deniskin was a close friend of the traitor Volodin. You remember the affair. . . . Volodin was interrogated and put under house arrest by the Chairman himself. My instructions are to silence Deniskin at all costs."

At that moment one of the men went to the wooden panel on the wall. He pressed a catch and swung the panel so that it was reversed, flush back against the wall.

Through the two-way mirror, in the inner hidden room they could see Deniskin lying on a bed.

Deniskin surfaced into semiconsciousness. His head was pounding. He reached automatically in the darkness toward the bedside lamp. A searing pain tore through his head. Instinctively his outstretched hand went to the pain: a lump and what felt like an encrustment of dried blood high up on his forehead.

His hand found the lamp switch. The sudden burst of light brought jagged pain to his eyes. He stumbled to the window and threw open the drapes. Outside he saw the cars in the street below. Thank God! He was still in America.

But—he swiveled around and looked at the room. It was big, with a high ceiling . . . like his Moscow apartment. And the bed, the bedside table with *his* lamp on it, and two of his most treasured possessions—his wife's photograph and an ivory statuette of Tolstoy—were there. Even the bookshelves above the bed were the same.

It was like a movie set. And all the props were real. His mind whirled. Where was he?

The door opened. The tall young woman with the black hair came in.

Without speaking, Jane walked across to a chair, picked it up, and placed it beside the bed.

"It's good, isn't it, comrade?" she said in Russian as she sat down. "A perfect replica of your apartment."

Deniskin rose to his feet and moved unsteadily toward the door. Jane spoke without turning her head. "Where are you going, old man? There's no way out. This is a KGB house. You are surrounded by good friends. . . ."

Deniskin returned to the bed. Something about this assertive young woman, no older than his youngest daughter, made him feel foolish. Like a boy. "It's not a replica," was all he could think to say. "These things are mine."

"Of course," she answered. "Authenticity was essential. Everything was flown over from Moscow, even the bedspread. But then, that was particularly important. It features very prominently in the action."

"Action?" he repeated, bewildered. "What do you mean?"

She took a large envelope from her briefcase and, slowly drawing some photographs out, dropped them carelessly onto his lap. "Look and you'll see how important the bedspread was."

Deniskin stared at the photographs, stupefied. Suddenly, the vomit spurted from his mouth. He leaned forward, still retching, though his stomach was empty.

Jane calmly got up and went to the washbasin. She returned with a cloth. As she wiped up the vomit she mocked him. "Come, come, old man. I didn't know traitors were so sensitive. Did you really think you could betray your country and get away with it? You should have known better."

He spoke with difficulty, through thick, distorted lips, trying to suppress his revulsion of the degrading things which had been done to him while he was drugged. "Lies, all lies. No one will believe I am a homosexual."

"If we release these photographs everyone will believe you are a homosexual," she replied.

"Lies," he repeated again in disgust, trying to rid his mind of the sight of the rape of his body. But there was something else nagging at the back of his mind which he couldn't put his finger on. He shook his head in an effort to clear it from the effects of the drug. He looked around the room again. Then, slowly, it dawned on him. "Why here . . . in New York . . . my apartment . . . and those—those vile photographs?"

Jane smiled. A cruel smile. She had no compassion for a traitor. "I'm glad you are regaining your senses, old man," she said. "It's quite simple, really. You see, the boy in the photographs was blackmailing you when you were in Moscow. Don't you remember?"

Deniskin passed a weary hand over his face. If he could only get rid of the stupefying drowsiness in his head he could cope with this arrogant young woman who was playing with him— work out what she was getting at. "I remember no such thing," he mumbled.

"Oh, but surely you remember, comrade," she taunted. "He was a student at the university. He came to the notice of the police because his lavish spending was not in keeping with his status as a student. He was interrogated two days before you came to New York. At first he would admit nothing. He was released and followed. The first thing he did was warn you. It's no good denying it. He has since confessed everything. So has the student who took the photographs. They have also told us about the young boys they procured for you . . . at a price. The state prosecutor has all the evidence he needs. The trial starts tomorrow. You will also be tried as a pederast *in absentia*. We have arranged to give it maximum publicity."

Deniskin massaged the back of his neck and breathed deeply, desperately trying to think clearly. "What—what are you getting at?" he stammered. "It's all lies."

"It's obvious," Jane answered. "We have no option but to totally destroy your reputation and credibility."

"Why in God's name should—"

"Because you have already given information to the Americans." Jane cut him off like a whiplash.

"Not yet, I . . ." He stopped in midsentence. But it was too late. She had led him into a trap and he had fallen for it. Now she had the answer to the question she had approached so obliquely, taking advantage of his already confused mind and the shock of the photographs.

She was speaking again. "Shall I complete your sentence, comrade?"

He said nothing.

"You were waiting until your speech to the American League of Freedom to betray your country."

He remained silent, but they both knew it was the truth.

"Now listen to me carefully, comrade," Jane continued. "We have a proposition to put to you and you have a choice to make."

"What choice?" Deniskin's voice was hoarse.

"You will deliver your speech and this is what you will say: You will tell your American audience that there *is* real freedom of expression and thought in Russia. You were kidnaped, drugged, and hypnotized by the CIA. You are a Russian patriot and whatever you said under hypnotism was false. You want to go home to Russia."

Deniskin could scarcely believe his ears. "But that is ridiculous! Who will believe me!" he exclaimed.

"It doesn't matter if they believe you or not. They will have to let you go."

"And then?"

"When you return to Russia you will lose all your privileges ... dacha, car, and so on. However, a small pension and an apartment in Kiev have been arranged for you. Regrettably, you will not be permitted to visit Moscow."

Deniskin smiled faintly. "In other words, I am to vanish into oblivion."

"Yes. Ill health will be the reason for your early retirement."

"And if I agree," Deniskin asked, "how will I account for my escape from you?"

"Tell the CIA you were seized by the KGB, just as it happened, and driven toward Kennedy airport. The car skidded off the highway and crashed. You were cut on the forehead and mildly concussed. You have the gash on your forehead to prove it." She pointed to it. "But your two captors were severely hurt and you managed to escape. You ran until you collapsed—delayed concussion. You contacted the police as soon as you came around."

Deniskin shook his head wearily. "Too many lies ..."

"You needn't worry," she assured him. "They'll believe you. When they check they'll find a car *did* skid off the highway near the airport and there *is* blood inside and some of it *is* yours."

"I need time. To think. To decide." Deniskin put on a show of bravado.

"You have no time," Jane retorted. She turned to go. "Pull yourself together, old man, and do what I say. A car is waiting to drop you near the airport."

When she had gone he lay back, exhausted. His whole body began to shake. Had he really believed it would be easy to defect ... *knowing what he did*? She was right: no one would believe the words of a pederast. His humiliation—and his disgrace— would be to no purpose. Yet if he did not speak the truth, the very system against which he had finally rebelled would have triumphed and destroyed him. Suddenly he felt very old.

He clasped his arms around his thin chest and began to rock from side to side, a low moaning coming from his quivering lips. At that moment he would have welcomed the tranquillity of death, where there were no impossible decisions to be made, no agony of mind ... just peace.

The four men behind the two-way mirror got to their feet and stretched their legs. The resident was smiling. "The girl was good, eh?" he said to Sakov.

Sakov nodded.

"Would you like to see her now?" the resident suggested.

Sakov remained silent for a moment. "No. I will wait until after the rally. Get me a seat near her."

"Certainly. But why? There is nothing more for the girl to do. Deniskin has no choice. He will give us no more trouble."

"Perhaps you are right. I hope so," Sakov said thoughtfully. "But the way a man will behave is never one hundred percent predictable until he is dead. Who can tell what will go on in that man's mind during the next ten hours?"

"Very well, Colonel, as you wish."

"It is what I wish," Sakov answered.

As the crowds gathered in the auditorium, Senator John Hurst took his seat behind the table to the left of the lectern that occupied the center of the stage. He poured himself a glass of water and looked out across the vast hall lit by a myriad of small lights sunk into the high dome of the ceiling.

Above him, across the entire frontispiece of the stage, the words THE AMERICAN LEAGUE OF FREEDOM boomed out in four-foot-high red letters.

The publicity buildup for Deniskin's appearance had been fantastic. For two days the public had been bombarded by television, radio, and press, urging them to watch the network prime-time transmission of Deniskin's speech. Thousands of invitations to hear him speak had gone out. Exactly how it had all been set up so quickly, the senator didn't know. But he did suspect where the money and the organizational know-how had come from: the CIA. But he didn't mind.

A lot of people didn't think too highly of the CIA. The senator agreed that they did some pretty stupid and irresponsible things at times. He also knew America needed the CIA, and that they were no worse than the intelligence services of other countries. The only difference was that the CIA's mistakes and misdemeanors were made public. A pity, he thought.

The front rows were filling with White House representatives, congressmen, and U.N. delegates from many countries. Anatole Deniskin was not just another defecting Russian intellectual: he had been the chief Party spokesman and propagandist for the Soviet government. This defection was like the Pope announcing he had become an atheist.

Jane Mantel walked toward her seat on the edge of the aisle exactly ten rows from the front. Her feelings were a mixture of satisfaction and curiosity: satisfaction with the job she had done so far; curiosity to see how Deniskin was going to react.

The resident was completely confident Deniskin would toe the line. He had congratulated Jane on the way she had handled her work. Jane wondered about the resident. He was foolish to be so certain about Deniskin. She had been trained never to rely on human behavior. She had taken the necessary precautions. . . . Time—another few minutes—and she would know the answer.

"Jane Mantel!" She turned quickly to see the man who had grabbed her arm. For a second she hesitated. Should she respond or should she pretend not to remember him? She decided to respond; it would cause less fuss. "Ed—Ed Peterson, what on earth are *you* doing here?"

They were standing in the middle of the aisle, people streaming past them looking for their seats. Ed Peterson held her arms, smiling with pleasure.

"Doing? I'm covering Hurst for the syndicate. Looks like he's made the headlines at last."

Jane squeezed his hand. "I'll see you after it's all over, huh?"

He grinned. "You bet."

She moved on. She had no intention of seeing him. It would be simple enough to lose him in the crowd.

Ed Peterson returned to his seat across the aisle and six seats back from Jane. He wondered how she felt . . . seeing him again. Nothing, he supposed. She'd got up and left him still sleeping that night nearly a year ago. No good-byes, no address. A one-night stand. Ships passing in the night. He wished it had been that easy for him. It hadn't. It had taken her just two hours to shatter a belief he had formed from long experience: Beautiful women make lousy lovers. Jane Mantel had given him the most exquisite pleasure he had ever experienced. Ever since, he had sought and bedded a succession of women, looking for that same experience, always disappointed. Always hoping, but never expecting, to meet the woman who had briefly given him such contentment only to leave him . . . so discontented.

The two giant clocks on either side of the auditorium showed five minutes to go. Peterson waited, eager for it all to be over, his eyes riveted on Jane.

Sakov, three rows directly behind Jane, had watched the encounter with no more than mild interest. A woman as beautiful as she would have many admirers. With equal lack of concern he saw her get to her feet, move into the aisle, and drop her bag, spilling the contents. In a state of obvious confusion, she bent and picked up the usual assortment of clutter found in a woman's bag, then returned to her seat.

The man in the roof had already counted ten rows back along the aisle seats. It wasn't going to be any bother at all. That morning, wearing overalls and carrying a tool kit, he'd taken the back stairs to the top of the building, entered the roof of the auditorium, and removed one of the myriad of light fittings, exposing a round hole ten inches in diameter. He'd have preferred the hole to be bigger, but it would do. He saw the speck below drop something in the aisle, then move back. Fine, he'd got the right seat.

The lights dimmed.

Senator John Hurst rose to make his speech of introduction.

Deniskin, sitting behind him, heard nothing. His mind was whirling to a crescendo of agonizing conflict. The truth, the truth, the truth! But what was the truth? What was he but a pawn being torn apart by the CIA and the KGB?

As he mounted the podium, the audience rose to its feet with a spontaneous outburst of applause. He heard nothing. Unseeing, he stared into the ranks thronging the vast auditorium. Silence fell.

His face white with strain, he began: "My friends . . ."

He peered out into the darkness, knowing that in his audience were many friends and many enemies of his country . . . all hanging on his every word. And at that moment he knew he could not commit the ultimate treason. He would speak the truth. The struggle and anguish of mind was over: he had made his choice.

He stood erect and continued:

"There is in Russia today a man very few of you here have heard of. He is my comrade Volodin. I speak to you now in his name. He sends you a warning. A plot is being organized in Russia which will very soon—"

And then it all happened, very suddenly. Jane took a powder compact from her bag, snapped it open, and raised it to her face. She pressed a small button on its base. The man in the roof saw the tiny stab of light coming from the blackness below. His finger squeezed once, twice—and once again. And then Deniskin was dead, very dead, with all the peace of mind he would ever need.

At first a stunned silence of incomprehension. Then pandemonium. Ed Peterson jumped to his feet. He had not heard a word the late Anatole Deniskin had said; his eyes had been on Jane. He had seen her raise the compact to her face and the faint flick of light catching a few stray hairs at the side of her head. But it didn't mean a thing to him. He had only one thing on his mind—not to lose Jane Mantel. Not again.

She had been quick out of her seat by the aisle and was already opposite him, engulfed in a flood of screaming, crying, frightened people, fighting their way to the exits.

Peterson grabbed the jacket of a man in the next row and hoisted himself onto the top of the seats. Then, using the heads and shoulders of the people on either side of him for support, stumbled along the seat tops like a drunken wire-walker and jumped into the midst of the flood in the aisle. A woman screamed with pain as the heel of his shoe caught her hip. And then like a maniac he fought his way up to Jane and grabbed her around the waist. "Stay with me," he yelled before her elbow sank into his stomach. And then something hit him on the back of his neck and he was unconscious.

He woke up in hospital with allover bruises and three broken ribs. He was one of thirty-seven people nearly trampled to death in the panic. Another five hadn't been so lucky.

CHAPTER
EIGHT

Reactions to Deniskin's assassination were mixed. The FBI and the CIA had no doubts about who had been responsible: the KGB. But there was no chance of nailing them with it. It had been a contract job.

What the FBI and CIA couldn't figure out was why the KGB had done it. The most plausible explanation seemed to be to discourage other prominent Party members from defecting. This theory was backed up by the Russian press. *Pravda* and *Izvestia* both attributed the assassination to criminal Russian émigrés who, it was claimed, had formed a conspiracy to murder any prominent Soviet who defected. This palpably ridiculous assertion was not for overseas consumption. It was for the benefit of their own top people, who would have no difficulty reading the clear warning between the lines—the penalty for defection at the top was death.

The American press took their normal line of complaining about the deficiencies of their own security services. How had it been allowed to happen? they wanted to know. It was clearly evident the security services had blundered again. Maybe if they took time off from invading the privacy of ordinary American citizens they might just be able to protect one Russian defector.

Neither government addressed the other about the matter. The Kremlin had no wish to. Washington had no evidence.

For two weeks Sakov sweated it out in the Washington embassy worrying about Jane Mantel. He had quarantined her from all further KGB contact of any kind. He was keeping her under twenty-four-hour visual and electronic surveillance. He had to be absolutely certain Jane Mantel was not a suspect of any of the American security services.

Everything seemed normal. Jane Mantel was carrying on with her life as if nothing had happened. She was taken out by two men—by one to a Broadway hit, by the other to dinner at Parks. Neither of these escorts fitted the description of the man Sakov himself had knocked unconscious at the Deniskin affair.

Colonel Sakov was a careful man. The FBI would have registered his reentry to America and his new appointment to the embassy. They would certainly suspect he was KGB. They probably knew he was—more than half the embassy staff were.

So he had waited before instructing the New York resident to contact Jane. Sakov had to move cautiously. In a meeting with Jane Mantel, *he* would be the security risk. A motel near Chester roughly halfway between Washington and New York was the appointed place.

Using a false identity, Sakov hired a car. After driving around town for an hour, he headed out on the highway to Chester. Twenty miles from his destination, he turned off the highway and drove down a small road for about a mile before taking a rough track leading through a wood. He stopped by the black Plymouth parked to one side among the trees. He nodded to the man standing by the Plymouth, then got in it and drove it back to the highway. Five miles from the motel a blue Chevrolet was parked by the roadside. He stopped, lowered the window, and took the key from the outstretched hand of the agent who had already checked into the motel and thoroughly searched the chalet. Twenty minutes later he parked by the chalet, situated out of sight of the office, and let himself in. Jane Mantel was due to arrive in half an hour.

Ever since she had received her instructions from the resident, Jane had anticipated her meeting with Sakov with growing impatience. She had been exhilarated by the Deniskin affair. She, Anna Zasoravna, the schoolteacher from Rostov, had destroyed a traitor and enemy of her country. She had tasted power and it had been sweet.

Jane parked by the chalet and walked toward the door.

Sakov was watching her through a slat of the closed venetian blinds. For an instant he felt pride. She was Madison Avenue. She was Sardi's. He could see her swinging along Fifth Avenue. She was every American cliché about sexual attraction you could think of. She was every man's fantasy of a "million-dollar broad." And she was *his* creation. Plus, he admitted to himself with a smile, a little touch of capitalism. She had used her short time in

America to good effect—to put the finishing touches to his work.

He opened the door. "Welcome, comrade," he said. They shook hands and he waved her to the chair next to the table lamp, then he drew the other chair close to her and sat down. He wanted to see her face—every moment, every shadow of expression.

"May I congratulate you on your handling of Deniskin," he began. "You acted just in time."

"You saw it?" she answered with surprise.

"Yes."

Jane knew better than to ask how or why.

"It went without a hitch," he continued, ". . . even in the auditorium. You arranged all that?"

"It was simple."

"Not even one little hitch," he repeated, his eyes fixed on her.

Jane hesitated for a second. The way he had spoken, it was impossible to tell whether it was a statement or a question. But if he'd been there, he would know. "Not one," she answered.

Sakov nodded, but she could tell something was bothering him.

"You had no trouble getting out in the panic?" he asked mildly. "Quite a few people were hurt, I believe."

"No more than anyone else," Jane answered.

Sakov nodded again. He was satisfied *she* was in no way concerned about the man who had pursued her. But *he* still was not satisfied.

"Tell me," he said. "Who was the man who spoke to you before Deniskin's speech? The man who grabbed you as you got away after the shooting?"

"Him!" she exclaimed, at last aware of what had been troubling Sakov. "A young man I met months ago when I was familiarizing myself with my legend."

"Why was he so keen to get hold of you?" Sakov persisted quietly. "He could have got himself killed the way he chased you."

Jane considered the question. "You remember I had a sex problem," she said.

"Yes."

"I used this young man to see if I had finally overcome it . . . in the field, not just in a sex school."

"And have you?"

"It would seem so." Jane smiled. "He was certainly hell bent on getting a second helping."

Sakov laughed and impulsively leaned forward and touched her hand. A gesture of camaraderie ... or affection. And much to her surprise Jane found she didn't mind.

Then Sakov continued, his face serious. "Too keen, perhaps, comrade. Where does he come from?"

She told him.

"His name?"

"Ed Peterson."

"His address?"

Jane frowned. "I don't know exactly. It's three or four blocks west of a bar called Harry's. An apartment block. But you don't have to worry. He's really not important."

Sakov grunted. He would check on Ed Peterson.

He got to his feet and began to pace up and down without speaking. His leg was troubling him again. A dull ache.

Not for the first time, Jane wondered about his limp. How had he got it? The war, she supposed. But *exactly* how? Perhaps one day he would tell her. Perhaps ...

At last he sat down and leaned toward her. "You remember Senator Hurst, Chairman of the American League of Freedom?"

"Of course."

"It is our intention to promote his political aspirations by every means possible."

Jane gasped in astonishment. "His aspirations!" she exclaimed. "His one aspiration is to warn his people against what he calls the immediate threat of Soviet military aggression. Are we to help him do that!"

"Yes," Sakov replied flatly. "And there is no need for you to understand why. You can safely leave that in the hands of the Politburo."

Jane was silenced by the enormity of what he'd said: that his orders, and hers—whatever they were to be—were part of an operation directly authorized by the Kremlin.

When she spoke it was in a whisper. "And my part in this, comrade?"

"A most vital part. But for now we will concern ourselves only with the first step. You are to get close to Senator Hurst—so close that he trusts you implicitly."

"How ... ?"

"Be patient and I will tell you. First you must get close to him. How you gain his trust is for you to work out."

Sakov was watching her face as he spoke. He saw no anxiety,

no doubts, no apprehension—only intense concentration and, beneath it, the controlled tension of her excitement. He was pleased with what he saw. He continued:

"The senator has a nephew named Brennan, Michael Brennan."

Sakov reached into his briefcase and took out two plain-covered files and handed them to Jane. "Take these with you and study them. One contains all you need to know about Brennan and his business affairs. The other, some very interesting information about a man named Robert Adams. Adams is the key to Brennan; Brennan is your entrée to Hurst."

He leaned back to stretch his leg, which was starting to ache once more. Then he produced a small file which he handed to her. "This contains details of how you will communicate with me, including the cipher you will use. You will see that all your written communications will be sent to an address in New York. From there, they will be delivered to me by courier. I will communicate directly to your New York address, using the same cipher. For additional security—and this is not contained in the file—you and I will misspell exactly three words in every communication. You understand?"

"Yes. It's perfectly clear."

"Good. In an extreme emergency you may telephone me at the embassy from a pay phone. Ask for extension three-four-eight . . . three-four-eight. A man will answer. Identify yourself by the code name Samual, then give him the number of a pay phone where I can call you back and the exact time you will be waiting for the call."

Jane nodded to indicate that she understood.

He got to his feet. "That is all for now." He extended his hand.

Jane rose, frowning. "There are no further instructions?"

Sakov understood what was behind her question. He stepped forward and rested his hand lightly on her arm. "No, comrade. *No* further instructions. You are part of the largest intelligence service in the world, but in this assignment you are on your own. You have been selected because you have the necessary talents, instincts, and cunning. But only *you* can know how best to apply them."

They shook hands and Jane left.

Immediately when she was back in her apartment Jane got busy opening the Mike Brennan file and memorizing the facts and figures about his business. Then she opened the Adams file.

She soon realized how he could be the key to Brennan. The question was, how to insert the key?

The answer to that lay in Brennan's personality and character. He was young, highly ambitious, and a true entrepreneur. A high flyer. He would play his hunches and make quick decisions.

Jane made her plans.

CHAPTER
NINE

Three days after Sakov's meeting with Jane, Ed Peterson walked down the steps of the hospital and caught his breath as the freezing wind bit into his bruised and battered body. It had been all right in the soothing warmth of the hospital bed. He had been impatient to get out. But now the wind came as a sharp reminder that three of his ribs were healing, but were not yet healed, and that his bruised flesh had not recovered from the pummeling it had taken as hundreds of people had fought their way out of the auditorium while he lay unconscious on the floor.

As his feet hit the sidewalk, a searing pain shot up from the base of his rib cage, reminding him of the elbow which had crashed into his midriff the instant he had grabbed Jane Mantel. A deliberate, skillfully delivered blow, with enough force to stop him in his tracks if the surging flood of people behind him hadn't carried him forward.

Once again he felt the anger rise within him. She didn't have to do that.

He started up the crowded street, twisting his head slowly from side to side, then reached up and massaged the back of his neck. And that was another thing. A blow which would have felled an ox on the back of his neck. Bastard! Whoever he was.

And why? Why should he have been singled out for such tender loving care?

All in all, Ed Peterson was not in a good mood. He was mad as hell and the focus of his anger was Jane Mantel. The first time he'd met her she'd taken him on a mind-blowing sexual trip. And that had been as calculated and skillful as the blow to his stomach.

He didn't much care for the way he was being messed around.

Just who the hell did she think she was? He was going to find out.

He stopped in front of a jewelry store, looked in the window, then went in. When they'd taken his watch off in the hospital it looked as if it had been trampled by an army.

He needed a new one. A newspaperman was naked without a watch—like he'd lost his sense of balance. No reference points. No times, deadlines, around which to concentrate the rest of his life.

His suit had been cleaned and pressed by the hospital. They were helpful like that; they'd do anything . . . for money.

The man behind the counter cast an experienced eye over him and reckoned he was worth around two hundred dollars. He produced a suitable range for him to choose from.

"I want a watch," Peterson said irritably. "Not a piece of god-damn jewelry. One in the window. Fifteen-forty. Plain and simple with a card which says the hands will go around at *exactly* the right speed for at least a year, *guaranteed*. I'll have it."

The man looked sour as he fished the watch from the window. He took the twenty-dollar bill and handed him the change. "It's Japanese, you know," he said, shaking his head disapprovingly.

"Right," Peterson answered. "A people who could sink our Pacific fleet in two hours flat should be able to make a little thing like a watch."

"I was there," said the man, looking as if he'd been slapped in the face.

Peterson strapped on the watch. "So they missed you . . . nobody's perfect."

Outside, he still didn't feel any better. He felt worse. Why did he have to make cheap cracks like that?

He knew why.

Jane Mantel.

He caught the noon flight and reported to his boss at exactly half past five. "How you feeling, Ed? They tell me you were lucky to get out alive."

Peterson grimaced. "Not sure I did, Josh." He lowered himself gingerly into a chair. "Fact is, the hospital said I was to take things easy for a few days. Make sure the ribs knit properly."

Josh looked at him sharply. Ed Peterson was not the kind of man to exaggerate his problems. There had been that time when he was on the police beat. He'd chased a couple of hoodlums who'd just killed an old man at a filling station. Taken a shot from a .38 in the shoulder and kept chasing halfway across town. Caught one and half beaten him to death before the cops pulled him off. Two days later he'd walked out of the hospital, leaving the doctor yelling his head off. Back at his desk, one arm in a sling, he typed with the fingers of one hand. If Ed Peterson said he wasn't feeling good, then he wasn't feeling good.

Josh stroked his bald head with the palm of his hand, examined his fingernails, looked out of the window, then said, "Get yourself home and into bed. Come back when you *know* you're alive."

Peterson got to his feet unsteadily. "I'll do that, Josh."

Back at his apartment he threw a few things into a bag, then went down to his car. Thirty minutes later he was out of town, heading west.

At nine o'clock the next morning he parked at the side of the administrative block on the campus. Three hours later he came out with a list of names and addresses of all the students who had graduated in the same year as Jane Mantel.

He returned to his hotel and sat by the telephone with the list on his knee and a pencil in his hand. First, he eliminated the men. He might have to go back to them later, but girl friends were more likely to have kept in touch.

He ticked off the names of all the girls with addresses in the city. About half. It was a near-certainty at least two-thirds of them would be married by now. Still, if they'd been living with their parents while at the university, he could get their new addresses from the parents. Some anyway.

First off, he dialed information and got the out-of-town number of Jane Mantel's address.

He dialed and listened to the buzz at the other end. A woman with a high-pitched voice answered: No, she herself had only lived there a year. Come from the West Coast. And no, she'd never heard of the name Mantel.

He replaced the receiver. He hadn't expected to be that lucky.

He started dialing the city numbers. "Miss Benson?" he asked. "Yes."

"I'm trying to locate a young woman name of Jane Mantel. She graduated the same year as you. Can you help?"

"Jane Mantel?" Then a long pause. "Yes, I remember her."

Peterson's pulse quickened. "Can you tell me where she is now?"

A laugh. "I'm afraid not."

"Do you know where her parents are?"

Another long pause, then: "As I recall, they're both dead. An automobile accident."

"Can I come and see you?"

"What for, Mr. . . . ?"

"Peterson. Ed Peterson."

A note of caution in the voice, "How would it help, Mr. Peterson?"

"I don't know, Miss Benson. But if I can talk to you, something might come up."

"Why is it so important . . . Mr. Peterson?"

He couldn't answer that. He didn't know for sure himself.

Sex.

Anger.

Curiosity.

Some kind of chemistry he couldn't understand.

"It *is* important, Miss Benson. Will you see me? I'm at the Liston Hotel. How far are you?"

"Half an hour's drive. But . . ."

"I'll be right with you." He slammed the phone down before she could refuse him.

"I guess you're the mysterious Mr. Peterson." Judy Benson had a relaxed smile, an open face, and straight blonde hair. Wholesome looking.

She showed him into a comfortably furnished sitting room. He looked round for signs of a man: there weren't any.

She was watching him. "To satisfy your curiosity, Mr. Peterson, I live alone. I like it that way. If you have it in mind to rape me, go right ahead. Only you'd better know about the dogs first."

She whistled. "Princess! Queen!"

Two muscularly sleek Alsatians appeared from behind the sofa, where they'd been lying out of sight. They came to her side, tails wagging, tongues hanging out, showing brilliantly white fangs. She patted them and they followed her to her chair and settled down on either side of her.

"Now. Jane Mantel," she said. "Why should I help you?"

Peterson seated himself across the low table from her. He'd thought about it on the way over and decided the truth, or as near as he could get, was the best approach.

"You mean you've lost her," she said when he finished.

"You could put it that way."

"Sort of careless . . . losing women." A gentle, teasing smile.

"I don't make a habit of it," he rejoined. He knew what she was doing: playing for time while sizing him up. There was more than a touch of shrewdness in the clear blue eyes of Miss Judy Benson.

"Mr. Peterson, I'm afraid you're going to have to tell me *exactly* why you want to find her. She's not the kind of girl to handle trouble."

Peterson frowned. "Could you explain that?" he asked. From his knowledge of her, Jane Mantel could handle all the trouble she was ever likely to get.

"She is an emotionally disturbed girl, unless she has changed. I don't know all the details, and I wouldn't tell you if I did, but her home life was far from ideal. It made her withdrawn, unable to establish relationships. I guess I was about the only person who took the trouble to get to know her. It may sound condescending but I felt sorry for her."

Peterson laughed. "Then she's changed one helluva lot."

Judy Benson slowly shook her head. "I doubt it. These things go pretty deep. To be perfectly honest"—her eyes pierced him— "I wouldn't have thought you two had much in common."

"You reckon she's too beautiful for me, huh?" Peterson was amused.

Judy Benson rose from her seat, went to the bookshelf, and withdrew a photograph album. She flipped the pages, found the place she wanted, passed the album to him. "The photograph at the top left," she said. "Which one is Jane Mantel?"

He studied the photograph: a bunch of kids in their late teens, in bathing suits, crowded around a boat by a lake.

He kept looking. "She's not there," he said finally.

She leaned over him and pointed to a thin girl with long, dangling hair, pinch-faced, flat-chested.

"That's not her," he said flatly.

"Then you've got the wrong girl."

Peterson tried to make sense of it. Perhaps the resemblance was there . . . just. The same kind of similarity there'd be between Leonardo da Vinci's Madonna and an attempted copy by a not-too-promising first-year art student. A travesty of the original. "When did you last hear from her?" he persisted.

"Not long after graduation. I had a postcard. From Dresden. East Germany."

"After that?"

"Nothing. I haven't heard from her since."

Then, the way it happens, a couple of cells in Peterson's memory bank made a seemingly pointless connection.

But a connection—East Germany and Deniskin.

"What subject did she major in?" he asked.

"Russian."

Abruptly his newspaperman's mind woke up and he asked another question. "Did she have any political views? More than the usual student bit, I mean?"

Judy Benson shook her head. "No, less than normal, I'd say. She had enough trouble straightening herself out, without trying to put Washington right."

There was a long silence, then:

"Come to think of it, she *did* get a bit close with one professor. Taught Russian history. Took her troubles to him a couple of times. Professor Wolfe—that was his name."

"You mean she had—"

"Heavens, no!" Judy protested. "Nothing like that. Nothing physical. He was a kind-hearted little man and could spot a student with emotional problems a mile off. He gave them support, that kind of thing. Personally, I thought him a bit intrusive. But he helped Jane. I must be fair to him."

"Is he still on campus?"

Her candid face clouded as she said, "It's sick really . . . him being so concerned about other people's troubles. He committed suicide."

He would, Peterson thought to himself with irony. He stood up, thanking her for her trouble, and the three of them—she and the two dogs—showed him to the door.

Back at his hotel he made more calls. He stopped after he'd contacted two more women who'd known Jane Mantel:

"Do you know where she is?"

"No."

"How would you describe her personality?"

"Timid . . . kept to herself."

"Would you say she was attractive?"

A long pause. "No, plain, really."

On the long drive home his ribs were jabbing at his inside and Jane Mantel was hammering at his brain. Now—added to sex—anger and curiosity. He had a mystery . . . and a challenge. What more could any man ask from a woman? If he wasn't careful she just might become a bit of an obsession.

He walked into his apartment and stopped dead in his tracks.

It was a wreck.

Drawers, clothing, papers all over the place. Pictures slashed. Black paint daubed over the walls. Sofa, cushions, mattress ripped open trailing their soft white entrails over the floors.

"Jesus H. Christ," said the police sergeant who arrived in reply to his call. "Someone sure as hell unloaded a lot of hate in here."

CHAPTER
TEN

Mike Brennan walked through the door of his new premises on Madison Avenue with the confident air of a man who knew where he was going and how he was going to get there. Brennan Associates were doing well.

He ran a lean outfit—all muscle, no fat. Only thirty-five people on the payroll, each one a real professional. He paid and he paid well. All he demanded in return was blood. And there were plenty of willing donors.

Brennan Associates were making a name for itself in the Avenue. They didn't win any art awards for their ads, but they sure as hell made sales for their clients. He was proving his approach was right. No crap. Tell the public the truth about the product. Talk to them like they'd got half a brain and they loved it. Why not? Who likes to be insulted! The days of selling creams with dreams were long gone.

Young Americans were well educated about advertising; the manufacturers and their advertising agencies had better grow up with them if they wanted to stay in business. That was his sales pitch and it got clients. Now he wanted the big one: the blue-chip account to give him the reputation to get into the big league. It wasn't going to be easy, but if it was easy who wanted it anyway?

He waved hello as he passed the receptionist. She was a honey. One thing hadn't changed in the advertising business: clients liked to see pretty girls around. He stopped briefly as he caught sight of the girl sitting in one of the reception chairs. That was another thing that hadn't changed—the impact of a beautiful woman. He walked on into his office.

"Good morning, Mr. Brennan." His secretary placed the mail on his desk.

"Good morning, Miss Baker. Any messages?"

She looked at her pad. "Only three. Mr. Sangster said for you to call him sometime this morning. It's not urgent. But his wife's had another idea he wants to talk to you about—would you believe!"

He groaned. "I would. . . . What else?"

"Mark Vardy in media said you wanted to see the latest Nielsen ratings first thing." She handed him a typed sheet of figures. "And there's a young lady waiting out in reception to see you."

He raised his eyebrows. "What about?"

"She won't say."

"You asked?"

Miss Baker looked at him reproachfully. "Of course. But she still won't say."

Brennan was irritated. "You go right out there and tell her, 'no say, no talk.' Okay?"

He watched Miss Baker glide her ass out of the door and regretted for the hundredth time his own self-imposed rule not to touch the in-house merchandise. The only time you mixed business with pleasure was when the clients wanted it that way.

Two minutes and Miss Baker was back. "The lady says, 'no talk, no business.' "

His head jerked up in surprise. "You mean she wants to talk business!"

"I don't know what she means, Mr. Brennan. I'm only carrying the messages."

"Okay. Get her in." He glanced at the Nielsen figures. Jesus! Only five percent rating for the Lansdown Show. The client would throw a fit when he found out. He'd start listing all the *good* agencies who'd been talking to him recently.

"Miss Mantel," Miss Baker said as she showed Jane in.

"Sit down, Miss Mantel, . . . and Miss Baker, ask Mark Vardy to come and see me."

Coolly, Jane scrutinized Mike Brennan. The features of his face were mobile and alert. Imaginative, certainly, but with a shrewd and hard business streak. But was he superstitious? She'd soon find out.

He was waiting for her to speak.

"I want to work for you," she stated baldly.

He raised his eyebrows, "Yeah. What at?"

"I don't know. I want you to train me."

"Sorry, Miss Mantel. Go to one of the big agencies. They've got the fat to waste time training people. I don't train anybody. They come to me fully trained, the best, then I make them better. No way do I let enthusiastic amateurs loose on my clients to learn by their mistakes. Clients don't pay me for mistakes."

He should have been feeling mad. She had to be out of her mind thinking she could waltz into his agency, con her way into his office by hinting about business—bait no adman could refuse —then just sit there asking to be trained. Nobody could be that stupid. Thing was, she didn't look even a little bit stupid. And that was why he wasn't feeling angry. Whatever the beautiful Miss Mantel wanted, it wasn't just to waste his time.

"What's really on your mind, Miss Mantel?" His eyes narrowed.

"I have a proposition to make," she replied. "We both want something. The situation with your agency is. . . ." She ran through his clients, their billings, and their business prospects. Mike Brennan was staggered by her knowledge. The business analyst in the KGB rezidentseya had done a good job.

"I've got to admit, Miss Mantel, you've succeeded. I'm impressed. I guess that's what you wanted. Now, what's your proposition?"

"You're sweating for the biggie. The blue-chip account to take you into the top league. You could get it tomorrow, like a miracle, or it could take two years, or it might never happen, right?"

"Right."

"Suppose I tell you that if you take me on, you've got a good chance of getting that account within six months."

"What d'you mean, I've got a good chance!" he snapped. He wasn't in the mood for playing games.

"I mean exactly what I say," Jane answered calmly. "If you hire me—normal salary, nothing on the side—you have a good chance of getting the account that takes you into the big league. No guarantees, just a good chance. All you can lose is a few thousand dollars to pay me for six months. If you don't get the account you fire me. Is that too high a price for a good-luck talisman?"

"That's ridiculous!" he exploded. "It's the craziest proposition I've ever heard."

Jane got up. "If that's how you feel, Mr. Brennan, I guess I'll just have to try another agency. Only don't hate yourself too much when you hear about some big account going to the competition."

She was halfway to the door. "Wait a minute. Sit down, will you. I haven't said no, have I?"

Jane sat down again, and looked at him expectantly.

"You've got to admit," he began, "it's not every day some beautiful lady floats into my office and says hire me and maybe, just maybe, you'll hit the big time. What's a guy supposed to do with a proposition like that?"

He knew what he was *supposed* to do. Throw the lady out. But she'd got through to him. He wasn't superstitious, but he knew he'd be grabbing the trade publications for the next six months, sweating in case he read the bad news about some other agency getting the big break. And then he'd be checking to see if a Miss Mantel was on the payroll. Jesus. It would be worth hiring her to buy himself peace of mind.

"You want to tell me more about this account I might be so lucky to get if I'm so crazy to hire you?"

"No," she answered.

"I didn't think you would."

Miss Baker called through to say Mark Vardy was waiting to see him about the Nielsen ratings. "Have him come in," he said, and turned to Jane. "You're hired. You start now. You start by learning how come we buy our biggest client into a program that gets a five percent rating."

Three months later Bob Adams, president of one of the biggest advertising spenders in the country, got a telephone call.

It was no accident Bob Adams was president of the corporation; his wife Martha owned eighty percent of the stock. This was why he had married her after her first husband, who had built the business, had gotten himself drowned in a hurricane while fishing off the coast of Florida.

Bob Adams was well pleased with his position. He liked the power and the money. Only problem was his wife was sort of narrow-minded about sex. She had spelled it out: if she ever caught him in bed with another woman, he'd find himself out of marriage, out of a job, and out of money.

So he had to be careful about his extramarital sex. Very careful. He restricted this activity to when he was on business trips out of the country.

His secretary put the call through. "A Mr. Shaw for you, Mr. Adams. Says it's personal."

"He's not selling insurance or charity?" Adams snapped.

"He says not, sir."

"Okay. Put him through."

"Mr. Adams. Do you want to be divorced?" Mr. Shaw had a foreign accent, European probably. He also had a novel way of introducing himself.

"Who the hell are you?" Adams challenged angrily.

"It doesn't matter, Mr. Adams. But you remember Copenhagen. The twenty-seventh of July four years ago, to be exact."

Suddenly Adams wasn't angry. He was apprehensive.

"What about Copenhagen?" he asked cautiously.

"I want to talk to you about it. There may be a way we can keep it from your wife."

"Keep what from my wife?"

"You remember, Mr. Adams. If you have forgotten, I have something to remind you. Meet me in Casey's bar at six-thirty." The phone went dead.

Adams began to sweat.

He did remember Copenhagen. And the "live show."

He remembered the big room downstairs, the walls covered with glossy blowups of porno photographs. The place was packed with men, a few accompanied by women either laughing nervously or trying to look cool like the whole thing was a bore. Then the blue films on one wall while the waitresses served drinks with nothing on their minds except getting the change wrong. What a rip-off! Then the show starts upstairs and he can hardly find room to stand. The guys sitting at the front must have come with the dawn.

Then a couple of young kids appear on the stage naked. What a routine! How athletic could you get? The audience is dead silent; they can't take it. The two kids are the only ones getting real kicks. She's laughing *at them*. And he's so proud of his joint he keeps pulling it out and flashing it at them. The show ends and they all go downstairs, depressed as hell. They grab for the drinks and then for the girls who drift in out of the wall. He gets a cab back to his hotel. Boy, he feels terrible as sin. Asks the driver to drop him off at a club. Gets bombed. Three in the morning and some broad hustles him into bed.

He arrived at Casey's promptly at six-thirty, ordered a drink, and stood at the bar.

"We should sit down, Mr. Adams." He had a neck like a bull, dead eyes, and was holding a glass of beer.

They sat down. "I guess you're Shaw. What do you want?"

"A small favor. In return for which these photographs will not be mailed to your wife." He passed four photographs under the table.

Adams looked at them, keeping them under the table. She could have been the girl in Copenhagen. She could have been anyone. But his wife would know who the man was.

"How did you get them?" he asked hoarsely.

Shaw stared at him, his face expressionless. He had spent his life looking at frightened little men. "That doesn't matter. All that matters is how you can prevent your wife getting them."

Adams felt sick. "How much?" he asked.

"Not money, just a small favor. Move your advertising account. Ask five agencies to—what do you call it?—pitch for your account. Include Brennan Associates, and make sure they get the account. That's all."

Adams couldn't believe what he was hearing. Advertising agencies would do a lot of things to get business, they had to; but not this, not blackmail. He said, "Listen, if this ever gets out, even a rumor, Brennan will be dead. He must be out of his mind."

Shaw leaned over the table. "You listen to me," he said. And when Adams met his eyes he saw cold savagery and violence. "The only person who can let it out is you. If that happens, these photographs will be released. And that will only be the beginning of your troubles . . . Mr. Adams."

Shaw sat back. His tone changed to one of reassurance. "But you have nothing to worry about if you do as you are told. Brennan Associates has a good reputation. People will think you are smart moving to an up-and-coming agency. And nobody, I repeat, nobody at Brennan Associates or anyone connected with your company knows anything about this. If you were foolish enough to disregard my advice and say anything to Brennan Associates, they would deny any knowledge of our little agreement. Without evidence against them, you would be in a most awkward situation. The courts do not look favorably on unsubstantiated allegations of blackmail. Now, good-bye, Mr. Adams. I hope we shan't have to meet again."

Shaw got up. Adams watched him shoulder his way out of sight through the crowded bar. He could only think of one thing —Mafia. Why they should want him to move his account, he couldn't begin to imagine. Some people said the Mafia were big potatoes, some said they were a bunch of adolescent hoodlums. Either way it didn't matter. They were big enough for him.

One week later he called Mike Brennan to his office and gave him the good news. He was looking for a fresh approach to his advertising and was asking a number of big-name agencies to work up their ideas and pitch for the account. In addition, he was offering Brennan Associates a chance to compete. He had checked out the work they were doing and they might have that extra freshness he was looking for.

From the way Brennan reacted Adams knew he was either an all-time great actor or he really didn't know anything about the Shaw setup.

Brennan called the key members of the agency into his office. It was going to be eighteen hours a day, seven days a week, he told them, and they were going to get that account. They did.

It took him three weeks working flat-out to get everything set up to handle the new business—hiring more help, getting more office space, and laying on all the facilities Adams's account was going to need. Then he took off and spent a week at Palm Beach making up on his sleep, soaking up the sun, and wondering about Jane Mantel.

First thing back in his office, he pressed the buzzer and told Miss Baker to get the Mantel girl up.

"I owe you something," he said as she sat down.

Jane looked at him as if she didn't understand.

"We got it. The big one. The ten-million-dollar baby."

"I had heard," Jane teased him.

"What would you like?" he asked. "Two weeks in Acapulco, Bermuda, all expenses paid and a new wardrobe to fill your baggage?"

Jane laughed. "That's very kind of you," she said, "but all I want is to keep my job. That was the agreement we made."

"Ah no," he protested. "You're my good-luck girl. You need special treatment."

"All right then," she said, "there is something you can do for me. . . . Speed up my training. I want to move into a job where I meet clients and where I'm more involved with the total operations of the agency."

Brennan looked doubtful. Giving presents was one thing; being unbusinesslike was another. She hadn't enough experience to be let loose on the clients. But she had the personality and the confidence, that was for sure.

"Okay," he said. "I'll make you assistant on a couple of small accounts and we'll see how it goes."

"Thank you, Mr. Brennan."

"But there is a condition," he added quickly.

"A condition?"

"Yes. You have dinner with me tonight to celebrate our success."

"That would be a pleasure," she replied.

He picked her up from her apartment at seven-thirty. As he tooled the Ferrari downtown he said, "Off duty, Miss Mantel, it's Mike." Then he grinned. "You, Jane." They arrived at Bussaco's. The maître d' greeted him warmly and escorted them to their table. A small group in an alcove to one side was playing unobtrusive jazz. The meal was the best. Jane turned her head as she heard the level of conversation rise suddenly from the direction of the service door. The maître d' followed by the chef in his high white hat and carrying a tray were making their way in solemn procession toward their table. As they got closer she saw the cake on the tray and the group started to play "Luck, Be a Lady Tonight."

Deftly the maître d' cleared a space and the chef, with an enormous smile of pleasure, carefully placed the cake before her. It was an incredible piece of artistry: icing, fruit, and candies skillfully used to decorate the cake with symbols of luck—a four-leaf clover, a model of a pixie, a horseshoe, sprig of heather, black cat.

Mike Brennan handed her the knife. "You do the honors, lady luck," he said.

Jane cut two enormous slices and handed him one with a flourish. "Thank you, Mike. What a wonderful idea."

Reaching in his pocket, he produced a flat leather case and handed it to her. Jane stared at it.

"Open it, lady luck, it's for you."

It was a gold medallion on a long, gold neck chain. She looked at it, puzzled.

"Don't you know what it is?" he asked, surprised.

She shook her head.

"A Saint Christopher, the patron saint of travelers . . . or he used to be, anyway. He protects travelers from all kinds of evil."

"It a lovely present, Mike, but why a Saint Christopher?"

"Because, lady luck, I don't know where you have been, and I don't know where you're going, but I do know you are going somewhere. You, lady luck, are a traveling lady."

Jane looked at him thoughtfully. "That's an odd thing to say," she said.

"I know," he answered, frowning slightly. "And I don't know why I think it. Call it intuition. The same intuition which made me hire you, maybe."

"Maybe it was," she answered, and changed the subject. "Where are *you* traveling, Mike? What do you want to achieve? Don't you want into politics? Like that uncle of yours—John Hurst? Sounds like he wants to change the world."

"You've got to be joking. He figures the Russians are going to change it for us. He's out of his mind."

They laughed and he called for the Dom Perignon. That night Jane slept alone but she felt well pleased. Mike Brennan was hooked; like all men on the way up, he was lonely. He would fall for any woman who understood he had a soul and who had the strength to break through and reach for it. Soon she was on the new business team. Her keen intelligence, her charm, and her beauty made a formidable combination. New business came in as fast as they could handle.

Next time he phoned to ask her out she said:

"Let's take it easy tonight, Mike. Have you ever had real Hungarian goulash?"

"How would I know?" he joked. "The way they use synthetics these days I don't know how long since I had *any* real food."

"Then you're in for an experience. My apartment, seven-thirty. Real Hungarian goulash—satisfaction guaranteed or your money back."

"It's a deal."

He arrived with flowers and a smile. "They're for my supper. I can't sing," he said.

The meal was simple. She made it that way deliberately. No obvious seduction. Candles, soft lights, sweet music, and the alarm bells would have exploded in his head. A simple linen tablecloth with a red-and-white checked pattern, a steaming pot of goulash, French bread, a big bowl of salad, and a bottle of Macon rouge; then a selection of French cheeses, coffee, and cognac.

After the meal they sat and talked about the agency. He'd grown into the habit of discussing major campaigns with her.

They finished sorting out the outline plan for Adams's new campaign and he was just about to launch into another project when he saw she was looking at him with gentle amusement.

"Mike," she said softly, kneeling by his chair. "I'm going to give you a vacation. I'm going to make love to you."

He stared at her in amazement. "You're what!"

"I'm going to do what I've wanted to do since that first time you took me out and gave me the Saint Christopher. I'm going to give you a present . . . all the love I know."

He couldn't believe it. "Hold on. I'm the guy around here. I make the love. I know about women's lib, but there's a limit." He sat up in the chair.

She put her hands on his chest and pushed him back, gently. "Well, now you're going to find out about male lib. You don't have to prove a thing. . . . Just do what I say and enjoy it."

She found his hardness and then began the first real sexual trip he had ever experienced. She used every technique, every trick she had learned at such cost at the training school near Moscow. Parts of his body came alive in ways he had never experienced. In the end he was lost in a paroxysm of sensations, his body totally in her possession.

He lay by her side looking at the beautiful curves of her body and thinking that if Aphrodite had ever existed that was how she would have looked . . . and this was what she would have known about love.

"Traveling lady," he whispered, *"where* did you come from?"

And then he made love to her. And then they made love together. And for Mike Brennan it was discovering the thrill of love for the very first time. . . .

For Jane it was one step nearer Washington . . . and John Hurst.

CHAPTER
ELEVEN

Sakov had been right: Adams had been the key to Mike Brennan. But as time went by, Jane found it was not going to be so easy to take the second step: Use Brennan as her entrée to his uncle, Senator John Hurst.

Brennan liked his uncle well enough as a man, but as a politician it was different. Brennan had an aversion to politicians that verged on paranoia. "For Christ's sake," he'd say, "politicians are a bunch of goddamn pirates. When they want your vote they throw promises around like confetti. But once they've gotten themselves elected, what do they do? Spend your tax dollars like it's Monopoly money and somehow—just somehow—fix it so they get rich doing it. Jesus! If there was any justice half of them would be in jail. . . . Yeah, sure, I know Hurst is different. But that doesn't stop him boring the pants off me with all that political crap he gives out with."

No way was Mike Brennan going out of his way to see more than he had to of Uncle John Hurst, senator.

Six weeks passed before Jane got her first opportunity. It was early morning. They were in Brennan's apartment. For Jane it had been a long night's work; for Brennan, another beautiful sex trip.

Brennan yawned, stretched lazily, slid out of bed, and padded off to get the mail. He threw a clutch of letters onto the crumpled bed and opened the top one. He groaned as he read it and passed it to Jane. "How the hell do I get out of this?" he said.

Jane read the short letter. It was from John Hurst's wife, Cathy —an invitation for Mike to join them in Washington for a family July Fourth celebration. He could bring "a friend" if he wanted to.

"You don't get out of it," Jane said. "You put up with it and suffer. Besides," she continued, knowing she had him in a receptive mood, "I'd like to get out of New York. I haven't been to Washington in ages."

"Not being in Washington is about the nicest thing that can happen to a person. Almost. . . ." He grinned and reached under the bedclothes for her smooth thigh. "But if you want it, we'll go. Only if that uncle of mine nails me and talks politics I'll strangle him."

"It's illegal," Jane said.

"Not between two consenting adults," he said and pulled her soft, warm body against his.

July Fourth was three weeks ahead. Jane acted swiftly. She had to. A family gathering was no place to work on Hurst. Cathy would have to be her first target. Somehow, she'd have to score in that one day: build her own relationship with the Hursts, so she didn't have to depend on Mike Brennan.

Jane contacted Sakov. What did he know about Hurst's wife? When the information came she was more than a little surprised just how much he did know about Cathy Hurst—her likes, her dislikes, and her main interests, especially her deep interest in art. Perhaps even more valuable, a psychiatrist's rundown on the personality of the senator's wife. One section of the psychiatrist's assessment took her attention particularly: "Our experience of Miss Jackson . . ." Jane paused, wondering what experience he was referring to, and how and why it had been before Cathy had married Hurst. *Miss Jackson!* She read on. ". . . indicates that while she is capable of displaying great self-reliance and inner strength, she is attracted to people who are apparently stronger than she is in the sense that they are more overtly projective and assertive. This trait is not uncommon among women who . . ."

Jane gave a slight nod of satisfaction. This was vital information. There would be no time to study Cathy before she made her play. She would have to hit it off with her from the word go. Now she knew exactly how to do it.

Two weeks after July Fourth, on the eighteenth and for that one day only, Stenburg's famous collection of Impressionist paintings was to be on show to the public in New York—viewing by invitation only. Jane had read an advance announcement in *The New York Times*, where it was described as one of the great up-coming cultural events of the year. Art galleries all over the world were waiting with indecent impatience for old man Stenburg to die so they could pay astronomical prices to get hold of some of the few remaining Impressionist paintings still in private hands.

Jane called Bob Katz into her office. Katz took care of the pastoral side of the agency's client relations—like fixing first-night tickets, and girls, and a few other activities of a more bizarre nature.

"Bob, I want two invitations to this Stenburg thing," she said handing him the copy of the *Times*.

Katz scanned the write-up quickly and said, "You're joking. Since when did we have clients with taste . . . this kind of taste, I mean," he said with a smirk, stubbing the paper with his forefinger.

"Since now," Jane said sharply. "It's a new account I'm after, it's big, and it's confidential. I want those tickets."

The smirk faded and Katz pulled a wry face. "It's not going to be easy and it's going to cost. I'll have to find out whose got those invitations, then come up with a couple of them who are not too long on culture and very short on cash. And it could still cost a thousand bucks."

"Sort of a challenge." Jane smiled.

"You could say that."

"But you can do it." A statement.

Katz shrugged. "Have I ever failed?"

"Knew I could rely on you."

"You bet. I'll get them . . . even if I have to kill for them." A laugh.

He got them.

Jane had other things to do. Aided by a phenomenal memory and four days at home in bed with a feigned bout of summer flu, she thoroughly absorbed six books on the history of art.

Sally Burton, Jane's secretary, also found herself saddled with an unusual job—searching through back copies of the *Congressional Record* looking for any speeches made by Senator John Hurst. She found a couple and Xeroxed them.

"You interested in this stuff?" she asked, handing the copies to Jane.

"Why not?" Jane answered. "Even senators have friends."

Sally gave a knowing look. "Friends in business with advertising accounts to hand out?"

Jane nodded. "And it's confidential. Absolutely."

By the time she and Mike left for Washington, Jane was confident. She had all the ammunition she needed.

It was a small gathering. About twenty in all—family plus a few friends. The midmorning sun was blazing down and the temperature already in the high eighties as they stood chatting, drinks in hand, in the garden of the Hursts' Georgetown house.

The conversation was light and punctuated by family in-jokes. Not a time to be serious.

Jane appeared to be listening attentively to Cathy's young brother, Jim, a tall, fair-haired youngster whose posture seemed unnecessarily, and unnaturally, upright. As if he was standing at attention. He had graduated from Annapolis Naval Academy the previous month.

He was telling Jane how the statue which the midshipmen at the Academy called Tecumseh was known as the God of C—C being the lowest pass grade. And how they all used to salute the statue with one hand and toss pennies at it with the other to bring them good luck.

Jane laughed at his story and chided him about our future naval commanders still relying on superstitions, but she was thinking about John Hurst. She had seen him go into the house and over Jim's shoulder she was watching for him to come out again.

Hurst came out carrying a bucket of fresh ice. Jane watched as he crossed the lawn toward the rustic wood drinks table.

"Excuse me one moment, Jim," she said. "I need more ice in this drink of mine."

"Let me—" Jim started, but Jane had moved away too quickly.

"Just what I need," she said to Hurst, pointing at the fresh ice.

"Help yourself before it all melts," he said. "The forecast says it's going to reach a high of ninety-five."

Jane reached for the ice. "Almost as hot as that speech you made in the Senate a few weeks back . . . the one about the arms talks in Vienna," she said.

Hurst's eyebrows came together in a puzzled frown. "How did you know about that? It didn't even make the press."

"It made the *Congressional Record*."

Hurst's frown deepened. "You read that! That puts you ahead of most of us congressmen."

"When I have time, I do," Jane answered. "I like to know what's *really* going on. Not the way it comes out in the media."

She smiled broadly and, placing her hand on Hurst's arm, said, "You see, Senator, I don't trust you politicos to look after my interests. Not when it comes to dealing with the Russians." She dropped a couple of ice cubes into her glass and winked. "Keep talking, Senator . . . and keep it hot." She left him staring after her.

Jane Mantel had sown a seed.

A small one.

But she knew the time would come when it would grow and bear fruit.

Jane joined Cathy, who was talking to a friend of Hurst's— something in oil—and his wife.

"You know what would be perfect on a day like this?" Jane said. "A long cool drink of sangría."

"Sangría?" Cathy queried.

"You mean that Spanish hooch?" the oilman said.

"What's it like?" Cathy asked.

"Beautiful," Jane replied. "Come on, Cathy, I'll make some for you. You'll love it." She ran toward the house.

"What do we put in it?" Cathy asked when they reached the kitchen.

"Nothing complicated. A couple of bottles of cheap red wine, brandy, lemonade, sugar, and fruit. Anything you've got . . . apples, oranges, lemons, pears, peaches, anything."

Cathy went to get the wine and brandy while Jane started chopping up fruit from the blue bowl on the kitchen table.

"Pour the wine and half a bottle of brandy into a jug," Jane said when Cathy returned.

"Half a bottle of brandy! Pow! Mixed in with the wine it'll knock the legs from under them."

"Sort the men out from the boys, you mean."

"And you hard-drinking advertising ladies from the rest of us women," Cathy replied with a laugh.

Jane paused, the knife sliced halfway through an orange. "You know," she said looking out of the kitchen window into the garden. "I think I envy you, Cathy. It's so peaceful here. Not like New York. That's a madhouse."

"It's kinda mad in Washington too. Scratch the surface and you'll find a bag of neurotic worms."

"Maybe," Jane mused, still gazing out of the window. "But looking at all the beautiful flowers out there, and your family enjoying themselves, reminds me of one of Renoir's paintings.

Full of brilliant colors and happy people. Soothing. Relaxing. *Safe*. . . . Ugh, not at all like New York."

"You like Renoir and the other Impressionists?" Cathy asked with surprise. It wasn't what she expected from a high-powered advertising woman. Not from a woman "attached" to Mike, whose appreciation of art was limited to the pictures on C-notes and upward.

Jane considered the question for a moment. "Well, to tell the truth," she said, "I really prefer their precursors. You know, Constable, Turner, Courbet, Corot, and the other Barbizon painters." She swiveled to face Cathy. "I keep promising myself to see the Corot collection at the Corcoran Gallery here in Washington. It's about the finest in the world." She shrugged. "Well, that's New York for you, I guess; there never seems enough time to do the things you really want to do. Never mind," she added with a sigh of resignation, "let's get the show on the road and put this sangría together."

The sangría was a great success.

So was Jane's ploy. Cathy went for it in a big way. It had been a long time since she had met anyone as knowledgeable and as enthusiastic about art. In fact, she thought with a wave of sadness, not since Carl.

That evening they stood with the crowds on the grassy slopes of the Washington Monument and watched the spectacular fireworks display. In the car on the way back to Georgetown for a nightcap, Jane suddenly said, "Cathy, you know Stenburg's collection is on show in New York in a couple of weeks. If I can get tickets, how about the two of us going along?"

"I'd love to. But how on earth can you get tickets? It's by invitation only."

"You leave that to me," Jane said. "I'll have you picked up at the airport, we'll have lunch somewhere nice, take in the exhibition, then I'll see you back to the airport. Okay? No arguments."

Cathy smiled warmly. She liked Jane. Very much.

CHAPTER
TWELVE

It was early October in Washington.

Jane Mantel sat down on a bench in Lafayette Square. The fierce heat of midsummer had passed and now the brown leaves on the trees were a blaze of golden richness in the warm sun of an Indian summer.

The people in the square had about them an air of relaxation, as if conscious that the respite between the humid heat of summer and the bitter winter to come was brief and to be enjoyed.

Jane watched two old men playing checkers on a bench nearby. They were moving the pieces with precise, unhurried movements. For them the struggle of life was over. It was too late to change anything; the need for striving, gone. They were enjoying the Indian summer of their lives and they were content.

But Jane Mantel was not content.

She glanced at her watch—11:05 A.M.—and bit her lip with irritation. Cathy was late. They had arranged to meet in the square at eleven o'clock, then walk the one block up Pennsylvania Avenue to the Renwick Gallery and visit the new exhibition of modern art.

But Jane's discontent went far deeper than Cathy's lateness.

Three months had passed since their first meeting and they had become close friends. Every week or so they would meet in Washington or New York and spend the day together going to the theater, concerts, and art galleries.

Jane had grown to like Cathy. And even, at times, in her inner loneliness, to envy her. To envy her leisurely, civilized way of life, her obvious love for her husband—a relationship with a man she herself would never know; could never know.

She looked at her watch again—11:20. It was unlike Cathy to be late.

The two checker players were carefully putting the pieces into a shining black wooden box. They rose to their feet slowly and ambled off.

A young man in his early twenties sat on the bench next to Jane and made a pass. She turned icy eyes on him. He got up, swore at her, then moved off with affected nonchalance.

Jane calmed herself. She must be careful. She had overreacted; something she must never do with Cathy. But her impatience and frustration were beginning to wear on her nerves. She had been on close terms with Cathy for three months and still she had got no nearer to Hurst! Almost as if Cathy were deliberately keeping her away from him.

And Cathy was, but for reasons Jane could never have guessed.

Cathy knew she was doing it—keeping Jane to herself. Jane had made her interest in politics plain enough. She had hinted, more than once, how much she would like to talk with people like her father, Senator Jackson, and her husband, Senator Hurst. But Cathy was stalling, clinging to the exclusiveness of their friendship for as long as she could.

She had tried to explain and justify her behavior to herself. She wondered if it was because something about Jane reminded her of her brief life with Carl—bringing feelings of bittersweet nostalgia which were hard to resist. Perhaps this was it. And at moments when she thought this, she felt ashamed and reproved herself for her selfishness.

But she continued to keep Jane to herself. For the truth went deeper, much deeper.

Cathy was almost certain she could not bear her husband's children. The worry and anxiety had destroyed her self-confidence, leaving her desperately insecure. Buried deep in her subconscious was the fear that a woman as beautiful and intelligent as Jane was a threat—a threat to be kept away from her husband.

It was 11:30 A.M. Jane got to her feet and walked toward the exit to find a phone. Maybe Cathy had forgotten about their appointment.

She heard her name called and turned to see Cathy hurrying toward her.

"Thank God you're still here," Cathy gasped.

One look and Jane knew something was wrong. Cathy's face was deathly pale, the features drawn and pinched; her eyes had a wildness about them.

"What is it?" she said. "Something's wrong."

Cathy remained silent.

"Come on, honey. I can see it in your face. Tell me," Jane coaxed, steering her back to the bench.

Cathy slumped down and stared at the ground.

She remained silent for a long time, her face averted, still staring unseeing at the ground.

Suddenly she took a deep breath and turned to look earnestly into Jane's face. "All right. I'll tell you," she said, her voice empty, hollow. "I can't have children . . . ever."

"What do you mean?" Jane asked quietly.

Another long silence. Jane waited.

"I've just come from the doctor," Cathy said at last. She broke off.

Jane had to bend forward to catch her whisper:

"I've been having tests. The doctor called me early this morning and asked me to drop by. He sounded so cheerful, I thought it was going to be all right. . . . When I got to his office he told me. No children . . . ever."

Cathy jerked forward and buried her head in her hands. Her shoulders shook as she sobbed. "Oh my god, Jane. What am I going to do?"

"Calm down." Jane put her arm around Cathy's trembling shoulders. "I know how you must feel, but it's not the end of the world. It happens to millions of women. They get by. Learn to live with it. Adopt children. . . . Have you thought of that?"

"Yes, I've thought about it. Hundreds of times. It's not that simple."

"I didn't say it was simple, honey. But it *will* work out for you."

"*You don't understand!*" It was almost a shout; desperate, plaintive. Cathy was staring at Jane wide-eyed, the tears streaming down her face.

Jane took hold of Cathy's hands and squeezed them gently. "I *do* understand. I promise you."

Cathy shook her head slowly. "How can you understand? You don't know. I've already had a baby—before I married John. In Switzerland. The baby . . . and the father . . . they were killed in an accident."

Jane's mind flashed back to Sakov's report on Cathy. There had been no mention of this part of her past. Did the KGB know? Had they even been involved in it in some way? Every instinct told her there was a good chance the answer was yes. So why had Sakov deliberately withheld the information? Should she probe Cathy to find out more? No, this was not the time. There was an obvious question to be asked. She said:

"How can you be sterile . . . if you've already had a baby?"

"I don't know. Not the details. When I asked the doctor if he was absolutely certain, he started to say something about my Fallopian tubes, but I couldn't take it in. I went numb. Dead. I walked out of his office in a daze." She took the tissue Jane held toward her and dabbed at her cheeks with shaking hands. "How can I tell John?" There was desperation in her eyes.

"That's the least of your worries," Jane reassured her.

Cathy grasped Jane's hands. "No—no. That's what you don't understand! John doesn't know about my baby. I've never told anyone. *Nobody* knows about it. It was *my* past. *My* secret. It couldn't harm John. They were both dead. There was no need to tell him. I didn't want to risk hurting him and . . ." She hesitated for a moment. "I suppose deep down I was afraid of losing him if I told him."

"You don't have to blame yourself, Cathy," Jane said. "What you did was perfectly natural."

The pressure on Jane's hands was suddenly released. Cathy's shoulders heaved as she took another deep breath. "Only now he's got to know. It would be cheating not to tell him—now that I can't give him children of his own."

Jane's mind was racing. If Cathy told John Hurst, he might start looking into Cathy's past. He was an ambitious politician. He would want to be sure there was nothing his political enemies could use against him. And if her instincts were right, and the KGB had been involved in some way with Cathy's past, there was no knowing what damage such an investigation might do. Until she could check with Sakov she had to play safe.

She squeezed Cathy's hands. "I know you're terribly upset, honey, but don't you think it would be pretty selfish to tell John about what happened in Switzerland? It may make *you* feel better, but what about him? How do you think he's going to feel— knowing you had kept it secret from him? It would hurt him very deeply."

Cathy was staring at Jane. "Oh god, I hadn't thought of that."

"I know," Jane said sympathetically. "You haven't had time to think clearly about anything yet. But believe me, it's best you let past history stay buried. For John's sake. It's going to be painful for you, but you owe it to your husband."

A tight smile came to Cathy's swollen face. "It's true, isn't it? About our past sins catching up on us so we have to pay for them."

"Well, I don't know about sins," Jane said. "But I know it would be very wrong for you to hurt your husband unnecessarily just to ease your own conscience."

"Better I hurt than he does." Cathy was nodding agreement.

"That's what you would want, isn't it?"

"Always."

"Then you have no choice. You have to keep your secret," Jane said with finality.

"You're right, I know," Cathy answered. "Thank God I spoke to you in time." She smiled, the relief showing as the color began to return to her face. "You know, when I left the doctor I just walked around in a daze for a while. Then I remembered you were here, waiting. A friend."

"That's what I like to think I am," Jane said. "Now let's find a cab and get you home. You're in no shape to look at pictures."

They walked toward H Street.

As Cathy pulled the door of the cab shut she leaned out of the window and spoke to Jane. "You are my friend, Jane. And it's a secret, huh? What happened in Switzerland. Just you and me."

"A secret," Jane said. "And call me if you want someone to talk to. Anytime."

Jane waved as the cab pulled away. She had a smile on her face.

Two days later the phone rang in Jane's apartment. It was Cathy. "It's all right," she said, the happiness in her voice unmistakable.

Jane listened while Cathy bubbled on excitedly about how understanding and sympathetic John had been. They would think about adopting children. But he was in no hurry and there was nothing to worry about. Then they had made love, and now that all her anxieties had gone she felt closer and more in love with him than ever.

Then Cathy said, "We're having a small dinner party. Just my parents, John, and me. It's at my folks' place and we'd like you and Mike to join us. Would you like that? With two senators you'll be able to talk all the politics you want."

Jane controlled her excitement. She guessed it was Cathy's way of saying thank you for helping her when she'd been so unhappy. It was the opportunity she had been waiting for so long.

"You know how much I'd like it," she said. "Only you know how Mike is. If he thinks he's going to be trapped with a couple of senators, he'll take to the hills."

"I'll take care of him," Cathy said. It was the answer Jane had fished for. "I'll call him and give him the choice of any day in the next four weeks. Once he knows there's no way out, he'll give in gracefully, you'll see. We'll make it a week on Thursday. Okay?"

"Marvelous," Jane said. "I'll leave it to you."

Jane replaced the receiver, poured herself a large vodka, downed it, then sat at the desk by the window. Unlocking the bottom left-side drawer, she took the small steel box from inside and dialed the combination lock open. Inside was the special cipher Sakov had given her.

The message she encoded to Sakov was long: requesting an urgent meeting with him and listing a string of facts and information she wanted. As Sakov had instructed, she deliberately misspelled three words. She addressed it to the New York address Sakov had given her, then went out and slipped it in the mailbox.

Four days later she received a reply. Decoded, it instructed her to go to an address in the Bronx at eight o'clock the following evening.

Sakov was waiting for Jane when she arrived at the old brownstone house in the Bronx. He greeted her formally, then took her coat and gestured for her to sit down in one of the low, cushioned chairs in the comfortably furnished room. But despite the formality of his greeting, she had not missed the way his eyes had flickered over her, taking in every detail. His training, she wondered, or something more? She couldn't tell.

Still standing, Sakov spoke. "You'll be glad to know your athletic boyfriend, Peterson, seems harmless. We took his apartment to pieces. Nothing was found."

"You took him seriously?" Jane laughed.

Sakov's thick eyebrows came together in a frown as he looked down at her. "Yes, comrade, we're in a very serious business."

Jane bit her lip. He was right: she should have known better than to joke.

Sakov studied her for a moment in silence, then sat down and said, "Tell me, comrade, in your message to me you asked for a detailed military appraisal of the comparative nuclear power of our country and America. Why?"

Jane got straight to the point. "Because I've been invited to a dinner party at which Hurst will be present. Hurst is not a fool. His hard line against our country is not based on unthinking emotion. I have read his speeches. He is fully informed of the details of the rapid growth of our military strength. If I am to impress him, I must be able to talk his language. I must be at least as aware of the military facts as he is."

Sakov was pleased. Jane Mantel was proving every bit as skillful and thorough as he had hoped. The easy and obvious way for her to pursue Hurst would have been to use her power as a beautiful and exciting woman. She had not fallen into that trap. Hurst would not be immune to her charms—no man could be— but it would take far more than that to gain his confidence and respect.

Sakov pointed to the thick blue folder on the table by his chair. "You will find all the information you need in there. You may use any of the facts; none of them are classified. They are available to anyone who takes the trouble to search them out from published sources."

Jane considered carefully how she should phrase her next question. "There is another matter," she said. "Hurst's wife had an affair of some kind when she was in Switzerland at school. She had a baby by the man, but he and the baby were killed. Did you know?"

Sakov ignored her question. "How did you find out?" he asked.

Jane told him, then repeated her question. "Did you know?"

"Yes," Sakov said.

"Is it important?"

"Yes. It is *very* important, comrade. And while I must congratulate you on becoming such a close confidante of Hurst's wife, I must warn you that under no circumstances must you reveal this information to anyone. Is that clear?"

"Yes, comrade." Jane knew that as far as Sakov was concerned the subject was closed. But she persisted. "May I ask why such a vital part of Cathy Jackson's life was omitted from the information you sent me about her? I *must* know everything possible about the people I am dealing with."

"On the contrary, comrade. You *must* know only what I choose to tell you," Sakov rebuked her coldly.

"But—"

Sakov spoke again. "Let me tell you a story, comrade. A cautionary tale, you might call it. There was once an officer in our service, a young man with little experience. He recruited an American woman to work for him. She was extraordinarily beautiful." Sakov paused and studied Jane's face for a moment. A slight smile relaxed his stern features. "Possibly even more beautiful than you, Anna." And in that instant Jane knew that the young officer Sakov spoke of had been himself.

"This officer and the American woman fell in love," Sakov continued. "And in the intimacy of the bedroom, he was foolish enough to tell her things she should never have known. Unfortunately, the woman later became infatuated with another man. A dangerous man." Sakov paused again, then continued, "Inexperienced as he was, the young officer knew he had no choice. . . . He killed the woman he loved."

Jane's eyes were locked on Sakov's face. She found that she was holding her breath. She felt the pounding of her heart. A shiver passed down her spine. "And you would do that to me?" she whispered.

"I would do that to you, Anna . . . if it was ever necessary," Sakov answered, his eyes without expression.

CHAPTER
THIRTEEN

Cathy was as good as her word. She talked Mike into the dinner date with her parents. Not that it was all that difficult: Mike knew when he was trapped and gave in without a fight.

"You two girls cooked this whole thing up between you," Mike said accusingly to Jane in the cab to catch the late-afternoon shuttle to Washington.

"Mike!" Jane looked at him with wide-eyed innocence. "Would I do a thing like that?"

"You betcha." Mike grinned. "Wouldn't be surprised if you haven't been working on Cathy all along to fix this little political soirée. You're the only woman I know who reads the political news before she gets to the gossip column."

"That's because you've been mixing with the wrong kind of women."

He laughed. "Maybe you're right at that."

As they approached the Hursts' residence in Georgetown, where they were going to stay overnight, Mike grabbed Jane's arm and said, "Now, remember—if I suddenly collapse into a coma, or get an attack of uncontrollable coughing during dinner, don't bother sending for the doctor. I'll give you the diagnosis right now—an acute surfeit of political crap."

They laughed.

"Lovely to see you," Cathy greeted them warmly at the door. "Glad you could come," she winked at Jane. "Come on in. I'll show you to the guest suite so you can freshen up before we go over to my folks. John's been held up. He'll join us there."

Half an hour later they drove the short distance to the Jacksons'.

During the predinner cocktails Senator Bill Jackson asked Jane about her work and listened attentively to her answers. A tall, silver-haired man with a ruddy, healthy complexion and twinkling blue eyes, he was noted for his charm and courtesy. Rightly so.

By contrast, his wife Betty was definitely on the plump side, with a well-preserved, smooth-skinned face that spoke of many hours of massage, beauty treatment, a whole warehouse of creams, and maybe just a bit of surgery.

She bustled in and out of the living room and the kitchen in a state of totally unnecessary agitation. "You know," she said to Jane, "I must have entertained thousands and thousands of people but I still worry about how the food's going to turn out."

"And I'll bet you've never had a failure yet," Jane replied.

Betty smiled appreciatively. "Well, no, I guess not. But there's a first time for everything, you know." She set her drink down and retreated to the kitchen again.

Shortly after eight-thirty John Hurst arrived. Jane noticed the lines of tiredness etched around his eyes. He took a martini from Bill Jackson and sank it quickly. "That's better," he said.

"How's the campaign going?" Jane heard Jackson ask.

She edged closer to join the two men. She knew about Hurst's midterm election the following month and had assumed it was little more than a formality. Cathy had never indicated otherwise. It came as a blow when Hurst said:

"It's going to be a close thing. Back home the folks reckon I spend too much time on foreign issues and not enough looking after them."

"They may have a point, John," Jackson replied.

Hurst gave a wry smile. "I know. I'm going to have to spend the next month hustling and trading with every wheeler-dealer in the state."

"It's the name of the game," Jackson said. "Always has been."

"Yeah. And it's a game I can play as well as anyone," Hurst said. "But the pressure's gotten a lot worse since the President sent his boys flying all over the world taking the heat out of the international situation. Promising heads of state everything and anything so long they keep off his back till the elections are over."

"That's the name of *his* game," Jackson responded. "You don't need me to tell you that."

Betty Jackson came in and announced that dinner was ready.

As they moved into the dining room, Jane was worried. Very worried. She had relied on Cathy to keep her informed of Hurst's political situation. Not the details, but at least something as vital as his reelection prospects. It had been a mistake. A bad mistake. She realized why, now: Cathy had been too obsessed with her personal problems. But knowing why didn't help.

Jane pushed the problem to the back of her mind as she took her place at the table. She had to concentrate on her immediate task: to win John Hurst's confidence and respect; to sell herself, hard. It wasn't going to be easy. Hurst was hardly likely to be in the mood to talk foreign politics.

Jane sipped the mulligatawny soup. Delicious. The seasoning was just right. In fact, everything about the Jacksons seemed to be just right, she thought, looking around the large dining room. The dark grain of the oak-paneled walls was relieved by a tasteful selection of paintings, each one obviously chosen for its individual merit. The oval mahogany dining table occupied half the room and could accommodate twelve people. Comfortable upholstered armchairs and a sofa faced a splendid green marble fireplace, the empty hearth now filled by an elaborately hand-embroidered screen in rich colors. The flickering flames from the candles set in the candelabras placed at each end of the table made the silver cutlery glow with a rich warmth. A setting of perfect contentment. But for Jane, a battleground.

After soup, Bill Jackson sounded off at John Hurst. "I've been reading some of your speeches, John. For heaven's sake! Do you really believe the Russians aren't as scared of war as we are?"

Jane took a sip of wine and watched John Hurst's face closely. For a split second, she detected a flicker of anger. Then it was gone and he smiled good-naturedly.

"Come on, Bill," Hurst said, "quit baiting me. Let's give politics a rest and let the ladies talk."

"Oh no, please," Jane said hurriedly. "I'm really interested. How can anyone say the Russians are scared of war? Whenever they use force, they win."

There was a silence. Hurst looked at her with raised eyebrows.

He was about to kill politely any further talk of politics, then he paused. Jane Mantel was the one who read the *Congressional Record*. The one who had told him to "Keep talking . . . and hot."

Maybe it would be interesting to find out if she really knew what she was talking about.

The seed Jane had sown on July Fourth *had* grown. It had borne fruit—and at a crucial moment.

"Okay, Jane," he said. "The floor's yours."

"Well," Jane began, "take Southeast Asia. The way the Communists see it, that was an American military defeat."

Mike interrupted. "That's stupid. We just got plain sick to the stomach at what we were doing."

"It was horrible," Cathy joined in. "Bombing towns. Burning villages down. . . ."

"Well, yes," agreed Jane, "I wouldn't defend the *way* we fought the war, but look what happened when we quit. The Communists took over the whole of Vietnam and then the dominoes *did* fall—Laos and Cambodia. Next it'll be Thailand and Malaysia."

"Young lady," Bill Jackson said, "we Americans had no business being in Vietnam. Using force to make other countries do what we want isn't a very moral policy."

"It rather depends, Senator," Jane said pointedly, "how you measure morality. If you think it moral to stand by while the Russians enslave the world, then I guess you are right."

Cathy was listening, fascinated. Jane was talking more like a man than a beautiful woman—a pretty hawkish man at that. Like her husband!

"And now it's the same all over again in Africa," Jane continued. "The Russians have got the message: we Americans just don't want to get involved."

Betty clicked her fingers for the main course to be removed. Privately she congratulated herself on having decided not to cook a special pudding. That girl Jane had distracted her guests from the carefully prepared Chieveley chicken. They hadn't even noticed what they were eating!

Bill Jackson was speaking. "It isn't that simple, Jane. We must consider the legitimate right of countries to determine their own futures."

Jane replied with icy coldness. "With due respect, I would have thought that what *is* important is to consider whether we want a Communist world or a free world. If it's to be Communist, then nobody is going to have *any* legitimate rights."

Mike broke the tension. "Honey. It's not as bad as that, for chrissake. The Russians aren't exactly about to come storming up the Potomac River."

Jane ignored his clear signal to ease up. She had a job to do and she was going to do it. She didn't care if she ruined Betty's dinner party. She didn't care if the others were bored. John Hurst was listening intently and that was what mattered.

She pressed on. "If the Russians can't win any other way, that's exactly what they *will* do. Come storming up the Potomac . . . with nuclear missiles."

"Frankly, that's nonsense, young lady," Bill Jackson said. "It would be suicide and the Russians know it."

"I'm afraid it isn't nonsense, Senator; I only wish it was. The fact is, the Russians could *win* a nuclear war. Right now, if they chose to."

Jackson turned to Hurst. "My god, John, she's worse than you."

"May I explain?" Jane asked quietly.

"Surely, young lady . . . if you can."

"The whole idea of nuclear deterrence," said Jane, "the whole idea that both the Americans and the Russians would be wiped out in a nuclear war, is dangerous nonsense. It's one of the biggest myths of all time. If the Russians had just *one day's* warning of a nuclear war they would lose twenty million people. *We* would lose about one hundred forty million. Where's the deterrence in that, for heaven's sake? The Russians had twenty million dead in the war against Germany!"

"Explain that," Jackson growled.

"Sure," Jane answered calmly. "It's a pretty complicated subject but let's take some of the basics. For years we have been spending less than a hundred million dollars on civil defense. We think it's a waste of money. A joke even. But guess how much the Russians have been spending? About two *billion* dollars a year. Dispersing and protecting factories. Building massive nuclear-proof shelters near big cities. Not only to protect people, but stocked with reserves of food and essential industrial machinery needed to recover quickly after a nuclear attack. *All* Russians are thoroughly trained in civil-defense precautions, even the children. How to make simple but effective shelters against nuclear fallout. How to take health counter-measures after an attack. The mass evacuation of major cities has been planned down to the smallest detail.

She paused and looked for a moment at each person around the table. Then, very quietly, she said, "The Russian people are being prepared materially and psychologically not *in case* there is a nuclear war, but so they can fight it and survive it *when it comes.* They believe nuclear war is inevitable."

Bill Jackson broke the uneasy silence that followed. "That, young lady, is a matter of opinion. But even if you're right, we're taking civil defense a little more seriously now. Making plans for evacuating cities if a crisis situation arises, and so on."

"I'm not sure taking it a 'little more seriously' is going to make much difference," Jane said, looking at the senator. "We're twenty years and tens of billions of dollars behind already. But that's not the point. Everyone talks as if there is going to be time to evacuate—some big political crisis building up as a warning. It isn't going to be that way. When the Russians attack, it will be because the men in the Kremlin have made the calculated and cold-blooded decision that they can win. They'll make damn sure there is no crisis, no warning. The time to watch out for the Russians isn't when they are being difficult; it's when they are talking too much about peaceful cooperation. That will be the prelude to war. And the only people who will have any warning will be the Russians. They'll know when it's going to start . . . to the second!"

"*If* the Russians wanted a war, they might do it that way," Jackson conceded. "But their country would be devastated, even if most of their people survived. They'd have to be out of their minds to do a thing like that."

"Are you *so* sure about that?" Jane replied slowly. "Look at it from the Russian point of view. Get into *their* minds. I said they'll attack us if it's the only way they can win. But there is one thing even more certain than that—they'll attack if it's the only way they can save themselves from *losing.*"

"I don't follow you," Jackson said flatly.

"We're opening up our relations with China. Right. We, and the rest of the West, can't wait to do all that beautiful business with the Chinese. Billions of dollars to build them into a modern industrial power. . . . *And* we think it's smart because it will give the Russians something else to worry about. They'll worry all right. And there is only one possible conclusion they can come to. They *have* to destroy us before we help build China into a superpower. A power that is totally hostile to them." She paused, her eyes riveted on the senator. "Do you honestly believe the Russians are stupid enough to sit back and watch that happen? Their country *will* be devastated when they attack us. But they'll think of it like a man having a leg amputated so he can keep on living."

Jane knew she had pushed her luck far enough. She turned to Betty with a dazzling smile. "I *am* sorry, Betty. I know I go on a bit sometimes. May I try some of your Camembert cheese now?"

When they moved into the spacious sitting room for coffee and liqueurs, John Hurst maneuvered to sit next to Jane.

He sipped his brandy and looked at Jane speculatively. "That was quite a speech. I'd like to have heard more! Pity you had to stop," he said.

"I'm not so sure about that," Jane answered, smiling. "Your Senator Jackson, he's a darling, a real gentleman, but I don't think he cares too much for my brand of politics. Not many people do."

"I do," Hurst stated.

"Now you're being polite," Jane replied.

"No. Seriously, I'd like to hear more of your views."

She told him.

When she had finished, he asked thoughtfully, "I don't want to sound impertinent, but how come a busy advertising girl knows so much?"

"The whole subject fascinates me," Jane said. "The outcome of the struggle between ourselves and the Russians will decide the future of the world for decades, maybe centuries to come. I learned Russian at college and I like to read the Russian news_ papers. You know . . ." Jane paused for a moment. "It's a pity more of you people in Washington can't understand Russian. You'd be surprised how much those newspapers reveal about what the Russians are up to . . . if you can read between the lines. Often it's what they *don't* say that's more important than what they do say." Jane laughed. "I guess I'm a bit of a screwball."

"I wouldn't say that," Hurst replied. "I'd say you're a very unusual young lady."

Jane smiled, then she looked at him earnestly. She had to be sure. "It's *really* serious? Your reelection chances?"

" 'Fraid so," he replied grimly.

He left her and went to sit beside Cathy, his mind still on Jane Mantel.

A remarkable woman, he thought. Not only did she talk fervently and with conviction, she knew the facts. During their conversation she had shown she was as familiar with the lexicon of nuclear weapons—circular error and kill probabilities, weapons yields, gamma radiation, guidance systems, and so on—as any member of the Senate Armed Services Committee he could think of.

Late that night when they had left the Jacksons and gone home, Cathy sat at the dressing table in the bedroom taking off her makeup. "What did you think of Jane?" she said to Hurst as he came out of the adjoining bathroom in his pajamas.

"She's one helluva smart lady," he said.

"I don't understand what she's doing with someone like Mike," Cathy said as she carefully removed her eye shadow. "Mike's nice enough. He's a lot of fun. But I wouldn't have thought he was, well . . ." She searched for the word. ". . . sophisticated enough for someone like Jane."

"You never can tell about people," Hurst replied. "But I can tell you this. I wouldn't mind having someone half as talented as she is on *my* staff. She's got brains, she knows her stuff, she even speaks Russian. And her looks aren't exactly a handicap."

"Hold on, John! You're making me feel jealous." Cathy swiveled to face him.

He came to her, cupped her face in his hands, and looked into her eyes with tenderness. "You, my darling Cathy, are the most beautiful and adorable woman in the world. The one I love."

Cathy melted inside as they embraced.

On the way back to New York Jane feigned a headache. Reluctantly Mike Brennan dropped her off at her apartment.

She used a Broadway drugstore pay phone around the corner from her apartment and got through to the Soviet Embassy. A man answered extension 348. She gave her code name, Samual, the number of the pay phone, followed by three separate times when she would be waiting to take a call.

Nothing more.

She returned to her apartment.

It was urgent. Senator John Hurst was worried about his reelection prospects. Not as worried as she was, though.

Again she wondered why she had been ordered to back such a hard-line anti-Soviet. It didn't make sense to her.

But it had to make sense.

It had been sanctioned by the Politburo.

She picked up the telephone and called Cathy Hurst—ostensibly, to say how much she had enjoyed the dinner and to thank her for setting it up. In fact, to get more information on Hurst's situation. A plan took shape in her mind.

The second time she went to the pay phone, Sakov called. He instructed her to be waiting outside an address on Fifty-second Street at exactly eight o'clock.

Sakov returned to the embassy and ordered that a hire-car be waiting for him when he arrived in New York. He would use false I.D. papers but apart from that he didn't take any other security precautions.

He had been right. The FBI had at first put him under the keenest surveillance. But since he appeared to be inactive—and might actually be an advisor on North American affairs—they had left him alone.

The FBI had to be choosy.

One of the less well-known results of détente was that the number of professional KGB agents operating in America had dramatically increased. The agents *known* to the FBI were more than they could take care of. The FBI were running about like a bunch of firemen with ten fires and one hose.

At five minutes after eight, his car glided to a stop by the waiting figure of Jane. He lowered the passenger window and leaned across. She saw his face, and got in beside him.

"The meeting's in the car," he said.

They headed slowly down the street.

"Just how serious is it?" Sakov asked, giving her a quick sideways glance.

"Bad, and getting worse," she replied with a bitter laugh. "I just spoke to his wife. Even she's worried. Hurst is giving a press conference tonight. He's going right out on a political limb by advocating that America cease negotiating with us Russians, altogether, about arms limitations. Unfortunately that's about the one issue the Americans are unanimous over. They believe the agreements make economic and military sense—provided they bring about genuine parity in strategic nuclear weapons."

The car turned a corner smoothly and they entered a narrow, dark street.

Jane went on. "Hurst is a very stubborn and logical man. He believes sooner or later we shall attack his country, if we think we can win. He doesn't trust paper agreements about arms levels. He is convinced America's only real security is to have unassailable military superiority over our country."

Sakov, listening carefully, reached down and massaged his leg. It was aching again, the way it always did in times of stress. And Jane Mantel wasn't doing much to make things better, talking so calmly about Hurst's logic.

"Perhaps, comrade, you might have a logical solution to *our* problem?" His voice had an edge to it.

Jane stared straight ahead. "Yes, I do believe I have."

Sakov's hand came off his leg. He gave her another quick glance, then coughed impatiently.

Jane turned to peer at him in the dim light. His face was hard-set and grim. Jane had a plan, and a good one. She wanted to please this man. Not because he was her superior, but as a *man.* It was a strange sensation, one she had never experienced before. She waited while Sakov crossed an intersection, then she spoke brusquely.

"First, his wife told me the latest polls show he's only six percentage points behind the competition. Bad, I know, but not catastrophic. She also told me that in the last three midterm elections only forty percent of eligible voters used their vote."

Sakov stopped the car and put the lever in P. He turned to face her. "Your point, comrade?" he said impatiently.

"We give those people who don't usually use their vote a good *emotional* reason to turn out and vote for Hurst this time."

"Very logical, comrade. And this . . . emotional reason?" He was peering at her intently in the half-light.

She turned to face him and he was struck yet again by her classical beauty. "Most Americans," she said, "have three things in common, three things they respond to emotionally: they like the small man to win; nothing makes them happier than proving federal bureaucracy wrong; and they admire initiative. Right?"

"Go on," he prompted.

"I have a plan which will enable Hurst to play on all three of these emotions. A real live human drama with Senator John Hurst in the spotlight playing the hero!"

Sakov listened to her plan with increasing admiration. It was ingenious. And it *could* work—even though it involved the arrest on Russian territory of an American citizen.

But there was a problem, one she would not have thought of. He said:

"Supposing this man's arrest caused so much bad feeling it put our trade negotiations at risk? It is vital these negotiations succeed."

Jane spoke slowly: "With due respect, comrade, your psychological reasoning is at fault. It is *because* the Americans know how important the negotiations are to our country that the State Department will believe the arrest is genuine. It will not damage our negotiations."

Sakov was too much of a professional to be riled by her criticism of his judgment. On the contrary, he respected her all the more for it. She *had* thought of everything.

"You realize I'll have to clear it at the highest level?" he asked, noticing the pain in his leg was easing.

"Of course," she replied. "But time is short . . . critical. It must happen on the day before the election. We've got to get the people to vote for Hurst on an impulse. An immediate emotional response to what he has achieved."

"Yes, yes," Sakov agreed curtly, thinking ahead. "I'm sure you will exploit the opportunity to its maximum."

Jane's eyes narrowed. "Oh yes, indeed," she said.

Sakov started the car and they moved off. They drove in silence to the nearest subway. As Jane opened the door to get out she felt Sakov's hand on her own. She turned to face him. He was smiling. "I like your perfume . . . comrade," he said. "It suits you."

Jane felt herself blush. Another new experience for her. She got out and slammed the door.

A few minutes after midnight Sakov was back in the Washington embassy. He went straight to his office, sat at his desk, and drafted a message in longhand. He walked the two flights down to the communications rooms and handed it to the duty cipher clerk. "Top priority," he instructed.

Within an hour the long message had been enciphered, transferred onto magnetic tape, and squirted the 4500 miles to Moscow in three separate compressed radio transmissions of a few seconds duration each.

Half an hour later—ten o'clock the next day Moscow time—Zimin's eyes flickered along the lines of the message as he sat at the ornate desk in his third-floor office in Dzerzhinsky Square. He picked up one of the battery of telephones on the console, a direct line to the Kremlin.

The conversation was short, the point at issue the trade negotiations. A satisfactory conclusion was reached. Zimin picked up another telephone and spoke to Remizov, one of his eight deputies.

Deputy Remizov summoned the chief of the Sixth Section of the Seventh Department of the Second Chief Directorate. The Sixth Section had full details of all foreigners visiting the country. Certain visitors requiring special attention were photographed at passport control. Their photographs preceded them by wire photo wherever they went. This made sure enough time was available to put the visitor in hotel rooms or railway sleeping cars equipped with hidden microphones and cameras.

But Deputy Remizov knew that the U.S. citizen he needed was unlikely to be in this special category. It would be necessary to check out all Americans in the country but it would not be difficult.

If the man existed, the Sixth Section would find him.

The man did exist.

His name was Jack Stanach.

CHAPTER
FOURTEEN

The Aeroflot flight taxied down the runway at Moscow airport—destination Helsinki. Jack Stanach was tired. The kind of tiredness only men who travel the world living out of suitcases, flying from country to country, selling, selling and then selling, know about. You never got to see the country you visited—hotels, offices, government buildings, nightclubs were the same the world over. The people back home thought it was great: export director for one of the biggest chemical manufacturers in the country, one long holiday living off a fat expense account. Boy, they could have it.

Jack Stanach was glad to be leaving Moscow. He hated negotiating with the Russians. Everything took so long. It was always the same: nothing but committees, and none of them able to make a decision without referring to some guy you never saw. Then the evenings out, when the same stone-faced bureaucrats regarded it as their duty to drink "our American friend" under the table. Drinking Americans under the table was a national sport in Russia, or so it seemed. His business would take two, maybe three, days in any sane country. But he had expected that, no matter what, he would be a couple of weeks in Russia.

And that was the way it had started this time—slow. Nothing but objections. Nothing but arguing about problems that could only exist in the screwed-up minds of bureaucrats. Then suddenly, after only four days, everything had changed. Outstanding problems he had reckoned would take a week to clear up were sorted out in half a morning. He had wondered what he had done wrong. Maybe he had sold his whole goddamn corporation to them for a couple of cases of vodka, without knowing it.

The hell with it, he thought, as the plane thundered down the runway. Only one more stop, Helsinki, and then he would be okay. The Finns drank so fast you could get unconscious in an hour, but at least they got through business at the same pace—most likely so they could get back to drinking! But that was their problem.

Two hours later, as the plane approached the Gulf of Finland, he looked out of the window. Clear blue sky. He kept looking. There was nothing else to look at. Aeroflot might be the biggest domestic airline in the world but they sure as hell came bottom of the league for pretty stewardesses.

The intercom spluttered, then came an announcement in Russian. The plane banked steeply to the right. Stanach nudged the man next to him, a Russian who spoke a little English. "What's wrong?" he asked. The Russian looked at him morosely. "Bad weather, we land . . . Leningrad." Stanach looked back out of the window. The weather was so goddamn bad you could see for a hundred miles! He nudged the Russian again and pointed out of the window. "Bad weather?" He pulled a face. The Russian grunted, shrugged, and pulled another kind of face which said that if someone in authority said the weather was bad, then it was bad; the fact that it was the calmest, clearest day you ever saw was irrelevant.

They landed. He followed the other passengers into the concourse. Now what? A pretty girl wearing an Intourist badge approached.

"You speak English?" he asked her.

"Yes. What do you want, please?"

"A goddamn airplane," he said, then decided she wouldn't understand his tired humor. "What am I supposed to do to get to Helsinki?"

"Ah yes," she said. "Your airplane had a fault. You have to get another one."

"No, not a fault, bad weather," he corrected her.

"No, a fault," she said. "The pilot was being kind . . . not to give you fright!"

"Oh," he said.

"Yes," she said. "Now you go through Customs."

"I do," he said. "Why?"

"Because you change airplanes," she explained.

"I see," he said, not understanding—but who ever understood the way the Russians did anything!

"I will help you," she said. And she did. She guided him to

where his baggage would arrive, then talked to him politely about his visit to Russia. When he had collected his baggage, she took him to the customs officer. Then she disappeared.

The blank-faced customs officer asked him to open his baggage and he wondered why the Russians looked so goddamn serious until they had half a bottle of vodka inside them. He opened his case. The officer riffled through it and pointed to a brown paper parcel at the bottom. "What is that, please?" he asked.

Stanach looked at it and frowned. "I don't know," he said.

"You will open it, please," the officer replied.

Stanach thought. And he thought, a bomb! "You open it," he said, and walked away to stand behind a concrete pillar nearby.

And then two men in uniform took him by each arm and steered him back to the customs officer. "You are under arrest—drugs," the officer said.

They drove him into Leningrad and shut him in a cell. He asked to see the American consul because he was very frightened. The Russians only planted drugs on people when they wanted to be very nasty. They said they would inform the American consul, but he was still very frightened.

Sakov put down the message he had received from the Center in Moscow, a look of satisfaction on his face. Everyone had acted with commendable efficiency. The only "suitable" American from the senator's state had been Jack Stanach. To get him arrested in time, before John Hurst's election, had meant curtailing his negotiations in Moscow, so they could get him into a situation where his baggage would be legitimately searched. The drugs had been planted when his plane was deliberately diverted to Leningrad. The right arrangements had been made in New York. The stage was set.

Now it was up to Jane Mantel.

Jane worked late that evening, then went over to Mike Brennan's apartment.

"Hi, hon. What kept you?" he greeted her.

"You know how it is," she joked, "pressure of business."

He grinned. "That's what all the girls say. Drink?"

"Sure. I need one."

He looked at her sharply. "Client problems?"

"No. Just tired, I guess. These last few months have been pretty tough."

He nodded and handed her a drink.

"Mike," she said, sinking back into her chair, "I'm going to take a few days' break. I've had it."

"Sure, why not?" he answered doubtfully. "You've fixed things at the office?"

"Yes. That's why I'm so late."

"What did you have in mind—somewhere in the sun?"

She shook her head. "No. Washington."

"Washington! You must be crazy."

"It's what I want."

Mike groaned. "Seems you've been talking to that uncle of mine too much. If you don't watch out, you'll get bitten by the political bug. If it gets into the blood it can be fatal!"

"I want somewhere really quiet," Jane said, "not a hotel. Do you think I could stay at your uncle's place? He'll be back home drumming up the voters. I'm sure he wouldn't mind. I know Cathy wouldn't."

"No. *He* won't mind at all. I'll call him and fix it. But how about *you*? It won't exactly be exciting on your own."

"That's what I want . . . peace and quiet. And all those beautiful boring books of his to read myself to sleep with."

"Okay. If that's what the lady wants. But you know Cathy's with him. He needs all the help he can get. A lot of people don't think he's going to make it back to Congress."

"He'll make it," Jane spoke abstractedly.

"That famous intuition of yours?"

"You could call it that." She smiled widely.

On the plane the next morning Jane searched the newspapers. She found what she was looking for. A headline: SOVIET DRUG TRIAL FOR AMERICAN. She settled down to read:

An American businessman, identified by Soviet papers as Jack Stanach, is to go on trial accused of drug offenses which could send him to prison for up to ten years. Embassy officials said today that Stanach was arrested at Leningrad airport while in transit to Helsinki. He has been charged under Article 78 of the Criminal Code of the Russian Federation with smuggling five pounds of Asian "brown sugar" heroin. Russian officials say the source of the drug is thought to be one of the several places Stanach recently visited in Asia, probably Kuala Lumpur.

Jane put the paper down satisfied.

She took a cab to Hurst's house in Georgetown and put her things in the guest room.

The election was in five days' time. She had estimated it would be two days before the senator realized he had to return to Washington.

At shortly after four o'clock the next day she got the call from Sakov. He told her the agent keeping tabs on Hurst had telephoned to report the senator had caught a flight to Washington.

She relaxed, made herself a drink, and turned on the television to pass the time while she waited.

Shortly after eight-thirty in the evening, she heard him come in and up the stairs.

John Hurst stopped when he saw her and looked blank for a second. Then he smiled wearily. "I'd forgotten you were here."

"I was expecting you," she replied.

"Expecting me?"

"Yes. The Stanach business. I read about it in the papers yesterday."

"But how did you know . . . ?"

"What else could you do?"

He shrugged. "What else!"

"Sit down while I fix you a drink. Scotch? Then I'll get you something to eat. The biggest, juiciest T-bone you ever did see."

They ate in silence. She could see he was exhausted. A tough election campaign . . . and now this Stanach affair.

She poured a couple of brandies. "D'you want to talk? . . . How bad is it?"

"About as bad as it could be."

"Are you certain Stanach isn't guilty? The Russians have picked up a few Americans recently . . . genuine drug smugglers."

"I know," he said. "I also know Jack Stanach . . . since we were kids together at school. He's not guilty. I'd stake my life on it."

"And you've come back to Washington because you're getting nowhere with the State Department."

"That's what you guessed, isn't it?"

"Yes."

"That's pretty smart thinking. You're right. The department wants me off its back and I've the opposition back home laughing themselves all the way to a victory. Guess what they're throwing at me: 'You're the guy who talks tough about the Russians, so now's your big chance. Show us. Get Stanach out!' "

"That's not very fair," Jane said sympathetically. "If the State Department can't do anything, what can you do?"

He sighed. "Lesson number one in politics. Forget fairness. What grabs the voters' emotions counts—and right now Stanach's the big emotional honeypot. My switchboard is jammed . . . and the language! I'd thought I'd heard it all. I was wrong."

"Could be you used some pretty strong language on the phone to the State Department yourself," Jane teased.

"You bet; but it didn't help. Only chance of moving those deadheads is to knock their doors in and jump right down their throats . . . starting tomorrow."

"I wish you luck," Jane answered, getting up to clear the dishes. "Go get some sleep now—you'll be needing it!"

He had left the next morning when she awoke. She had a good breakfast, read the papers, then went downtown to buy an outfit for the election celebrations. It was a pity she had to let John Hurst sweat it out with the State Department for another day. But she wanted him really softened up.

He returned shortly before seven o'clock, looking dispirited.

"How did it go?" she asked, handing him a Scotch.

"Bad. Sometimes I wonder whose side the department's on! Now they have it figured that, no matter what I say, Stanach *is* guilty."

She raised her eyebrows inquiringly.

"The Russians," he explained, "are negotiating to renew trade contracts . . . grain, machine tools, things they need badly. To the department, that means one thing. It proves Stanach's guilty. They're saying I'm crazy to think the Russians would risk upsetting us with a phony arrest when there's so much at stake in the trade negotiations."

Jane suppressed her satisfaction. It had worked the way she had told Sakov it would. She said, "I think I know how you can get Stanach released."

"You what!" Stark disbelief showed on his face.

"Listen. There's nothing special about Stanach—he's not CIA and he doesn't have military information the Russians need. Right?"

"Right."

"So the Russians want him for a trade-off. Like having money in the bank. They'll give him a long sentence and hold him until they want to exchange him for something or somebody they want from us."

"How does that help?" he said impatiently.

"Because if he was special we'd have to offer a high price for him. Since he's not . . . I think I've got the right price."

"Price?"

"Yes . . . information. Something which will persuade the Russians to release him."

"Like what?" he asked guardedly.

"The information is for you and only you. No one else is to know—especially the State Department. I want your word on it."

There was a long pause, then he said, "You mean this information might interest the State Department and you want me to withhold it from them?"

"Yes. It might be of interest to a lot of people, including the FBI and the CIA. But if you do what I'm going to suggest, it won't make any difference whether they know about it or not."

"No way do I give my word over something I don't understand."

"You must trust me."

He shook his head. "Sorry, Jane, I can't. Not if it affects national security . . . and that's what it sounds like."

"Not even if it guarantees you'll be reelected?"

"Not even that."

"You're being a very difficult man, John Hurst, do you realize?"

He smiled. "I've heard it before."

Jane studied him for a while as if she were trying to make up her mind. "Okay," she said at last. "If you agree it won't affect national security—once you know what I'm talking about—will you keep quiet?"

"Of course . . . *if* I agree."

"Right. Then listen. These trade negotiations have reached a pretty delicate stage. The Russians are asking for an awful lot. And it looks as if they're going to get it all . . . unless anything goes wrong."

"What could go wrong?"

"A lot of people are opposed to the deal, say we're giving the Russians too much. The slightest suggestion the Russians are doing anything underhanded would give them all the ammunition they need to blow the whole deal apart. Right?"

"I'm listening," he said.

"I make it my business to win the confidence of women who have influential husbands. Get really close to them. You know how it works: I build a personal relationship with the wife, then Mike meets the husband socially and takes it from there. Contacts—that's the name of our game. You never know who's going to be useful. One of the women, who shall be nameless, is the wife of a top-ranking member of our negotiating team. She's having an affair with the senior Russian trade official on their team."

John Hurst looked at her in amazement. "That's dynamite!" he exclaimed. "Who is she? I want names."

Jane was reluctant. "Keep it private, won't you?" she begged. "It's Reginald Brown's wife. Jennifer Brown. You know her?"

Hurst nodded. Jane went on, "Jennifer Brown told me the whole story. How she was infatuated with the Russian and couldn't leave him alone, but if it ever came out it would ruin her husband, who she still really loved, et cetera. I suggested she throw the Russian out and take a long vacation; someplace where there's plenty of willing beachboys."

"And?"

"She's still seeing him. And that gives you a perfect opportunity to get Stanach out of trouble and create some A-one publicity for yourself. At the same time you'll break up a relationship which could become a danger to national security. . . . You can never tell how these things will develop."

"Keep talking."

"To start with, you want Stanach's arrest and the failure of the State Department to do anything blown up as big as you can in all the media. Use all your contacts. I'll get the agency to work on it. Then you announce you're going to Moscow personally, to see what you can do to help. We'll make the national media with a human-interest story like that. The State Department won't like what you're doing, but they can't stop you. When you get to Moscow, you tell the Russians you *know* Stanach is innocent. They'll politely tell you he's guilty and suggest you keep your capitalist nose out of Soviet judicial procedure. You then suggest, equally politely, that they keep their embassy staff from out of the beds of the wives of prominent U.S. trade negotiators. That's when they'll stop talking and start listening. You then mention this name."

She took a piece of paper with the name of the Russian trade official from out of her bag and handed it to him.

"Which is when they ask me to *prove*"—John Hurst glanced at the piece of paper—"Feliks Bogachev is being a bad boy."

"Right. But you don't have to prove it. All you do is tell them you will be in Moscow for twenty-four hours. And, if by the time you leave they haven't found out they have made a terrible mistake arresting Stanach, you will feel it your duty when you get back home to inform the State Department of Feliks Bogachev's love life."

"What happens then?"

"In Moscow—panic. They'll start squirting radio messages to the Russian Embassy over here to find out what's going on. Feliks Bogachev will confess and be shipped straight back to Russia. You'll be told you are quite mistaken about Feliks. However, on further investigation, they have found that Stanach was arrested due to an administrative error and the people concerned will be severely punished."

"Suppose Feliks doesn't confess?"

"He will. He'll know if he does he'll end up sweeping the streets in Moscow. If he denies it, and it comes out later, he'll end up sweeping snow in Siberia."

"How can you be so sure it will work?" Hurst said.

"Look at it from the Russian angle," Jane replied. "If they don't release Stanach, the trade negotiations bomb out. They haven't any choice. And," Jane persisted, "what have you got to lose? Even if you don't get Stanach out, going to Moscow and trying will do you more good with the voters then hanging around the State Department."

John Hurst looked at her silently, then a smile spread across his face.

"You certainly are a remarkable young woman, Jane Mantel. I don't know if this plan of yours will work, but for dreaming it up you ought to be working for the CIA or the State Department even."

Jane laughed. "Maybe I should at that," she answered, "but it's not what I had in mind. I want a favor from you. . . . If the plan works and you're reelected, I want to work for you."

"Did I hear you correctly?" His tone was mild.

"Look—you know I'm sold on your brand of politics. So what am I doing selling cornflakes and girdles when I could be doing something I really believe in? And I'm sure I could be useful to you."

Hurst was looking at her. There was no mistaking she was serious. And she didn't have to persuade him she could be useful. But there were other considerations. He said:

"What about Mike and the agency?"

"I've given it a lot of consideration," she replied. "Mike and I are fond of each other, but nothing more. As far as the business is concerned, I've done him a lot of good. But he's more than capable of looking after himself. Besides, he knows he's going to lose me sooner or later. He's prepared for it. Mike's no fool."

John Hurst couldn't argue with that. "All right," he said, "I'll think about it . . . *if* your idea about Stanach works."

"Thank you," Jane said. Then she grinned. "The only thing you have to worry about is you may be getting a real crook off the hook. Maybe Stanach *is* guilty."

"Not a chance," he answered.

It happened the way she had predicted. The KGB acted out their part in Moscow and John Hurst returned in triumph with Stanach. The network news featured them arriving at Kennedy airport. The polls said twenty percent of the American public would have good reason to remember the name of John Hurst and the way he stood up for the rights of the individual American citizen, when the State Department had quit.

The only person who didn't get any satisfaction was embassy trade official Feliks Bogachev. He was bundled onto a plane for Moscow with two hours' notice. The official explanation was that he'd suddenly been taken seriously ill. John Hurst knew better!

So did Feliks Bogachev. But the only explanation he received was that his removal was "necessary." He tried to object. Hadn't he served his country well by almost wrapping up one of the most favorable trade deals ever? Yes, they agreed, but it was still "necessary." What Feliks would never know was just how well he *had* served his country—by having an affair with a woman he had never met!

In the Jefferson Room of the Sheraton Hotel, nearly five hundred people stood absolutely still, as if frozen in the embrace of the silence that filled the room.

In exactly twenty-nine seconds the results of the election would be announced.

Senator John Hurst and Cathy stood side by side on the platform. The senator's face was drawn, a white line of tension around his tightened mouth. The strain of the campaign—his dash to Moscow—now this suspense. He moved his hand imperceptibly till it found and held Cathy's. A gentle squeeze told her more than words could.

In fifteen seconds they would know.

At the back of the room, close to the door, Jane waited. Each person in that packed room had something to gain if the senator was reelected: promotion, a job kept, or just plain satisfaction.

But no one had as much at stake as Jane Mantel and the KGB.

As the results were announced the room erupted. Cathy threw her arms around her husband, hugging and kissing him with joy. The senator took a white handkerchief from the breast pocket of his dark-blue suit, wiped the sweat from his forehead, and stepped forward to the microphone. He spoke for a couple of minutes, then gave up, his voice drowned by the cheering, whooping, laughing crowd. The liquor began to flow and the reporters closed in on him.

"Senator, sir, would you care to say more about how you got the Russians to release Jack Stanach?"

"No, sir, I would not."

"But, Senator, people would like to know."

"So would the State Department," someone near the senator quipped.

An outburst of laughter.

"Senator, you've got one helluva story there."

The senator couldn't resist it. "I have . . . but you haven't." Then he added, "I'm sorry, but some things are better not talked about. Let's just say I've got the two things I most wanted—my good friend Jack Stanach back home safely, and myself back to Congress."

Ed Peterson withdrew from the crowd around the senator. Jesus! Was he supposed to make a lead story out of that? Didn't the guy want the publicity? He moved toward the back of the room.

Outside in the lobby Jane Mantel had got her connection on the telephone to Washington.

"Yes," a voice said. It was Sakov.

"He's in," she stated and hung up.

Jane pushed her way back into the crowded room. The senator was still on the platform surrounded by jubilant supporters. Cathy was by his side, tears of happiness in her eyes.

As she forced her way to the platform Jane caught sight of Ed

Peterson. He was scowling. For a split second she was startled. Then she remembered. Of course he'd be here—a political correspondent and supporter of Hurst. She turned away sharply but was too late. Peterson had seen her. His expression changed to a broad smile.

"Got you," he triumphed as he grabbed her arm. "And this time make sure you keep that elbow to yourself."

"My elbow!" Jane looked suitably surprised.

"Yes, your elbow. Last time we met you half killed me with it."

"Oh!" she said, as if some understanding was just dawning in her mind. "That was *you*!"

"I've the scars to prove it." He bent over in mock pain.

"I'm so sorry." She smiled her lovely smile and he was entranced all over again. "I had no idea. But you know how it is in a crowd. A girl has to protect herself. You'd be surprised where the men put their hands."

"Show me," he suggested.

Jane glanced toward the platform. John Hurst was tactfully edging toward the steps.

She put one perfectly manicured hand on Peterson's shoulder. "Wait for me here, Ed," she breathed. "I've got to have a quick word with the senator."

"Wish you more luck than I had," Ed replied with feeling.

She turned from him.

"And don't run out on me," he added, "or I'll put a professional investigator on you this time." He bit his tongue with annoyance. That had been a damn-fool thing to say!

Jane froze. Then she swiveled around on him. "You'll what?" she spoke icily, slowly.

He grinned. "Relax. It's not exactly an insult."

"What isn't an insult . . . Ed?"

"Why, trying to trace you after you'd elbowed me and left me for dead."

But she was looking at him in a way he didn't understand. It was unnerving.

"Listen—all I did was look up some of your old university classmates," he protested.

She treated him to another lovely smile. "Okay. I'm flattered. You relax, Ed," she said. "I'll be right back."

She threaded her way to the platform and spotted Mike Brennan in the middle of a group of celebrators. He had his arm around the waist of a pretty brunette who was wearing a campaign sash. Mike was laughing raucously. She noted with satisfaction he was already half-drunk.

On the platform she embraced Cathy. "Isn't it wonderful," she enthused.

"Wonderful," Cathy echoed, her face flushed with excitement. "I still can't believe it."

She moved to the far side of John Hurst. He saw her. "Excuse me, Sam," he said, turning from the city mayor who had been telling him how he had always known the senator would come out ahead and how he really did believe they had to watch those Reds—and a whole lot of other lies.

John Hurst looked steadily down into Jane Mantel's face. "Thanks," he said, his eyes expressing the fullness of his gratitude.

"We made a deal," Jane said. "Now I'm working for you full time."

"Sure you want it?" he asked seriously. "Sure you've thought about it enough?"

"I'm sure," she answered.

"It's a deal," he said. "I only hope you know what you're letting yourself in for."

"Nothing I can't handle," she assured him with her smile.

She returned to Peterson. "Let's get out of here." She linked her arm under his. "It's too crowded and I'm starving."

He took her to a small Italian restaurant around the corner from the hotel.

Jane kept the conversation light while they ate. When the coffee came, she said casually, "Did I tell you I'm going to work for Hurst?" It would seem odd if she didn't mention it and he would soon get to hear about it anyway.

He stopped stirring his coffee. "You . . . in politics!"

"Why not?" She laughed in mock hurt.

"Well, I don't know." He gazed at her flawless face. "I guess you just don't look the part." But that wasn't what he was thinking. He was recalling Judy Benson telling him how she had shown no interest in politics at the university. He was recalling how not only Judy but two other classmates had described Jane Mantel as a plain girl. And a timid one too.

"How am I supposed to look?" Jane parried.

He smiled faintly. "Just beautiful, I guess. Just as you are!"

"Thank you," but Jane sensed some unease. He was puzzling about her. It was time to make her next move.

"Aren't we wasting valuable time?" she purred, parodying her first invitation to him in the bar so long ago.

"You bored again?" He grinned right back.

"No . . . impatient." She smiled at him.

"Let's go," he said.

They reached his apartment and he undressed hurriedly, eager, his penis hard with anticipation. She stood watching him but made no move to remove her clothes.

"Come on," he urged. "I thought you were impatient."

She undressed slowly, sensuously, watching the growing excitement in his eyes. Naked, she stood at the end of the bed and began gently massaging herself. He lay, transfixed, torn between the urge to pull her down on him and the erotic sight of a beautiful woman manipulating her own body. And all the time her eyes were fixed on him and he saw the frenzy in them as her pupils widened with the excitement of her power: he was a helpless animal, the whole of him in that one swollen, demanding organ.

The vaginal juices began to flow in her.

She moved onto the bed, then sat astride his thighs and inserted his penis into her warm vagina. He started to thrust. "Keep still," she whispered. Then it happened. Something he had never experienced before.

With her body completely motionless, her vaginal muscles were rhythmically contracting, relaxing, contracting, around his penis. It was the most incredibly sensuous sensation he'd ever experienced—weirdly erotic. The two of them, absolutely still, yet the muscles inside her, warm and soft, gently then firmly, bringing him closer and closer. . . . He moaned and closed his eyes, conscious only of the life within her, giving him such exquisite pleasure.

Then slowly bending backward, she placed the tips of the fingers of her right hand just behind his testicles and pressed. His orgasm hit him like an explosion. His whole body jerked violently and uncontrollably. For an instant he passed out—*la petite mort,* the little death that comes occasionally to women, and very rarely to men, after orgasm.

He opened his eyes, his chest still heaving for breath. *"Where did you learn that?"* he gasped.

She was by his side, gently wiping the perspiration from his brow with the sheet. "A talent." She smiled gently. And she remembered the little Indian girl with the angelic eyes who had told her about it at the sex school, saying, "But it will take you many, many hours of practice to master the art. Where I come from, our mothers teach us."

Jane had practiced and for many, many hours.

"Like witchcraft." He spun the words hazily.

"Better than investigating?" she teased, running her fingers over his chest.

"Investigating . . . ?" he repeated, puzzled for a moment. "Oh that! Forget it. It was a crazy idea I had I could trace you by talking to girls you'd known at the university." He started to caress her full breasts.

"How did you make out?" she persisted.

He gave a wry smile. "Not too well. I found one girl who'd known you, name of . . ." He paused, trying to remember the name. Jane held her breath, desperately hoping it was one of the classmates Professor Wolfe had briefed her on.

"Judy . . . er . . ." he said.

"Benson," she cut in.

"That's the one. Nice girl, only not too helpful. Can you imagine? She described you as shy and sort of plain-looking. Even had a photograph of you. . . ." He looked at her admiringly. "Boy! Who said the camera never lies."

"I was a late developer," Jane pouted. "Ever hear the story of the ugly duckling?"

"That was a fairy story; you're more like a miracle."

Jane laughed. "They happen."

"They sure do. . . . Then there was this Professor Wolfe. I thought he might give me a lead."

"Yes?" Jane arched a delicate brow, seemingly faintly disinterested.

"Only he committed suicide."

"Oh dear, I am sorry to hear that. He was such a nice man." She wondered about it. Suicide, or had the KGB plugged a potential crack in her cover story? She might never know.

He started to bite her nipples, gently. She cupped her breasts for him. "And that's all you found out?"

"Yeah . . . except you went to Dresden in East Germany. From the same woman . . . Benson . . . Judy. . . . You sent her a postcard."

He raised his eyes to her face. "Why d'you go to a boring place like that?" His eyes returned to her breasts and he began to roll her protruding nipples between his fingers.

Jane was grateful for the time. She had to think fast. "What do you mean, *a boring place like that*?" she said indignantly. "Don't you know they produce the most famous and exquisite china in the world! In Dresden. I had a thing about it at the time. I wanted to see it being made."

His attention drifted from her breasts as the faintest of queries lodged in his mind. "*In* Dresden?"

"Naturally."

"Naturally," he repeated and his attention returned to her breasts.

Her hand reached down for his penis.

They made love again . . . and again. But not like the first time.

That was rationed, something they always came back for. She'd keep it as an insurance policy. Peterson had found nothing to damage her cover story but, working for Hurst, she was certain to meet him again. And you never knew.

The dawn was breaking as she left. She gave him her New York address and a promise she'd let him know the new address when she moved to Washington.

Peterson made a decision. There was a position coming up shortly in the Washington bureau of the syndicate. With a lot of hard work and a little luck he could probably swing it his way.

He's sure as hell try.

He found it hard to concentrate the next day. His mind kept wondering back to every little detail of the night. Christ, she was incredible. Out of this world.

Every little detail.

What was it?

Peterson had an encyclopedic memory; he knew more useless facts than anyone he'd ever met. But he couldn't be sure.

He went up to the reference library and took down the encyclopedia: *A–D*. He flipped the pages. DRESDEN CHINA. He read:

"Popularly believed to come from Dresden in the German Democratic Republic but in fact manufactured from local kaolin in the small town of Meissen, Pop. 51,000, 14 kilometers NW of Dresden."

He read no further.

That was what had prompted him to ask: "*In* Dresden?"

Why had she said *naturally*?

If she'd been there, she'd know better.

CHAPTER
FIFTEEN

A room in a house in Washington. A very special house. A safe house, used to entertain guests who required luxurious but discreet entertainment; to impress them or to reward them.

The man examined the small round table with an experienced eye.

Everything was in place. The silver cutlery perfectly and symmetrically laid out. The vase of pink-and-white carnations carefully arranged and set exactly in the middle of the table. At each of the two place settings, glasses of different shapes—small vodka glasses, tulip-shaped champagne glasses, and large, bulbous brandy glasses—gleamed in the soft light.

The man made a fine adjustment to one of the two candlesticks strategically placed at the edges of the table so as not to impede the vision of the two people who would occupy the comfortable high-backed chairs.

The man moved the laden drinks trolley a little nearer one of the chairs, then carefully wiped away a few drops of water he noticed on the neck of the magnum of champagne in the ice bucket.

All was ready.

The man went out to the kitchen to check with the chef.

Sakov entered, quickly looked over the table, then, satisfied, stood with his back to the open fireplace which was glowing with red coals. He glanced around the room. The walls were covered with tapestry wallpaper, the motif a variety of exotic birds with much, but delicately colored plumage. On two of the walls hung gold-framed mirrors which had once graced the château of a long-dead French nobleman—as had the rest of the elegant furniture.

The man showed Jane Mantel in. Sakov advanced to meet her

and kissed her warmly on each cheek. "Welcome and congratulations, Anna," he said.

Jane was a little taken aback by the enthusiasm of his greeting and by the use of her Russian name. She took in the luxury of the room and the table for two, and looked questioningly at him.

"You deserve it, Anna," he said, reading her look. "You have done well. Now sit down"—he gestured toward the sofa at one side of the fire—"and tell me of your success with 'our' senator."

With swift, graceful movements she settled herself on the sofa. She began to recount what had happened, all the while conscious that Sakov had not gone to such lengths merely to reward her. She had done her duty. Nothing more.

Sakov listened without interrupting. When she had finished he rose and pressed a button on the wall. After a few seconds the man who had taken so much trouble with the preparations appeared with a trolley of hors d'oeuvres. "Shall we sit?" Sakov held Jane's chair, inviting her to the table.

Once they were seated he nodded toward the man. "You need not worry about Ivan," he said. "He is one of us. By day a chauffeur at the embassy, on occasions such as these the perfect butler and waiter. There are other occasions"—Sakov waved a hand airily—"many other things to be done. He has many and diverse talents. Is that not so, Ivan?"

The man gave a tight smile. "That is correct, Comrade Colonel."

Jane looked at the man Ivan. She doubted that was his real name. He was dark and swarthy. From the south, she guessed, Turkmenia or Tadzhikistan. Despite Sakov's assurances, caution made her remain silent while he served them and filled their champagne glasses.

It was not until he left the room that she spoke. "There is one thing which I have not mentioned yet." She sighed. "It's tiresome, I'm afraid. Peterson is becoming inquisitive."

Sakov's eyes narrowed. "Inquisitive? Explain."

Jane told him.

He remained silent and thoughtful for a few minutes. Then he said, "I don't like it. Particularly his knowing of your supposed visit to East Germany. No. I do not like it at all."

"I can handle him." Jane spoke with all the confidence of a desirable woman.

"Perhaps. But newspapermen have long noses and big ears. They are trained to scent out hidden meanings, inconsistencies, conspiracies." He fell silent once more, wrestling with this irritating, and maybe dangerous, problem.

At last he spoke briskly. "I shall let you have another passport. Identical with the one you already possess but with the visit to Germany recorded in it. Keep both passports. *And,* comrade, you will immediately make yourself familiar with Dresden china. Always remember, it is the details, the minutiae, the unexpected coincidence that we have to be most wary of. Things we can plan for, things we can foresee, can be controlled. But a speck of unseen dust falling into a delicate but vital part of the most meticulously designed and constructed machine—that speck of dust will destroy it."

"I have already taken precautions," Jane said. "I have purchased two books on china and I shall read them most carefully."

Sakov smiled at her. "Forgive me. I should have known you would not overlook such a thing. It is good and I am pleased. Now you are working for Hurst, this Peterson knows where to find you. If I am not mistaken he will not leave you alone. You have, my dear Anna, acquired a most enthusiastic and unwelcome admirer."

Jane smiled with a tinge of malice. "I shall do everything to discourage him, as you can imagine."

While the man Ivan cleared the table and served the main course Sakov kept the conversation general. When they were alone again he raised his glass. "And now, a toast to the *next* President of the United States," he said. "I give you . . . Senator John Hurst."

Jane's hand remained arrested, frozen in the air, the glass some six inches from her lips. She stared at him, eyes wide, her mouth open in startled disbelief.

"What did you say?" she asked, her voice a mere whisper. "Hurst? President?"

"That's what he wants, isn't it?"

"Of course. He's a very ambitious man."

"Well, we are going to make sure he achieves his ambition. Now perhaps you understand the importance of your assignment."

She was numb with amazement. She understood nothing.

"Drink, Anna, drink," Sakov urged with a broad smile.

She took a small sip and replaced her glass on the table. She regained herself sufficiently to ask, incredulously, "Why Hurst? He hates us."

Sakov became serious. "There are two answers to that—because there are two questions. The first question is, why the *man* Hurst? You will be told that answer in good time. The second question is, why a man with Hurst's political views?"

Jane couldn't contain herself. "Yes. *Why* an anti-Russian politician? *And* Hurst is completely preoccupied with foreign affairs. American presidential elections are decided on home issues."

"Exactly. But we cannot influence American domestic affairs."

Jane shook her head vigorously. "I don't understand."

Sakov explained. "Suppose that at the time of the next election the Americans have to regard foreign policy as the major election issue. And suppose the one man who has foreseen this is Hurst, eh?"

Jane struggled to follow his meaning. "*If* that were to happen, then Hurst would no longer be out on a limb. He would be a messiah. And we could influence, *manipulate*, what he does?"

"Precisely."

Jane now grasped the enormity of what he was proposing. "A drink, comrade," she said, pushing her glass forward.

He filled it to the brim, watching her carefully.

She gulped it down unceremoniously.

"May I be allowed to know *how* we can make foreign policy a major election issue?" She sounded quite breathless.

"Not only may you ask, it is *necessary* for you to know. . . . We are making certain military preparations which threaten the Americans and we cannot hide them." He paused and looked at her sharply. He had her total attention. "There are, of course, even more important preparations, which they are not aware of. Fortunately, the Americans place too much confidence in technology . . . satellite surveillance . . . and there are many things technology cannot detect."

A conspiratorial gleam began to glow over the soft bloom of Jane's face.

Sakov continued, "We are going to make moves in various parts of the world—southern Africa, northeast Africa, Southeast Asia, and elsewhere. You will be given prior knowledge of what we are doing. At first, small things. You will pass them on to Hurst as predictions. He will find your predictions turn out to be right; he will come to trust your judgment. Then you will give him more important information—information he can use to support his hard-line foreign policy. Very soon, people will no longer regard him as an anti-Soviet alarmist. He will be stating specifics which will be proven to be true. By the time the presidential election comes, he will be the man of the moment. The right man at the right time—like Lenin, Roosevelt, Churchill, Eisenhower, and many others. Men made great by events."

Jane stared at this man whom she had respected for so long. Now he was exciting her with his power. "But that will damage our country." She had to protest.

A sardonic smile spread over Sakov's face. "No," he assured her. "Unless we threaten America or Europe *directly* we can do pretty much what we like anywhere else. They may try to stop us with their money. . . ." He shrugged. "But, they'll never try to stop us by force—not after Vietnam!"

Jane was silent for a moment. Then she asked: "How will I explain to Hurst how I get this special information?"

Sakov smiled. "Nothing succeeds like success. Your success with Stanach has already established your credibility with Hurst. It has demonstrated that you have your own private contacts and perceptive judgment of how we Russians behave. You would be surprised how highly he thinks of you."

Jane looked at him sharply. "How do you know that?"

"We have heard him talking to his wife about you," Sakov answered matter-of-factly.

"You mean you have bugged his house?"

"Of course. And his office."

"Isn't that taking a risk?" she asked.

"Come, come, Anna, I think we can leave that to our experts. After all, they bugged the American Embassy in Moscow for twelve years before it was discovered. I think we can rely on them to manage one unsuspecting senator."

"Of course, comrade." She shrugged off her doubts.

"Now," Sakov continued, "we come to the first step in *our* election campaign for Hurst." He talked at length, giving Jane details about a White House advisor named Seaford Lent. Jane listened attentively.

Finally Sakov summed up. "Through this Lent operation we will achieve three things. We will build Hurst's public reputation. Increase his trust in you. And last, and most important of all, undermine public confidence in the present President. Clear?"

"Beautifully clear," Jane answered, her eyes sparkling.

"Good," Sakov replied, and filled the vodka glasses. "A toast, comrade. *Rodina!*"

Jane tossed back the fiery liquid in one swallow. Then, quite unexpectedly, she felt the tears coming to her eyes. It had been a long time since she'd heard the word *rodina*, a word no Russian can hear without an emotional gut reaction. *Rodina*—her motherland, her country, her Russia.

Sakov's voice was low. "You miss your country, Anna?"

"Till I die," she murmured, her beautiful head bent forward.

Sakov put his hand on her shoulder. "Cheer up, Anna. You may be home sooner than you think." He picked up the bottle of vodka and moved to the sofa by the fire. "Come, Anna, we will get drunk together like good Russian friends."

They drank as only Russians do. . . .

They talked.

Both, of Russia.

She, of her life before she became an illegal.

He, of his wife and family.

Jane couldn't be sure but, for the first time in her life, she might have been touched by jealousy as he talked about his wife.

There was a silence broken only by the sound of the fire. A hot coal fell deeper into the glowing ashes and burst into flame, sending shadows dancing on the walls of the dimly lit room.

Jane looked at Sakov as he stared unblinking into the dying fire. She saw the strong profile of his face—the high cheekbones and forehead, the firm set of his chin—and she wondered once again about this man. A man who had been capable of killing the woman he loved, yet who talked of his wife and family like any other man. Could such a man, she asked herself, could such a man *really* love?

Sakov leaned forward, still staring into the fire. He began to talk, answering her unspoken question. Reading her secret thoughts as he had always been able to. He spoke slowly and with great care. It was important she understood. "This life of ours, Anna—this life we have chosen, are indeed honored to live —it is not easy. It demands great sacrifice."

"The loneliness, you mean," Jane said.

"Yes, that. But far more. It calls on us to sacrifice our souls, to lose our humanity."

Jane listened intently. She had not expected him to talk of souls and humanity.

"A good agent must be cynical about human nature. He must be constantly on the alert for the hidden signals which betray human weakness and folly. No. It is deeper than that. He must make it his business to look only for the evil inherent in man, to dig it out, prey on it, exploit it in any way possible. It is dirty work, Anna. Inevitably it corrodes the soul. To look only on the darker side of human nature is to make a mockery of love."

"But you loved once. . . . You told me."

"Yes. When I was young."

"And will this happen to me . . . this corrosion of my soul?"

"In time, yes. But for the moment, you are an innocent."

"Innocent!" Jane felt bewildered. "How can you say that when you know the things I do?"

"Because you have faith. You believe in the Party, in communism, in your country. When you lose that faith you will no longer be an innocent."

"And you. Are you saying you don't believe?"

"For me it is no longer a question of faith. I see all people as the same—weak, greedy, evil. All people, whether Russian or American. I am a Russian. Therefore I chose my country. . . ."

Jane would not let him finish. "I do not think that is true," she interrupted softly. "May I tell you what I think?"

Sakov nodded. He had not once lifted his eyes from the fire, had not once looked at her.

Jane drew a deep breath. "I think you are telling me this because you do not want me to . . ." She faltered a little but then went on. ". . . because you do not want me to have any feelings for you. Apart from our cause and comradeship."

"I think I've said enough—we must not become maudlin from too much vodka, you and I." Sakov spoke evasively, his head turned toward the fire.

"Look at me," she pleaded, forced by some inner need which drove her onward. "Please. Look at me."

It was some moments before Sakov moved. Slowly he raised his head. An eternity of time seemed to pass before his gaze met hers. Their eyes locked and held.

At last Sakov spoke. "I have nothing to bring you, Anna. Nothing."

In the morning Jane awoke, cold and stiff. She'd fallen asleep on the sofa. Sakov was standing over her, his face clean shaven, his eyes clear and alert. He smiled. "Now, Anna," he said. "The man called Seaford Lent. You remember your instructions?"

White House advisor Seaford Lent closed the door behind him, leaving President Dale alone in the Oval Office.

The President rose to his feet and went to the window overlooking the Rose Garden. He slammed his fist into the palm of his hand. Goddamnit! He'd do it. It made sense.

Seaford Lent's policy proposal for the Mideast was about the smartest thing he'd heard in a long time. It was going to be tough to handle, though. Every darn political commentator in Washington—in the world—would call it a series of bumbling gaffes. To hell with them! You didn't get to be president without being able to take a little heat.

The President sat down again. He hit a button on his desk. He wanted the Secretary of State to come and see him. The State Department was going to hate it. They had done everything possible to oppose Lent's appointment to the White House. Not because he wasn't bright; nobody would deny him that. But because he was unreliable. According to State, you couldn't take Lent to a cocktail party—let alone a meeting of heads of state—without a high probability he would upset everybody, starting from the top. The President had to admit they had a point: Lent was eccentric, moody. But he was bright, brilliant sometimes; and for that the President could put up with his erratic behavior.

As Seaford Lent climbed into his car to leave the White House, he was feeling good. Very good. He'd come up with the Mideast solution—while he was shaving, would you believe! What was more, for once—in fact, for six consecutive months—he'd got the stock market right.

His only vice, playing the market.

It had been an expensive vice. He bought when he felt good and sold when he felt bad. And whatever else the Dow Jones did, it did not follow the moods of Seaford Lent.

But, six months ago, it had all changed. Now, he was a winner.

He turned off New York Avenue down 12th Street. He was on his way to see Dr. Bitner, his once weekly visit.

According to his psychoanalyst, Dr. Bitner, Lent was a manic-depressive on a two-month cycle of "highs" and "lows." Which meant when he was on a high he would spark off brilliant ideas faster than anyone could follow them, speak in short bursts, feel happy as hell, and go about the place quietly laughing and singing to himself. Then he'd slow down and sink into a low—the depths of despair, not talking to anyone, drinking, and think of no ideas except maybe he should kill himself.

Sad.

A typical manic-depressive.

Seaford Lent was sensitive about his complaint. He didn't

want people to know. Particularly he didn't want State to know. He got his kicks from making them look stupid and he wasn't having them throwing the mud around saying he was out of his mind half the time.

That was why he liked Dr. Bitner.

The doctor understood about privacy.

Lent went through the discreet door, was greeted by the discreet receptionist, and was immediately shown into a discreet waiting room. When he left, it would be through a back door. Dr. Bitner's patients didn't meet one another.

The doctor was in the discreet business.

Profitable.

His prices were high and he got bonuses for some of his patients.

He got a bonus for Lent.

"How are we today?" Dr. Bitner had a foreign accent and his voice was lugubrious, matching his sad brown eyes with the dark circles under them. He'd fled Hungary after the uprising in 1956.

Dr. Bitner, psychoanalyst, was one of forty-eight KGB agents who had used the uprising as a cover to infiltrate the West.

"Fine, fine . . . just fine," Lent assured him, running a bony hand through his long white hair. He laughed. "To tell you the truth, Doctor, I don't know why I come and see you."

"It's best," the doctor answered.

Lent sat on the couch. "I guess I owe you some money," he said, his keen blue eyes darting about the room.

"There's no hurry," the doctor demurred.

"I owe you," Lent insisted.

"Very well then," the doctor answered.

Lent jerked to his feet, strode swiftly to the window, and looked out. "Do you know why I'm going to pay you?"

The doctor said nothing.

"Investment consultant—Johnson Stafford. I'll give you his address." Lent returned to the couch, groping feverishly in his pockets. "Hell, I don't have the address. I'll mail it to you."

"Most kind," the doctor answered.

"Sent me these mail-shots . . . you know . . . usual thing about how good he was. Had a special package deal—commodities. Kept sending them . . . these mail-shots. So I began to try them. Fantastic! Hardly ever put a foot wrong."

He groped around in his pockets again. "Where in damnation is that address!"

"It doesn't matter. Mail it to me."

"Better be quick," Lent said, getting to his feet and pacing up and down in front of the doctor. "He gave me a tip he says is a once-in-a-life opportunity to make a killing. Put every cent I've got into it . . . and a lot more. Even got my married kids into it."

"I'm sure you've done the right thing," the doctor reassured.

"You bet."

Lent started to whistle a tune, then stopped abruptly and pointed a finger at the doctor. "Know what? Just put the President right . . . the State Department!" He burst out laughing. "I shit them."

He turned to the door. "I'll be off now, Doctor. Got work to do."

"Your tablets," the doctor reminded, handing him a white package.

"Oh yeah. Thanks."

He left . . . by the back entrance.

He hadn't mentioned paying the doctor again.

He'd clean forgotten.

The doctor didn't mind. He picked up the telephone and dialed. A high-pitched whine was the signal. He began to talk: a precise description of Lent's state of mind and what he'd said. At the other end of the telephone a tape slowly wound.

He didn't know who the recipient of his message would be.

He didn't care.

He was well paid.

Into a Swiss bank.

No tax.

And if he did have to leave the country in a hurry, he'd know where to go . . . and how to live.

There were many people in Washington who required his services. Discreet. They talked . . . in confidence. Through Dr. Bitner, the KGB had a direct line to the innermost secrets of the private lives of highly placed government officials and politicians. They found the information . . . helpful.

Dr. Bitner finished his message.

Half an hour later Sakov was listening to the tape.

It was Sunday afternoon. Early that morning Jane had phoned to tell Hurst she had some new ideas to put more muscle behind his presidential campaign. Hurst had said to come over in the afternoon so they could talk.

Now the three of them—Jane, Hurst, and Cathy—were seated in easy chairs around a low table in Hurst's spacious Georgetown house. It had been a long session. The table was covered with typed documents and sheets of scratch paper with notes.

"How about a drink?" Cathy suggested.

Jane nodded.

"Large ones," Hurst said.

Cathy got up and went to the paneled bar. She was convinced Jane was right.

Hurst wasn't so sure. Jane had suggested the time was right to step up the anti-Russian content of his platform. She had even gone so far as to predict some imminent Russian moves in Africa he could hone in on.

Hurst met Jane's cool eyes and shook his head slowly. It was too risky to go out on a limb on Africa the way she had suggested. She was being too specific. If her predictions were wrong, every political opponent and commentator would tear him to pieces.

Cathy handed him a large Scotch. He set it down on the table, leaned back, and stretched his arms above his head. "I think it's best we play the African thing cool for a while yet," he said, looking at Jane. "You could be right, but if you're not"—he chopped one raised arm down onto the back of his neck—"it's my head that goes."

Jane smiled. "Okay, John, if that's the way you want to play it . . . cautious . . . it's your decision. But you'll regret it. I'm right and I know it."

"We'll see," Hurst answered, and turned the conversation to discuss other ways of boosting the media exposure he was getting.

They talked on for a while, then Jane said, almost casually, "You know what would really grab the headlines? Warn people of the growing threat from the KGB. The possibility they will— may have already—penetrated the White House."

"That's going too way out," Hurst objected.

Cathy looked anxious. Jane, in her enthusiasm, was going too far—the White House!

Jane leaned forward. "Did anyone think it possible that German Chancellor Willy Brandt would be forced to resign because they discovered his chief advisor was a KGB agent? Or that U.N. Secretary General U Thant should have had Viktor Lessiovsky, a KGB agent, as a personal advisor? Or that the West German government in Bonn is so riddled with spies we might just as well send a copy of NATO defense plans direct to Moscow? Or that our own U.S. Army Lieutenant Colonel Whalen, assigned to the Joint Chiefs of Staff, should turn out to be a Soviet spy?"

Jane reeled off another half-dozen examples of proven KGB penetration of the highest Western military and political circles, then concluded: "The Russians are the best chess players in the world. They know it's not enough to know what pieces—weapons —your opponent has. To win, you have to know what he is thinking, how he will respond to *your* moves. That requires agents in the highest places. The White House has to be their top-priority target."

Hurst was thoughtful. A general warning about the KGB . . . nothing specific. . . . It couldn't hurt. It couldn't rebound against him. And it *would* get the headlines.

"Okay," he said. "We'll fly that one. I'll call a press conference."

Jane sat back, hiding her feelings of triumph . . . and irony. She'd just given some of the best advice he, or any other American, could hope to get. But by the time he *really* knew it, it would be too late.

Six weeks later, Sakov listened to another tape from Dr. Bitner. Lent was in a low, a severe depression. The worst he had had. Even the tablets weren't helping this time. The doctor knew why. He knew what was in those tablets. Nothing!

About the only thing holding Lent together was his financial success. A week ago his investment consultant had said his big play was looking good. It was something to hold on to.

Sakov switched the tape off and summoned an embassy chauffeur. The man, Ivan. He gave him his instructions.

Then Sakov picked up the phone and spoke to Johnson Stafford, investment consultant extraordinaire.

Most *extraordinaire*.

Most successful.

He had taken part in the great Russian grain coup in the early seventies. He, and other Russian "friends," using all types of espionage, including microwave intercepts of conversations between American commodity dealers, had quietly and cheaply purchased billions of tons of American grain before the authorities knew what was going on.

It had been a once-only operation.

But there was still plenty of work for Johnson Stafford.

The work included Seaford Lent.

He listened to Sakov's instructions; replaced the phone, then picked it up again and dialed.

Lent was slumped in a chair, still in his pajamas, an empty glass in his hand. It was early afternoon. His daily housekeeper had gone at noon while he was still in bed. He was quite alone. He had been alone since his wife died five years ago.

The mornings were always the worst. Wake up from a drugged sleep feeling nothing but empty despair. Getting out of bed seemed too difficult, too demanding. Purposeless, anyway. The simplest actions—dressing, washing, and so on—became impossible tasks . . . pointless.

He couldn't even begin to operate till he had a half-bottle of whiskey inside him.

He heard the telephone ring, distant. It was right by his side. He made no move. Five minutes later it rang again. He fumbled for it, knocking the receiver onto the floor. He slithered down off the chair and lying, clutched the receiver to his ear.

"Mr. Lent . . . Mr. Lent . . . are you there?"

A noise like a moan.

"*Mr. Lent*, this is Johnson Stafford."

A faint gleam of hope, of purpose, flickered in Lent's fuddled mind. "Yes," he said.

"I'm sorry I have bad news for you."

No answer. Lent's mind hadn't taken it in.

"Mr. Lent . . . *are you there?*"

A low groan. "Yes."

"Your investment has bombed. . . . I'm sorry. . . . It happens . . . particularly with commodities. . . . *Of course, you knew the risks.* . . . Ninety thousand dollars by the end of the week."

"My god! I can't. I haven't a cent. . . . Time?"

"No, Mr. Lent, this is a cash business. No time." The voice was harsh, cruel.

"Impossible." The word, though slurred, was clear.

A long pause.

"I might have a friend who can help you, Mr. Lent."

"Who is he?"

"A friend. . . . I'll speak to him. If he agrees, I'll send him around to see you."

"Yes," Lent said. The receiver fell from his hand.

For five hours . . . the bottle . . . open another . . . stare at nothing. No feeling, no thought. Ninety thousand dollars. . . .

The doorbell rang. The sound reached his ears. He ignored it. It kept ringing. He had to stop the noise. He fumbled his way into a robe and went to the door.

The man Ivan introduced himself. "We have a mutual friend, Johnson Stafford. My name is Abdul Hassan. May I come in?" He smiled politely.

Memory stirred. He stood aside and let Abdul Hassan into his room.

"Drink?" he asked abstractedly. He filled his own glass.

"Forgive me, no. My religion does not permit it."

Lent peered at the man . . . Arab.

The man spoke. "Our friend tells me you have an urgent need of money."

Lent remained silent.

But, yes, he had an urgent need. Without it he would be bankrupt. Without it he would have no career. He would have nothing. Be nothing. And the money he had persuaded his children to invest. *They* had an urgent need.

"Let me explain myself," the man said. "There are certain governments who have a great deal of money. They have intelligence services which also have a great deal of money but very little experience. These intelligence services are called upon by their governments to produce results. They find this very difficult. You can help them. They will pay you well, very well. . . ."

Lent listened. The man said he would come back the next day.

Lent thought about it. What harm could it do. Low-grade classified documents. Years out of date. Everyone knew the facts anyway!

And he had an urgent need.

It would be all right just as long as he could organize himself to get into the office and get the copies.

The next day the man returned. He began reading through the documents carefully, glancing up from time to time at the almost inert body of Lent slumped in the chair opposite him.

There were ten documents in all. He read five, then he asked

Lent if he could use his toilet. Lent waved vaguely toward the door and muttered something unintelligible. The man went swiftly upstairs, found the bedroom and the box of sleeping tablets next to the bed. With a gloved hand he emptied the box, putting the tablets in one pocket, the box in another. Then he found the toilet, flushed it, and returned downstairs.

He entered the room and, as he passed Lent, knocked his half-filled glass from the table near him. He apologized, picked the glass up with the gloved hand, turned his back on Lent for a moment, and tipped the powdered contents of a phial into Lent's glass. He dropped the empty box of sleeping tablets on the floor and gently kicked it under Lent's chair. He picked the bottle of whiskey up with the gloved hand and poured some into the glass. Lent turned his half-glazed eyes toward him and mumbled his thanks.

The man sat down to read the remaining documents. When he saw Lent had consumed a good half of his drink, he stopped reading and opened his briefcase. He took out nine bundles, each ten thousand dollars, and dropped them one by one on the floor in front of Lent.

Then the man took the documents, slipped two of them under his chair, and put the other eight in his briefcase. He grasped hold of Lent's lifeless hand and shook it. He let himself out.

It had all been so easy.

Like giving candy to a kid.

It was the next day.

President Dale's eyes were calm, belying the tension which gripped his stomach. His gaze left the bunch of fresh-cut flowers standing on the columns between the northernmost window of the Oval Office and the door leading to the secretaries' room.

He looked directly at Press Secretary Bill Crawford. "That *is* my Mideast policy," he said emphatically.

The press secretary was rigid, a sheaf of notes in his small hands, his thin face flushed. He raised his hand and adjusted his spectacles. A nervous habit.

"Yes, Mr. President, it makes sense to *me*. But it won't satisfy those correspondents I'll be facing in"—he glanced at his watch—"nine minutes."

"The hell with correspondents! *You* deal with them. Bat them off. I'm trying to run a country, not a press bureau. I pay you to do that."

The press secretary rose. "Yes, sir." He reached the door, turned as if to speak, then changed his mind and hurried out.

The President let out a long breath and swiveled to stare at the flowers again. They did something to reassure him the whole goddamn world wasn't completely insane.

A buzz, and he leaned over and pressed a switch. "Mr. President, Mr. Hatford would like to see you. Says it's urgent."

"Send him in."

Chief Aide David Hatford came in, a heavy frown on his deceptively cherublike face. He looked ten years younger than his forty-three years.

"What is it?" the President asked, pointing to a chair.

"Seaford Lent's been found dead." The aide spoke bluntly, flatly.

The President hunched his shoulders in query. "Dead! How?"

"Looks like we choose between suicide and an accident. An overdose of sleeping tablets with too much alcohol. It's lethal."

The President sighed and leaned back slowly in his chair. "I guess it was always in the cards with a guy like that. Brilliant but moody."

The aide nodded. "There's just one peculiarity."

"Peculiarity?"

"He was found dead this morning by the woman who does his cleaning. Apparently he was slumped in a chair, a three-quarters empty bottle by his side and an empty box of sleepers on the floor. As I say, suicide or an accident. And here's the crunch—"

But the President had interrupted, raising his hand. "Hold it a minute. I want to hear this." He flipped a switch on his desk. Voices from the West Lobby where the press conference was being held came through the speaker in the console beside the President.

The President listened, a wry smile on his face. The press secretary was doing a great job. He wasn't giving a thing.

"I'm not going on that."

"No comment."

"I have nothing to add."

"You've got a better answer?" The sound of laughter.

"Let's wrap that one up."

He turned back to his aide, leaving the speaker on and giving it some of his attention. "Look, I'm sorry about Lent. I really am," he said. "So a few people will snipe at me about hiring advisors who could be said to be unstable. The usual mud. Nothing I can't ride out. No big waves."

"Could be a bigger wave than you expect," the aide started, but the President silenced him again. He'd caught the name *Hurst* on the speaker. "Smart-ass bastard," he said sourly.

The press secretary's voice came through the console speaker: *"Would you mind repeating that question? I didn't get it all."*

The press secretary was stalling for time and the President knew it.

The correspondent's voice came through again. *"In view of Senator Hurst's recent suggestion that the White House must be a prime target for hostile intelligence services, would you care to comment on the fact that presidential advisor Lent was found dead this morning with ninety thousand dollars in his lap?"*

A long pause.

The press secretary replied, *"I have no knowledge of Advisor Lent's death. Are you suggesting his death could be in any way ... connected with espionage?"*

"No, sir, I asked if you had any comments on the situation."

"Yes. Your question is highly improper. No further comment."

The President hit the switch and the speaker went dead.

"Wha-at was that all about?" The President stared accusingly at his aide.

"I'm trying to tell you—Lent was found with ninety thousand bucks. It's the dough that they're on to. There's already talk of a payoff.... Espionage."

The President shook his head slowly. "No ... not Lent. I'd never believe it."

"I agree," the aide replied, "but that money? Lent had a king-size brain, but one big problem. He played the market ... badly. Everybody knows it. He's got no rich family. How come the ninety thousand ... and in his lap!"

The two men looked at each other in silence.

At length the President said, "I want a full situation report in two hours. Everything our Washington police, or anybody else, know. And shut the lid tight on this thing until we know what's going on. No releases. Nothing."

The aide rose to go. "And," the President continued, "find out why that correspondent asked the question."

The aide grimaced. "He'll say ... it was a hunch. If he's got sources, he's going to protect them."

The President was tight-mouthed. *"Then lean on him.* The po-

lice, the Revenue Department, the Justice Department, the FBI
—drop everybody on him . . . hard! You know what the sonofabitch has done? He's sown seeds of suspicion in people's minds.
I want it stamped out, dead! Before it starts to grow."

The detective sergeant from homicide division showed Jane
Mantel his I.D. and sat down on the metal chair across her desk
in the small office in the Senate Office Building.

He looked at her speculatively and wondered what a beautiful
broad like her was doing in a two-bit office . . . in politics, working!

"Miss Mantel," he said, "we'd like your cooperation."

Jane's face was expressionless. "Yes."

"We've spoken to a newspaperman name of Ed Peterson. He
tells us you gave him information which prompted him to ask an
unusual question at the press secretary's conference this
morning."

"He told you?" Jane had fed the story to Peterson.

"He told us."

Jane laughed. "So much for the right of the press to protect
their sources."

"He was most cooperative."

"You have ways of making them talk," Jane mimicked a German accent. But that wasn't what she was thinking. The deal
she'd made with Ed Peterson was that he *would* tell his source.
When the thing blew up and filled the media, she wanted the
fact that John Hurst had predicted this to be in all the headlines.

"I said he was most cooperative, that's all."

"Okay," she nodded, her shining hair swinging forward.

"He said you told him about the money."

"And you mean there wasn't any?"

"I didn't say that."

"So there was?"

"I didn't say that either. I'm not here to discuss the evidence."

"Evidence as to what?" She beamed all innocence at him.

"What I'm saying, Miss Mantel, is that until the official verdict
I'm not at liberty to discuss the circumstances surrounding the
death."

"So why are you here?"

"I want to know what made you suggest to Ed Peterson that
there was money involved. And why you suggested there might
be more to his death than straight suicide."

"Is there?"

"I'm asking the questions."

"And I don't have to answer them."

"You don't have to, Miss Mantel, but under the circumstances it might be smart if you did."

"Why?" Jane snapped. "The way I see it Lent committed suicide. That's all the information you've released to the press. Right? If there are any complications, you have the evidence, not me. Or are you hiding anything?"

"We like to check all the angles."

"Angles?"

"Possibilities."

"You mean there was money."

He gave her a hard stare. "You're not being very cooperative, Miss Mantel."

But Jane could easily outstare him. "Sergeant," she said, "I'll tell you where to find your cooperation . . . in your own division."

The sergeant did a double take.

"How many people are working on this investigation?" Jane asked. "How many know the . . . circumstances, as you call them, surrounding Lent's death?"

"A half-dozen maybe."

"Then ask *them*," Jane retorted. "I got an anonymous call from someone claiming to be from your division. He said money had been found *and* that on the day of his death Lent took copies of certain classified documents from the State Department. Only a couple were found in his home. And if you want to know how cooperative I've been, I *could* have mentioned those documents, only I didn't. And the more I listen to you, the more I think maybe I should have."

The sergeant shifted uncomfortably in his seat. The Chief of Detectives had said to keep the case tight. Nothing was to get out until it had been cleared by the top brass. And here he was talking to some broad who already knew it all. Or as much as anyone did . . . so far.

"Could you describe the man's voice?"

"Yes. Muffled. He was disguising it."

"Why would he call you?"

"He didn't. He called Senator Hurst, only he was out of the office."

"Why the senator?"

"Because," Jane bit off her words, "Senator Hurst is about the only person around who takes Russian espionage seriously. And maybe, just maybe, you've got one man in your division who's got enough sense to agree with him. Who doesn't go along with cover-ups ... not when they involve national security."

The sergeant got to his feet. "Thanks, Miss Mantel."

Outside her office he let out a long breath. Boy. Women! When they were hard, were they ever hard. He started to think about the men in the division.

Ed Peterson had begun his Washington bureau job with a scoop—thanks to Jane Mantel. She had told him the information came from Senator John Hurst, and Peterson made no secret of his source.

He spent that afternoon at the Press Club. The only topic of conversation was Lent. The consensus of opinion was that Lent might be a peculiar guy but no way was he involved in espionage.

One thing was certain: There was more to come out.

Peterson called Jane to thank her for the big tip-off. She asked him over to her apartment off King Street out at Alexandria, across the river from Georgetown.

She welcomed him with a smile. She was elegantly dressed but not overtly sexy, he noted.

"Ed, before you sit down, fix the drinks, will you? Scotch for me." He went to the small cocktail cabinet by the wall.

"You seem to be getting along well with John Hurst," he said.

"Working pretty hard," Jane agreed.

"And you're getting damn good publicity."

She gave a light laugh. "That's my job."

"I'm following up on this Lent business. You started me on it and I'm going to see it through. There's got to be proof, Jane. I mean, about the payoff ... that dough."

He handed her a drink, sitting opposite her in order to see her face quite clearly.

"The FBI will handle it," said Jane. "And you were right to put that question. If Lent was involved in anything then it will come out. If he wasn't, his name will be cleared. It will be your story, Ed."

"It's got to come out," Peterson insisted. "I've a good hunch there might be an attempt at a snow job."

Jane looked at him reprovingly. "Ed Peterson, we've met after all this time and all you can talk about is shop. Come on, now ... tell me how you've been," she coaxed.

He talked, all the time aware she was watching him . . . not looking at him. It was weird. Nothing tangible. But it was there.

He'd made a reservation at the Embers for nine o'clock. He kept one eye on the time. At half past eight he suggested they get going. He was anxious for a change of scene, of atmosphere. Then maybe she'd relax.

She got to her feet. At the door she stopped. "I nearly forgot. I've something to show you."

She took him by the hand and led him to a small alcove at one end of the room. It was lined with shelves on which were an assortment of ornaments—brass, pewter, silver, and china. She picked one up. A five-inch model of a woman in a crinoline dress, delicately colored.

"My latest acquisition," she said proudly. "Isn't it exquisite? . . . Dresden china."

"From Dresden," he said.

Somehow he knew what her answer would be.

"Well, not literally. It's manufactured in Meissen, near Dresden. But I guess you wouldn't know that. Most people don't."

The Embers was exactly right. A comfortable atmosphere of prosperity. After dining, they danced in the lounge to the music of a trio.

Relaxed, pleasant.

Very nice.

Except all the time she was keeping him at a distance. The conversation impersonal. While they danced, she stiffened very slightly when he held her close. Very slightly, but the message was clear.

The brush-off. The gentle good-bye.

So when she asked him to get her a cab as they left, he wasn't surprised. She'd said it all. Nicely, but unmistakably. Leaving Peterson with the feeling he'd been used.

The next day President Dale stared at the headlines with stark disbelief.

HURST'S ALLEGATIONS OF KGB WHITE HOUSE PENETRATION JUSTIFIED

He read aloud to Chief Aide Hartford: " 'In an article yesterday *Pravda* attacked the President's new Mideast policy. Reference was made to American cooperation with Israel during the Yom Kippur war. In substance, nothing was revealed that is not already well known. However, what is startling is that the article contained *extracts from secret exchanges* which took place during the war between the State Department and Israeli leaders. There can be no doubt that the Soviets have had access to secret U.S. government documents.' "

The President read on in silence, quoting, from time to time, the more sensational bits from the report: "The peculiar circumstances surrounding the recent suicide of White House Advisor Seaford Lent. . . . Why has the White House made no statement? . . . What other more vital information might Lent have leaked to the Russians. . . ."

The President threw the paper down. "The bastard Russians! They've done it deliberately. To discredit me." The President thumped the table. "The dirty conniving bastards! Why did they do it? And that sonofabitch Hurst . . . !

"Mr. President," the aide interrupted. "Forget the Russians *and* Hurst. We've got other problems. The shit's hit the fan and we're standing right under it."

Ed Peterson reacted to the same news with somewhat different feelings. Feelings about Jane Mantel, who'd given him the tip-off.

The woman who didn't look like her photograph.

The woman who had changed personalities.

The woman who didn't know about Dresden china, then suddenly did.

And then his mind went back to the Deniskin killing. The way it always did, for some unaccountable reason. When he thought about her. There was something there. Something in his mind. Something he'd missed.

And then he thought about Hurst.

The man who'd pulled off a miracle with Stanach but wouldn't talk.

The *only* man who was going to gain from Lent's suicide.

Questions—no, not questions—shadows. . . . Meaning?

There was no meaning, no pattern, no conclusions.

Nothing.

Shadows.

Doubts—no, nothing as concrete—shadows.

Not even shadows.

Feelings.
Something not right.

Senator Hurst put the newspaper down on the breakfast table.
He went to the telephone.
"Morning, Jane," he said.
"Morning, John."
"Seen the papers?"
"No," she lied.
"Go and get one. I'll hang on."
Jane put the phone down and stood still for two minutes. She
picked the phone up. "I've scanned it," she said. "Fantastic!"
A thoughtful pause, then, "Yes, but I wonder how much dam-
age Lent has done we'll never know about?"
"At least the White House will tighten up their security now."
Another thoughtful pause. "Why d'you suppose the Russians
did it? Confirmed Lent's guilt?"
"They'll have had their reasons."
"I don't doubt it."
"Anyway," Jane said cheerfully, "it's done you a lot of good."
"You're right. You'd think the Russians were on our side!"
She laughed. "That'll be the day."
"See you at the office," he said. "And thanks for your idea . . .
about building up the KGB threat."
"Everyone gets lucky sometime," she said.
Hurst put the phone down.
Luck, no. Jane Mantel had an instinct, a sixth sense about the
Russians. And her predictions about their moves in Africa *had*
proved right.
He'd follow up on some of her other ideas.

CHAPTER
SIXTEEN

From the top of the mountain two figures could be seen, about half a mile apart, inching their way down the snow-covered slopes toward the bottom of the valley. Their apparently slow progress was deceptive, an illusion created by the great distance. In fact, the two skiers were traveling at between twenty-five and thirty miles an hour.

One was a tall woman, elegantly clad in a dark-blue ski suit. Long hair flowed from under her deep-red ski cap. The grace and élan with which she negotiated the rock-hard icy slope spoke of the perfect tone and suppleness of her muscles, particularly those of her long legs. She was clearly enjoying the descent.

By contrast, the other figure, although progressing at the same speed, was doing so more by determination than skill. His face was grim, and when his skis thudded over the inevitable icy bumps, he grimaced as if in pain. Altogether, there was something ungainly about his posture.

The previous few days had been unusually warm for late January, thawing the surface of the snow. But now a sharp drop in temperature to ten below had turned the surface into a treacherous sheet of ice.

Three-quarters of the way down the long sweep of the mountainside stood an isolated clump of firs. Perhaps a hundred trees in all, they formed a minute dark blotch against the dazzling white. Slowly the two figures converged on this blotch, then disappeared out of sight amongst the trees—the woman first, followed several minutes later by the man.

She was waiting, smiling, at his approach. At first he didn't speak, removing his skis, then bending one leg at the knee several times. "That's better," he said at last, brushing the snow from his ski jacket.

"You did well. You only fell once," Jane said.

"Twice," Sakov admitted with a grin. "I'm out of practice . . . *and* I'm too old for this sort of thing."

Jane Mantel smiled. *"I* don't think so."

Sakov produced a silver hip flask. "First, a drink," he said. Jane took a small sip. Sakov threw back his head and drank deeply.

"Careful, comrade, or you'll never get down the rest of the mountain . . . not on your feet," Jane chided cheerfully.

Sakov began, "I am going to Moscow to make a full report on the situation with Hurst. The primaries start in five weeks and Chairman Zimin will want a definite statement of Hurst's prospects for the presidential nomination. I need your opinion before I go."

Jane gave him a verbal report ending with: "The major problem is that the Americans are an overconfident people. They've never been invaded. They honestly do believe that no matter what happens in the rest of the world *they* are safe, protected by miles of ocean and their superior technology. Honestly!" She grinned at him.

"Then we must act quickly to disillusion them," Sakov said. And he too was grinning. "Something to jolt them out of complacency, eh?"

Jane suddenly became intense. "We-must-*frighten*-them. Make them understand they are vulnerable. Nothing less will shake their confidence."

"Someone will have to be sacrificed," said Sakov. "Someone they will listen to and believe. One of our top people. A military man, perhaps." He paused. "I will arrange it when I get to Moscow," he said.

Major General Vladimir Orlov was in a good mood. He stood in the big bay window of his second-floor office watching the muffled figures scurrying along the Moscow street below. The snow was already six inches deep and still falling. It was going to be a hard winter. But the general's mind was not on the weather. He had been ordered to report to the office of Marshal Baturin. It could only mean his promotion had come through.

He had earned his promotion. If anything, it was overdue. He was not a conceited man, but the work he had done preparing contingency plans for the Middle East was brilliant. The complexities of the political situation in the area plus the saturation of certain countries with advanced weapons by the Americans made it a strategist's nightmare.

He crossed to the corner cupboard where he kept a bottle of Starka vodka reserved for special occasions. He deserved his promotion and he deserved a glass of Starka. He gulped it down in one swallow, felt the kick, and was even more pleased with life. Climbing into his car to be driven to see the marshal, the invigorating glow of the vodka was still with him.

As the car drove slowly along the snow-covered roads, the thought did drift through his mind that it was rather unusual for promotion to be bestowed in person by a marshal. But then his record *was* outstanding and personal congratulations were not out of order.

The marshal's office was warm, the decor and furnishings comfortable. He accepted the marshal's invitation to be seated and wondered if it was too much to hope that one day he might have such an office. The marshal spoke:

"First, comrade, may I congratulate you on the work you have done. It is excellent. Now—the reason for our meeting . . ." The marshal had spoken briskly but abruptly halted.

Orlov felt a thrill of excitement run down his spine as he waited for the marshal to complete the sentence.

". . . you are going to defect to the Americans."

Orlov looked at the marshal, dumbfounded.

"You are going to defect to the Americans," the marshal repeated, "and you had better be quick about it; we have no time to lose."

Orlov recovered his senses enough to understand the marshal's words, but not their meaning. "Defect . . . to—to the Americans. I don't understand," he stammered.

"It will be explained to you by the KGB," the marshal replied, unmoved by Orlov's consternation. He had ordered hundreds of thousands of men to their deaths during the war with Germany. The discomfort of one man did not move him greatly. He continued, "I have been instructed by the Party to inform you that as of today you will come under the direction of Colonel Sakov of the KGB. You will obey his orders to the letter and without question."

"But, Marshal . . ." Orlov started to protest.

"Major General," the marshal said curtly, "I know nothing of this matter. I suggest you go directly to Sakov at KGB headquarters. He is expecting you. He will enlighten you as to your future."

Orlov got to his feet in a daze. "Dzerzhinsky Square," he muttered hoarsely to his driver.

All thoughts of his expected promotion had gone from his mind. Defect! Why? Why him? What for? He thought of his family. *Once he left the country he would never see them again!* He sank back and closed his eyes. He loved his wife and children.

When Orlov entered his office, his face deathly pale, almost unable to coordinate his movements, it came as no surprise to Sakov. He knew of the marshal's reputation for being brusque to the point of callousness. Orlov sank into a chair and looked at Sakov.

Sakov spoke quietly and reassuringly. "Comrade, I am aware of the contribution you have made to the military preparedness of our country. Unfortunately, by one of those savage ironies of fate, it is this very fact which has led to your selection to perform an even greater service to your country."

Sakov could see Orlov becoming calmer, some of the color returning to his face. He continued, "You have been told by the marshal you are going to play the role of a defector. However, it is not a life sentence. We will get you out of America and back to your country within a year."

Orlov's face relaxed; he sat forward more confidently in his chair.

"Further," Sakov continued, "although the question of your promotion is academic at the moment, you will of course be promoted . . . backdated to preserve your seniority on your return. You may also be honored in other ways. In the meantime, your family will be taken good care of."

A new anxiety occurred to Orlov. "Will my family be told I am not a *true* defector?"

"No, I am afraid not. It would be too dangerous. Under the stress of your disgrace they might reveal your innocence. You will not see your family again until you return to Russia."

Orlov looked stunned. "You mean, I cannot see them before I leave?"

"Regrettably, no," Sakov replied. "We can take no chances. Even unwittingly you might intimate to your wife in some way that your defection is not genuine."

Orlov was a professional soldier and a committed Party member. His whole life had been one of self-discipline. At first, the sudden turn of events—from the satisfying anticipation of promotion to the chilling prospect of playing the role of a defector—

had completely disoriented him. Now his mind was rapidly adjusting to the full import of what was happening. He had been selected to carry out what was obviously an assignment of the greatest importance to his country. He dismissed all thought of his family from his mind. He looked at Sakov calmly. "And what exactly is my mission?" he asked.

Orlov listened to Sakov with growing incredulity.

"But, comrade," he exclaimed, when Sakov had finished, "what you are proposing can only do our country the greatest damage. I don't understand."

"There is no need for you to understand," Sakov replied. "Now let us concern ourselves with arranging your defection."

"It will not be easy." Orlov was doubtful. "When the Americans check they will find I am a happily married and a successful career officer. Why should I defect? They would not believe it was for ideological reasons alone."

"Precisely, comrade. That is why we are providing you with a bitter, personal grudge against our system." He flipped open a file. "Major General Viltov—he worked closely with you on your contingency plans for the Middle East."

Orlov nodded.

"His contribution was important in matters of logistics, but the strategic concepts were yours. Moreover, he is junior to you in length of service." Sakov paused for effect. "But he has one great advantage over you: his wife is the daughter of a member of the Central Committee of the Party."

"Advantage?" Orlov queried.

"Yes, advantage. He is going to get the credit for your work. . . . He is also going to get your promotion."

Though Orlov knew they were talking about a fabricated cover story for his defection, the hurt and resentment showed in his eyes. "But the American intelligence services will soon find out it is not true," he objected.

"It is true, comrade. His promotion *is* being announced in a few days." Sakov permitted himself a smile. "He is going to be a very surprised man. That is not all. He has been having an affair with your wife."

Orlov started. Sakov's calm and easy way of talking about fiction as if it were fact, the ingrained habit of years in the KGB, had again caught him unprepared. "That's not true," he protested vehemently.

"Calm yourself, comrade. Of course it is not true. But several of your military colleagues have just heard very convincing rumors that it is true. Fortunately, you will not be put in the embarrassing situation of seeing them again. They have received orders posting them immediately to positions in East Germany and Poland. Although your defection will not be made public, we will ensure these officers hear of it. They will be working with officers of the Polish and East German armies whom we know to be agents for NATO intelligence services." Sakov smiled again. "We like to leave a few NATO agents free—they are a most useful means of passing false information to our enemies. We will ensure these agents hear of the reasons for your defection. Party nepotism has robbed you of your due recognition and promotion and given them to a man who is having an affair with your wife. You are very bitter, comrade. It may surprise you, but personal resentments are a more frequent cause of treachery than ideological beliefs."

"What about my family?" Orlov asked.

"Ah, your family. They will have to disappear. I am arranging for them to be sent to a small town near Kiev. They will be well treated, but they must leave Moscow. CIA agents in the American embassy will expect them to be arrested for questioning. We must satisfy their curiosity."

Sakov did not tell Orlov that, to make it completely authentic, his family would be arrested in the middle of the night and with a maximum of disturbance. Talkative neighbors would confirm the arrest. His family *would* be well treated but they would have no idea why they had been moved or where Orlov had gone.

Orlov was thoughtful. "How do I get out of the country? It isn't easy. You KGB see to that," he added.

Sakov smiled. "Yes, we are efficient, comrade. But it has been arranged. As a follow-up to your planning operations you are going on a personal inspection of our frontier with Iran. Incidentally, you will be leaving tonight." Sakov spoke casually and was pleased to observe that Orlov showed no signs of perturbation at the imminence of his departure. Orlov had emotionally accepted his new role and was reacting positively.

"Your story to the Americans is this," Sakov continued. "The day after you arrived on the Iranian border you were telephoned by a friend in Moscow and told that Major General Viltov has been promoted instead of you. You were also told that the major general got drunk at his celebratory party and was indiscreet enough to let slip what you had recently come to suspect—that he was having an affair with your wife. Naturally you were very upset. You had been betrayed by your wife, by a brother officer, and by the nepotism of the Party. You decided to defect while you had the chance—while you were on the frontier with Iran, an area you knew well, an area where your papers allowed you to travel at will."

"Except across the frontier—the KGB guards will see to that," Orlov said, with a touch of sarcasm in his voice.

"The border guards will help you. The fact is, you will be traveling with false papers. I have them here." Sakov indicated a drawer in his desk. "As far as the guards are concerned, you are a KGB agent slipping into Iran. They will show you where to avoid the Iranian guards."

"And once I am in Iran?" Orlov questioned.

"You will make your way to Tehran. There you will go to the American Embassy and ask for political asylum."

"That is all?"

"Yes. You will find a change of clothes in the car which is waiting to take you to the airport. They are civilian clothes. The KGB border guards would hardly expect a KGB agent destined for Iran to be using the uniform of a Soviet officer. It is imperative that even our own people do not know the true nature of your mission. It is too important to take the slightest security risk."

Sakov opened a drawer in his desk and took out an envelope. He handed it to Orlov. "Your papers," he said. Then he extended his hand. "Good luck, comrade. Do not fail."

Orlov sat silent behind the driver as they drove out to the airport. He was glad to see it had stopped snowing. Briefly he wondered what his family would think of his defection. He pushed his anxieties to the back of his mind. The task before him would require every bit of guile and concentration he could muster. He was still staggered by the enormity of the implications of his assignment. They appeared so disastrous to the interests of his country that they could only be the prelude to some event of much greater moment.

Three weeks later John Hurst had a call from Ben Hudson of the CIA. Could he see the senator as soon as possible? It was urgent.

Ben Hudson was of medium height, slightly built. He had a stuffy, studious air: a real detail man at first sight. But the light-blue penetrating eyes behind the rimless glasses took in John Hurst and his office with one quick glance.

"What can I do for you?" John Hurst asked pleasantly. What's so urgent?"

Hudson came straight to the point. "We have a very interesting situation, Senator. A senior Russian army officer has defected. We've checked out his story and we can't fault it. He's given us some military information we already knew and a little extra we didn't." He paused, looking uneasy.

"So?" John Hurst encouraged him.

"He's sitting on something else he won't tell us. . . . He says he doesn't trust the CIA."

John Hurst suppressed a smile at Hudson's obvious embarrassment. He said, "So what can *I* do?"

"He says he won't give us the information because he knows how security services and governments work. They suppress information from their people if they think it's going to embarrass them politically. He says it's like that in Russia and he's certain it's like that in America."

"Smart guy," said Hurst.

"Yeah." Hudson did not sound amused. "Only we want to know what the hell he's sitting on. I think it's vital to national security, Senator. And he's ready to talk."

"So why are you telling *me?*"

"Because . . . the only person he will tell is *you*," Hudson answered, trying not to sound too sour.

"Why me? How would he even know I exist?"

Hudson sighed. "Senator, you've nearly as good press coverage in Russia as you have here—only it's not quite as flattering. He figures if he tells you, the American people are sure to get to know. And he wants us to know."

"What? Have you any idea what it's all about?"

Ben Hudson shook his head. "None at all. Only it's big. I'm sure of that. I've been closeted with him for three days, talking, and if I'm any judge of people, he's no joker."

"Okay, then bring him here and let him talk. What's the problem?"

"We want a guarantee that if he spills anything likely to endanger national security it won't reach the press without our say-so."

John Hurst got up from behind his desk. "It's a deal," he said.

The relief showed on Hudson's face. "Only, I'm the one who's going to decide what is and what is not vital national security. And I'll have my own interpreter."

Hudson's face fell. "I told them at Langley that's what you'd say. For chrissake, why do I waste my time!" He sounded exasperated.

"Because that's what they pay you for," Hurst answered unsmilingly. "Well?"

Hudson got to his feet. "I'll have him here eleven o'clock tomorrow morning. And one thing, Senator—try to remember the CIA's not always wrong, will you?"

"Okay. And you try to remember—you're not always right."

When Hudson had gone, he called Jane Mantel into his office and told her what had happened. She would be his interpreter.

"That's marvelous news," she said with a wide smile. "It couldn't happen at a better time. The New Hampshire primary's only one week off. And this may be just the one break you need."

"Hold it," John Hurst protested, trying to cool Jane's enthusiasm. "I haven't the faintest idea what the Russian's going to say or whether I can use it. It may be nothing new."

Eleven o'clock next morning, there were four people present in John Hurst's office: Hurst himself, Ben Hudson, Jane Mantel, and Orlov. The interview was to be taped.

Orlov was confident. He had convinced the CIA of his authenticity as a defector. During the days of interrogation, they had checked on his cover story in Eastern Europe, Moscow, and Iran and it had held. He looked at the people around him. He wondered how they would react to the bombshell he was about to lob into their midst.

John Hurst spoke. "General, this interview has been arranged at your request. May I suggest you start the proceedings."

Orlov cleared his throat and began to speak, pausing from time to time for Jane to translate. "My name is Major General Vladimir Orlov. Until I left the Soviet Union three weeks ago, I was engaged in the preparation of contingency plans for various military eventualities. Unfortunately one such plan has now become operational. . . ." He paused for dramatic effect.

He needn't have bothered; the men in the room had stopped breathing The Russian writer Deniskin had hinted at something like this. Now they were getting the facts.

Orlov was in no hurry. The information he was about to reveal was so frightening, he must ensure there could be no doubt of its authenticity.

He said, "Let me explain why I have left the Russia I love so much. I am a Communist, but I am a Russian first and foremost. It is because I love my people, my country, my Russia, I come to warn you. The leaders of my country have embarked on a course of action which will be successful in the short term but which will, inevitably, lead to a full-scale war between our two nations in the not-too-distant future. My earnest hope is that you will be able to forestall these plans and preserve the peace so the people of our two great nations may reach a true understanding."

Orlov paused for the full effect. And then he gave it to them.

"Senator Hurst, this is what I am here to tell you. To warn you. *In approximately three months' time, we will totally destroy eighty percent of the oil facilities in the Middle East.*"

Utter incredulity registered on their faces. Nothing in Orlov's long preamble had prepared them for this: that Russia, without warning or provocation, was planning—no, *intended*—to go for the jugular of the energy resources of the Western world.

John Hurst broke the silence. "How?" he snapped.

"By retargeting some of our intermediate and intercontinental nuclear missiles." Orlov shrugged. "We are like you; we have plenty to spare."

Hurst knew the answer to his next question, but he wanted to get it on the record. "General, exactly what does Russia expect to gain by such an open act of aggression?"

"Many things," Orlov replied. "It will take several years to restore oil production in the Middle East. The economies of Europe will be in chaos, making the advance of eurocommunism irresistible. Other countries, including Japan, are dependent on Middle East oil. What you call the 'free world,' Mr. Hurst, will be in ruins while we would remain as strong as ever. As you know, my country produces *all* its own oil."

"And you think America would let you get away with it!" Ben Hudson erupted.

"What would America do?" Orlov replied coolly. "Attack Russia and start a full-scale nuclear war? No, no. I think she would rather accept economic chaos in Europe and other parts of the world. Your country would have many problems. Your economy would be crippled but you would survive. You have your strategic oil reserves to help you."

Orlov sat back and surveyed the confused faces about him. He was pleased with his performance. As he had expected and Sakov had warned him, they were having great difficulty digesting what he had told them. They were finding it hard to believe Russia could be so brazenly ruthless. But he was finding it hard to understand why they were *so* surprised. After all, his country had always been ruthless when it was necessary, or when it was opportune. They *must* know that. Once they got over this shock they would believe him. Why should he lie about something so devastating? They would not be able to find a reason. He wondered if the Americans had made their own contingency plans for such an eventuality. He wasn't the only one in the room asking himself that question.

Ben Hudson broke the uneasy silence. "I suppose you can substantiate the existence of this plan?" he asked.

"Not with documentation," Orlov answered evenly. "*You* will recall the circumstances under which I left my country. I had no time for such preparation. But since I devised the operational plan, I can give you sufficient technical data to convince you." Orlov spoke with confidence. He had made such a plan.

Orlov rose to his feet. Ben Hudson spoke to Jane. Orlov was to go with the two CIA agents who had been waiting outside. Hudson would see Orlov later for a detailed rundown on the operation.

When Orlov had gone, Hudson turned to John Hurst. "No way does this leak out," he stated emphatically.

"Why not?" asked Hurst. "Don't you believe him?"

"I don't know. He's checked out A-one so far, but I'll have a better idea when I've talked to him some more—and when military intelligence has grilled him."

"Why should he lie?" Hurst persisted.

"How the hell would I know?" Hudson snapped. "The point is, if this breaks, all hell will be let loose. There'll be a panic."

"Maybe we could do with a bit of panic," Hurst said pointedly.

"Look. At least give me a chance to notify the White House and the Pentagon. That's reasonable, isn't it?"

"Well, I . . ." Hurst began.

But Hudson broke in. "Senator, you know how government works. It takes time for consultation, for chrissake."

"Afraid I can't go along with you, Ben. If the White House hasn't an answer to this one, then it should. Maybe what Orlov says is true and maybe it isn't. What's important is Russia is strong enough now to start playing nuclear poker any day she feels like it. Seems to me we should know what kind of game *we* play before we have to sit down at the table. If we don't, then maybe this will teach us to learn fast."

Hudson sighed. "Okay. If that's the way you want to play it. I can't stop you. I hope you know what you're doing."

"I do," said Hurst. "There's no other way."

Later that day Senator John Hurst called a press conference. The following morning the early copy of *The Washington Post* read:

RUSSIAN GENERAL WARNS HURST OF RUSSIAN NUCLEAR STRIKE.

Ed Peterson stared at the photograph. He'd read the headline about Hurst and Orlov and the full story below. But for some reason he didn't understand, his eyes kept returning to the photograph.

As a supporter of Hurst, he was glad the senator had got the lucky break. With the New Hampshire primary less than a week off the timing couldn't be better. It had finally got through to people that Hurst could be right!

He whistled, an irritating little tune that wouldn't leave him. The same way the lucky breaks for Hurst kept happening. Not only his predictions about Russian moves—they had all come true—but there was Stanach, Lent, and now Orlov as well. Each event perfectly timed and tailored to fit the needs of Hurst's political progress—as if Hurst had a direct line to the Kremlin!

It was almost uncanny. In some way he couldn't formulate, it was deeply disturbing.

He focused his whole attention on the photograph and another thought floated into his mind. The Deniskin killing. Now, why should that have suddenly come back to him? There were three people in the photograph: Hurst, Orlov, and Jane Mantel.

Since Jane Mantel had given him the sweet good-bye that night at the Embers, he had contacted her several times. Her response had always been the same—polite but negative. He sent her flowers and she called to thank him—politely. Twice he'd met her at cocktail parties, and once at a tennis party given by Hurst which was by way of being a fund raiser rather than a sporting event. She had talked to him on those occasions. As long as he kept the conversation to politics or Washington gossip she had been friendly, she had been charming. But any sign he was attempting to move the conversation into more personal areas and she'd jumped right ahead of him and frozen him out.

The photograph was a head-and-shoulders shot. Hurst and Orlov were full face, Jane Mantel to the right of Orlov with her back to the camera, her head turned slightly toward Orlov. To the left of her, the photograph showed the edge of a window.

Peterson put the paper down. He had been assigned to cover Hurst during the primaries and he would be seeing a lot of Jane Mantel. He wondered if this would give him a chance to get through to her. It was odd, he speculated—not for the first time —that a young woman who was so sexually experienced should appear to have no sex life in Washington. On the few occasions he had met her, there had been no sign of a male escort. What was more, he had made inquiries about her personal life. She didn't appear to have one.

Just one more thing about her that didn't make sense.

He picked up the paper and his eyes went to the photograph again. A streak of reflected light, perhaps from the window, caught the side of her hair, highlighting it.

He picked up the telephone and dialed.

"Hi, there . . . Ed Peterson," he said.

"Hello." Jane Mantel's voice was flat.

"I was wondering if I might talk to you . . . on a strictly professional basis." He emphasized this. "You know, a few details about the way the Orlov thing was set up so I can do a follow-up story."

There was a silence. At last she said, "If you don't mind wasting your time, come around about eleven o'clock. I have fifteen minutes then. But I doubt you're going to get anything you can use."

She was right.

She hadn't anything.

On the way out of her office he turned back. Her blonde head was already down reading something on her desk. "Ever think about that guy Deniskin?" he asked.

There was a pause before she raised her head. Then she did and said, "Why?"—her voice perfectly natural, controlled.

"Oh—I don't know . . ." he answered. And he meant it.

"It's an odd question," she said.

He found he was looking at her intently. "I guess it is," he agreed. "Don't know what made me think of it." He turned away and went out.

Jane waited a short while, then she left the office. She made her way to the nearest pay phone. She dialed.

The first time it could have been an accident.

The disco was in K Street. The time, 2 A.M.

Peterson had parked a couple of blocks away. They walked.

They'd met in a bar. She was a fun girl.

She took his mind off Jane Mantel.

He opened the passenger door for the girl to get in, then walked around the front of the car to the driver's door. A parked car pulled out from twenty yards up the street. He stood still, flat against his car to let it pass. It all happened in three seconds.

First the awareness that the car was accelerating like a racing start, the wheels screeching as they tore into the road surface. *Crazy goddamn idiot,* he thought. He waited for a second for the car to pull out into the road away from the line of parked cars. He knew he was clearly visible. Then came the split second of disbelief as he realized he *was* clearly visible but the car was *not* pulling out. It was heading straight toward him! There was nowhere to go except up. He jumped like he'd never jumped before. As his body hit the hood he felt the whole car rock violently as the speeding car ripped down its side.

The girl flung herself out of the car and started screaming.

For half a minute he lay on the hood, shaking with shock. Then slowly he rolled off onto the ground.

Numbly he looked at the huge dents and at the streaks of clean metal, stripped of paint. He tried to imagine how his body would have looked if it had still been there, squashed between the two cars. He felt sick.

He was still standing there and the girl was still yelling when the patrolmen arrived.

Peterson explained what had happened. As best he could.

"Could you identify the car?"

"Black sedan," he answered. "Buick . . . I think."

"No chance you got the number."

"Sure I did."

The patrolmen gave him looks of surprise.

"I see things, and things I see, I remember," Peterson said.

He gave the number—New York plates.

He got a call the next day from police headquarters to tell him the plates were from a car reported stolen in New York State the previous day. Not a Buick, a red Chevrolet.

Peterson couldn't figure it out. The driver *must* have seen him.

Maybe he'd been drunk or spaced out. In which case, he'd certainly been unlucky. The guy could have hit any one or all of the cars parked along the street. Why pick on the one he happened to be standing by!

He was still thinking about it the next evening when he parked his not-so-good-looking car and walked toward his apartment. The man came out from behind a tree a short way ahead of him. Every muscle in his body tensed as the adrenaline coursed through his veins.

Nature's instinctive response to danger.

The man moved slowly toward him.

Six feet away and the dull glint of a knife flashed in the man's right hand. Held low, ready for the swift upward strike that would take it to the soft gut below his ribs.

He knew he had only one chance—to do the unexpected. The man would be expecting him to stop, hesitate, perhaps say something. He remembered the only thing he knew about knife-fighting—go for the knife, always the knife, never the man.

He closed to three feet, then suddenly stepped to the left side of the man. The knife swung outward toward him, but late and he knew it was coming. His right hand grasped the wrist holding the knife before it reached him. As the man moved his body to face him, he brought his knee up straight into the groin.

The man doubled up, the strength taken out of him with the pain. That second was all he needed. He wasn't an expert in unarmed combat. Only a few tricks he'd picked up in Vietnam. He'd used up all his tricks; his assailant probably knew a bookful of them.

He ran.

He reached the outer door to his apartment and fumbled for the key. Then in the dim light coming from the glass pane above the door, he saw it. A chip of brick flying out of the wall a foot to the right of his head. And then there was a whine in the air and he *knew* what that was. He'd heard it too often in Nam. A bullet.

He dropped to his knees, got the door open, threw himself inside on his stomach, then turned onto his back and slammed the door shut with his feet.

Upstairs in his first-floor apartment he grabbed the phone and called the police. He poured himself a large bourbon.

Half an hour later the detective sergeant sat down in the low comfortable chair opposite him from the sofa. He had pale-blue eyes and was looking at him with an expression which said exactly nothing.

"I'll have Ballistics check it."

"For chrissake, what for?" Peterson objected. He'd shown the sergeant the brick with the fresh chip out of it when he'd let him in the door.

"So I'll know it was a bullet," the sergeant answered flatly.

Peterson was exasperated. "You mean it just fell out in front of my eyes and the ricochet I heard was all in my head or something?"

"No. You *say* it was a bullet. When Ballistics have examined it I'll *know* if it was."

Peterson slumped back in his chair. "Next you're going to tell me if you have one very dead body, you don't know it's dead until the medical examiner tells you."

"It's not the same, Mr. Peterson."

"Okay, okay. But for the sake of the argument let's suppose it was a bullet."

The sergeant crossed his legs, blinked twice, and said, "I'm supposing."

"Then it doesn't make sense. The guy comes at me with a knife. Now, I don't *know* he means me any harm but it's a fair bet. Right?"

"A fair bet," the sergeant agreed.

"So maybe he wants my wallet," Peterson continued.

"Maybe."

"Then why does he take a shot at me? Muggers don't operate that way. They'll threaten you, pull a knife or a gun on you, beat you half to death. But *not* take a shot at you after you've gotten away."

The sergeant uncrossed his legs, hitched up his trousers at the knees, and worked with his eyes to produce a look of patient understanding. "May I ask some questions now, Mr. Peterson?" he said.

"Why not? You get paid for it."

"Tell that to my wife."

"I'm sorry," Peterson said. "I guess I'm a bit edgy."

"Okay—did you get a good look at this man?"

"No. It was too quick and too dark."

"But he wasn't young? Not a kid?"

"No."

"Black?"

"No."

"How about dress?"

"Hard to say. He was wearing a long topcoat."

"Nothing way out?"

"No."

"So although you can't describe what he *did* look like, what he didn't look like tends to exclude him from the usual categories who wave knives around to get their hands on other people's wallets."

"I guess so."

"Then, Mr. Peterson, providing you're not lying or imagining things and *supposing* he did take a shot at you, I'd say it's likely someone tried to kill you. Just—plain—kill—you."

"That's ridiculous!" Peterson exclaimed. "Why would anyone want to do that?"

The sergeant smiled, without humor. "I suggest *you* think about that, Mr. Peterson. We've only just met. I don't know the kind of company you keep."

"Not *that* kind of company, I promise you."

The sergeant looked at Peterson in silence. "Haven't you missed something, Mr. Peterson?" he asked quietly.

"Missed something?" Peterson's eyes narrowed. "Like what?"

"You see a piece of brick flying through the air, you hear a ricochet. . . . What's missing?"

"Jesus!" The full implication of the sergeant's question hit him. "No sound of a shot . . . a silencer!"

"You've got it, Mr. Peterson. Now you know why I want Ballistics to check that brick. If you're right, the guy was no amateur. He came with the full equipment."

"But why try and kill me with a knife first?"

"Just an idea, but maybe he wanted it to look like a random street killing. And if he'd succeeded with the knife and removed your wallet and other valuables, that's what it would have looked like. The fact he took a shot at you—if Ballistics says he did—means he was awfully anxious to see *you* dead."

Jane's eyes were icy with controlled rage. "I hope they send that bungling idiot Ivan to Siberia."

Sakov calmed her. "He is already on the flight home and I have no doubt he will be suitably punished."

"I'll kill Peterson myself," said Jane.

"You will not," said Sakov. "It would be far too dangerous."

"Then what?" Jane snapped.

Sakov stood up and began to pace around the room in the safe house in Arlington where they had hastily met. He stopped and turned to face Jane. "Our decision to eliminate Peterson was the right decision at the time. His question to you about Deniskin was odd. Why should he ask such a question—out of the blue and out of the context of your conversation?"

He began pacing once more. "However, it would be too dangerous to kill him now. The police must suspect that a deliberate attempt was made on his life. Even under the most favorable circumstances, a further attempt on his life would be too risky—unless we have absolutely no option. You both leave for the New Hampshire primary tonight. Correct?"

Jane nodded.

Sakov paused and cleared his throat as if reluctant to ask his next question. "I take it Peterson is still . . . attracted to you?"

"Yes. I can do what I like with him," Jane answered without hesitation.

"Then you will marry him," Sakov said.

"Marry!"

"Yes. He will be easier to deal with—having him close to you where you can keep on eye on him."

"I'd rather kill him," Jane said.

"Eventually that may happen too," said Sakov.

CHAPTER
SEVENTEEN

In the aftermath of Orlov's startling revelation, the New Hampshire primary was a walkover for Hurst. He took the next two primaries in Massachusetts and Florida by storm, and from then on the bandwagon rolled. Six months before New Hampshire, the professional politicians would not have put one red cent on Hurst. Now they climbed aboard his bandwagon—boots, saddles, shirts, and all.

Four weeks after the Orlov incident the Russians revealed the "true" reason for his defection—a personal grudge. They flatly denied that they had, or would ever have, any intention of interfering with the oil supplies from the Middle East. But the doubt was still in people's minds and they turned to Hurst.

The man who understood the Russians.

He was nominated presidential candidate on the first ballot at the national convention in Chicago.

Peterson had been more than glad to leave Washington for the primary in New Hampshire. He had convinced himself he had no enemies—not the kind who would try to kill him. And he had other things on his mind. Following Hurst around kept him close to Jane Mantel.

Acting on Sakov's instructions, Jane was encouraging Peterson. It was like putting flame to kindling. Peterson was totally obsessed with Jane, his worries about her temporarily buried, overwhelmed by his desire for her.

They were married after the Oregon primary.

With the national convention in Chicago over, John Hurst agreed for Jane to take a short break . . . a delayed honeymoon.

Jane wasn't going to waste it.

Since their marriage Peterson had not said anything about her past or Deniskin. But the honeymoon would give her the perfect opportunity to force him into looking at these things. To finally check out if he had any hidden worries and, if he did, he would die.

And this was why Sakov had chosen the little-known island of Lanzarote, located two hundred miles off the coast of Morocco, for their honeymoon. Somewhere it would be easy to arrange for Peterson to disappear, if necessary . . . someplace where the American police would know nothing about it.

The morning after their arrival Jane and Peterson lay on the warm sands of the Playa Blanca at the southern tip of the island. The hot sun beat down from the azure sky. A short way out to sea a shoal of flying fish skimmed across the sparkling water.

With long sensuous fingers Jane massaged the sun cream into the strong muscles of Peterson's thighs. He groaned and stirred. He raised himself on one elbow and nodded toward the gleaming white villa behind them.

Jane took him by the hand and led him down the beach. Together they plunged into the warm water and swam out to sea. Then she pulled his trunks down and, clasping her thighs around his waist, guided him into her warmth. The sensation in the water was a special kind of thrill he'd never experienced before. Then, her bikini in one hand, she pulled away from him and dived down into the shallow clear-blue sea. He followed her naked body down and grasping her narrow waist entered her again. Their bodies entwined, they slowly rose and broke the surface gasping for breath. She gave him time to recover, then dived again. . . . Twenty minutes later they swam slowly back to the beach. Peterson collapsed onto the sand, exhausted. It had been the most erotic experience of his life; the sensations, out of this world.

They spent two days in the sun, in the sea, in bed. On the third day they hired a taxi in Arrecife—a very old yellow Mercedes driven by a handsome young man called Pepe. Half Spanish, half Moroccan, the features of his face were strongly chiseled. For a thousand pesetas he would be at the disposal of the señor and the beautiful señora for the day.

On the way out of town they passed women dressed in traditional island costume. Long black dresses with long sleeves—the sun was for tourists. Atop their heads, wide-brimmed hats and a shawl which came down to cover the sides and lower half of their faces.

Jane turned to Peterson. Touching his arm she pointed to the women. "Look how they hide their faces," she said. "That's what I wanted to do when I was young. I was so plain."

He leaned across and kissed her tenderly on the cheek. "Never mind, my darling, you know what they say: *'Pour être belle, il faut souffrir.'* " And Jane saw nothing but love in his eyes.

That evening at dinner, he laid his hand gently on hers. "I've been thinking, Jane. Would you like to start a baby?"

"Why not, after we get back and the election is over," Jane said. "I don't see why a career woman should miss out on children. I can manage both."

"Waiter!" Peterson called out. "Champagne... French."

"Sí, señor." The waiter hurried off.

"I've never been happier in all my life," said Jane. "And to think, all this would never have happened if you hadn't seen me at that awful Deniskin thing." She looked tenderly into his eyes ... and all she saw was love.

Peterson squeezed her hand and was thoughtful for a moment. "You know," he said, "I wonder why John and Cathy haven't had children." He laughed. "Apart from anything else, it's good politics. The Presidential Family stuff."

"Didn't you know?" Jane said. "Cathy can't. It sounds complicated. There's something wrong with her Fallopian tubes."

"I had no idea."

"It makes her pretty unhappy at times," Jane went on. "She told me about it sometime when we were swapping intimacies. You know, the way women do. I feel so sorry for her."

The champagne arrived and they talked on about their future.

Next day they wandered along the narrow streets at Arrecife looking at the shops full of souvenirs. Peterson pointed to an array of crude pottery—vases, bowls, ornaments of all kinds—decorated with bold, bright colors. "Not *quite* as delicate as your Dresden china," he laughed, holding up an enormous vase.

"Not quite," she answered. "But I'd like it. A small memento!"

"It's yours." He grinned.

Jane turned away as he began to count out three hundred pesetas to pay. She was glancing toward two men nearby dressed like typical tourists. They weren't. They were an assassination team from Department V of the KGB.

He's no threat, she was thinking.

She made no sign to the two men.

Peterson could live.

But as Peterson went to hand the money to the eager shop-keeper, he paused and frowned. Dresden! As if something deep down in his subconscious had triggered off a disturbing signal. A warning!

"Hurry up, Ed." Jane's voice penetrated the dark, fleeting shadow in his mind. He turned to her and once again was over-whelmed by his love for her as he saw her standing in the bright sunlight—tall, elegant, her long blonde hair lifted by the gentle sea breeze, softly caressing her lovely face.

The shadow of doubt receded into his mind . . . leaving only a trace of a mystery. Something still unresolved.

CHAPTER
EIGHTEEN

It was ten-thirty in the morning when Zimin's chauffeur approached Sakov at Moscow airport. Having identified himself, he escorted Sakov to the waiting limousine. He spread a thick, brightly woven afghan over his passenger's knees before getting into the driver's seat.

The message Sakov had received twenty-two hours earlier in Washington had been brief. Chairman Zimin required to see him. There was no explanation.

As the car approached the center of the city Sakov felt his pulse quicken. He had nothing to fear . . . nothing he knew about. Everything was under control. Hurst was doing well. The latest polls showed he was only a couple of points behind the President. The only danger had been Peterson, but now that Jane Mantel had married him she could watch him like a hawk.

Neither the FBI nor the CIA had any suspicions. How could they? That was the beauty of the whole operation. Pressures had been applied, events manipulated . . . all at long range. On the political level. It was inconceivable that the Russians would want to promote the political career of a hard-line anti-Soviet like John Hurst.

Nevertheless, Sakov *was* tense.

Zimin had that effect on people . . . all people.

Sakov saw the route they were taking. He leaned forward and spoke to the driver through the open glass partition. "Chairman Zimin's apartment?"

"Yes, Comrade Colonel."

He sat back and began to take long, deep breaths to relax himself.

Zimin was standing by the window as he entered. He turned to greet Sakov. The smile was faint but it was there. "Sit down, Colonel," he said, gesturing toward a sofa at the far end of the room. Sakov watched as Zimin seated himself in the high wing-backed chair opposite. For an instant it occurred to him there was something obscene in the contrast between the power this man wielded, the universal fear he engendered, and his physical frailty. In stature Zimin was like a small boy. Sitting bolt upright, thin hands clasped between thin knees, his feet hardly touched the floor. But the impression was only momentary, for Zimin's eyes were now upon him: calculating, ruthless, unforgiving. He spoke: "You have heard the rumors, Colonel."

Sakov frowned. "Rumors?"

"Yes. Concerning Lensky's appointment to lead the Party."

Sakov nodded. The rumor of Lensky's pending appointment had reached the embassy in Washington several weeks before, but it had come as no surprise. It was common knowledge that big changes were imminent within the Politburo. With most of the existing leaders in their seventies, the fight for succession had been going on for several years. Lensky was regarded as the man most likely to emerge at the top. The time was right for him. He had the backing of the military and the neo-Stalinists in the Party. They shared his views—that the time for détente and compromise with capitalism was over. It had served its purpose well enough. They had gained the breathing space needed to build their military strength.

"Then you know we shall be at war with America in the near future?" Zimin continued calmly.

"A nuclear war?"

Zimin smiled. "No, Colonel, it will be more complicated than that. Amongst other things, your assignment will see to that.

"What do you know of the Volodin affair?" Zimin asked suddenly.

"A little," Sakov replied. "Some years ago he made a speech to the Ukrainian Party Congress. He predicted war with the Americans, didn't he?"

"Correct, Colonel . . . Volodin is a very clever man. Before becoming our leading ideologist he was a senior member of the State Planning Commission. He knows a great deal about the way our economy works. In his speech to the Congress he predicted the economy would stagnate. The reasons were what he called 'in-built deficiencies': lack of real incentive for the people to work hard or be efficient. He also said this stagnation would coincide with Russia's gaining military equality with the West."

There was a silence. Zimin appeared to be preoccupied with

his thoughts. Sakov waited patiently for whatever was to follow.

At length Zimin began to speak again. "Volodin put forward the view that such a confluence of events—economic stagnation and military strength—would tempt our leaders to take the path of war. Not war for war's sake, you understand, but war as the preferred alternative to admitting to the people that the Party, *that communism*, had failed. And, as if that was not enough to condemn him, he went even further."

Another pause.

Another silence.

"He went even further," Zimin repeated. "Volodin actually singled out Lensky, a fellow Ukrainian and member of the Politburo, and said, 'If that man is in power when this happens, I promise you our country is doomed to the most horrendous war in history.' "

Sakov shifted uncomfortably in his chair. Zimin was waiting for a reply. What could he say? A war because communism had failed! That was ridiculous . . . and unthinkable. Yet Zimin had given no indication of what he himself was thinking. Sakov decided to play safe.

"I take it there is no love lost between Lensky and Volodin." He forced a laugh.

"Hardly. Lensky wanted to have him shot. However, I was able to intervene and reduce the sentence to one of house arrest for life. You see, Colonel, when I interrogated Volodin, he convinced me he was right. And I thought a man clever enough to do that should not be fed to the worms. He might come in useful one day."

Sakov forgot his caution. "You mean he was right? Right about the failure of the economy? And war being the only way out. It's preposterous!"

Zimin's sneer was cold. "You are an expert on such matters, Colonel?"

"No. But—"

"Then stick to what you know about," Zimin silenced him. "Volodin *was* right. The estimates for the next five-year plan put the growth of our economy at less than two percent a year. I call that stagnation. More important, so does Lensky."

Sakov remained silent. Any excitement he might have felt was soured by the knowledge that war was not to be the deserved triumph of communism. War born out of communism's failure? A political expediency to preserve the power of the Party? He must not think about it. He was an officer and an officer's duty was to obey.

"Why so silent?" Zimin misread Sakov's thoughts. "We are going to have that war. And Volodin is going to help us win it. It is he who will guarantee that your Senator Hurst becomes the next President of the United States."

Zimin stood up.

"Come with me and witness the first and last act of Volodin's contribution to your plans." Zimin was smiling, a sadistic tightening of the mouth but nothing in the eyes.

It took them an hour to reach Volodin's dacha. As they got out of the car Zimin turned to Sakov. "You will say nothing, absolutely nothing. You understand, Colonel."

Volodin was tall with a slight stoop. His long gray hair was combed straight back lying flat on his head. There was an air of dignity about him, Sakov thought, a characteristic not commonly found amongst senior Party members. He greeted the two men with restrained politeness as he showed them through to a large, comfortably furnished library.

"To what do I owe the pleasure of your visit?" he addressed Zimin.

"I need your help to prevent Lensky from becoming First Secretary of the Party," Zimin answered.

Sakov hid his surprise. Zimin had assured him Lensky's appointment was a fact!

Volodin's face clouded with concern. "You mean his appointment is a real possibility?"

Zimin nodded gravely. "More than a possibility, comrade. But with your assistance we may yet stop him. Your warning did not go unheeded, comrade. Many fear Lensky will plunge us into war with America just as you predicted."

"It must not happen." Volodin rose to his feet in great agitation. "Don't they realize, even if we defeat America, our country will be devastated, our industry destroyed. The Chinese have been waiting and praying for this to happen. They will flood across our frontier in their millions and we will be powerless to prevent them."

"Calm yourself, comrade," Zimin said quietly. "You know you do not have to convert me to your way of thinking."

Volodin sat down and began to run his fingers through his hair.

"Your views still command great respect amongst the more liberal element of the Party," Zimin continued. "And I myself am also not without influence. What we need is forcefully to remind these people of the dangers of Lensky's policy. This is why I have come to see you."

"What can I do . . . a prisoner?" Volodin spread his arms in a gesture of helplessness.

"The pen may yet prove mightier than the sword, comrade. You must write a personal letter to Lensky, a plea from the heart as well as the mind, to reconsider his aggressive plans."

Volodin's face fell. "Gladly, but what good would it do? Lensky will spit on it."

"It will not be for Lensky's eyes alone, my friend. You will give the letter to me and before it is delivered to Lensky, I will have copies made for distribution to all senior Party members throughout the country."

Volodin's pale face lit up. "You could arrange that?"

"Of course, comrade." Zimin paused and lowered his eyes as if uncertain how to express what he was about to say. Then he looked directly at Volodin and, speaking slowly, said, "I must warn you I intend to make certain nobody knows I am responsible for leaking copies of the letter. The consequences for me could be . . . fatal, if it became known. But as for you"—Zimin shifted uneasily in his chair—"I cannot guarantee your safety. Even if we stop Lensky, it is more than likely he will still be powerful enough to take his revenge against you."

Volodin smiled. "I appreciate your honesty. But I did not expect to live after my speech to the Ukrainian Congress. I owe my life to you. I am not afraid to die now."

"You are a brave man," Zimin replied quietly.

"Not brave. It is harder to live with a bad conscience than to die with a clear one. If I can do *anything* to prevent our country being destroyed, I must do it. I have no choice."

"A brave man," Zimin repeated in a murmur, his eyes lowered.

Volodin was on his feet again, his eyes bright, eager to begin his task. "When do you want this letter?"

"Now. There is no time to be lost," Zimin answered.

Sakov sat by the edge of the blue tiled swimming pool, his feet dangling in the water. Looking across the lawn and the flowerbeds beyond, he could see Volodin's head bent over the desk by the window in the library. In front of him, Zimin was methodically swimming up and down.

Volodin had asked for one hour to write the letter and Zimin had suggested that he and Sakov take some exercise while they waited. It was late September and the temperature not much above fifty. Sakov shivered. It would be warmer in the water but somehow he couldn't bring himself to share the same water with Zimin. There was a deep coldness within Sakov. He did not know why Zimin had asked for the letter, but he did know it would never be distributed. And he knew that Volodin, who was indeed a brave man, must be writing his own death warrant.

A shout came from the library window. Volodin had finished.

"Come, Colonel," Zimin spoke from the water, "let us see what this patriot has written."

They dressed and returned to the library. Volodin was standing beside the desk at the window. "I have written in Ukrainian," he announced. "It will add to the impact. . . . As you said, an appeal from the heart, from one Ukrainian to another to set politics aside and think of our people."

A slow smile spread across Zimin's face. "Excellent, comrade, it will add to its authenticity."

Volodin read aloud, translating into Russian as he went. He finished and handed it to Zimin, who said, "Thank you, *comrade*, that will do very well."

Zimin turned to Sakov. "Fetch one of the guards from the gate."

Sakov hurried to the command and returned with the guard.

"Come here," Zimin ordered the guard.

The man approached. "Your pistol," Zimin commanded.

The guard removed the pistol from its holster and handed it over.

Without hesitation and without speaking a word Zimin fired four times. For a split second Sakov saw the horror in Volodin's eyes before they went dead and his body hurtled backward with the impact of the bullets and crashed through the window.

Sakov stared dumbly at Zimin.

"He was a traitor," Zimin said, his face expressionless. "His house arrest was merely a stay of execution. I thought he might be useful one day. I was right."

As Sakov hurried up the steps to board the Aeroflot plane which was to take him back to America he felt the relief flow over. He had no stomach for cold-blooded political executions.

In his briefcase were two copies of Volodin's letter—one in Ukrainian, the other a translation into Russian.

CHAPTER
NINETEEN

The Director of the CIA let out a low whistle as he finished reading a copy of Volodin's letter to Lensky. He looked up at his Special Assistant. "What do you think?" he asked. "Is it genuine?"

"I don't know," the assistant answered. "All we know at present is that there *was* a Party ideologist named Volodin. He used to write regular articles for various Party publications. Some years ago the articles suddenly dried up and as far as we know nothing has appeared under his name since."

"How did we get hold of the copy?" the Director asked.

"One of our embassy attachés was stopped in the street in Moscow. It was all very hurried. The guy refused to give his name. Just handed the attaché an envelope, then disappeared into the crowd. As simple as that."

The Director raised his eyebrows. "A plant?"

"Could be," the assistant replied. "Only problem is, why?"

The Director gazed thoughtfully through the window at the barren trees surrounding the CIA headquarters at Langley. "Yeah . . . why?" he echoed. "Why would the Russians want to warn us they are going to attack us? Off the top of my head I can't think of one good reason."

"The Chinese?" the assistant suggested. "Maybe it was a Chinese plant. Could be they're trying to twist our arm so we'll increase our economic aid to them by throwing another Russian scare into us."

The Director gave a tight smile. "If they are, they've sure as hell succeeded. *I'm* scared." He got to his feet abruptly. "Check on every angle," he said to the assistant. "Meantime, I'm going to see the President. No matter what, Dale must know . . . and now!"

At ten o'clock that night the Senate Office Building was almost deserted. Jane Mantel ripped the typed sheet out of the typewriter and scanned it quickly.

Two days ago Sakov had given her an English translation of Volodin's letter. It was this she had just copied onto a piece of Hurst's office stationery.

Jane sat for another half an hour and learned it by heart. Then she locked the copy she had just made in the desk drawer. The original she took along the corridor, tore into small pieces, and flushed down the toilet.

As she entered the apartment, Ed Peterson switched off the television. "Boy! Hurst certainly works you hard." He kissed her.

Jane flopped into a chair and sighed. "With two days to go before the TV debate on foreign affairs, it's hardly surprising."

Peterson fixed them both a drink and sat beside her. "You know, a lot of people figure Hurst's playing up the Russian scare too hard," he said, handing her the vodka martini.

"I know it," she answered. "But it's *his* platform and if he gets off it, he's nowhere to go. Hurst's only chance is to push foreign affairs." She sounded despondent.

Peterson looked at her with concern. "Do I detect a note of disenchantment?"

Jane sipped her drink. "Not really . . . but I'm scared he's beginning to bore people. There's a real danger his campaign will go off the boil before the election."

Peterson took her hand. He'd never heard her talk like this. "Don't worry, honey, it's going to be a close thing, but I've a hunch he'll pull it off." He was trying to comfort her but the truth was he thought Hurst was going to bomb out.

Jane sighed again, then smiled at him with forced cheerfulness. "Well, we'll soon know," she said. "The television debate will settle it one way or the other. He's not going to let up one bit on the Russian thing. If the voters have had enough, it's going to scream out from the polls."

The morning of the debate Jane arrived early in her office. She riffled through the mail. Among the hundreds of letters, she found what she was looking for: an envelope addressed personally to Hurst in a childlike handwriting and marked MOST URGENT. She smiled and placed it on top of the pile. She took the mail through to his office and returned to await his summons.

At three minutes after eight her intercom buzzed. It was Hurst. Would she come in right away?

He handed her two pieces of paper. "That's Russian, isn't it?" he asked. "What the hell's it all about?"

She took the two pieces of paper. The top piece was a half-sheet of yellow lined paper. On it was a short message in the same childish handwriting she'd seen on the envelope when she'd checked the mail. It read:

Hit him with it tonight.
Your friends at the CIA.

She flipped over to the next sheet. It wasn't in Russian; it was in Ukrainian. Only someone who spoke the language would know the difference. Jane didn't speak Ukrainian, which was why she had memorized the translation the previous evening.

She pretended to translate, hesitating from time to time over a sentence to make her performance seem authentic.

When she finished, Hurst's face was a study. "If it's genuine, it is political dynamite!" he exploded. "Who is this Volodin character?"

Jane paused as if thinking. "I'm not certain," she replied, "but if I recall correctly he used to be a Party ideologist." Then her face flushed with excitement. "You realize what this means? . . . You've got the President stone cold! It's dated six weeks ago, before Lensky's appointment. The Administration must have been sitting on it. It's hotter than the Orlov affair."

"Hold it a minute," Hurst warned. "How do we know it's the real McCoy?"

"Would someone dream up a thing like this?" she answered. "They'd have to be out of their minds. Even the CIA aren't that irresponsible."

Hurst remained silent.

"Look," Jane went on. "This letter means Lensky is almost certainly planning a military attack against the West. Maybe only Europe. But that's enough! It's exactly what you have been telling the voters for years." She almost shouted, "And the Administration has been hiding it!"

Hurst was weighing up the situation. "I'm not sure they could do anything else. If they released so much as a hint of it, all hell would break loose and that wouldn't help anyone."

Jane hid her exasperation. "Particularly it wouldn't help the President. He wouldn't stand a chance in the election if it came out."

"I am fully aware of that," Hurst answered. "However, this may just be too hot to disclose on television."

"You don't have to go into the details. Just put the President on the spot," Jane urged. "For heaven's sake, it's a gift!"

Hurst seemed unmoved. "I'll think it over. Meantime, let me have a written translation. And every detail you can get on this Volodin."

"Sure." She rose and walked to the door. Here she turned and spoke coolly. "One school of thought would certainly agree you are right to protect your integrity by not using this information. But another school of thought would just as certainly point out that there is the overriding need to protect your country." She waited, poised and determined.

"It's my decision," he replied grimly.

The television debate went out from Washington at ten o'clock that night. As the crowds gathered in the hall you could feel the hum of excitement. It was make or break for Hurst and everyone knew it.

As President Dale and Hurst mounted their respective rostrums at either side of the platform they both looked drawn and tense. Something more than the exhaustion of the long campaign.

The President had been badly shaken by the contents of the Volodin letter. Maybe it was phony and maybe it wasn't; he had no way of knowing. The whole affair was unnerving, a state of mind that had not been helped by a telephone call he had put through to the Director of the CIA less than twenty minutes ago.

"Anything new come up?" he had asked.

"Nothing substantive, Mr. President. But there are a couple of pointers which don't look too good. We've tracked down a professor at Harvard who met Volodin at a conference over here eight years ago. He invited Volodin to dinner. Volodin wrote a short note thanking him. The professor kept the note as a memento and the handwriting checks out. . . .

"Another thing. We've been doing some pretty hard thinking out here and the way we see it, if it was a plant by the Chinese or the Russians—God knows what for—they'd have written in their official language. The fact it's in Ukrainian tends to support its authenticity as a man-to-man personal letter. Like I say, nothing definite. Just pointers."

The President had put the phone down and taken a couple of shots of whiskey to calm himself. He decided the best way to counteract the worry in his mind was to take the attack to Hurst. Nail *him* for facts.

Sitting in the audience, Jane had never felt so tense in her life. Everything . . . everything she had worked for hung in the balance and the most she had gotten out of Hurst was, "I'll think about it. . . . I'll play it by ear."

The audience fell silent. The debate began. The President led off with five minutes to encapsulate his foreign policy. He ended:

"It is my firm belief that because of the measures to strengthen our defenses the possibility of a Soviet attack on *any* area crucial to our national security can be no more than a figment in certain people's minds. And, I might add, the Soviets themselves are far too realistic to indulge in such fantasies."

Hurst spoke next. Through the blaze of the television lights he could sense he had lost his audience. They had heard it all before. And he knew the millions of viewers would be feeling the same way.

The debate was thrown open. The President put the first question. "Senator Hurst, have you got any evidence *at all* to support your assertions about the Soviet's intentions?"

Hurst was silent. He was recalling Jane's words. Which was more important—his integrity or his country?

"Mr. President," he said, "I would like to answer that by asking you a question." He turned from the camera and looked straight at the President. "Can you assure the American people that *at this very moment* you have absolutely no evidence to suggest *even the possibility* the Soviets might be *contemplating* some military operation against us?"

Hurst's question came out of the blue and hit the President like a line drive between the eyes. Hurst knew! The question could not have been framed the way it was without knowledge of the Volodin letter. The cameras were on him, picking up the beads of perspiration breaking out on his brow. The President couldn't think how to answer the question . . . for a brief moment he couldn't think! The wild desperation showed in his eyes . . . to millions!

He heard himself say, "It would not be in the interests of national security. I can't answer that."

There were gasps of astonishment from the audience.

An honorable man's political career had been ended by four words.

"I can't answer that."

Everyone knew who the next president would be—the candidate who had asked the one unanswerable question. Two weeks later, John Hurst won the election and became President-elect of the United States.

For Jane Mantel, it was a night of triumph. Shortly after midnight she left Hurst's party for another celebration. It was with Sakov. The location: the special safe house where he had dined her before.

This time the table was spread for a typical Russian celebration with *zakuski*—hors d'oeuvres—and chilled vodka. Salted herring and vodka, marinated mushrooms and vodka, salami and vodka, caviar and vodka, and a half a dozen other dishes . . . and vodka. With each shot of vodka they took it in turns to propose a toast.

Finally Sakov could think of no more toasts. In desperation he offered, "Here's to your good friend Peterson . . . your beloved husband."

The smile went from Jane's face. Her eyes met Sakov's and he saw the pain. "You think it has been easy for me?" she said, her voice tight.

Sakov was still smiling. "Of course, Anna . . . with your beauty and your training, how could he resist you?"

Jane knew he had deliberately misunderstood her. She hid her hurt and put her arms around his neck. "Do *you* find me attractive, Comrade Colonel?"

"The most attractive agent I have ever handled," Sakov laughed.

Jane pressed her thighs against him. "That's no compliment," she said.

"It's all you're getting from me." Sakov's voice was suddenly hoarse.

Jane forced herself to smile. "Really, dear Colonel. Then let's see how good you are at resisting temptation."

She climbed onto the table and slowly, deliberately, lingeringly stripped. She stood naked and glorious. "Look, Colonel, am I not better than the whores they provide you with at the embassy?"

Sakov looked, his eyes feasting on the beauty of her body. And for the first time since her sexual education in Moscow, Jane was embarrassed by a man's gaze. Their eyes met and Sakov saw beneath her smile, the vulnerability, the pleading.

His face clouded. "Get down, Anna." His voice was angry.

She stood naked before him, her eyes averted from his.

"Listen to me, Anna." Now his voice was serious but the anger had gone. "You may have to act the whore for your country, but never, never degrade yourself for me."

Jane raised her eyes to his. "But what can I do? What else can I give you but my body? I must be close to you at least in some way."

Sakov took her head in his hands and pressed his lips to hers. And then his hands and lips moved urgently yet tenderly to her breasts and he was on bended knees before her. She stood transfixed, her eyes closed as her body yielded to his power. And for the first time in her life she abandoned herself to a man. *She wanted to be taken.*

He led her to the sofa, then left her waiting there and fetched his glass. Draining down the last of the liquid he stood over her, his eyes watching her body, examining, probing. She writhed under his gaze in an agony of suspense. Her breath was coming fast, a hoarse moan escaped from her throat. He turned down the lights low and rapidly undressed.

He made love to her with a gentleness she had never known until he had brought her to an ecstasy of burning, consuming, demanding desire. She was possessed by him and she cried out, wild meaningless cries, as he brought her to her climax.

She lay still clutching him with a desperate joy. "Is that love?" she whispered.

"Yes, my dear Anna. *That* is love," he said softly. She began to rock slowly until she felt him growing inside her again . . . and a low moaning came from her parted lips.

PART
THREE

CHAPTER
TWENTY

The letter had been delivered by hand to their Georgetown house early that morning as they were preparing to leave for the White House and the Inauguration ceremony. There had been no time to read it, as John was impatient to be going. Cathy had stuffed it into the pocket of her coat to look at after the Inauguration. But as they drove to the White House with their escort, acknowledging the waves from the people in the streets, crowded even at that early hour, she felt a curious urge to open the brown envelope with only her first name printed by hand on the front.

The White House Chief Usher showed them upstairs, to the presidential quarters, and she noted with pride the commanding set of her husband's jaw as he strode through the rooms. He left her, to take a look at the Oval Office, and, sitting near the window, she opened the envelope.

A set of color photographs slid onto her lap from between the single-page letter. She looked at them, one by one, not believing, not disbelieving, her mind unable to take in what she saw. The first photograph was of a smiling man fondly holding a small baby in his arms. Neatly hand-written underneath was, *Anette–6 months–Riga.* The man *was* Carl, the little baby *could* be Anette. The next photograph, *Anette–3 years–Odessa,* a little girl in a blue summer dress stood beside Carl holding his hand and smiling up at him. In all, seven photographs taken at three-year intervals. The seventh, *Anette–18 years–Moscow.* It was still Carl, even more handsome with the passing of time; the girl, a tall attractive brunette. It was not hard to believe it was her own daughter. The features, the coloring were so like her own.

But it was the last photograph which added a sinister note to her confusion. A collection of various objects neatly arranged on a green cloth-covered table, the caption, *Cathy and Carl.* And she remembered that day, all those years ago, when she had locked her bedroom door and opened the baggage Hans had sent from Vienna. And how she had thought, *Poor, dear foolish Hans,* as she found everything which would remind her of her life with Carl had been removed. They were all there, in the photograph, even her white-lace wedding gown draped over one corner of the table. She could no longer doubt it *was* Anette with Carl in the photographs. *And they were alive!*

Her hands trembled as she opened the letter:

Dear Mother,
    I know this will come as a great shock to you, but we are alive. We're both in Washington, Daddy and me.

Love,
Anette

CHAPTER
TWENTY-ONE

While the letter was being read by Cathy in Washington, Phase
One of the Russian plan was already beginning in Europe.

The Russians were working to a rigid time schedule. Every
second counted. . . .

The first Westerner to know what was happening was a British
Officer, Brigadier General Kenneth-Smythe. As a member of the
General Staff, Allied Forces Central Europe (AFCENT), it was
his duty and doubtful pleasure to be one of the NATO observers
assigned to monitor the Russian maneuvers, which were taking
place in the northern sector of East Germany.

The general did not like vodka. Or, to put it more accurately,
vodka did not like him. It was a vicious and malevolent drink. It
burned your throat, tore your gut, then kicked you in the head.
Quite unlike the soothing and mellowing behavior of Scotch, to
which he was somewhat partial.

He had arrived early that afternoon at the small town of Stenburg, in East Germany. He had been briefed by a dour Russian
colonel, who seemed more concerned with explaining the political reasons for the maneuvers than with military details. But
these Russian chappies were all the same: obsessed with politics.

The general had to admit the Russian colonel had a point. The
bellicose utterances of the new American President were not
exactly calculated to be soothing to Russian ears. It was not surprising they wanted to test out their ability to reinforce their
front-line positions in the event of a NATO attack. The general
knew damn well NATO had absolutely no intention of attacking
the Russians. The American President might have that kind of
thing in mind, but NATO staff knew it would be suicide. Still, the
fact was the Russians were damnably suspicious chaps. Their

convoluted minds would scent out a threat behind even the friendliest of actions—no doubt the result of too much communism, mixed with too much vodka.

Now, in the officers' mess, the general was being dined by his Russian hosts. He braced himself as the senior Russian officer got to his feet to propose yet another toast of friendship. The general rose unsteadily and emptied his glass in reply. That was when he knew, if the honor of the British army were to be preserved, that he must absent himself from the proceedings; fresh air was what he needed.

He bowed formally to his host and made what seemed to him to be a pretty dignified exit. Certainly it did not justify the ill-concealed and adolescent sniggers which accompanied his departure.

Outside, the night was still and clear. A thin layer of snow covered the ground and the surrounding buildings. He breathed deeply, hoping it was not true that there was only one thing more lethal than vodka—vodka and fresh air.

He decided to take a quick walk, get the old circulation going, clear the head and lungs. He reached the gate in the high wall surrounding the officers' quarters and came face to face with two Russian troopers. They said something to him in Russian. "Brigadier General Kenneth-Smythe," he replied. The guards' eyes took in the gold braid and red tabs on his uniform, and the rows of medal ribbons. They exchanged glances. "Brigadier General Kenneth-Smythe," he repeated in his most authoritative manner, and walked on, leaving the guards muttering.

About three hundred yards ahead he saw the long, low outline of a building with dimly lit windows. The men's barracks, he supposed. And to the left, set on its own, a small, brightly lit building. That would be his target. A brisk walk there and back would work wonders for the old constitution.

He set off boldly. Halfway to his objective, to his right, he caught sight of the silhouettes of rows of tanks parked between the officers' mess and the barracks. They were menacing in their stillness. He shivered. For General Kenneth-Smythe knew about tanks. And he recognized the squat silhouette of Russian T.72 tanks. Nasty brutes. With their 125-mm laser ranging guns, more than a match for the underpowered British Chieftain or the almost obsolete German Leopard I.

As he approached the brightly lit building he saw, leading toward it, a lineup. Curious, he hurried forward. The open door at the front of the lineup was jammed with Russian troopers. He pushed his way through, getting no more than a mildly hostile grunt from the men around. Inside, they had all stripped off their greatcoats and tunics and, holding them under their right arms, stood with their left arms bared, shirt-sleeves rolled up.

At the head of the lineup, two men in white overalls were rapidly injecting each man with a hypodermic.

The general stood watching, a questioning frown on his face. One of the men in overalls, turning to take a fresh hypodermic from an assistant, saw him. He stiffened and stared at the general. Straightening up, he advanced toward him, his eyes scrutinizing and wary. He spoke in Russian.

The general shook his head. "English," he said.

"Oh ... English," the Russian answered slowly.

"NATO observer," the general said brusquely.

There was a long pause, then the Russian spoke: "You come to observe our influenza vaccinations?"

"Flu?"

"Yes ... flu, as you call it. Very bad in winter. We keep our men fit. But come," he said, taking the general by the arm, "it is not military business." He nodded his head sharply and the men at the entrance made way as he guided the general out. "I am sorry, I am very busy." He waved his arm at the long lineup outside. "You will excuse me please."

The general walked slowly back. Funny chaps these Russians, he thought, vaccinating their men on the eve of maneuvers. His surprise was quickly replaced by a nagging worry. What was it? Something he had read—in the latest field manual—or was it an intelligence report? Why should the Russians inoculate their men just before maneuvers? Some of them would be knocked out by the reaction. It wasn't right. The general's trained mind worried. *What was it?*

At five the next morning the general was awakened by the thunderous roar of the Russian tanks as their engines burst into life. He heard the unmistakable clanking of the steel tracks as they moved off. His frightening suspicions of the night were replaced by horrifying certainty. The door of his bedroom was locked.

Twenty minutes passed and his door was unlocked. Two Russian soldiers directed him by gestures along the corridor, down the stairs, and into a waiting car. Two and a half hours later he was in a cellar, already full of other NATO observers.

"It's crazy," an American general was yelling. "Why are we here? Who do they think we are?"

"I think we may be prisoners of war," said Kenneth-Smythe.

"Are you crazy too?"

"I think it's war. And worse than that. It's probably CW," said Kenneth-Smythe.

At the mention of CW there was a silence. Every man present knew it stood for chemical warfare.

A German officer pushed his way forward. "CW? What kind? Blister? Blood? Nerve?"

"Nerve."

Again, silence. They were all familiar with the NATO terminology: "blister" for chemicals which attacked the skin and eyes; "blood," the bloodstream; "nerve," the nervous system.

"But they wouldn't dare," a voice objected from the crowd gathered around Kenneth-Smythe.

"Why not?" he replied. "They've dramatically increased their production of rocket launchers and they're far more advanced than we in the development of new gases. Since rocket launchers are the best method of delivering nerve gas, it does rather add up."

"What about world opinion?" the same voice protested.

"Christ! Maybe he's right. Since when did the Russians care about world opinion?" It was the American general speaking. "All they care about is winning." He looked intently at Kenneth-Smythe. "What makes you so sure? About it being war, and CW?"

"Because," Kenneth-Smythe answered quietly, "I saw their tank crews being inoculated last night. They claimed it was against influenza. Nobody but an idiot would believe that and . . ."

"And we know they can immunize their own men against certain nerve gases," the American finished for him, a sour look settling over his features.

"Precisely."

"Jesus Christ!" the American said. His voice became hollow with strain. "We've only got one answer to their CW . . . nuclear warfare."

"Only *half* an answer," Kenneth-Smythe corrected. "By the time we get clearance to use nuclear warheads, the Russians will have a dozen divisions in West German territory. And that's one place we can't use nuclear weapons."

"Jesus Christ!" the American repeated.

"Quite so," agreed Brigadier General Kenneth-Smythe.

The giant E-3A, a Boeing 707 with a huge radar tower on top, cruised noiselessly thirty thousand feet above West Germany, its radars probing deep into Communist territory to the east. Part of NATO's Airborne Warning and Control System, its sensitive "look-down" radar would detect low-flying aircraft trying to slip in low beneath the vision of land-based radar the second they took off from their airfields.

In addition to a flight crew of four and some of the most advanced electronic equipment in the world, the Boeing carried a complement of thirteen radar and control operators under the command of "Bird" Colonel Crankshaw. In the event of a Soviet air attack, it would be his task to control the operations of the entire NATO air defense system.

Sergeant McCarthy glanced at the large segmented radar screen in front of him. Everything normal. The precision clock on the instrument panel read 0800 hours. He grunted with satisfaction—Golanski would soon be around with hot coffee. He could do with it. After a four-day furlough in Frankfurt, a guy got awful bushed.

Clasping his hands behind his neck, he pushed his head back and yawned. As his gaze returned to the dark surface of the radar screen, he jerked forward. A dozen bright pinpoints of light had appeared on the eastern extremity of the screen. He screwed his eyes shut for an instant. When he opened them, the number of pinpoints had doubled. "Holy Jesus," he whispered. His hand shot to the intercom switch connecting him with Colonel Crankshaw.

Sergeant McCarthy was the first to see the lead flight of some nine hundred Russian aircraft as they streaked westward toward the German frontier.

Private Kurtz, of the West German 15th Armored Artillery Brigade, looked at his watch. Exactly eight o'clock. From the guardhouse, he saw his relief making his way toward him. He started to walk to meet him, then stopped dead in his tracks. A sound like the onrush of a screaming wind filled the air. The ground shuddered, as the noise of muffled explosives reverberated from all around. He stood absolutely still. The approaching guard began to weave from side to side as he walked. Then his head fell forward, his knees buckled, and he crumpled to the ground. Kurtz rushed to help him. He never made it. A floating dizziness filled his head. The strength drained from his arms and legs and he lost control of his muscles. The rifle fell from his hand. He fell to his knees and collapsed on his face in the snow.

The two West German soldiers lay unconscious, oblivious to the spasmodic twitching of their arms and legs. And so it was for thousands of soldiers and civilians on a fifty-mile front.

Phase One of the Russian military master plan had begun. . . .

CHAPTER
TWENTY-TWO

While the Inauguration ceremonies in Washington gathered momentum, a special agent of the CIA in Geneva, Switzerland, made a shattering discovery—a piece of information so potentially explosive that he had to see the new President of the United States, John Hurst ... urgently ... secretly.

Two seemingly unconnected events had recently brought L'École de Lystre, the finishing school Cathy Hurst had attended, to the attention of the CIA....

The first event was the discovery by Jeff Ryan, head of research at the Ace Electronics Corporation in California, that his daughter Mary was using a 35-mm Pentax camera to take copies of highly classified documents.

He took work home most weekends. This particular weekend his briefcase contained complete specifications of the latest modifications to the guidance system of the long-range Cruise missile. They hadn't cracked all the problems of linking the on-board minicomputer to a Satellite Global Positioning system, but they were making good progress.

The discovery that his daughter was overly interested in his work had been all too simple—one of those accidents of fate.

Thirsty, he had got up for a glass of water in the middle of the night. The light was on in his study. And there she was, the contents of his briefcase neatly spread on his desk, copying them with the Pentax. And with Mary was her husband Franz, an Austrian she had fallen in love with when she'd been at L'École de Lystre.

The FBI investigation revealed it to be a typical KGB operation. Franz persuaded his wife Mary that the only way to preserve world peace was for the East and the West to be equal in strength. Soon America would have a long-range Cruise missile. Russia must have one too. It was necessary for peace. Mary swallowed it. She would swallow anything from Franz. She was deeply in love with him.

The second event was rather more dramatic. A Lufthansa flight from Frankfurt was hijacked by members of the Berlin Red Army Faction—a terrorist organization dedicated to the violent overthrow of capitalism. In return for the lives of the eighty-seven passengers, they demanded the release of six imprisoned members of the Berlin RAF plus six million deutschmarks. The German government stalled on the negotiations until the hijackers were tired, then a specially trained German commando unit stormed the plane at Ankara airport.

Five of the seven hijackers were killed. Of the survivors, one was a German girl of twenty-four, the daughter of a senior government official in Bonn. She admitted she had been persuaded to join the Berlin RAF by her lover, one of the dead men who was identified as a KGB agent.

She had met her lover four years previously while she was at L'École de Lystre.

These two events had taken place within a month of each other. And that was how an observant CIA employee at Langley came to notice the unlikely coincidence that both girls had been persuaded to work against the West by KGB agents they had met while at L'École de Lystre.

Jim Settler, an old friend of John Hurst's, had traveled for the CIA quite a bit. He had headed up the Company's stations, first at Brussels, then Paris, and now Geneva.

He received instructions from the Western European Division of the DDP (Clandestine Services) to check out L'École de Lystre and put the staff under heavy surveillance, particularly Madame Leberge. For three months nothing unusual was observed. Then, one Friday morning, Madame was followed to a small out-of-town restaurant where she lunched with a tall man with rimless glasses and a bushy moustache. The agent who observed this meeting had the good sense to follow the man, not Madame, when they parted.

The man returned by a circuitous route to the Russian Embassy. He was later identified as a cultural attaché.

That was all that was needed for alarm bells to start ringing in Jim Settler's head. L'École de Lystre catered to the daughters of the rich and mighty. There was no, absolutely no, reason for its owner to meet with a Russian Embassy official. Unless . . . !

What scared Settler half to death was that scores of American girls had passed through this school over the years. How many were being used by the KGB? How many dormant, waiting to be used?

If the school had records he *had* to get them.

Members of the Clandestine Services of the CIA have many friends . . . associates. Among them are a fair proportion of prostitutes, illegal moneychangers, drug peddlers . . . and burglars. This kind of association goes with the work.

So it was that Jean Goutier, a burglar of considerable skill, found himself being offered a great deal of money by a stranger to perform a very menial task, for a man of his standing in the profession.

Demeaning though it was, Goutier accepted the job because it *was* a lot of money and he *would* be paid in advance. Of course, the stranger had explained, if he took the money and failed to do the job he might never work again; it was possible he might never breathe again. But that was fair.

Nobody makes a school burglar-proof . . . not in Switzerland. The safe was old. He opened it and found what he was looking for: a file containing lists of girls' names going back over the years. He placed the file on the floor and methodically photographed the pages with the special camera the stranger had given him.

He met the stranger again, returned the camera to him, and expressed the sincere hope that he might be able to help him on some future occasion.

In his office Settler looked at the prints. Right back from 1935. Girls' names.

He checked for the names of the research chief's daughter and the hijacker's. He found them. They were underlined. Rapidly he turned over the prints, and found lists of girls' names going back through the years. Jesus H. Christ! Some of the most influential names in politics and industry in Western Europe and America were underlined.

He turned over more prints. Then he saw it!

It couldn't be. *It mustn't be!*

Christ! She was the President-elect's wife now!

Cathy Jackson. *And her name was underlined!*

He knew what he had to do. Maybe it was her and maybe it

was another Cathy Jackson. And maybe it didn't matter anyway. The names might only be targets, not all successful operations. But until he found out he wasn't going to let it go any further. He owed it to John Hurst.

That afternoon Settler dictated his report to the chief of the Western European Division of the CIA. Attached was a typewritten list of the girls' names. But Cathy Jackson was not among them.

He put one copy of the report in his pocket, then he told his secretary he would be away for a few days in Frankfurt. No, he didn't want a flight reservation, he was going to drive. He'd contact her when he could; he might be moving around. He gave her a secretive smile and she understood. It was that kind of business.

His trip to Washington was going to be a secret . . . between him and his old friend Hurst. And Jim Settler hadn't forgotten that, although the President's power might be limited in all kinds of ways, he could still reward his friends for services rendered. Promotion to Langley or a position in the White House. Who could tell?

CHAPTER
TWENTY-THREE

President Hurst was tired.

After the Inauguration, there had been the post-Inauguration lunch, then two hours of standing, watching the parade. After that, the series of eight Inaugural Night parties he and Cathy had to attend. A heavy day, made more exhausting by the air of veiled hostility he felt from many of the people as he moved amongst them.

Nothing had been said. Not much anyway. The bearded young kid standing outside as he left the lunch holding a placard: REMEMBER MCCARTHY. And the state governor, clutching a glass as he swayed unsteadily on his feet, smiling viciously: "You going over the top first, Mr. President?"

John Hurst was glad it was all over. So was Cathy. She had resolved not to say anything about the photographs until the Inaugural proceedings were finished. Two more days of receptions! She wondered how she was going to hold out. The tension already showed in her face.

They got back to the White House at 1:30 A.M. and went straight to the bedroom. At 1:59 A.M. he smiled at Cathy as she clambered wearily into bed. "Only two more days and you can relax . . . and I can get down to real work. It'll be like a holiday compared to this." She returned his smile with an effort and sank back into the bed, gratefully shutting her eyes. It was easier to hide her feelings that way. He turned to switch off the lights, and the telephone rang. He reached for the receiver.

"Mr. President?"

"Yes."

"I'm sorry to disturb you but we have Party Leader Lensky on the Hot Line from Moscow. He says it is urgent he speak to you immediately."

Hurst flung himself out of bed. "What's that?" he shouted.

Cathy raised herself on one elbow and listened apprehensively.

"Lensky . . . from Moscow, Mr. President."

"I'll be right with you," he said brusquely.

"Who was that?" Cathy asked as he grabbed his robe.

"Lensky. From Moscow."

Cathy's eyes widened. "What does he want?"

"I hate to think," he answered over his shoulder as he went through the door.

All kinds of fears flooded Cathy's head. For one desperate moment she thought Lensky's call might be connected with the letter from Anette. She dismissed the idea. There could not possibly be any connection.

While President Hurst raced to the Oval Office, two thoughts flashed through his mind. One, that Secretary Lensky was the first Russian leader to speak English fluently—to enable him to understand the Western mind better. Russian translations could never accurately reflect the nuances and subtleties of the original English, he claimed. At Lensky's request, the recently revised Hot Line Agreement had included the installation of a voice capability, in addition to the encoded teleprinter system already operating. Accordingly, this facility had been built into both satellite links—the American Intelsat system and the Russian Molniya II system.

The other thought was the one which alarmed him. The revised agreement had *not* changed the understanding that the Hot Line would only be used in times of emergency.

In the Oval Office, an aide handed him the receiver.

"President Hurst," he said into the phone.

Speaking in heavily accented but clear English the Russian leader began. "Good morning, Mr. President. I am glad your Inauguration celebrations kept to schedule. My advisors assured me you are a most punctilious man, and would be back in the White House by 2:00 A.M. your time. My regret is that our first conversation should have to be of such a disagreeable nature."

The President tensed. The line was crystal clear. Lensky's voice could have been in the same room.

"I have to inform you," Lensky continued, "that precisely five minutes"—there was a pause—"and forty seconds ago, the forces of the Warsaw Pact launched a defensive attack against NATO forces in Western Europe."

"A *what?*"

"A defensive attack," Lensky repeated, unperturbed, and continued. "Only after the most careful considerations of all possible consequences did we decide we had no alternative but to take this action to defend the territorial integrity and chosen way of life of our allies in Eastern Europe."

The President kept listening while he hurriedly scribbled a note and handed it to the aide: *Summon meeting NSC immediately—include Joint Chiefs of Staff.*

"It is clear to us that under your leadership America is determined to threaten the sovereignty of our allies in Eastern Europe.

"We have moved to protect them against your planned aggression. You have given us no choice. . . ."

The President knew it was not the time to take issue with the twisted polemics of Communist propaganda, but he could contain himself no longer. "Who the hell do you think is going to believe that!" he interrupted angrily.

"All the peace-loving nations of the world, Mr. President," Lensky answered calmly, then added caustically, "Read your own speeches, Mr. President, and you will understand that you have been provoking this European war."

The President bit back his anger.

Lensky's voice droned on. He was obviously reading from a prepared text:

"Mr. President, before you undertake some precipitate and unwise action, there are a number of essential facts you must know. Firstly, on the Central Front we are using nerve gas. An area of fifty miles by ten miles deep has already been saturated and our troops are occupying it. I tell you this because there will be a state of great confusion at the front at present. It will be several hours before your intelligence assesses the precise nature and strength of our attack.

"However, it is vital *you* know immediately—before you decide on any action—the gas is one of the milder varieties available to us. It does not kill; its effect is short-term. There will be a few deaths. Some people are particularly vulnerable to the effects of the gas. But that is nothing compared to the hundreds of thousands who would have died if we had launched a nuclear or even a conventional attack."

The President beckoned to the aide who was on another telephone frantically trying to contact members of the NSC. He passed him a second note: *Get an expert on chemical warfare to attend meeting.*

Lensky was going on:

"The second thing you must be clear about, Mr. President, is that if you use nuclear weapons against our forces in Western Europe or against our supply lines and bases in Eastern Europe, we shall retaliate instantly. A deluge of missiles, already targeted, will descend on NATO forces in Europe, including Great Britain. The responsibility for millions of casualties, including civilians, will be *yours and yours alone.*"

Lensky paused to give full impact to his words. Then said: "That is not a threat, Mr. President, it is a certainty. I hope you believe me."

"I hear your words," the President replied.

"I am glad, Mr. President. Because at this precise moment, my ambassadors are communicating the same information to the heads of state of all NATO countries. I think they will be as concerned as we are to save their people from catastrophe."

The President scribbled another note and handed it to the aide: *Get Supreme Allied Commander Europe, based Casteau, Belgium, on phone immediately. Get some more help in here!*

Lensky was still talking: "Finally, Mr. President, and most vital of all. I would urge you not to contemplate a nuclear first strike against the Soviet Union itself. Your advisors will tell you we can absorb such a strike. Even if it is directed against our nuclear-missile installations, we can retaliate with enough force to destroy your population centers.

"The fate of the world is in your hands, Mr. President. Act wisely. The lives of millions depend on your decision."

There was a high-pitched buzz, then silence.

The President sat back and closed his eyes for a second. "Who've you contacted?" he asked the aide.

"I've got Joint Chief of Staff General Preston. He's at home getting hold of an expert on chemical warfare. He'll be right over. Some of the others are still on the town celebrating your inauguration, sir."

"Where's Secretary of Defense Synton?"

The aide grimaced. "I just spoke to his wife at home. She doesn't know where the hell he is. Says she had a headache and left him at a party at the Mayflower Hotel. I've got people looking."

"Who haven't you contacted?"

"Secretary of State . . ."

"I'll handle him," the President cut in, and reached for the phone. Chief Aide John Watson bustled in, a flush on his normally pallid face. "What's going on?" he asked breathlessly.

The President looked up. "We've got a war on our hands," he answered flatly.

Watson went bug-eyed. "A war?"

"That's right," the President replied. "You remember. One of those old-fashioned things that couldn't happen anymore . . . to America."

When Lensky put the telephone down on President Hurst the Inaugural Night party at the Sheraton-Park was in full swing. A dozen big-name celebrities from Hollywood, sports, and music mingled with fat cats, party moguls, academics, journalists, and the hopefuls—the seekers after top-level jobs. The hell with the President; it was party time!

When Jane and Peterson entered the ballroom late, the noise from the revelers was deafening. The traffic jams had made party-hopping almost impossible but they'd managed to take in the Mayflower, the Kennedy Center spectacular, and the Corcoran Gallery. The Sheraton-Park was to be their last stop.

Jane looked around and spotted comedian Herti Artman surrounded by a group of hilariously laughing people. Herti had put in a lot of sweat fund-raising for Hurst.

Jane was grateful for his help.

She really was.

She was grateful to anyone who had helped Hurst. More than they would ever know.

But throughout the celebrations her excitement and sense of achievement had been tempered by the knowledge of what was yet to be done. The King was in position, but for the checkmate, the Queen had still to be moved.

She touched Peterson's hand. "Get me a drink, Ed; I'll be over there with the mob around Herti."

Peterson made his way unsteadily to the bar. He'd been matching Jane drink for drink. He wished he hadn't; the room was swimming and the messages from his brain telling his feet where to put themselves were getting fouled up somewhere along the line. He changed direction, found the men's room and, leaning over a basin, splashed cold water over his face. For a few minutes he stood breathing deeply, then summoning all his powers of concentration, set out determinedly for the bar. He made it and ordered a vodka and tonic for Jane and a straight tonic for himself.

A heavy arm fell on his shoulder. He jerked around to see Harry Gaunt slumped over the bar, glaring up at him with bloodshot eyes.

"You conniving sonofabitch," Gaunt spluttered.

Peterson did a double take, then realized Gaunt was drunk, very drunk. He had a right to be: he'd just lost a forty-thousand-a-year job as a White House staffer for the ex-President.

"What's that supposed to mean?" Peterson said, removing the arm from his shoulder.

"It means your man Hurst won the election on a low-down, goddamn trick, that's what, buddy." He thrust his face close to Peterson.

"For chrissake, what the hell are you talking about?" Peterson glanced impatiently toward the bartender.

"The Volodin letter . . . that's what I'm talking about. He should never have come out with it. Not on television."

Peterson felt his anger rising. "Why the hell not? He had hard evidence. A copy of the original letter."

Gaunt gave him a leery look. "You goddamn liar. The President only got news of it himself the morning of the debate. And you say you had a copy! Bullshit! The most you had was a tip-off . . . most likely from some smart-ass at the CIA."

"I tell you Hurst had a copy of the letter," Peterson answered heatedly. "I should know, for chrissake. My wife translated it from the Russian."

"She translated it? You lying sonofabitch! That letter was in Ukrainian. Not Russian!"

"You're drunk," Peterson snapped as he picked up the drinks from the bar.

He found Jane, her head thrown back, laughing at one of Herti's jokes. He caught her eye and signaled her to join him on the edge of the crowd.

"The Volodin letter," he said. "What language was it in?"

Jane stroked his cheek affectionately. "What's gotten into you, Ed? Asking a crazy question like that."

"I said, *what language was it in?*" He raised his voice and squeezed her arm so it hurt.

Jane stalled. "What language do you think, Ed?"

He squeezed her arm tighter. "*You* tell me."

She wrenched her arm free and stared at him coldly. "You've

had too much to drink, Ed. If you can't enjoy yourself decently, go home and get sober. I'll see you later."

The hotel manager came up hurriedly and whispered in Jane's ear. "Telephone for you, Mrs. Peterson. The White House. They say it's urgent."

Jane followed the manager up to his office. She knew what the call was. She'd attend to Peterson later. Meantime, she had to take his mind off that letter.

She took the call and hurried back to him. "Ed, I have to go right over to the White House. Don't tell anyone for god's sake or there'll be a stampede, but I've just heard the Russians have attacked in Europe. You'd better get around to the press bureau. I doubt if they even know!"

She left him standing. The way she always did.

Ed Peterson was a newspaperman and this was the biggest news of his life. Through the haze of alcohol his one clear thought was that he must get to the press bureau. Fast.

Jane would have to be left until later. Then he would force himself out of his obsession for her and take a clear look at the evidence. Force some truth out of her. Something . . .

CHAPTER
TWENTY-FOUR

3:30 A.M. One and a half hours after the Russian attack in Europe. The key members of the National Security Council had gathered in the Situation Room in the basement of the West Wing of the White House. The Vice President and the Director of the CIA were still to be located.

President Hurst had quickly briefed each on arrival so they could take whatever immediate action was necessary to alert their staff.

They dispersed themselves around the long conference table, their faces drawn, a mixture of tiredness and that special alertness which comes with tension and danger. The President spoke calmly.

"The Warsaw Pact, and that means Russia, has attacked NATO. You all know Lensky spoke to me on the phone. He told me what cards he's holding and how he's going to play them. We have to decide how much he means and how much he's bluffing. Before we do that, we need to take a hard look at our own cards so we know our own strengths and weaknesses. It's a kind of poker, only the stakes are so high you'd have to be sick in mind to call it a game."

Hurst gestured to an aide who was standing by a tape recorder. "First let's hear what Lensky said."

The machine replayed Lensky's telephone message to the President. The men assembled at the meeting listened in uneasy silence.

When the tape ended Hurst spoke: "Colonel Watz," he said, "as a specialist in chemical warfare, precisely how effective is this nerve gas? And do we have any answer to it?"

The colonel, a slightly built man with receding sandy hair, hunched his shoulders and looked at the President uncomfortably over the rims of his spectacles. "As a tactical weapon, Mr. President, it can be highly effective. Particularly when used against an enemy who has limited defenses against it and a low capability to retaliate with similar weapons."

"Are you suggesting we are in that position?" the President barked.

The colonel glanced nervously at General Preston, Chairman of the Joint Chiefs of Staff. "In my opinion, yes, Mr. President. We have known for years the Russians have been allocating substantial resources to research and development of these weapons. We know they are way ahead of us. We also know the Warsaw Pact has integrated special units within their battle groups to deliver chemical weapons. We have no effective defense against them."

The President looked at him grimly. "You mean we have been irresponsible enough to let a potential enemy get ahead of us in *any* area which could threaten our security?"

The colonel gave a slight shrug of his hunched shoulders. "I think the general is in a better position to answer than I am, Mr. President."

"I'm asking you, Colonel."

"Well, sir, my opinion, and it is only an opinion, is that we have been mesmerized by our greater technological know-how. We have concentrated our resources on weapons where we can apply that superiority. Increasing the sophistication of our missile systems, aircraft, and so on. The Russians are aware of this and have concentrated more on weapons where pure technology is not so important."

The President turned to Jimmy Ruddell, his newly appointed National Security Advisor. "What about it, Jimmy?"

Ruddell was well known for his outspoken criticism of the defense and foreign policies pursued by previous administrations. An alumnus of Harvard, he had not sought political office, preferring to use the neutrality of his professorship to attack what he called the "oversimplistic" attitude of America to defense and foreign affairs. He had made many enemies. Congress would never have approved his appointment to a cabinet post—which was why the President had brought him in as a member of the White House staff, saying, "You've knocked the system long enough, Jimmy, it's time you proved you can do better."

Ruddell leaned his huge frame forward in his chair—for there was a stark contrast between the precision and subtlety of his mind and the rugged exterior of his six-feet-four body—and spoke in a soft, relaxed voice. "The colonel is correct, but the problem goes deeper. Over the past ten years or so the Russians have been heavily outspending us on scientific research with weapon potential. Most of this expenditure will be unproductive. But they are gambling that one day they will come up with something which will make all other weapons obsolete."

Gray-haired Secretary of Defense John Synton fidgeted with a pencil while Ruddell spoke. He banged it down on the table. "Mr. President. We are supposed to be discussing a war which is *here* and *now* and with today's weapons. I suggest we don't waste any more time talking about past mistakes and future possibilities. We have crucial decisions to make . . . and fast."

The President looked at him coldly. "I appreciate your impatience, John. However, before we decide what we are going to do, we have to assess how far the Russians are prepared to go. Is this the big gamble? Or, because they think they'll have greater comparative strength in five, ten years' time, will they back down if we call their bluff? To answer these questions we *have* to look at the past and the future." He turned again to Ruddell. "What do you think? Is this the big one?"

"Maybe. Probably. Two things make it probably. One: They're ahead of us in conventional weapons and they match us in both strategic and tactical nuclear weapons. Overall, therefore, they have an edge on us. They're ready and we are not.

"Two: They can't afford to wait for a possible breakthrough with some new weapon. Their people have had just about all they can take sacrificing their living standards for military expenditure. They're getting sick of the whole Party setup. And the new leaders in the Politburo know it. Lensky's only way out is to unite the country by war. It's a technique as old as history itself. The Russian people have been psyched into a state of mind so they'll respond to a call to their patriotism without giving a thought to the consequences."

"General," the President addressed General Paul Preston, Chairman of the Joint Chiefs of Staff, "how do you see the situation?"

Paul Preston, tall, dark-haired, could have been ten years younger than his fifty-six years. He glanced at the notes on his pad and rose to his feet. He spoke in a monotone and without emotion. He could have been reading a store's inventory.

"First, I have already taken the following action:

"The Strategic Air Command is on full alert. That covers all strategic bombers and land-based intercontinental ballistic missile squadrons.

"A general alert has gone out to all services throughout the world. All leave has been canceled.

"Additional elements of the Second Fleet (Atlantic), including our new Trident ballistic missile submarines and other Cruise missile submarines and surface vessels, have been ordered to stations closer to Western Europe and Russia.

"Dual-based army units at present in the U.S. have been ordered to prepare for airlift to Europe. So have divisions stationed in the U.S. with equipment already deployed in Europe.

"Our ten reserve divisions have been alerted to prepare for shipment to Europe. And mobilization of nine divisions and twenty independent brigades of the National Guard will commence 0800 hours today.

"Regarding the discussion so far," the general continued. "Theoretically, certain of our combat units undergo chemical warfare training. However, I would be misleading you to say it has a high priority. In any event no amount of training can be effective against a surprise attack with nerve gas."

The President held up his hand. "Just one moment." He turned to Colonel Watz. "Colonel, would you leave us now. Stay within call. We may need you later."

When the colonel left the room the President said quietly: "Okay, gentlemen, short of a nuclear strike, what do we do?"

"You'd better have the facts," began General Preston. "In northern and central Germany, NATO has thirty-one divisions, thirty-three if we include the two French divisions stationed in West Germany. Against this possible total of thirty-three divisions, the Warsaw Pact has sixty-nine divisions.

"The Russians will rely on high concentrations of armored forces and artillery to achieve a quick breakthrough. They're well equipped to do this. They have twenty thousand tanks on the northern and central fronts against NATO's seven thousand. They have double our number of artillery pieces."

Charles Pearce, Secretary of State, burst out with astonishment, "You mean they outnumber us over two to one in tanks and artillery. That's crazy!"

"It may be crazy, Charlie, but it's true," the general replied. "NATO has always assumed a *defensive* stance. Greater emphasis on antitank weapons. That's where we have superiority in quality—more lethal and precision-guided ammunition, higher rates of firepower. I can give you the exact figures."

"Okay, General," the President said, "forget the statistics. Can the Russians break through?"

"Yes. Our whole defense strategy rests on the assumption that the high concentration of our precision-guided antitank weapons would counter Russian tank superiority. The Russians have torn that strategy apart by using gas. The weapons are there, only the men to use them might just as well be dead! There's no way we can stop them on the frontier or anywhere near it.

"What happens now depends on reinforcements. The Russians have short land communications. It will take us twice as long to match their strength; to mobilize our manpower and sea-lift the equipment across the Atlantic. And the Russian navy might just have something to say about that! From Murmansk they can position nearly 150 anti-shipping submarines across our Atlantic sea route before we have one ship out of port."

"General, don't you think you're painting an overly negative picture?" the Secretary of State cut in sarcastically.

"I'm not in the painting business, Charles. My business is facts. So let's have some more. Airpower. I'd say on the central and northern fronts we bat about even. The Russians outnumber us two to one. But with our new generation fighters—the F15, F16, and A-10—we score on quality. There's just one snag. We're short of airfields. If the Russians go for them in a big way we could be in deep trouble."

"Aren't you forgetting our capability to reinforce our airpower in Europe, General?" the Secretary of Defense interrupted impatiently.

"No, sir, I'm not forgetting that. But there's no percentage in flying in a couple of thousand planes if they've nowhere to land and no support facilities. If we overcrowd our airfields, it will reduce their operational efficiency. And the planes on the ground will be sitting targets for the Soviets."

The President listened with growing concern while the general spoke. It was hardly news to him that NATO was highly vulnerable to a surprise attack. But hearing the facts spelled out like this was something else again. He said, "Short of using nuclear weapons, what action do you recommend, General?"

"There's only one possibility of stopping the Russians, Mr. President, and not much of a one at that. So far they've done all the right things. Especially attacking on our most vulnerable front, the north German front. The territory is flat. Hard to defend. Ideal for mobile armored forces. And the shortest route to allied capitals. It's also the weakest defended front."

The President interrupted. "You've got to be joking, General. Are you saying our most vulnerable front is the weakest defended!"

"Just that, Mr. President. It's defended by British, West German, Belgian, and Dutch forces plus a couple of American divisions—the Northern Army Group. There's nothing wrong with the troops. Trouble is, they all use different weapons—ammunition, vehicles, guns, planes, the lot—even different communication systems. They can't communicate with each other. Some can't even communicate directly with NATO's central command."

"You mean they can't fight as an integrated force?"

"Right, Mr. President."

"While the Warsaw Pact countries have standardized weapons, communications, and a unified command?"

"Right, again."

"Go on, General. Now what?"

"Our main line of defense is along the Weser River, about a third the way into western Germany. Only I doubt if we can hold it. Our plans relied on blunting a Soviet attack on the frontier before they got to the river. That hasn't happened. Now our best bet is to pull back our American divisions on the southern front in Germany into France and move them up north to stop the Russians on the French border with Belgium."

"We'll have to clear that with the French," the Secretary of State interposed. "We can't even move on their territory without their permission."

"Charlie," the President addressed the Secretary of State, "get on the phone right now and have your people find out where the French stand. Are they going to fight with us or not, and can we move our forces in their territory?"

"Yes, sir." The Secretary of State got up and moved to a phone.

"General," the President asked again, "in a word, what are our chances?"

"Bad."

"That's what I thought. And you all heard what Lensky said. We use nuclear weapons against the Warsaw Pact countries, *they* retaliate killing millions of civilians in Western Europe."

"That's a political decision, Mr. President. I'm here to give you a military assessment. And there's a very good military reason why we shouldn't use them. If we do, they can wipe out just about every airfield we've got in Europe, including Britain, without putting one aircraft in the air. They've deployed nearly a thousand intermediate- and medium-range nuclear ballistic missiles in Europe—including the land-mobile SS-20."

"General," the Secretary of Defense interrupted, "surely we could hit back with carrier-based aircraft and submarine-launched missiles?"

"We could. We can devastate Eastern Europe. The Soviets do the same to Western Europe. And their ground troops can still walk in and occupy Western Europe—what's left of it."

The President turned to National Security Advisor Ruddell. "What do you say, Jimmy?"

"The general's right, Mr. President. "We can't defend Europe with nuclear weapons. It's an illusion . . . always has been. Something the politicians use to fool the people. Unfortunately it doesn't fool the Russians."

"How about a limited nuclear strike against military targets inside Russia?" the President suggested. "Do you think that might convince them they've pushed their luck too far in Europe?"

"I doubt it," Ruddell replied. "My guess is we'd get it right back—with interest. Lensky means exactly what he says. He doesn't want a nuclear war but he's prepared to have one if he has to."

"Are we?" replied Hurst. He looked around the conference table. No one could tell him the answer to this question.

"Okay, gentlemen," he said sharply. "We try to hold them in Europe and, God willing, we'll stop them there."

CHAPTER
TWENTY-FIVE

The headline screamed: SOVIETS ATTACK NATO, but there was no hard information and no details; the situation was fluid.

In the taxi taking him downtown from Dulles, CIA agent Jim Settler threw the newspaper onto the empty seat beside him.

He felt a curious sense of unreality. From the well-ordered peacefulness of Geneva to this calm, seemingly uncaring normality of Washington. Yet three thousand miles away millions of men were engaged in a war of unprecedented violence; using weapons of a complexity and destructiveness difficult to comprehend, many untried in actual combat.

"You come from Europe?" the Washington cab driver asked him.

"Yeah."

"Just made it in time, huh?"

"Guess so."

"Those goddamn commies got it coming real good. They tread on our toes, we bite their heads off. Yes, sir, we sure do. *Right off*."

"You bet," Settler agreed, staring out of the window.

American people, American automobiles.

Everything normal.

No rushing; no excitement.

Nothing to show that in this capital city decisions were being taken—had already been taken—deciding the fate of hundreds of millions in Europe. And America.

And here in Washington, in the White House where these decisions were being made, was Cathy Jackson.

If she was under Russian influence!

She mustn't be!

But she was on the list!

He checked into the Hotel Ebbitt. He had selected it deliberately. It was central, near the White House, comfortable but not plushy. Not the kind of place he would meet people he didn't want to meet. People from the CIA. Not yet.

First he had to see the President. . . .

Urgently.

Two hours later Settler was still trying to get through to the White House. The ashtray beside the telephone was brimming with half-smoked butts, his unpacked suitcase on the bed where he had thrown it the minute he had gotten into the room.

The line to the White House was jammed.

Once again he dialed.

"Hold please," a voice said.

He held long enough to smoke another cigarette.

A click. "Yes."

"The President's appointment secretary. It's urgent," he said.

Another long silence.

"Yes?" A male voice. Abrupt.

"My name is Jim Settler," he spoke slowly and deliberately. "I am a *personal* friend of President Hurst and a member of the Central Intelligence Agency. I have just gotten in from Switzerland and I have vital information which I *must* convey *personally* and *immediately* to the President. It affects national security. Vitally."

A pause. "You'll have to tell me more. I can't go to the President on that."

"You will have to. *You must.*" He bit the words off.

"Mr. Settler, why not come through your Director if it's that important?"

"It's personal. Very personal. It concerns the President's wife."

Another pause. "Where can I contact you, Mr. Settler?"

He gave his address, then added, "I'd be grateful if you don't tell them at Langley I'm here. Don't want them crashing in on me. It's *very* personal to the President. *He* wouldn't want them to know. You understand?"

"I understand."

"Fine. When will I hear from you?"

"How about after the war?" The voice was caustic.

"Far too late. Does that give you some idea how urgent my business is?"

"I'll do what I can. I can't promise *anything*. The President is busy." He said this straight, no sarcasm—so straight Settler wanted to laugh.

The secretary put the phone down. Settler *had* got through to him. But there wasn't a chance in hell of fixing an appointment. He pressed a button on the console. He would try the President's wife. Maybe she knew the guy if he was a personal friend. And he'd said it concerned her.

In the hotel, Settler lit a cigarette and drummed his fingers on the small table. There had to be some way for him to bypass this hang-up and get to the President.

Four cigarettes later it hit him. For god's sake! He could get through to the White House by the back entrance. His old friend Ed Peterson was married to one of the President's counselors.

His call to Peterson at the press bureau was short, but enough to stress the urgency of the matter. Peterson agreed to meet him for a late lunch in an hour's time.

A couple of minutes later the telephone rang. He grabbed it.

The voice announced the President's wife was on the line. He hadn't expected this.

"Mr. Settler, I understand you have a problem. Can *I* help? The President may not be free for days." Cathy's voice was pleasant, friendly.

Settler thought fast. "That's most kind of you, Mrs. Hurst, but it's a strictly military matter. If you could contact the President and ask if he could take time out just to give me a call, I'd be mighty grateful."

Settler waited for it. "But, Mr. Settler. I thought it concerned *me.*"

"You!" he exclaimed and forced a laugh. "Not unless you understand missile systems, Mrs. Hurst. I guess there must have been a misunderstanding. Thanks anyway . . . and if you *could* contact your husband . . ."

"I'll see what I can do." She sounded disconcerted. The line went dead.

The restaurant was half full when Peterson slumped down wearily at the table. The wire services from Europe had been hot all through the night and he hadn't seen a bed for over thirty hours. The situation in Europe was still unclear—"fluid" was the way NATO spokesmen described it. There had been no time to even think about the episode with Jane at the Inaugural Ball. But with Settler's call saying he had to see him concerning the President and national security, his doubts and fears had flooded to the surface. Settler was CIA. Why did he want to see him?

Urgently.

About the President.

He was filled with a sense of foreboding.

Settler came through the glass door, looked around, saw him....

"How's the Company, Jim?" Peterson said with false jocularity as they shook hands. "Looks like some of your branches over there might be out of business."

"For Christ's sake, Ed, keep your voice down." Settler's own voice was tight. "And there's no time for jokes. I need your help."

He kept his voice low as he explained to Peterson that he wanted to see the President and why. He stopped talking twice. Once when the attractive young waitress came to take their order and again when the blond-haired young man with a fawn coat over one arm and TWA bag in his hand passed them to sit at the next table.

"Can you get your wife to help me?" he ended.

Peterson was troubled, his thoughts confused. His immense relief that Settler's business had nothing to do with Jane was mixed with the appalling suggestion that it was the President's wife who was involved with the Russians. But somehow he was still reluctant to help Settler through Jane. But how could he explain about his wife at a time like this? He had nothing concrete, nothing he could discuss with another man. And Settler was sitting on something which *had* to reach the President. Urgently.

He rubbed his forehead wearily and let out a long breath. "Okay, Jim. But if Jane says she can't help, then you'll have to go through official channels."

Settler remained silent while the blond-haired man from the next table brushed against him on his way out. "I know but—"

"Hold it," Peterson cut him off. "That guy's left his bag." He grabbed the TWA bag and weaved through the tables. He reached the street just in time to see the man getting into the back of a waiting cab. He dashed to the window and banged on it as the cab pulled away. Evidently the young man didn't see or hear him; he was calmly staring in front of him.

Peterson returned to the restaurant and handed the bag to the pretty waitress. "The blond fellow sitting next to us left it," he said. She thanked him and he rejoined Settler.

As he sat down he saw the waitress taking the bag to the service entrance.

That was the last he saw of her.

It was the last anyone saw of her.

The force of the explosion threw Peterson from his seat and sent him crashing across the tables. For a second he lost consciousness as his body thudded against the wall sending every ounce of air in his lungs shooting out from his mouth and nostrils. His ears were ringing but he could hear the screams coming from the smoke- and dust-filled room. There was a weight on his lap. Dazed, he looked down. It was a woman's arm, severed at the shoulder, a wedding ring on one finger. He threw it from him, overcome with revulsion.

Settler was crawling nearer, blood streaming from a jagged gash down one cheek. "How are you?" he gasped.

Peterson moved his arms, his legs. "Bruised, I guess, nothing worse."

"Listen to me"—Settler was shouting to make himself heard above the cries for help, the shrieks of agony filling the restaurant—"that bomb was meant for *me*. The guy with the bag followed me in. Right. There must have been a good fifty pounds of explosive in that bag. Enough to smear us all over the walls if it had detonated by the table."

A man careened out of the dust, hands clasped over his bleeding face. "I'm blind. Oh god, I'm blind," he yelled, and crashed into the wall behind them.

Peterson tried to get to his feet to help but Settler grabbed him by the shoulder. "Leave him, for chrissake," he shouted, "you can't put his eyes back."

Peterson sank down again, still dazed.

"I've got to hide," said Settler. "Can I use your apartment?"

Peterson nodded and reached for his keys while Settler took out a small black notebook, tore a sheet from it, and scribbled:

Add name Cathy Jackson—President's wife—to list of names on my report. He signed the note.

Taking the CIA report from his coat pocket, Settler tucked it, together with the note, down Peterson's inside pocket.

"You hearing me?" he asked in a shout.

Peterson nodded.

"If anything happens to me take what I've put in your pocket to the CIA. Got it?"

"Got it."

"And notify your wife I'm in your apartment. I must see her. Okay? She's not to tell anyone. *Especially not the President's wife or I'll have another bomb up my ass.*"

"What do you mean?" said Peterson, startled.

"For chrissake. . . . She's the only person who knew where I was. *Who knew I was even in the goddamn country.* Except for the appointments secretary and he's sure as hell not in this kind of business." He waved toward the shattered room and its occupants.

Settler took Peterson's apartment key and disappeared into the smoke and dust.

Peterson clambered to his feet and staggered through the debris, the moaning, and the screams. There were bodies and bits of bodies everywhere. His feet suddenly went from under him and he crashed to the floor. He put his hands to the ground to get up and felt the wet mass which used to be a head. The vomit spewed from his mouth as he stumbled blindly out into the street.

The sidewalk was jammed. Some standing, some lying on the ground—the wounded. Some helping, some screaming, some just plain curious. In the distance the noise of sirens approaching.

Peterson ignored the offers of help and started toward his office. It was only a block away. His head was whirling. Buildings, automobiles, people zoomed in and out of focus. He blundered into people but mostly they quickly stepped aside. He didn't look nice. His suit was torn, covered in dust, across his midriff was a bright splotch of blood where the arm had been. His hands were covered with the mess from the head on the floor.

Peterson's secretary screamed when she saw him.

He spoke a lot more steadily than he felt. "It's okay. All on the outside. I'm *not* hurt. Now calm down, will you, and get me some coffee."

She hurried out, glad to get away.

He went to the washroom and attempted to make himself look half-decent, except for the blood on his suit. He felt better . . . but not good.

She was staring at him as she handed him the coffee. "The bomb," he said, "you heard it?"

"We heard a bang, Mr. Peterson." Her eyes went wide. "A bomb!"

"Yeah. I'll tell you about it later. Right now, get my wife on the phone. Right away . . . and keep people out of my office. Okay?"

"You're sure you're all right?" she said.

"Never felt better," he answered with a thin smile.

He sat at his desk and sipped the hot coffee. It was comforting.
. . . Everything else was insane.

The President's wife! Cathy!

Settler *had* to be right. Who else could have known he was in
the country and where he was? The bomb *had* been meant for
him. It couldn't have been chance—some maniac doing his thing.

His secretary came through with the call. He picked up the
phone and explained the situation to Jane. She answered, very
cool and relaxed, "Don't worry, Ed, I'll take care of things. I'll
speak to the President as soon as I can, then I'll get right over
and see Settler. You take it easy for a while . . . till you've gotten
over the shock, then come on home. . . . We're going to need that
report he gave you."

Jane put down the telephone feeling a mixture of anger and
relief.

Anger because the KGB agent detailed to kill Peterson had
failed. The bomb had *not* been meant for Settler. After receiving
the call at the Sheraton-Park summoning her to the White House,
she had telephoned Sakov. They had agreed no further chances
could be taken. Peterson might, or might not, follow up on her
purported Ukrainian translation, but dead there wouldn't be any
doubt as to what he would do. Nothing.

Relief because she had known nothing of Settler or his information and if either had reached the President or Langley. . . .

Now she knew exactly what to do.

Jim Settler had been nervously pacing Peterson's apartment for
nearly an hour. The bourbon he had drunk had done little to
steady his nerves. He knew what he should have done. Head for
Langley the second after he wasn't killed by that bomb. The
situation was too hot to keep under wraps any longer.

As soon as Peterson arrived, he'd grab the report back from
him and go straight to the Director of the CIA.

The key sounded in the lock and Jane came in. She looked
concerned. "Are you all right, Mr. Settler? Ed's told me what
happened."

"I'm okay," he answered.

"You had a fantastically lucky escape."

"That's right. . . . Some others weren't so lucky."

"I know," she spoke with downcast eyes, taking a seat on the sofa. Settler sat on the low chair across the table from her.

"Mr. Settler, I'd like to get straight to the point," she said. "I've spoken to the President and he'll fit you in for a few minutes tomorrow morning. There is, however, one thing which particularly worries him. While he appreciates your consideration in coming to see him directly, he is anxious not to be seen to be going behind the back of one of his agencies."

Jane hesitated as if embarrassed. "What I'm saying is, has he your categorical assurance that no one else in the CIA has any knowledge of this matter you wish to discuss?"

"Absolutely not. There are no records, no conversations. Nothing to compromise direct discussions between the President and myself."

"Well, that's fine, Mr. Settler. Now if you'll excuse me for a few minutes I'll go and freshen up. Fix yourself another drink." She beamed at him.

In the bedroom she opened her bag and took out the package. She had stopped at a pay phone after leaving the White House and called Sakov. The code name for the package was "the ticket for the Kennedy Stadium," and her message to Sakov had been brief. "Deliver the ticket for the Kennedy Stadium *outside* my apartment *immediately*. Aunt May doesn't get out often. It will do her good."

When she arrived at the apartment she had parked, then stood on the sidewalk. A car drove up with two men inside. One man got out. He said, "I have the ticket for the Kennedy Stadium."

"Aunt May doesn't get out often. It will do her good," she had replied, and the man gave her the package. Then she had instructed him to park near the apartment and wait with his companion. She might need them later.

She opened the package on the bed: a six-inch metal tube about half an inch in diameter, open at one end and closed at the other, with a small protruding button an inch from the closed end: also a small yellow box containing two pills and two capsules.

In the bathroom she dissolved the two pills in a glass of water and drank it. She tidied her hair. Then, with the tube in one hand and the two capsules in the other, she went back to Settler.

He rose as she came in, and she walked over to stand in front of him. "Have you ever seen one of these?" she asked, showing him the tube. He bent over to look more closely. She pressed the button on the tube with her thumb and there was a faint plop, like a small stone dropping into water. She stepped back, crushed one of the capsules under her own nose, and inhaled deeply. Then she watched Settler.

Settler stared at her with mild surprise for a few seconds, then suddenly he went into convulsions. His face contorted with pain. He clutched his chest in agony as he gasped for breath, his skin becoming deathly pale. He sank to his knees, then collapsed, sprawled out on the floor.

All the outward signs of a massive heart attack.

Which it was.

The tube had contained a glass capsule of prussic acid. On pressing the button she had activated a firing device which crushed the capsule and sent the contents spraying out into Settler's face like a fine vapor.

The effect had been almost instantaneous. The vapor had entered his lungs and passed into his blood vessels, contracting them exactly as in a natural cardiac arrest.

Jane looked down at the dead body. She knew that very soon his blood vessels would return to normal. There would be nothing to show the heart attack had been artificially induced. The pills she had taken and the capsule she had inhaled were an antidote for herself in case she accidentally inhaled any of the vapor.

She went to the phone and dialed Emergency. An ambulance would soon be on its way.

She would behave as any normal citizen under the circumstances.

Ed Peterson felt unsteady on his legs as he got out of the cab. It was only one floor up but he took the elevator to the apartment. He opened the door and shouted, "Hi, honey."

"In here," said Jane.

He came into the living room and saw Settler's body out on the floor.

"He's dead," said Jane.

"Oh my god! ... How?"

Jane shook her head. "I don't know. I was talking to him and he just collapsed. I've called Emergency. I think his heart went."

He moved to Settler and bent down to look at him. Jane stood opposite across from the dead body. He looked up into her face. The light behind her caught a few strands of her hair at the side, highlighting them.

It was like another explosion, this time *inside* his head. All the repressed doubts and suspicions of the past erupted into his consciousness, triggered by that recollection of the light he had seen in her hair the instant before Deniskin's death. Thoughts whirled in his head like the debris from the bomb in the restaurant. He stared at her as the bits fell into place. Unanswered questions . . . but all pointing . . .

Deniskin!

The two attempts on his life.

Hurst's luck!

The Ukrainian she couldn't translate, but did.

The bomb. It had been meant for *him!*

Now Settler! The timing was too perfect. Unnatural. Like everything else which had happened.

Peterson knew.

He was staring at her, wide-eyed.

"You," he began, shocked by his realization.

The movement of her arm and the blow on the side of his neck came too swiftly for him. He fell forward, grabbing at her, clutching desperately at her skirt, trying to drag her down, too dazed to do anything else.

She pulled away from him. For a split second he saw the skirt, ripped off in his hands, then her foot crashed into his face, once, twice . . . then blackness. For him. But Jane kept on kicking—his head, his body—her eyes wild in a frenzy of revenge.

The body she'd had to please.

So often and in so many different ways.

Hatred blazed from her eyes as her foot crashed again and again into his groin.

Finally she stopped.

Looking down at the face covered in blood. She spat, "Pig."

Breathing heavily, she went into the bathroom and found the special combination-lock briefcase in the cupboard. She turned the dials rapidly, flipped open the lid, and removed the automatic with its silencer, screwing them firmly together as she returned to the living room.

She stood over him, the gun pointing at his head.

The doorbell rang.

Momentarily she was confused, lost in the orgasm of her savage revenge. Then she grasped the unconscious Peterson under the arms and dragged him through to the bedroom. Hastily she put on a housecoat and pushed the gun under the bedcover.

In the living room she took a quick look around to see if everything was in order, then went down the hall and opened the door.

"Where is he?" asked one of the ambulance men as they pushed in.

She pointed down the hall and followed them through.

The large black-haired ambulance man with the bull-neck took one experienced look at the dilated pupils of Settler's eyes and the cyanosed color of his face. "He's gone," he said. "How long since it happened?"

"About fifteen minutes."

"He's gone," the man repeated. "No chance." He addressed the second man. "Sam, go fetch the stretcher," then turned to Jane once more. "I'm sorry. Did your husband have a heart condition?"

"He's not my husband," Jane answered impatiently.

"Ah! A friend?"

Jane hesitated. She had to behave normally.

"He was a friend of my husband." She was straining to keep the tension out of her voice. "I just came in and he started to say something to me. Then he fell over. I called you at once. . . ."

In the bedroom Peterson was coming to. Through a mist of pain he could hear the murmur of voices from the other room. . . .

The ambulance man had taken out a pack of Luckies. "Mind if I smoke, ma'am?"

"Go ahead."

"Help yourself," He held the pack toward her.

"I don't . . . thanks."

"That's sensible." He stepped over Settler's body, sat on the sofa, and lit the Lucky. "People die in some pretty embarrassing places. Believe me, I know! Particularly when it's sudden. But I ought to tell you, it goes in the records . . . where they die."

"I don't follow you," said Jane.

The ambulance man took a long drag on his cigarette and blew smoke down at the carpet. It curled up and drifted across Settler's blue face.

Jane stared hard at him without speaking.

The ambulance man stared right back at her, his large head on one side. "Only trying to be helpful, Mrs. . . . You'd be surprised the trouble it causes, people dying in the wrong places. Know what I mean?"

"Yes. Now will you get the body out of here." Jane tried not to shout.

"Surely. Just as soon as Sam gets himself up here with the stretcher, we'll get him out."

In the bedroom Peterson was on his feet. He got to the window, opened it. He winced with the pain as he levered himself onto the sill, his legs dangling outside. When his feet hit the grass below it felt like his flesh was being torn away from his bones.

The man Sam had arrived with the stretcher. They placed Settler on it with elaborate and unnecessary care.

Respect for the dead.

When all men were equal.

The *only* time they are.

As Jane saw them out, the ambulance man was repeating, "Now, just remember what I said. It shows in the records."

Jane shut the door swiftly and dashed into the bedroom. She saw the open window. She grabbed the gun from under the bedcover.

When she looked out of the window, the men were sliding the stretcher into the ambulance.

There was no sign of Peterson.

"Who the hell are you?" The ambulance man was staring down at Peterson crouched low between the seat and the dashboard. He saw Peterson's blood-soaked face and let out a low whistle. "Holy Moses! Where have *you* been?"

Peterson spoke with breathless urgency. "I'm Ed Peterson. That man has been murdered and..."

"Geez," the ambulance man shook his head slowly. "I smelled something wrong with that dame."

"Get me out of here, fast," urged Peterson. "You're in danger too." He was grasping at the man's arm and squeezing with all his strength. "Understand, I *mean* it. You've got to get me to the CIA."

The ambulance man looked at him and believed him. "Get in the back," he snapped. "Give me room to get in."

Painfully Peterson crawled between the seats into the space behind the stretcher racks. The ambulance man heaved his bulky frame in and slammed the door. "Get moving, Sam," he said. "This one needs more help than the dead one."

Jane saw the ambulance shoot by as she came out of the house.

It clicked. She knew where Peterson was—the only place he could hide. She hurried over to the parked Chevrolet where the two men had been patiently waiting. "He's in that ambulance. Get him. Alive. . . . No witnesses."

The tires screeched as the KGB Chevrolet leaped forward. In the back the driver's companion lifted up the seat and removed the M60 machine gun from its hidden housing. He lowered the window.

The ambulance lurched around the corner from O into Thirteenth Street. "Okay, Sam," said his bull-necked buddy. "Take it easy now or we'll all be hospitalized." Sam slowed at the intersection with N, then cruised down to turn into M.

The Chevrolet pulled out to overtake, the barrel of the M60 six inches through the open window. A couple of yards past and a hundred rounds poured into the front tires and engine of the ambulance. The whole front of the vehicle suddenly sank. The hood flew open and bits of metal and glass shot into the air. The ambulance careened to a shuddering stop a few feet up on the sidewalk.

What happened next was too quick for the few pedestrians and passing drivers to recall clearly.

The man flung the M60 onto the seat and leaped out, an automatic in his hand. He wrenched open the ambulance door and shot the bull-necked man through the forehead before he had time to do more than turn toward him in amazement. Sam was slumped over the steering wheel, too dazed to move. The bullet from the automatic went clear through his head.

Peterson had been flung against the back of the driver's seat. On his knees he saw the man grab bull-neck's collar and heave him onto the street. Next he saw the automatic pointing at his head, then the weapon thudded onto his head and there was darkness.

Five seconds later his body had been hauled over the seat, dragged the few yards to the Chevrolet, and bundled onto the backseat. He lay unconscious on the floor of the car, a foot on his throat, a gun at his head.

He came to in a small basement room bare except for a bed and two metal chairs.

Sakov gave a slight smile at Peterson's battered and blood-covered body. "Well, well, you are in a mess, my friend," he said. "But you mustn't complain. You have caused us rather a lot of trouble."

Peterson rolled his head slowly toward the voice.

Sakov reached inside Peterson's pocket and removed Settler's report and his scribbled note. He glanced at them quickly, then grunted with satisfaction. Another man entered, a hypodermic in one hand. Peterson was too numb to feel the needle plunging into his arm.

Peterson was in the basement of a secluded old country house in Maryland not more than four miles from downtown Washington.

Amongst the other six recent arrivals at the house were Carl and Anette. As Peterson slipped into total oblivion they were passing time upstairs in a back room playing chess. Neither Carl nor Anette had been out of the house since their arrival in America six days previously.

The remaining four new arrivals were Sakov, the cultural attaché from the Russian Embassy and two chauffeurs from the same place. Sakov was in charge of operations, the attaché was a cipher expert and manned the two-way radio in touch with Moscow, while the two chauffeurs did odd jobs. Like killing ambulance drivers and flying helicopters.

They had moved into the house on the day before the President's inauguration. The day before the war had started and the Russian Embassy was closed.

Now the six new arrivals were waiting. Waiting for the war in Europe to end. Waiting for *their* war.

CHAPTER
TWENTY-SIX

Five days had passed since the Russian whirlwind attack against Western Europe had started. President John Hurst sat silent, his face grim and drawn. Across the table from him General Preston sat down as he finished his summary of the disastrous military situation.

Regardless of losses, Russian battle groups had stormed across the flat plains of northern Germany. For years these troops had trained to refine even further the *blitzkrieg* tactics developed by the Germans. Exhausted and depleted battle groups were not reinforced. They were withdrawn from the attack and replaced by fresh units so the remorseless attack could continue unabated.

Even the nights brought no respite for the outnumbered and disorganized NATO defenders. The Russians had perfected night-fighting tactics to maintain the momentum of their onslaught around the clock.

And what the NATO commanders had known and feared for so long proved true. The Russians had river-crossing equipment of unsurpassed engineering ingenuity. For the Russians, rivers were not barriers.

Now, in the north, the Russian forces were sweeping down from Holland into Belgium toward the French frontier.

In the south, a second attack had been launched and penetrated as far as Frankfurt.

The air battle had been one of attrition. The Russians had lost over a thousand aircraft. But they had achieved their objective: the almost total destruction of NATO's limited airfields.

The American forces from the south, struggling to move north to defend the French frontier, had encountered impossible obstacles. In Germany, elements of six Russian airborne divisions had been dropped to blow up bridges, railways, and supply depots. While, in France, the eurocommunists had called a strike, disrupting all communication systems.

"What now?" the President said to General Preston.

The general's face was bitter. "Now, Mr. President? . . . Now we get slaughtered." He was silent for a moment, then said, "Nearly two and a half thousand years ago a Roman named Vegetius said, 'Let him who desires peace prepare for war.' We should have listened."

An aide standing near the President spoke, his face tense. "Mr. President, Lensky's on the Hot Line from Moscow."

As the President took the phone the eyes of those around him were riveted on his face. Lensky spoke to the point and without emotion.

"Mr. President, you have lost the war in Europe. You have no choice but to accept our terms 'for peace.' "

"Terms!" The President's exclamation rang through the room.

Lensky continued. "Yes, Mr. President. If you do not, your forces will be destroyed and thousands of civilians will die with them. When your American divisions eventually meet our armies in the north, they will have no chance. They will arrive piecemeal. Our armies will be ready, waiting to annihilate them. Would your own people ever forgive you for sacrificing three hundred thousand American troops in Europe . . . to prolong by a few days a war you have already lost?"

"What are these terms?"

"Considering your situation, most generous terms," Lensky replied. "The Soviet government has no wish to cause unnecessary suffering. We seek to protect our own security, that is all. Our only demand is that all NATO forces lay down their arms and return to their homes.

"If you agree to these terms we will allow your American forces to proceed unimpeded to the French ports of Le Havre, Cherbourg, and Brest. From there you can evacuate them to America. They will, of course, leave all their equipment, including aircraft, intact in Europe. Those are our terms, Mr. President. They are not negotiable. You have one hour to give me your answer. If you do not accept, the fighting will continue until you are forced to submit. In that event I cannot guarantee when we will return your prisoners of war. It will take many years to rebuild the devastation in Europe! Good-bye, Mr. President."

The President put the phone down and turned wearily to face

those around him. "Lensky says we're licked in Europe. He's offered peace terms," he said flatly.

"And if we don't accept them?" said General Preston.

"We have to accept. Our only other option is to launch a nuclear strike against Russia. And you all know what that would mean. . . ."

CHAPTER
TWENTY-SEVEN

Peterson opened his eyes and saw the clean white ceiling of the small room. He blinked several times and shook his head to try to clear the muzziness. He sat upright in the bed and his hand went to his face. It was sore, encrusted with dried blood. He turned and saw the man standing by the bed watching him.

"Who the hell are you?" said Peterson. His tongue felt thick.

"My name is Colonel Sakov and I am an officer of the KBG," Sakov answered.

Peterson's brain began to function. "And . . ." he began, then abruptly fell silent. It was hard to say it. Hard to admit to himself he had been duped by Jane. *Hurtful* to acknowledge that her supposed love for him had been no more than a calculated piece of acting. *Humiliating* to know that his love for her had been used as a successful weapon against him. He forced himself to say it. ". . . And Jane has been working for you all along."

"Yes."

"The bitch!" Peterson's mixed emotions crystalized into anger.

"No, Mr. Peterson," Sakov answered quietly. "A very courageous woman."

"The hell she is. She's a goddamn traitor."

"She is a *Russian*, Mr. Peterson. An illegal agent working for her own country. Not a traitor."

"She can't be," Peterson protested. "She's as American as I am."

Sakov shook his head. "No. Russian. Why should I lie?"

Peterson sank back into the bed, trying to take in the truth. His hand went to his face again and he felt the bristly beard. His eyes shot to Sakov. "How long have I been here?"

"Four days. You have been under heavy sedation."

"Four days! What's happened in Europe? The war?"

"Finished. Over. NATO has been defeated."

Peterson stared at him in disbelief. "It can't be . . . so quick?"

"The fighting was a mere formality," Sakov replied with a shrug. "You lost that war years ago by doing too little to match the buildup of our forces in Europe."

There was a knock on the door and a man came in carrying a tray with two cups of steaming black coffee. Sakov passed one to Peterson and took the other himself. Then he pulled up one of the metal chairs and sat beside the bed.

Peterson sipped the coffee, trying to think.

The war in Europe.

And Cathy!

Jane in the White House!

What the hell was going on?

Peterson looked at Sakov, who was watching him keenly.

"You are possibly asking yourself why we haven't killed you," said Sakov. "Well, there is no longer any need for that, Mr. Peterson. In fact, I hope you will stay alive." He glanced at his wristwatch. "We will learn shortly if any of your people are going to survive. It will be their choice, Mr. Peterson."

"Just what are you doing?" said Peterson. "You and the KGB and Jane?"

"Jane Mantel is working to save the lives of millions of Americans," said Sakov calmly.

"Tell that to the marines!"

"We intend telling it to *all* the American people."

"Tell what, for chrissake? Stop talking in riddles," Peterson replied angrily.

"It is all quite simple, Mr. Peterson. We intend capturing your country without a war."

"You're out of your mind. . . . Capture us without a war? If you make one move against this country, we'll wipe you out."

"The voice of the average American, eh, Mr. Peterson?"

"You bet your sweet life it is."

"Be careful not to underestimate the intelligence of your people, Mr. Peterson. Let me give you the facts. We Russians have been preparing to defend ourselves against a nuclear holocaust for twenty years. Most of us will survive. Most Americans will die. And then there is Western Europe. We now occupy it . . . *and* its industry. We will emerge from nuclear war immeasurably stronger than you. Millions of American men, women, and children will have died for nothing. It is to stop such a futile waste of human life that Jane Mantel is working."

"Bullshit," Peterson said. "What can she do? The President and the military make the decisions. They'll press the button even if it means the whole goddamn world goes up in the air. That's the way they think and that's what they'll do."

"Precisely, Mr. Peterson. And that is why we propose letting the American people make their own decision. To live . . . or to die for nothing."

"How in hell's name . . . ?"

"We shall do it. A highly esteemed and respected American will explain the situation directly to your people. More important, it will be the voice of someone you all know puts humanitarian considerations above the blind, unthinking, Pavlovian responses of your military commanders. It will be the voice of a woman!"

CHAPTER
TWENTY-EIGHT

Cathy had heard nothing more of Anette or Carl since the morning of the Inauguration. Five days of unending torment followed.

Her emotions were mixed, confused, frightening. Again and again she examined the photographs, hoping desperately to detect some flaw which would show them to be fakes. Why that would make things less frightening, she couldn't sort out. If they were fakes, it could only have been done with some sinister intent. But what could be more sinister than this! Had their *deaths* been faked? Why should they reappear on the day of her husband's inauguration—from Russia! And even more terrifying; why the day before the attack on Western Europe?

There was no way she could even begin to understand. Nor could she find anything to indicate the photographs were not genuine.

She knew she must tell her husband. First she had put it off until after his inauguration. Then had come the war in Europe and the awful dilemma of whether to tell him, or wait until the crisis was over.

Jane had come to see her the morning after the Russian attack and she had blurted everything out and shown her the photographs. Jane had remained silent for several minutes and Cathy knew her cool, calculating mind was methodically examining the situation from every angle. Finally she had said:

"No, the President mustn't be told yet. He has to make some incredibly difficult decisions. Nothing must distract him. Anyway," Jane had added with a faint smile, "whatever these two ghosts of yours want, they'll make contact before they *do* anything. Why else would they have sent *you* the photographs to prove their existence?"

Jane had been right. She must wait for a more opportune time to tell her husband. Now that moment had arrived. The President had fallen into an exhausted sleep after days of tension relieved only by catnaps. It was early afternoon. As she paced the sitting room, clasping the envelope of photographs, she heard the faint sounds of her husband stirring in the bedroom suite next door. He came into the sitting room wearing a robe.

He smiled when he saw her. "Come over here and let me have a look at you. It's been so long, I've forgotten what the good things in life look like." She moved to him. He put his arms around her and looked into her face. Then his expression clouded as he saw the paleness of her skin, the dark rings around her eyes, the hollowness of her cheeks. He searched her face anxiously for a moment. "What is it, Cathy? What's wrong?"

Cathy's voice trembled as she fought to keep control of herself. "I have something very serious to tell you, John. Something that happened when I was a girl in Switzerland." She forced herself to look into his eyes.

Hurst remained silent for a moment holding her gaze, then he smiled. "What in the name of hell could be so serious about Switzerland that you have to tell me at a time like this?" He pulled her tight against him.

"I had an illegitimate baby," Cathy said flatly.

His arms fell from her and he looked at her in stunned silence. When he spoke his voice was hard. "Why have you never told me before?"

Cathy moved to a chair and sat down wearily. "It's a long story...." she began.

"I don't give a damn if it's a long story. Tell me ... all of it," Hurst snapped.

In a flat, empty voice she told him, not once meeting his eyes. "Can you ever forgive me?" she ended, looking up into his face with pleading eyes.

"Right now it doesn't matter a damn whether I forgive you or not. I want to know what those two, Carl and Anette, are doing here in Washington." He stood over her and said harshly. "Give me the photographs."

He looked at them quickly. "You're sure they're genuine?" he asked.

"As certain as I can be," Cathy answered. "I'd swear it's Carl. I can't be sure about Anette.... It could be. But the photograph of all my things ... they were mine."

Hurst pulled up a chair and sat facing her. "Now, listen to me.

I want you to go over every detail you can remember of your stay in Europe. Everything. No matter how personal or trivial."

Cathy closed her eyes, desperately trying to concentrate, projecting herself back to the day she had arrived at L'École de Lystre, so long ago. She began to talk. "The first day we had a lecture by the headmistress. Susan said—"

"Susan? Susan who?"

"Susan? She was . . ." Cathy stopped. An expression of horror crept over her face. "Oh my god," she whispered. "Susan was the only close friend . . . the only American who knew I was pregnant. Carl told me not to tell anyone. But I did tell Susan . . . and I told Carl I had told her. I can still see the look on his face. . . ."

Cathy was silent. At last she said, her voice trembling, "Susan committed suicide the day before she was to return to the States. She jumped out of a fourth-floor window. She was the most happy-go-lucky girl I've ever known. Oh my god, John. Do you understand? Maybe I killed her."

"For the moment that's pure supposition," Hurst said coldly. "I want more facts."

But Cathy wasn't listening. Her mind raced ahead, the pieces of a nightmare falling into place with terrifying clarity. Carl, always so kind and considerate—or was it calculation and conspiracy?

She said, "I thought Carl was wonderful—he could always fix things. Like me getting back late. Taking days off." She paused. "My god! I've just remembered. My form mistress actually encouraged me to spend a day alone with a man she knew nothing about. And L'École de Lystre was supposed to be the strictest finishing school in Switzerland! Do you realize what I'm saying?" Her voice rose in panic.

"Carl and the school were in cahoots. That's pretty obvious. Keep talking . . . *all* the details," Hurst persisted, ignoring her distress.

Cathy forced herself to go on. "Susan tried to warn me about Carl—the way he singled me out when we first met, knew my taste in art . . . knew how to arrange everything. Even," she added with an empty laugh, "how to get me pregnant though I was taking the Pill."

For an instant Hurst's face was bitter. "The birth," he said, "was it normal? No complications?"

"None."

Hurst was thoughful for a moment, then he said, "Tell me

exactly what happened when you were ill before the plane crash."

"I got terrible pains . . . shortly after takeoff. I . . ."

"Hold on a minute," Hurst cut in. "Did you eat anything unusual before takeoff?"

"No . . . only a tranquilizer. I didn't want it, but Carl and Hans insisted."

"Hans?"

"Sort of a personal manservant. He took care of Carl's arrangements. And mine. He's the one who removed all the personal things in the photographs before he forwarded my baggage. And I thought he was such a dear old thing. He'd been a prisoner of war."

"Whose? Whose prisoner?"

"The Russians."

They looked at each other.

"Go on," the President said grimly. "The pains."

"Terrible pains. We diverted to Munich. I was rushed to a private hospital and operated on for a burst appendix."

"What happened then?"

"Nothing. I was ill for quite a while . . . weeks. Then Hans told me about the crash."

Hurst got to his feet. "What this means for you and me, Cathy, we'll talk about later. Meantime, there are more important things to worry about. I want you to write down the names, the positions and occupations of everyone you remember meeting while you were in Europe. Addresses too if you can. And descriptions. Height, build, coloring—anything which might help identify them. I'll be in my study. Let me have the list the minute you're through."

Cathy rose and took Hurst's arm. "Please, John . . ." Her eyes were pleading.

"For god's sake, *leave* it for now, Cathy. We're in the middle of a world disaster and now you tell me the KGB have got their claws into you. Isn't that enough for me to be dealing with!"

Hurst took the photographs and letters and went into his study.

He made two telephone calls—one to Chief Aide John Watson.

"John, get the Directors of the FBI and the CIA over to my study. I don't care what they're doing. Get them. Now."

The other call was to Dr. Lance Stenburg, Cathy's personal

physician. "Lance, I want some information . . . in the strictest confidence."

"Yes, sir," the doctor murmured.

"Would it be possible while operating for peritonitis to deliberately interfere with the Fallopian tubes? Causing a permanent blockage and consequent sterility?"

There was a silence. The doctor was fully familiar with the medical history of the President's wife. "Mr. President," he answered, "on the understanding you appreciate I am not a gynecologist, I would say the answer is probably yes."

"Would an examination of the patient, several years later, reveal the fact that the sterilization had been deliberate?"

"Most probably not," the doctor answered.

"Thanks, Lance. That's all I wanted to know."

The President sat thinking in the quiet study, trying to figure things out. Ansil Crowther, CIA Director, and Art Solan, FBI chief, arrived. They listened while he spelled out the facts—all of them.

"Ansil," the President asked, "is it possible the whole thing in Switzerland could have been set up by the Russians?"

"Sure. It's *possible*. Her father an influential American politician. They'd figure there was a good chance she'd end up married to some guy who carried a lot of clout." He smiled wryly. "I guess they were right, Mr. President."

"But the odds! Why go to so much trouble on a bet that long?"

"The Russians don't gamble, Mr. President; they play the averages. Like the guy who propositions every woman he meets—the more he tries, the more he scores. Same with the Russians. They try to get leverage on as many influential people as they can. Just in case—in case one day it comes in useful. Americans in Europe are soft targets. A lot of ways they can be compromised. The KGB has thousands of files in Moscow full of embarrassing information. Most of it will never be used. Now and again they get lucky."

"I can't figure out what they're after," the President replied. "How do they think they're going to use my wife?"

"Mr. President," the FBI chief shifted uneasily in his chair as he spoke. "Mind if I ask a very personal question? I don't want to. Only it's important."

"Go ahead," answered the President.

"This Anette, she's your wife's only child. Do you think she might have some emotional hold over Mrs. Hurst? And—" He hesitated, changed position again as he braced himself to continue. "I have to ask this, Mr. President. Is it conceivable that *Carl Heindrick* has any hold over her? First love. Impressionable age. That kind of thing."

"Don't worry, Art. I know you're only doing your duty. These questions have to be asked," the President reassured him. "I've been asking them myself waiting for you to get here. Apart from not being able to have children Cathy's never shown signs of stress or unhappiness. But whether there's something way below the surface—some pull she isn't aware of herself—I couldn't say."

"Thank you, Mr. President."

"Right." The President became brusque. "Now let's fix the action. What we do know for sure is it's no coincidence the two of them are over here right now. With the Russians nothing is coincidence. Ansil, I want you to check all you can on the European end. I realize it's going to be difficult, especially now. Do what you can. Mrs. Hurst is preparing a list of all the information she can remember."

"It won't be easy, Mr. President," Ansil replied. "Our whole European setup has fallen apart. Agents are pulling out fast as they can. They're quitting Switzerland and Austria too. The Russians are moving in."

"You've still got some good men." The President's face was set.

"Sure."

"Use them."

"Art," he continued, "you find these two, Carl and Anette. Here." He pushed the photographs across the desk. "The last was taken recently. Find them."

"Mr. President," the CIA chief spoke, "may I suggest we do one other thing. Whatever the Russians have on their minds, chances are their next move will be to contact Mrs. Hurst again. It goes without saying she'll inform you the minute they do. But if you'll excuse me saying it, sir, your wife's emotions are being kicked around. I think her mail and telephone calls should be monitored. With her permission, of course, Mr. President," he added hurriedly.

"I'll speak to my wife. Meantime, Art, you make the necessary arrangements."

Art nodded.

The door opened and Cathy came in, holding several pieces of paper. The two men rose to their feet and acknowledged her greeting. There was a moment of embarrassment broken by the President. "You got it all down?"

"All I can remember," Cathy replied, and handed the papers to him. The President passed them to the FBI chief. "You and Ansil sort out the information you need between you. I don't have to tell you this is top secret. As top secret as you can get. And I want results. Fast."

They left carrying Cathy's papers, the photographs, and the letter. The President turned to Cathy.

"One other thing. What about your outside engagements?"

"I've already canceled most of them. They seemed frivolous at a time like this. Except for the American League of Freedom tomorrow."

The President winced. "I'd forgotten. Ironic, isn't it. I'm billed to speak to the American League of Freedom a few days after presiding over the enslavement of half of Europe. Kinda sick."

"Nobody expects you to keep the engagement. Obviously, you can't leave the White House at a time like this. That's why Jane feels it's even more important someone speaks to them."

"Jane?"

"Yes. Jane. You've forgotten. She's chairman of the committee."

The President sighed. "It seems a thousand years ago. B.C. Before communism." He smiled thinly.

Cathy continued, "She asked me yesterday if I would speak in your place. Keep the flag flying. Help reassure people. It made sense so I said I would."

"Makes a lot of sense," the President agreed. "Will Jane be there?"

"Yes."

"Okay, then. Only stick close to your security. Make it easy for them. If you don't lose them, they can't lose you. That's the way it operates."

The only good news to come the President's way the next day was the withdrawal of American troops to French ports. It was proceeding smoothly. The Russians were keeping their word and standing off; moving into French territory slowly, after the Americans left. Having taken Paris, the Russians stopped advancing, a hundred miles from the ports.

The rest of the news was bad. The worst came at nine o'clock that evening when he met with CIA chief Ansil Crowther.

Crowther sounded glum. "It's happened too fast. Since our Moscow embassy was closed down when the war in Europe started, the whole goddamn intelligence apparatus's been fouled up. Would you believe we've only just found out the Russians began secretly evacuating essential personnel from their cities six days ago!"

"Yeah, I'd believe it. Shows how carefully they planned this whole thing. Afraid we'd panic into a nuclear strike."

"Looks like they're still scared," the CIA chief continued. "You know the Kama River Truck Plant. The biggest truck plant in the world and stuck plumb in the middle of nowhere. Cost over seven billion dollars—including an estimated billion worth of machinery we helped finance."

The President nodded.

"The big joke *was*—they didn't have enough roads to put that many trucks on. Well . . . they've found them. The roads in and out of Western Europe are jammed with Russian trucks. Their forces don't need supplies. There's enough food, gasoline, you name it, in the countries they've occupied. Those trucks are full of Russian civilians! Valuable people—scientists, managers, administrators, university professors—the kind of people you don't want to lose. A column of trucks drives into a town. These people get out. Split up. Find a house. They present the owner with a letter from the Russian Occupation Authorities ordering them to house and feed them. And who goes back to Russia in those trucks? The same kind of people from Western Europe. They are being rounded up and shipped back to Russia."

The President had risen and was walking back and forth across the office. Finally he stopped and turned to the CIA chief, speaking his thoughts aloud. "If they're scared we'll hit them with a nuclear strike, it's good insurance to have their own valuable people, as well as half their army, in Western Europe. We would have to wipe out millions of our friends to get at them. Right?"

"Right."

"And if we hit Russia we kill the intellectual elite of Western Europe. They've got them as hostages. Right?"

"Right," the CIA chief agreed again.

The President returned to his desk and sat silent for several minutes, deep in thought. Suddenly he crashed his fist to the desk. "My god! There's another possibility. Maybe Lensky's been fooling all along. He's been busting his gut to convince us he doesn't want a nuclear war. Suppose he *does* want one. . . . He's in the strongest position he'll ever be to start one."

"Jesus! You could be right. Maybe Lensky's psyched us into figuring this whole thing round the wrong way." The CIA chief stared at the President.

"At that meeting of the NSC tomorrow morning, we take measures to meet every contingency we can figure," the President said.

The CIA chief gave the President a measured stare. "Including a nuclear strike against this country?" he asked.

"Yeah. Including that."

"The military have had that planned to the smallest detail for a long time."

"I know the military are prepared," the President said, "but the people aren't. When I go on television to the nation tomorrow at noon, my intention *was* to tell people to keep cool, the country was in for a long economic siege, lasting maybe decades. I'm going to change that intention. The people of America have a right to know it could be a lot quicker . . . a lot more violent."

The CIA chief let out a low whistle. "Jesus, Mr. President, you can't do that. You'll have a nationwide panic on your hands. They'll take to the hills, get out of the country, like there really is no tomorrow."

"It depends on how I do it," the President answered. "I want to condition their minds so if some catastrophe does happen, they can absorb it better. The Russians have been preparing their people for this for a long time. In this country the subject has been taboo. There's one thing you can't do in a democracy. Talk about the unthinkable. And history is full of unthinkable 'happenings.' "

"I only hope to god you can do it—without a panic."

"I can. And I will. We'll discuss it at the NSC tomorrow."

Shaking his head, the CIA chief left the President's office.

The President called Chief Aide John Watson into his office. "Alert all senior government officials to stand by for possible evacuation to Fort Ritchie and Mount Weather," he said. "And check on the readiness of the National Airborne Command Boeing at Andrews Air Force Base. No questions. Do it."

In her office, Cathy had finished printing the last of the three-by-five-inch cards she used as prompters for her speeches. She checked her watch—7:25 P.M. There was time to take a shower, get dressed, and have a bite to eat before she made it down to the American League of Freedom venue.

She felt better. The agony of waiting to tell her husband about Carl and Anette was over. It was good to be doing something positive.

Her staff had already left and she walked through the empty office toward the door. She stopped. A plain white envelope lay on the floor a few inches from her shoes. She picked it up. Her name on the front in a handwriting vaguely familiar. She tore it open and her eyes went straight to the signature at the bottom—Anette.

In cold fear she returned to her desk and read the hurriedly written letter.

> Dear Mother,
> Your husband's life is in danger. Carl is trying to stop it, only it will be too late.... Unless you help. We can't use the phone. It's being bugged. We must see you. There is no other way. Your husband will be dead by tomorrow if you don't help. You must slip your security tonight at the American League of Freedom meeting. This is what you must do...

Cathy stopped reading. Her immediate impulse was to take the letter straight to John. The panic gripped her—a terrifying jumble of confused thoughts and conflicting emotions as the guilt and fear she had been living under for days overwhelmed her.

She had thought *she* was in danger. Now it was the President himself. But how could John be killed . . . and by tomorrow? He wasn't going to be away from the White House.

Cathy clutched at her throat and stared in horror at the floor where she had found the letter. It had been pushed under her door by someone *inside* the White House. The appalling realization hit her. The killer must be on the inside!

Trembling with fear, she forced herself to sit down . . . to think. Why had Carl and Anette warned her? Who had delivered their letter? Was it the killer? Why would the killer warn her? None of it made sense. The one thing Cathy understood was that there was a traitor inside the White House who could kill John at any time!

The thought of losing John was too much.

She would do what the letter commanded.

It was the only hope she could see.

Whatever the risk, she would take it.

For John.

And if she acted rightly, with courage and resolution, she might save John and redeem her own past foolishness. For she knew that in some way she herself must have created this horrifying situation.

It was as simple as Anette had instructed her in the letter. The last thing security expect is for their charges to escape from them. . . . Cathy ended her speech. The audience applauded politely. No more. It had not been a good speech. The President's wife was too nervous. Her mind was elsewhere. The speech was disjointed, without authority or conviction.

Cathy descended the rostrum, then backed toward the drapes at the rear of the stage, keeping the applause going with little bows of acknowledgment. She turned abruptly and ducked through the drapes. She saw the door with the bolt on the inside. She slipped the bolt. Across the corridor, the door of the service elevator was open. Carl stood waiting inside. He stepped forward and, taking her arm, guided her swiftly into the elevator.

The night was cold. No one saw the two figures on the roof hurry toward the helicopter which had landed a few minutes before.

Carl bundled Cathy into the helicopter. Inside she looked at him, her face white. Then her arms were grabbed from behind and a hand forced a wet pad over her mouth and nose. Then darkness. The helicopter took off.

Five minutes later Jane stood on the deserted roof with the Chief of Security. They looked around helplessly.

"She must have had it all planned," the chief said. "We had no guard on that door. . . . It was bolted on her side. She must have been shipped off the roof by 'copter. There's no other way."

Jane nodded. "Okay. Now listen," she said urgently. "We've got to keep this under wraps. Clear *everyone* from the rear entrance of the building. Bring round the First Lady's limousine. Tell the management Mrs. Hurst is near collapse from exhaustion and strain. She wants to slip away quietly. She doesn't want anybody to see her. I'll come out surrounded by security and we drive off. And officer, tell your people to keep their mouths shut tight. The President would want it."

One hour later Jane was explaining to the stricken President what had happened. The only consolation in the whole terrible business was that Cathy's "escape" had been kept from the public. He was thankful to Jane for this.

Cathy opened her eyes and saw the large expanse of white ceiling above her. She turned her head and looked around. She was lying on a spacious, high-backed sofa in a modern, elegantly furnished living room. Across from her, sitting quietly in a chair, a young woman was idly flicking over the pages of a magazine.

The woman looked up with a slight smile. "I am Anette, your daughter," she said very calmly, with only a slight trace of a Russian accent.

Cathy's heart stopped.

Nothing could have prepared her for this meeting. This meeting with the girl in the photograph. This meeting with her daughter!

Stealthily, Cathy examined the girl's face. Yes, it was like her own, incredibly similar. The slightly tip-tilted nose, the wide-set blue eyes, the same chestnut brown hair clustered around the pretty young face.

"It's really true then, you weren't killed," Cathy heard herself whisper, afraid she would wake up and find it was a dream, the girl gone.

The girl laughed softly. "No, Mummy . . . you only thought I was killed."

She had used the word *Mummy* like a new and unfamiliar toy to be played with, but there was also something cold and cruel in her voice.

The girl closed the magazine and went on in that same playful tone, but now there was clearly a note of cruel jeering in her voice. "It was only a trick, Mummy . . . to make you think I was dead."

Cathy froze inside. "A trick?" she echoed. "What do you mean?"

"You will be told soon enough." Then the girl's manner changed abruptly and she smiled at Cathy with all the fresh brightness of her youth. "But we don't have to worry about that for now. . . . Aren't you glad to see me?" Eagerly, the girl leaned forward toward Cathy.

Hesitantly, Cathy reached out and touched the girl's hand. Then the yearning and buried grief of all those empty childless years suddenly welled up and overwhelmed her. Cathy flung her arms around her daughter.

Anette jerked back and broke free from her arms. "Don't paw me." She looked at Cathy with disgust. "It's bad enough I have to be here with you; I don't have to let you slobber all over me . . . *Mummy!*"

Cathy looked at her daughter in anguish. "Don't you feel anything for me?" she cried.

Anette tossed the magazine onto the sofa. "Feel?"

"For me . . . *your mother.*"

Anette laughed. "What should I feel for you? A stupid American cow who gets herself impregnated by the first man who takes the trouble to seduce her!"

Cathy's mind was reeling. For a second she almost wished her daughter *had* been killed. Then at least she would have had the memory of her baby and her brief happiness with Carl which she had secretly clung to all those years. This Russian girl horrified her.

"You can't be my daughter," Cathy cried. "You are lying to me. My baby *was* killed."

"It was just a trick. I told you." Anette was looking at her with expressionless eyes.

"I don't believe you," Cathy answered desperately.

"Carl will convince you," the girl snapped. "And you'd better believe him, if you want to save your husband."

At the mention of Carl's name, Cathy caught her breath.

"My husband, the President. Your letter said he was in danger. . . ."

"He is. In great danger."

"For god's sake, tell me. What is it?"

Anette went over to the window and looked out. "It's raining," she said.

"My husband. Tell me!" Cathy shouted at her.

Anette turned to look at Cathy with blank, indifferent eyes. "Carl will tell you."

"Then get Carl. Please. I beg you." Cathy broke down in helpless tears.

In five short minutes Cathy's emotions had been put on the rack and torn apart.

Anette looked at Cathy with distaste. "You are an hysterical old woman, aren't you. My sloppy, sentimental, bourgeois mummy," she added with disgust.

"Get Carl," Cathy implored. "Let me speak to him."

"Very well. If it'll stop your sniveling."

Anette went through a door into an adjoining room. Carl and Sakov sat on tall, plastic-covered kitchen stools drinking black coffee. Above them on the wall was a small television screen and, on the screen, a picture of Cathy in the room next door.

Sakov spoke first. "You did well, comrade," he said to Anette. "You have softened her up very nicely. Soon she will respond to any show of kindness. I have seen it work a hundred times. When you next see her, you will act the part of the most loving daughter any mother could wish for."

Sakov turned to Carl. "And soon, if you play your part properly, we will have the three of you together as one happy family. United to save America from us wicked Russians, eh?"

The two men smiled in complicity.

"Right. Let's get on with it," Sakov said. "Go in and act your part. You have exactly three minutes before I show myself."

Carl checked his watch, then slid off the stool.

Cathy's eyes shot to the door as Carl entered. Despite everything, she couldn't help herself; she was struck once again by his remarkable good looks, enhanced even more by the maturity of years. And the animal magnetism that had engulfed her so long ago when she and Susan had first seen him standing in the café in Switzerland.

But there was none of the old tenderness in Carl's eyes. His voice was hard as he pronounced her name. "Cathy."

Cathy was sitting rigid, her clenched hands grasping the edge of the sofa. Her voice was determined and controlled. "What are you and Anette doing here in Washington? Anette wrote me that John is in danger and you are trying to help. What does it all mean?"

Carl ignored her question. "Don't you think Anette has grown into a fine-looking young woman?" he said.

"She's a monster. And I imagine it's your doing," Cathy replied.

Carl considered her statement for a moment, then said, "She looks like you, but I'll admit her character is different. She has the advantage of good Russian blood."

Cathy's eyes locked with Carl's. "My husband?" she demanded fiercely.

"Ah yes, the President." Carl glanced at his watch. "It's very simple. If you do what we want, he'll live. If you don't, he'll die."

"What . . ."

At that moment the door opened and Sakov came in. Carl jumped to his feet and stood stiffly at attention. Without looking at Cathy, Sakov spoke to Carl. "I will be back in one hour, comrade. Take good care of this woman. You know what we want from her." Then he was gone.

"Who was that? What did he mean? . . . For god's sake, what *do* you want from me!"

Carl moved rapidly to sit on the sofa by Cathy. His hardness had gone and now he was looking at her with earnest anxiety. "Please listen to me very carefully. There are things being planned far more dreadful than you could ever imagine."

Cathy held her breath. Not trusting him. Not knowing what was going on. Not understanding this sudden change in him. But Carl went on as if compelled to confess to her. "First, I want to clear up the past so there's no misunderstanding between us. *Yes,* I am a KGB agent. *Yes,* what I did to you in Switzerland was a KGB plot. So we could use you in the future when the opportunity arose. *Yes,* the deaths of Anette and myself were faked." He broke off, staring at her. "I make no excuses for myself. The intelligence services of the world are at war even when there is military peace. I am a soldier in this war. My work is dirty. War is dirty. But there are limits even in war, crimes too monstrous to be acceptable. That's why I'm speaking to you like this."

Carl glanced at his watch again, then continued hurriedly: "As you know, we have new leaders in the Kremlin. Men who talk of détente but underneath are more ruthless than Stalin. Men who are not willing to wait for the slow disintegration of capitalism as predicted by Marx and others. Men who are prepared to attack your country and destroy it."

Cathy caught her breath.

"Yes, Cathy, attack your country. A nuclear holocaust in which millions of Americans and Russians die. But these new men care nothing for human life. Only the perpetuation of their own power and their own self-aggrandizement. Do you understand what I'm saying?"

"Yes, I understand what you are saying, but not why you are telling me," Cathy said.

"Because it explains what Anette and I are doing here . . . and what it means for you and your husband. We were sent here to trap you. After all, who else could have persuaded you to escape from your own security guards at a time like this?" He smiled

"I can't explain," Carl answered. "But I can swear to you that no harm will come to your husband, if you do what we ask." Then he gripped her arm again. "Remember, it's not only your husband's life that's at stake, it is the lives of millions of people in our two countries. In the name of humanity, you must deliver this speech and prevent this crime!"

Cathy was silent. She understood now what was at stake. But how could she make this decision? If she made this speech the consequences would be incalculable. . . . If she did not, millions might die. But how could she know she wasn't being used, tricked again, and it was all a Russian plot? A monstrous deception. . . .

At last she said, "I want to see Anette."

Carl looked startled. "Why?"

"Because you said your instructions were to be cruel to me. Anette carried out those instructions. You haven't. It doesn't make sense. I don't trust you."

Carl let out a long breath. "Anette had to do what she was told. That man, the one you saw earlier, is a very powerful person in my country. A man to be feared. He was in the room next to this, watching Anette on closed-circuit television. There, see . . ." Carl pointed to a small, round, shining object in the corner of the ceiling. "That is the lens of the camera."

"Why isn't he watching you now?" Cathy challenged.

"Because I am a seasoned officer of the KGB. He trusts me. But Anette is young and inexperienced. She might have been tempted to show you some affection."

"I still want to see her," Cathy persisted.

Carl looked at his watch and made a great show of being worried. "We haven't much time. Please, Cathy, trust me."

Cathy was silent.

"All right. If you insist." Carl went to the door and shouted Anette's name.

A second later Anette flew across the room and flung her arms around Cathy. "Oh, Mother, I'm sorry I was so hateful to you, but I had to do it. Has Carl explained?" She hugged her mother tenderly, her eager eyes searching Cathy's face.

"Yes, Carl has explained. If I can believe him," Cathy said desperately. "I don't know what to believe." She held Anette at arm's length and gazed intently into the girl's apparently loving and innocent young eyes.

"Please do what Carl says, Mother. Then we can see each other again."

The door opened. Sakov came in. Curtly he commanded Anette, "Get out."

With an imploring glance at her mother, Anette ran out.

Sakov spoke to Carl. "Well, has Mrs. Hurst agreed yet?"

"Not yet, comrade, but I think she will deliver the speech," Carl said.

"Think!" Sakov spat out the word.

Carl looked at Cathy, his eyes pleading.

Cathy faced Sakov. "I need time. I don't know if I can believe that even *your* government would do such a terrible thing."

"There is no time, Mrs. Hurst," Sakov snapped. "Have you heard of a small American town called Canton?"

Cathy looked puzzled. "No. Why?"

"It is in Illinois. A small town of two thousand three hundred twenty people," Sakov replied, then walked across the room and picked up the telephone. He spoke a few words in Russian, then turned to Cathy. "In exactly five minutes Canton will cease to exist."

"What do you mean?" Cathy gasped.

"It will be wiped out. No one will survive," Sakov said. "You see, Mrs. Hurst, you leave me no option. I must convince you of the truth of my government's intentions. If I kill two thousand three hundred twenty people you will believe me when I say we are not bluffing."

Cathy's mind reeled. Could it be possible they would do such a terrible thing?

Sakov's voice hardened. "Many more will die before this thing is over."

Something broke in Cathy. She was terrified by this man. "All right, I believe you!"

"I am sorry, Mrs. Hurst," Sakov said. "I cannot stop it now. If I did you would still not be certain we are serious. You must *know*."

He turned to Carl and nodded to the television set in the corner of the room. "Switch it on," he commanded.

Carl moved swiftly to obey.

Minutes passed. They watched the screen in silence. The program was interrupted and Cathy recognized the tense face of the newscaster who came into vision:

"This is an urgent news flash. Reports are coming in of a massive explosion in Canton, Illinois. No details are available. Stay tuned for further . . ." Carl switched off the set.

Sakov turned to Cathy.

"The reason, Mrs. Hurst, was an atomic explosion. We call them suitcase bombs. This one was deposited in the trunk of a car in a used-car lot and detonated by radio on my instructions. There are four more bombs waiting to be detonated on my orders, each in a larger town. I hope now you are thoroughly convinced my government is serious."

Cathy was in torment. All those innocent people dead. She had to stop this terrible man. "For god's sake, no more killing! I believe what you say," she shouted.

"Thank you, Mrs. Hurst," Sakov said, and left the room.

For the rest of that nightmare evening Anette and Carl stayed with Cathy. And despite the terrible cloud which hung over her, as she listened to their talk about Russia and Anette's plans to be a doctor, Cathy had to keep reminding herself this was all real. She was experiencing this with her daughter and her lover. In some weird way she felt they were a family. A family, torn apart, made enemies by fate, yet now conspiring together to prevent the destruction of the world by a demented power menacing both America and Russia.

When it was late, Anette gave Cathy a bedtime drink laced with a sedative. "Good night, Mother," she said. "When this is all over you must come and see us in Russia."

In the kitchen, Carl spoke to Sakov. "So you think she will do it, Comrade Colonel?"

"She will do it."

Carl frowned. "Can we be sure how she will react when the pressure is off and she is back at the White House with her own people? She is a very brave woman underneath."

Sakov smiled slowly. "That is why we have arranged that when she gets back to the White House the pressure will *not* be off her and she will *not* be with her own people. . . ."

It was 8:02 A.M. when Jane Mantel drove through the northwest gate to her office in the White House West Wing. Her black leather briefcase was on the passenger seat beside her. She wanted to be in early to check that there had been no change in the President's plans for the day. The guard called a cheerful good-morning.

In her second-floor office Jane stared out of the window. A pale sun was breaking through. It was going to be a beautiful day. The most beautiful day in her life.

At precisely 8:45 A.M. she picked up her briefcase and walked to the Cabinet Room.

In view of the crisis, the President had called for a full meeting of the NSC. Everyone concerned had to know what was going on.

The room was packed when Jane entered at 8:55 A.M. The Vice President; the Secretaries of State and Defense; the Directors of the Office of Emergency Planning, CIA, and FBI; the Chairman of the Joint Chiefs of Staff; head of the Strategic Air Command, and many others. They were standing in groups, talking in subdued voices, waiting for the President to arrive.

Jane looked around and saw the President's chief aide. She placed her briefcase against the wall just inside the door, and went up to the aide and asked him if he had any news of Cathy. He hadn't. Jane looked solemn and left the room.

At exactly 9:00 A.M. the President entered and went straight to his seat. The meeting began. The President spoke gravely. "I have reasons to believe our country may be in immediate danger. The Russians are evacuating their cities. My wife has disappeared under unusual circumstances. The explosion in Illinois last night was atomic."

A heavy silence filled the room. The President continued: "As you know, I am speaking to the nation on television at noon. Before then we've a lot of ground to cover." He turned to General Preston. "General, we'll start with your situation report on our military state of readiness."

At 10:45 A.M. Jane Mantel was leaving the White House. She turned down Pennsylvania onto New York Avenue. She approached the corner of Ninth Street. A car stopped just ahead. The door opened and Cathy staggered out. She looked bewildered. The car moved away. Jane pulled into its place. She leaned across, opened the passenger door. "Get in. Quick," she ordered.

"Oh, Jane, Jane," Cathy exclaimed as she climbed in and slammed the door.

Jane gunned the car and turned up Ninth.

"Is John all right?" Cathy said.

"Sure. Why not. I've just left him."

"Thank God," Cathy sighed with relief.

As she turned into H Street back toward the White House, Jane took an open envelope from the dash and handed it to Cathy without speaking. A quick glance was all Cathy needed; it was from Anette. "Delivered to you inside the White House?" she asked.

Jane nodded. "It's how I knew when to pick you up. We'll talk about it later. And about what happened to you. Right now, I want you back in the White House without any fuss. There's been no public announcement yet. It's better it stays that way."

They reached the West Sitting Room in the residence at 11:05 A.M. "Sit down," Jane snapped.

Cathy was startled by her changed tone, but nevertheless sat down.

Jane stood over her. "Now, listen to me. I know everything that's happened to you—your escape, your stay with Carl and Anette, *and the speech*. Everything."

Cathy's mind reeled.

"I know because I'm a Russian agent. Do you understand?"

Cathy shook her head. "No. No. I don't understand."

"I am Russian. I am your enemy. Everything was planned. I helped get your husband elected so we could do this. Now do you understand?"

"My husband," Cathy whispered. "Where is he?"

Jane looked at her watch—11:13 A.M. "I'll tell you about your husband in two minutes' time," she said.

Cathy closed her eyes. "Oh god," she moaned.

"God is not going to help you," Jane said through clenched teeth. "The Russians are the only ones who can do that now. Unless you deliver that speech, you know what will happen. Carl has told you."

"But you're Jane, my friend."

Jane raised her arm and slammed the back of her hand across Cathy's face. "Is that friendship?" she hissed.

Cathy reeled under the blow. But now she *did* understand. She blazed with anger. "You traitor," she screamed.

"No. Not a traitor." Jane's face was grim. "A patriot. A Russian patriot."

Cathy rose. *"Sit down,"* Jane commanded. "Remember, the fate of the country is in your hands. If you do anything to stop that speech, you will commit the most monstrous crime in all history."

Cathy gave a terse laugh. "That . . . from *you*."

"Screw your emotions," Jane snapped. "I've work to do. All I want from you is no trouble . . . and the speech."

Jane pulled a small gun from her bag. "Do exactly what I tell you or I'll kill you," she said.

"What's happened to John? Tell me!"

Jane looked at her watch again. "In exactly fifteen seconds he and the rest of your country's leaders will be gassed."

"Gassed." The word was a whisper as Cathy closed her eyes.

"Only temporarily . . . six hours or so," Jane said. "*If* the antidote is given in time."

At that instant in the Cabinet Room the President was in midsentence. . . . A muffled explosion stopped him. The briefcase Jane had left just inside the door hurtled through the air. There was a loud hissing as the gas was pressured through twenty small jets inside the open briefcase. Within seconds the room was filled with gas . . . just as the replica of this room in Moscow had been when the scientists of the KGB had perfected the device.

Inert bodies were strewn across the room. Some fallen forward onto the table, some slumped back in their chairs, some fallen to the ground.

In the West Sitting Room of the residence Jane continued: "Your husband will come to no permanent harm if you do what I say. His life is in your hands. I am the only one who knows the antidote for the gas. Now get on the phone and tell the President's press secretary to get up here. Tell him nothing else."

Cathy moved to obey. She made the call.

"When he gets here," Jane said, "tell him you have heard what's happened to the President. Tell him the President discussed his speech with you last night and you have a copy. And tell him you are going to deliver the speech in place of the President. That it's vital for national security you do. Convince him. . . . You know what's at stake."

The press secretary arrived. At first he hesitated. What authority did he have, et cetera? But now Cathy was fighting for her husband's life . . . and the lives of so many others.

"Are you questioning the judgment of the First Lady?" she said to the press secretary, her eyes blazing.

"No, but . . ."

"Then fix it. If you don't, the President and millions of Americans will die. Do you understand?"

The press secretary did not understand.

But he understood he had no choice.

There was no time to consult.

There was no one to consult with.

At 11:58 A.M. Cathy sat in the President's chair by the fire in the Oval Office.

She was oblivious to all around her.

Except for Jane.

The only one who knew the antidote to save her husband.

Cathy began her telecast, her voice hollow. "Fellow Americans, I regret the President is unable to speak to you at this moment. My reason for taking his place is that the future, perhaps the very existence of our country, is in the balance. What I am about to read to you is an . . . ultimatum . . . your government has received from the government of the Soviet Union. Before I read it, let me make one thing very clear. It is not a hoax. I beg you to believe every word I say. From this point on, I am reading the ultimatum."

Cathy cleared her throat and looked straight into the camera with expressionless eyes. Then she lowered her eyes and began to read.

" 'The government and people of the USSR have no quarrel with the people of America. It is your government which has consistently worked to undermine our country, not you, the American people. We understand this.

" 'On your part, you must understand we will not give in to you. War is now inevitable. In this war it will be you, the people, who will die. Your government, your military commanders, and the privileged rich have taken care to protect themselves. This is why we have arranged for your President's wife to receive and deliver our ultimatum, direct to you, the American people. Had it been left to your government, you would have had no choice. They would have plunged our countries into this war.' "

Cathy paused, choking. She reached for the glass of water, took a sip, and went on:

"I repeat, fellow Americans, I am reading this. Here is the Russian ultimatum: 'The United States will forthwith sign a treaty of friendship with the Soviet Union. Under the terms of this pact, all control of military and security forces will immediately pass to the Soviet Union. We will require your strategic nuclear forces to be dismantled immediately under our direction. . . .' "

Cathy's voice did not break again and she read to the end:

" 'That is our ultimatum. You have until midnight, eastern standard time, to accept our terms. Failure to do so will produce a state of war between our two countries. On the stroke of midnight, we shall saturate your country with nuclear bombs. Over one hundred million of you will die. If you launch a first nuclear strike against us before midnight, it will make no difference. Enough of our nuclear missiles will survive to destroy you. Your military commanders know this.

" 'The Russian people will also suffer. But, *our* government has done all it can to protect them. We have already evacuated our cities. For years we have been building nuclear shelters. Our people are thoroughly trained in civil defense. Your intelligence service knows these facts to be true. Twenty million Russians will die, but America will be destroyed. It is a price our people are prepared to pay for the final solution to our conflict. They do not flinch at the prospect.

"You now know war is the alternative to accepting our terms. The choice is yours. . . .' "

When Cathy finished her speech, everyone stayed quite still, frozen, unable to believe what they had heard.

But she was sitting there. The President's wife. *And she had said it.*

An ultimatum.

Surrender or fight.

Live or die.

Millions of men, women, children.

Cathy's eyes were full of hatred when she looked at Jane, who was standing close by her but just out of camera vision.

Before anyone could move, Jane grabbed Cathy and put a gun to her head. "Stay where you are, everyone," she shouted, "or the First Lady dies."

Holding Cathy tightly, she moved to the door.

Just outside the Oval Office a security man reached for his gun. Jane fired first. The security man took the shot in his chest. He spun around, crashed against the wall, and slithered to the ground. A crimson streak of blood ran down the wall.

They passed three more security men on their way to the helicopter pad on the South Lawn. They all obeyed Cathy's frantic warning: "Don't move. I'm all right."

The helicopter, with false U.S. military markings, came in low and settled on the pad. The KGB man beside the pilot flung open the door. Thirty yards away a White House security man grasped his gun with both hands, taking careful aim. The noise of the shot rang out. The KGB man at the open door of the helicopter grimaced with pain. Cathy screamed.

The Russian pilot reached over the seat, grabbed the M60 machine gun, and rested the barrel on the shoulder of his wounded companion.

"Keep still, comrade," he said, and fired. Thirty yards away, the shattered body of the White House security man was hurled up into the air as if sucked up by a hurricane. His body landed in a bloody heap six yards back.

"Get in." Jane was shoving Cathy up and into the helicopter. She followed quickly and the helicopter rose.

As it swept low over the Ellipse, Cathy screamed at Jane. "The antidote for my husband. For god's sake, you can't let him die."

"He doesn't need an antidote," Jane answered flatly. "I was fooling you. He'll recover in a few hours without any help."

From the rear window of the secluded house in Maryland four miles from downtown Washington, Sakov, Carl, and Anette watched the helicopter landing on the lawn in front of a wooden summer house.

Cathy came out first followed by Jane, pushing her toward the back of the house. Then the two men jumped to the ground and moved swiftly, shoving the wheel-mounted summer house forward and over the helicopter.

"Well done, Anna, well done." Sakov hugged Jane at the door. He turned to smile at Cathy. "And your performance, dear lady, was magnificent."

Cathy stared silently at him.

The two men came in. Sakov pointed to the blood-soaked sleeve of the wounded man. "Bad?"

"No, Comrade Colonel. But you should see the man who did it." He grinned.

"Get it cleaned and dressed," Sakov directed. "We leave as soon as it's dark."

The wounded man went into the kitchen.

"Take her down. Put her in with Peterson," Sakov said to the other man, nodding at Cathy.

Jane followed Sakov into the living room. He poured two stiff vodkas and handed one to her. She tossed it down.

"How are we getting out?" she asked.

"A flight plan has already been filed for a business trip tonight to Miami. We take off from a private airfield twenty miles from here; the helicopter will get us there."

"And?"

"Once near Miami the pilot of the jet will be persuaded to keep going . . . till we hit Cuba. It's only two hundred miles from Miami."

"If the pilot refuses?"

"Not very likely. But we have our own pilot along. He can fly anything."

Jane smiled. Then she grew thoughtful. "Won't the American air defenses be alerted? On the coast?"

"Don't worry, Anna," said Sakov. "By the time the American fighters get anywhere near us we shall be escorted by our own fighters from Cuba . . . flown by good *Soviet* pilots."

Jane held out her glass. Sakov refilled it. She raised the glass. "To Castro," she said.

Cathy stumbled into the basement room. She heard the key turn in the lock behind her.

She stared at Peterson. His swollen and smashed features.

"You—you know what's happened? My television . . ." Cathy's voice was still shocked.

"Yes," said Peterson. "They let me watch it. They drank champagne. I wanted to kill them. I still do. Jane and the others."

"The others?"

"A man. A Russian called Carl. And a young girl."

"What did they do to you?" she said. "How long have you been here?"

"Four days." He shrugged. "I found out who Jane really was and I tried to stop her. So here I am."

"Do you know how long they've been planning this?" Cathy said.

"No."

"For years . . . since I was a girl of twenty."

Peterson shrugged again. What did it matter how long. What about today! "Why did you do it for them?" he said. "People believe they're going to die if we don't give in. Christ! What's going through their minds right *now*. . . . *Panic!* The whole country."

"Do you think I don't know?" said Cathy. Her hands were clenched tight, nails digging into the palms. She rocked in her anguish. *"You think I don't know!"*

Peterson turned his head sharply toward the door and grabbed her arm. "Be quiet," he whispered.

They listened in silence.

Footsteps were coming down the wooden stairs to the basement.

"Do what I tell you," Peterson whispered. "Sit on the bed and cry. Got it?"

Peterson moved soundlessly and stood beside the door. "Cry," he whispered urgently.

Cathy put her hands to her face and began to sob noisily.

The key turned and the door opened wide, hiding Peterson. Carl came in followed by Anette. He saw the hunched shaking figure of Cathy and he paused. Reaching inside his jacket, he pulled a gun from his shoulder holster. He whipped around to face the door.

"Come, come," Carl said. "I'm too old a hand for games like this." He smiled.

Anette pushed the door shut, revealing Peterson.

Cathy peered through her fingers. Carl's back was four feet from her. She must do something. She lunged forward with her outstretched hands, the whole weight of her body behind her. Carl, knocked off balance, plunged forward toward Peterson. Immediately the side of Peterson's hand came down on Carl's wrist like an ax. The gun clattered to the floor a few inches from Cathy's sprawled body. She seized the gun and scrambled to her feet.

"Don't move." Her voice trembled. She pointed the gun directly at Carl.

"Oh come along, Mummy. Don't be so silly." It was Anette, a contemptuous smile on her face. "Give the gun to me. You know you're too frightened to use it." She took a step toward Cathy, her hand outstretched to take the gun.

"Stop." Cathy's hands were shaking.

"You really are being ridiculous, Mummy. You wouldn't kill *me*." Anette moved a step closer.

"I—I . . ." The words froze on Cathy's lips.

"There. That's more sensible, Mummy." Anette was near enough to touch Cathy.

Cathy fired. A red blotch appeared at the waistband of Anette's white dress. For an instant Anette looked at her mother in disbelief. "I didn't think you would . . ." Her voice trailed away. Blood spurted from her mouth and she crumpled to the floor.

A low moan escaped Cathy's lips before she fainted. The gun fell beside her.

Peterson threw himself full length, snatched up the fallen gun, whipped over onto his back, and fired straight into Carl's moving body. The bullet tore the left side of his head off. He crumpled on top of Peterson.

Peterson shoved the body away and got to his feet. He stood at the door listening, expecting it to open any moment and men with guns to come rushing in. But there was silence.

Cathy had dragged herself to the bed and was lying with her face hidden in the blanket. She was crying hysterically.

Peterson shook her. She raised her head and looked up, her eyes glazed with pain and horror.

"Mummy!" Peterson prompted. "What did the girl mean?"

Cathy stared unseeing at him, then her head sank to the bed again.

Anette was writhing on the floor. She would die but it would take time. Peterson had seen men die of stomach wounds in Vietnam—before the medics could get to them with morphine. No one deserved that much pain. He pointed the gun at her forehead, shut his eyes, and fired. He looked at Cathy, but if she had heard the shot she showed no sign.

She was still in shock, beyond reach.

He looked at the carnage in the room.

He had to leave her.

At least she was safe in here . . . for the moment.

He left the room, locked the door, and put the key in his pocket.

Taking the steps three at a time he reached the ground floor. He stopped and listened. Still silence. They must be outside. He went through the first open door. A bottle and two glasses stood on a table by the window. He looked out. Darkness was beginning to fall. Men were pushing a small building like a summer house clear of something—a helicopter!

He saw Jane and Sakov coming across the lawn back to the house.

Peterson stood behind the open door. He heard their footsteps along the corridor and down to the basement. The sound of banging on the locked door. The muttering of voices. Then two shots as they blasted the lock.

Footsteps hurried back up the stairs. Doors were flung open along the corridor. It was Jane who came in first.

Peterson grabbed her around the waist and stuck the muzzle of the gun against her head. He pulled her tight against him.

"One move from you, you bitch, and you're dead," he said between clenched teeth. Jane stayed rigid against him.

Sakov came in, a gun in his hand. "Ah, Mr. Peterson, you've been busy in the basement." If Sakov was surprised or shaken it didn't show.

"Move back," Peterson snapped.

Sakov obeyed. He took a step back, his gun still leveled at Peterson and Jane.

"Drop the gun," Peterson ordered, "or I kill Jane."

Sakov looked at him and Jane. He fired.

The bullet grazed Jane's throat and smashed into Peterson's shoulder. The gun went off as it dropped from Peterson's hand. The bullet thudded harmlessly into the floor.

Jane tore free, her hand to her throat, her face white with fury. "Kill him," she screamed at Sakov.

"No," Sakov replied quietly.

Peterson was holding his wounded shoulder.

Sakov's calm authoritative voice explained, "Perhaps you will now understand us Russians, Mr. Peterson. The balance of power has always been with us—as it is with me now. I was prepared to kill a woman, Jane, my comrade, fellow Russian, the one I love. Would you do that?"

Sakov shook his head and turned to leave, then paused and added, "Your President will be regaining consciousness now. The gas is only effective for a few hours. He and his advisors will be trying to control the situation. But it is a situation beyond control. You see, we have done what we set out to achieve. We have bypassed your government controls on information and decision-taking. Now that the people of America know they are in a position of nuclear checkmate, they will not wish to die. They are already voting with their feet. Now all we await is the final surrender from your President."

"You mean, American surrender?" said Peterson.

"Yes," Sakov replied. "You had better hope for it."

Sakov turned abruptly and, supporting Jane, he left.

Clutching his wounded shoulder, Peterson went down to the basement to get Cathy.

"It's all right now. Take my hand," he said.

Like a child she obeyed him. He guided her carefully around the two bodies and out of the room. He led her up the stairs and out of the house through the front door.

The highway at the end of the drive was jammed, both sides with traffic all heading the same way. Out of Washington. It was panic. Flight from the capital. Not a place to be at midnight. . . .

Peterson kept his left arm around Cathy as they walked by the side of the road past the endless stream of traffic moving in the opposite direction.

They approached a car stopped off the side of the road, a man bent over the open hood frantically fiddling with the engine. A young boy with a toy gun stood watching him. Military music blared from the car radio. In the back of the car, a jumble of possessions—loose clothing, bags, a fur coat, papers, a jewelry case, everything thrown together. A little girl about six sat on her mother's lap in the passenger seat, crying.

The boy saw Peterson and Cathy. He pointed the toy gun at them and made a noise like a machine gun.

The man turned. "Know anything about these goddamn things?" He pointed to the engine.

"Not a thing," Peterson answered. Then he spoke to the woman through the open passenger window. "Any news?" he asked.

"Nothing yet," she answered.

"Come on, Cathy," Peterson said.

"Where in damnation are you going?" The woman peered at them out of the window. "Washington's no place to be. No way. . . . There's nothing we can do."

Peterson and Cathy walked on.

There would be a way.

They had to find it.

To find it and work it out.

Millions would want to surrender. To save their lives. But there would always be enough who would fight.

They would have to fight.

For America. . . . For the freedom of the world.

Washington was the place to be at midnight.